Charming Puckboy

Also by Eden Finley and Saxon James

Puckboys

Egotistical Puckboy
Irresponsible Puckboy
Shameless Puckboy
Foolish Puckboy
Clueless Puckboy
Bromantic Puckboy
Forbidden Puckboy
Possessive Puckboy
Stubborn Puckboy
Charming Puckboy

CHARMING PUCKBOY

EDEN FINLEY & SAXON JAMES

First published in the United Kingdom in 2026 by

Canelo, an imprint of
Canelo Digital Publishing Limited,
20 Vauxhall Bridge Road,
London SW1V 2SA
United Kingdom

A Penguin Random House Company
The authorised representative in the EEA is Dorling Kindersley Verlag GmbH. Arnulfstr. 124,
80636 Munich, Germany

Copyright © Eden Finley and Saxon James 2026

The moral right of Eden Finley and Saxon James to be identified as the creator of this work has been asserted in accordance with the Copyright, Designs and Patents Act, 1988.
All rights reserved. No part of this publication may be reproduced or transmitted in any form or by any means, electronic or mechanical, including photocopy, recording, or any information storage and retrieval system, without permission in writing from the publisher.
No part of this book may be used or reproduced in any manner for the purpose of training artificial intelligence technologies or systems. In accordance with Article 4(3) of the DSM Directive 2019/790, Canelo expressly reserves this work from the text and data mining exception.

A CIP catalogue record for this book is available from the British Library.

ISBN 978 1 83598 585 4

This book is a work of fiction. Names, characters, businesses, organizations, places and events are either the product of the author's imagination or are used fictitiously. Any resemblance to actual persons, living or dead, events or locales is entirely coincidental.

Printed and bound in Great Britain by Clays Ltd, Elcograf S.p.A.

Look for more great books at
www.canelo.co | www.dk.com

CHAPTER ONE

LACHIE

I don't know how this always happens to me. Every. Fucking. Time.

There I am, minding my own business, catching my breath during a low moment of a HIIT run, thinking about dicks and fantasizing about riding my next one, and the next minute, there's a furry creature whimpering at my ankles. Not even the sexy kind of furry either.

The soft meow and head rub against my calf is adorable though. I pick up the stray cat, and she settles in my arms. Her white calico coat might be covered in so much dirt she looks mostly brown, but the orange and black spots are still visible. And with the way her swollen stomach contracts against my chest as she purrs, I know exactly what's happening and where I need to take her for help.

The poor thing is in labor and must not have a safe enough area to give birth. There are probably bears around here, and she thinks I'm her best hope. That's the only reason a stray would approach a human.

If *I'm* her best hope, we're all in a world of trouble.

Then again, as my brothers and teammates tease me about all the time, I'm not any random human. I'm the animal whisperer. If I weren't a future hockey god, I could've become a vet. I probably would have too.

For some unknown reason, ever since I was little, any animal, big or small, would be drawn to me.

Growing up, I became known at the local shelter as a real-life Disney Princess. I'm home in Colorado for the summer, which means I'm about to deliver yet another needy animal to them. All I have to hope is that one of the guys who works there has moved on in the three years since I was last at the facility.

Sam has been at the shelter forever—he started when he was eighteen and I was twelve. I was already well-known around the shelter by that point, but it was Sam who coined the Disney Princess moniker after he asked me if I was kidnapping the animals I brought in. I swore until I was blue in the face that they all approached me.

I was infatuated with his smile back then, and nothing has really changed over the years.

The reason I hope he no longer works there is because of the last time I saw him at the shelter. In a rare moment where the animals weren't on my side and I had nothing to bring to him, I decided to go in there and show him that now that I had turned eighteen, I was obviously the sexiest man alive and he should throw himself at me.

I mean, what's sexier than a fresh-faced eighteen-year-old telling the guy he has a crush on that he's now of legal age? All of my confidence and determination left me when Sam only replied with, "Happy birthday. So, what animal brought you here today?" Considering what a red flag it would have been if he *were* interested, I've stopped hating him for not immediately dragging me into the back rooms.

I guess it's lucky that back then, with all the pressure of not wanting to draw too much attention to my sexual identity, I didn't answer with something like "The animal in my pants." I'd so do that today if he asked me the same question.

Which I hope there's not a chance for him to do because he won't be there. He won't.

I get back to the trailhead where my brother's car is waiting for me, and if this cat gives birth in Easton's G-Wagon, I won't have the chance to die of embarrassment at seeing Sam again. I'll already be dead.

Not that I have a real reason to be embarrassed. He was so oblivious to my attempt at a come-on, he'd have no idea I practically threw myself at him. Or maybe he did know but ignored it to let me down gently.

And I'm back to anticipating embarrassment.

As soon as I'm sitting behind the wheel, the fear of the cat giving birth all over Easton's seats goes away because she immediately climbs out of the footwell on the passenger side and jumps up and into my lap.

Why can't I find a man who is this much of a stage five clinger?

At least Easton's interior won't get birthing fluid all over it, and my life is safe once again. Apart from having to, you know, get to the shelter safely with a damn cat on my lap.

Somehow, I manage, and as mamma cat's mewls get louder, I don't even have time to worry if I'll see Sam again. I rush her inside, and something like a mix of relief *and* disappointment hits me when I see a young girl behind the counter instead of Sam.

She glances up at me, sees the dirt-covered mess in my arms, and gasps. "Oh no. What do we have here?"

"I think she's in labor? I found her out by the Green Mountain Trail, where she was spooked by something. She hasn't wanted to leave my side since she saw me."

A loud chuckle comes from behind me, and I freeze.

"The Disney Princess has returned."

His voice is like butter, and I hate it. I hate it because I still react to it.

I turn toward him, and he pulls back as if in shock. I don't think I've changed that much in three years. My hair is still short and messy, though I have finally gained the ability to grow stubble, so that's something.

It's entirely possible I'm reading into it because as fast as it happens, he unfurls that killer smile of his that has always made me weak.

"I was beginning to think you'd moved. It's been way too long since you brought in an animal." Sam gasps. "Have you been cheating on us with another rescue?"

If I think I still look the same since the last time I saw him, it's nothing compared to how exactly the same he looks. He's late twenties now, isn't he? Shouldn't he have wrinkles and shit? Okay, so my older brother Connor is of a similar age, and he doesn't have wrinkles. Sore knees and aching hips from years of hockey, but no wrinkles.

Sam's hair is a darker shade of brown than mine, his five-o'clock shadow looks like more than the pathetic stubble it takes me three days to grow, and his warm brown eyes are as inviting as his smile.

And here I am, tongue-tied around him like I always have been.

While Easton was spending his teen years lusting after our older brother's best friend, I was fantasizing about the day the boy from the animal shelter would look at me the way I've always looked at him ... with maybe less drool.

"Princess?" Sam cocks his head.

I shake out of my stupor. "Sorry, what?"

"I asked if you'd moved. You haven't been here in ..."

"Three years," I say. While I've only been in the NHL for two years, I spent that year between the ages of eighteen and nineteen living and breathing hockey, so I wasn't around. Hockey workshops, camps, and playing for the juniors was my only focus so I could be ready for when they called my name for that first overall draft pick. "I moved for work, but I get summers off, so I'm home with my parents at the moment."

"You go into teaching or something?" He approaches me, his sleek and toned arms almost bursting out of his tight khaki shirt, but as he reaches for the cat, she hisses and struggles in my arms. He backs up. "As I thought. You're going to have to bring her out the back. I don't feel like having my arms shredded today."

I'm thankful I didn't have to answer the question about work because the last time I was here and I mentioned I was going to be a pro hockey player, he'd muttered something under his breath about hockey players being dicks. Or that's what it sounded like, anyway.

"Follow me." He walks toward swinging doors with "employees only" written on it and takes me into the back, not where the adoption cages are but where there are medical supplies and animal food and everything else a shelter needs to provide animals with basic needs.

Sam grabs a square frame that's leaning up against a wall and some bedding and towels and then leads me through another door into a small empty room with cement flooring.

Mamma cat is panting now, but Sam is busy setting up a whelping box for her in the corner.

"See if she'll let you put her down in here."

As soon as I lay her on the warmth of the bedding, she begins kneading the material and purring.

"I think she's getting close," I say, still kneeling beside her.

"That's what he said." Sam chortles.

I laugh and then stand.

Sam's eyes get caught on my shirt. "You, uh, might want to change. You've got blood and probably amniotic fluid all over your tank top."

I glance down. "At least it's on me and not in my brother's car. He should have a shirt in there I can change into on the way home. Thanks. You got her from here?"

"Should be all good. The plan is to leave her alone to do her thing. Thanks for bringing her here." His eyes roam over me, almost like he can't stop himself. "It was good to see you again."

Little delusional Lachie has to be imagining the way he looks me up and down. Right?

Yeah, I'm not letting myself run away with those kinds of thoughts again. All those times coming in here with the fantasy of him saying, "You look so grown up now," and then some porno track playing in my head as I imagine him pushing me down and fucking me in a very unhygienic animal environment are no longer allowed.

"I'm sure I'll be back at some point over the summer," I choke out and turn to leave the way we came in.

But then momma cat makes a horrible sound and jumps out of her whelping box to follow me.

"Uh-oh. Looks like you're not going anywhere. You're her emotional support human."

There could be worse ways to spend an afternoon, but if I don't get Easton's car home soon, he's going to— As if on cue, my phone starts vibrating in the pocket of my running shorts.

I don't even get the chance to say hello before he talks. "Where are you? I thought you were going for a quick run. Where is my car, and if you say in a ditch, you'll be in a ditch next time I see you."

It's obvious in the quiet room that Sam can hear everything because his shoulders shake with silent laughter as he hangs his head. He gets on the floor, trying to *pst pst pst* the cat back into the box he made for her, but she won't let him anywhere near her.

I kneel back down, resting the phone between my ear and shoulder, and I pick her up, moving her to the bed just in time for one of her babies to be born. Instinctively, she knows what to do and starts cleaning the kitten while I talk to my brother.

"I'm at the animal shelter because—"

"Oh God. Is it another llama? It's a llama, isn't it?"

Sam's head snaps in my direction so fast I know I'm going to have to explain the llama thing all over again as soon as this call ends. No matter how many times I say I drunkenly stumbled across one of those animal trailers with a llama in it and don't remember the rest, no one believes me.

"It's not a llama. Get Connor or your boyfriend to bring you to the shelter to get your car. It's in perfect condition. No birthing fluid or anything got anywhere."

"What the fuck?"

Oh. Right. Probably didn't have to tell him that part. "Gotta go. About to deliver some babies." I end the call and place my phone on the ground, refusing to look in Sam's direction.

"So ... There was a llama?"

Ugh. Here we go again.

CHAPTER TWO

SAM

Holy pig on a bike, Princess went and grew up. I keep shooting him looks from the corner of my eye, trying not to swallow my tongue or give in to the swoop that hits my gut every time he makes eye contact with me.

He has to be the hottest man I've ever seen covered in amniotic fluid. He's the hottest in general, but that *should* be a turnoff. It isn't.

This is so inappropriate.

I rub the palms of my hands against my eyes to give them something else to do. The cat lets out a low mewl again, but it's fine. We don't technically have to be here.

Well, according to the cat, Lachie has to be, but I don't.

Knowing that doesn't make me stand and leave any faster.

"Tired?"

The rough, confident voice washes over me and completely derails my plans not to glance his way. Let's face it, the plan was shaky at best. I meet his gray eyes, and the smile that pulls at my mouth is effortless. "Just calculating how many animals I'm going to have to deal with if you're home *all* summer."

"It's not like I ask for them to find me."

"But they do anyway."

He leans in closer. "I guess it's lucky I know a big, strong animal shelter man to bring them to."

Oh, hello. Was that flirting? The delivery was shaky, but straight men don't usually call other guys big and strong …

right? How long has it been since I hung out with a straight man?

"Unfortunately for you," I say, playing it off, "Mattias isn't in today. I'll have to do."

"I can't believe you still work here."

The words come out like a stray thought, one that doesn't expect an answer. Maybe he doesn't mean to be judgmental, but I've had this conversation too many times not to get defensive. "Why not? Good pay, good benefits, and access to all the animals I want. Not all of us are a magnet for them."

It's a question I get a lot, so my answer is prepared. Having been employed here for all ten years of my working life, people can't understand why I don't have ambition. Why I don't want *more*. I'm still struggling to work out what *more* is supposed to be code for. I'm only a manager reluctantly, and even doing the absolute bare minimum desk work is a killer.

Here, with the animals, is where I'm meant to be.

My gaze strays back to Lachie. Having eye candy walk into the place doesn't hurt either.

"So where have you been?" I ask, to the background ambiance of labor. "If you're home every summer and you're *not* cheating on us with another shelter, does that mean your pied piper bit has ended?"

Lachie waves a sexily large hand toward the cat. "Clearly not."

My question hangs between us, and the longer he tries to ignore it, the weirder it feels. "You know I'm joking. You can go to whatever shelter you want."

"No, it's not that. I haven't been home as much as I should have been. I've been … establishing myself. New careers and all that."

"Makes sense. Where are you based?"

"Missouri." Before I can ask anything else, Lachie looks down. "This shirt is really gross."

"So take it off." It's supposed to be a casual suggestion, but it somehow doesn't come out that way. We make eye contact, and the way my blood heats is ridiculous. I haven't had this kind of instant attraction to someone in years, and it's uncomfortable because I knew him as a kid, but the man crouched beside me is nothing like I remember.

Lachie whatever-his-last-name is tall, lean, and—judging by his smirk as he reaches for his shirt—completely confident.

He pulls the material over his head, and even though I tell myself not to, I immediately look at his chest. He's all lean muscle, with a long chain that hangs between them. Between his styled light brown hair, pierced ears, and the million rings he's wearing, I'm trying my hardest not to drool.

"Maybe you should try to leave again." The croak in my voice makes me cringe.

"I dunno ..." His gaze flicks to the cat and back to me again. "I think I'm stuck here."

He sounds like he wants to be.

I want him to be.

But also, I really don't.

I'm at work. I'm professional.

Usually.

I will *not* look at the sexy man's nipples while I'm on the clock.

"Right. So. We'll wait for her to have her kittens ..." Why is my voice coming out like this?

"What have you been doing since I was last here?" he cuts in.

A sigh echoes through my brain, and I give in to the urge to sit on the floor. Lachie joins me. Like we're settling in until the cat says we can leave. "Working. Training." I can't help myself. "Giving back to my community."

He tilts his head. "*Your* community?"

"I volunteer for a queer charity and run community days, things like that. We have a half-marathon coming up."

"Can I help? I mean ... I love running."

"Sure."

"And fucking dudes."

I choke on air. Of all the things I'd been expecting to come out of his mouth next, it wasn't that. The blushing, stuttering kid is long gone, and I couldn't be more grateful. Considering I'd been trying to get it out of him subtly, this works a *lot* better for me. Still, for as confident as he is, there's a hint of nerves in his expression as he waits for me to answer. And catch my breath.

"Same. On *both* things." Then I have to add, "But the event is a family day, so we'll only be doing one of those things there."

"Ahh ..." His smile grows. "We'll make plans to do the other thing another time, then."

I love it when guys are direct, but this has caught me completely off guard. When I'd gotten ready for work this morning, in the world's most boring uniform in existence, I did not expect this. I'm still battling the ethics of being on the clock and knowing him from when he was a literal child, so I don't even know how to respond to that.

Do I want to fuck him?

Absolutely.

Should I?

I need someone else—not him—to give me the answer to that.

So I deflect.

"How do you know I'm not already taken?"

He shrugs. "If you are, it must be part of your relationship, given you begged me to take my shirt off."

"If you think that's begging, I might need to have a word with these guys you've been fucking. They obviously have no clue what they're doing."

"How much time do you have? It's a long list."

"I see you've been putting the last three years to good use."

"A man's gotta have a hobby."

"I think hobbies are usually reserved for things like reading. And knitting."

"Riding's a hobby."

I almost choke-laugh again. "Not the riding you're talking about."

I'm so insanely curious about him. He's moved away, had the time of his life, and now he's magically back in my animal shelter? Is the universe really dropping a sexy, flirty guy in my lap?

He's only home for the summer, so—

No. Stop.

I need to talk to Ethan and figure out if this is even something I should be thinking about. My brain is too swamped with lust to be capable of a rational decision.

"So tell me more about the running." I don't want to let the flirting go, and he clearly doesn't either, but he lets me move things along.

"I'm an active guy. I figure it will help stop me from being lazy this off-se—summer. A half-marathon sounds like a good time."

"I've been trying to rope my friends into this for years and never have any luck. Ethan always claims I'm trying to murder him by cardio."

"Ethan's your boyfriend?" He's fishing. He doesn't hide that he's fishing.

"Best friend and roommate."

"Roommate, huh? *That* kind of roommate?"

"We've never fucked," I answer dryly because he's not the first and won't be the last to ask. "We're ... incompatible."

"Am *I* his type?"

"He's into bears."

"So that's a no, then. Guess you'll have to do."

That gets a real laugh out of me. "I'm not as easy as you think I am."

"We'll see. I haven't heard a no yet."

"I haven't given one. Yet."

He gestures to his torso, and *damn it*, I'm looking again. "We've already basically made it to first base. You have me half-naked."

"Again, I *really* need a word with whoever you've been sleeping with."

"Is that jealousy I'm sensing?"

"Disappointment. I—" Before I can take that sentence into dangerous territory, there's a tap at the doorframe that pulls both of our attention. Two men, I'm assuming his brothers since they're both similar-looking to Lachie but less hot, walk in, and one of them catches my attention. He's familiar in an abstract way, and as I'm puzzling through why I know him—*please* tell me I haven't hooked up with one of Lachie's brothers—his gaze collides with mine, and his face twists into a sneer.

"Ready to go?" he snaps.

Lachie glances back at the cat, who's apparently done. Three tiny kittens are feeding, and she's lying there exhausted. "The cat won't let me leave."

"The cat will be fine," the asshole answers.

His other brother smiles. "It didn't take long for bossy Connor to make a reappearance. Though two whole days since Lachie's been in town might be a record."

"Shut up, I'm not being bossy," he says like he's defending himself while his tone does the complete opposite.

Lachie doesn't make a move to obey. "I told Easton to grab his car and go. Why are you even in here?"

"Wanted to make sure you're okay."

Judging by the look that takes over Lachie's face, this isn't new behavior for Connor. "I'm *fine*."

"Good. Then get up, get in the car, and I'll drive you home."

Lachie and Easton exchange a look, and Easton says, "He was fine until we pulled up here."

"I'm still fine," Connor bites back. "Like Lachie's fine, and you're fine, and Sam is fucking fine. But we have places to be, so let's go."

Sam? I'd assume he read my name tag in the two seconds he spent glowering at me, but that sounded like he *know* knows me. And doesn't like me.

Oh God, I *did* fuck Lachie's brother, didn't I?

Connor. *Connor.* Con … nor. That name doesn't ring a bell, but of my sexploits over the years, it's not like I got half their names.

This confirms it, then. Can't go there. I know making it through a family is fun for some people, but that isn't me.

"Maybe we should all go," I suggest, wanting to get as far away from the potential mess I almost unwittingly made. "Let her sleep."

Once again, Lachie checks on the cat, but it doesn't look as though she's paying him any attention. He eases himself up off the floor, and when it's clear we're leaving, Connor turns on his heel and disappears, the three of us left behind.

"Sorry about him," Easton says. "He forgot to have his lobotomy this morning."

Wanting this to be over, I wave my hand like it's no big deal. "I get grumpy before coffee too. It's fine. I have to get back to work."

They follow me out of the room, and Easton passes me, but Lachie grabs my arm, pulling me to a stop.

"This marathon thing. Do you want my number so you can send me the details?"

That is *not* what I'd use his number for if I had it, and I'm not about to get between brothers.

"You know what, I think we'll be okay with this one. I'll give you the heads-up if we plan something else while you're in town."

Then I duck into the back hallway that leads to my office before he can reply. It doesn't stop him from calling after me though.

"But you didn't get my number."

I pretend I haven't heard him.

Even though it's all I can concentrate on for the rest of the day.

CHAPTER THREE

LACHIE

Okay, I think I have whiplash. One minute, we're flirting, actively making plans to fuck, and the next minute, he's backing away. All because of my stupid brother. Or maybe he wasn't flirting but placating me in case I turned out to be one of those guys who react badly when rejected.

I run our entire interaction over in my head again. Dear God, I'm one of those people who read into everything and twist every sentence.

"I like fucking dudes, but this will be a family event, so we won't be doing that."

What I heard: "But I'd love to do that afterward." What he actually meant: "Me too, but not you."

He probably still sees me as that kid who would always come in with an injured or lost animal and would then stammer through every excuse under the sun to stay and help. Need a volunteer to clean cages? Happy to. Need someone to scoop all the poop in the dog yard? Give me the baggies.

"Lachie," Connor barks from the main entrance to the shelter. "Hurry up."

I snap out of overanalyzing every word that left Sam's sexy mouth and force my feet to move. When I catch up to them in the middle of the gravel parking lot, I stop and snap, "What was that in there?"

Connor turns to face me. "Why don't you tell us? Where is your shirt, and why were you undressing in front of *that guy*?"

"Why do you care?"

Easton's the one who answers. "Because he's Connor. He always freaks out at the thought of us having sex. Which is really weird for a brother to think about. Just FYI."

Connor rolls his eyes. "You know it's not that. Lachie still isn't out to the media yet, and that guy in there would probably sell the story for whatever he could get."

"Why do you keep saying 'that guy' like you know him?"

"I *do* know him," Connor says and then looks down at his feet. "He's ... he's the one who flirted with Parker while we were adopting Conishkin. I was right there, and he—"

Easton laughs hard.

"Why is that funny?" I ask.

"Yeah. Why is that funny?" Connor folds his arms.

"Don't try to be on my side now," I say.

Easton's laugh settles to a chuckle. "Connor has gotten so used to being controlling over our lives, it's not enough for him now. He now has to control random strangers' lives too." He stands upright and puts on a deep voice, mocking Connor. "No, Mr. Hot Animal Shelter Man, you can't flirt with my boyfriend. Or my brother. You get no one. Be destined to be alone forever!"

Connor gestures to Easton. "See, he gets it."

Easton face-palms. "I wasn't agreeing with you, you dick-face."

"You're the dickface."

And these two say I'm immature. "Well, thanks for cockblocking me. Who's taking me home?"

"I'm not taking you anywhere until you tell me where your shirt is," Connor says.

"It's still inside. It has pussy juice all over it, so I don't want it." Did I purposefully use a phrase that would make both my brothers squirm? Of course I did. It works too.

Connor screws up his face. "I don't want to know anymore."

"You see, brother, the way birthing works is—"

He holds up his hand. "Got it. Don't need the details. Thanks. Get in the car."

"I might go with East—"

"Like hell, you will. You put a laboring cat inside my baby, and now it's probably covered in pussy juice!"

At the absurdity of that sentence, we all pause. Silent. Blinking. The only sounds to fill our ears are those of the birds in the rustling trees. And then, simultaneously, the three of us burst into laughter.

"You're so lucky no one was around to hear that," Connor says, his eyes welling. But then his laughter dies, and I can't help wondering—not for the first time in my life—how Connor can switch back into serious mode so quickly. It takes a whole lot of effort for me to be serious at all.

"Come on, get in the car." Easton nods toward his G-Wagon, and I take that as forgiveness for putting his "baby" in danger from the big, scary possibility of a stain.

As we climb into our seats and he starts the engine, he says, "You're lucky you got rid of your shirt, or you would be going home with Connor."

"Thank ... you?"

"You're welcome. Also, ignore him. He's getting better about his controlling side—sorry, 'protective' side, as he likes to call it—but he still has lapses of judgment. Especially when it comes to us."

"You mean me."

"Huh?"

"Ever since you started shacking up with his best friend, he's moved all his focus onto me. How are you and Knox doing? Is he so annoying to live with that you want to break up? Because then Connor would be busy fussing over you and Knox, and I can sleep with whoever I want."

"You can do that now. Like I said, ignore Connor. Or do what I did when I finally had enough." He grins. "Punch him right in his stupid face."

No matter how annoyed with him I get, I could never do that. "Do you think other families are like ours? Is this normal brother behavior?"

"I have no idea. Maybe you should ask Asher Dalton when the Collective is in town. He has a billion brothers."

Oh, right. The Queer Collective vacation is in Colorado this year. In a few weeks, Denver is going to be overrun by some very loud, over-the-top, drunken hockey players. They are my people.

Though, to be honest, I sometimes don't feel like I'm one of them. I'm the outsider, the youngest, and the only single one of them. It's like I'm a kid again, being allowed to hang out with the cool kids because they're my brothers' friends. They're welcoming and accepting, and I look up to those guys, but ... a few of them are nearing retirement age. My career is in its infancy.

"When are they getting here again?" I ask. Because I have an idea of how to get Sam's attention.

Apparently, I'm a slow learner, but if I can make a big deal out of his marathon thing, be the hero who brings in dollars and media coverage ... maybe he'll see that not only animals love me, but that I'm actually a loveable guy. And by loveable, I mean fuckable.

"Two weeks."

I quickly take out my phone and check the shelter's website to see if the fundraising event is on there. They have a tab for community events, and thankfully, the half-marathon is listed there.

"How much do you think the Collective guys will hate it if I make them all run a half-marathon while they're here?"

"Not at all. Especially if you put a wager on it."

"What kind of wager?"

"Tell Ezra that if he beats everyone in the race, he can choose the group activities for the whole trip."

"And if anybody else wins?"

East glances over at me. "Ezra won't get to plan anything. Trust me. They will all be dying to stop Ezra from having that kind of power."

Yeah, that checks out. The entire Collective seems to find Ezra annoying as hell. Me? He's kind of my idol.

I could never tell him that though. It would go to his head, and his husband might kill me, but still. I don't see anything wrong with wanting to be Ezra Palaszczuk when I grow up.

Everyone else would probably tell me to get therapy about that.

CHAPTER FOUR

SAM

"But he's really, really pretty," I stress, like I haven't said that enough since I got home.

Ethan guffaws—which isn't a way I'd ever described a laugh until I met him. "Still don't see the appeal."

"Okay, picture you met a thick, hairy man, with pretty eyes, fun banter, and who could bench-press even you." Ethan's a competitive bodybuilder, and the guy is scarily large.

My best friend instantly turns to jelly. "Dark hair?"

"Of course."

"Missing teeth?"

That pulls me up short. "*Wha*—you know what, sure."

"Damn." He drums thick fingers on the counter. "But … no. Brothers are off-limits."

"Completely off-limits?" I push, even though I already know the answer myself. "No loopholes?"

I get one of Ethan's rare, serious looks and know that I'm not going to be handed my free pass to assholery. "Don't mess with family, bro. You're better than that."

He's right, of course, but I'd really hoped he would have come up with some super-wonderful plan that hadn't occurred to me in all of my horniness. I'm proud of myself for walking away, but I can't lie and say that it wouldn't be nice sometimes to not care about being decent. It would be a fast way to lose Ethan though.

We met after high school, and while he can easily afford his own place from prize winnings and sponsorships, he doesn't like being alone. I pointed out you're never alone if you have pets, but with all the animals I end up bringing home with me, either to rehab or from being too young or sick to be left alone, and with Ethan having to travel for competitions, we haven't been able to commit to one.

"Technically, I don't actually know that I slept with his brother," I remind him. "I'm assuming. Based on the attitude and the death glares and the way he wanted his brother away from me as fast as humanly possible."

"You definitely fucked him."

"But maybe I didn't."

"Except you probably did."

I swear and scrape my hands back through my hair, then check the fridge for a beer. There's nothing there, of course, because neither of us drinks unless we're out, but I could really use something to take my mind off Lachie. And his soft-looking hair. Those smooth, lean muscles. The teasing way he'd hold my gaze ...

I swear again.

"It's your fault," Ethan says. "You shouldn't be so hot. You do nothing for me, but in your work uniform, you've got the whole rough Robert Irwin thing going on, and people seem to like that."

"I look nothing like him." My hair is a lot darker, for one. And for two ... well ... I'm *not* Australian. Though I don't know what that has to do with looks.

Ethan tips his hand side to side.

"*Nothing.*"

"Maybe we should get Lachie's opinion on this." Ethan scoops up his phone, and the tiny sunflower charm swings. "What's his last name?"

"No idea."

"No ..." He splutters. "*Girl.* You want to marry this man, and you don't even know his last name?"

"I want to fuck him. Not marry him."

"*Oooh*, fuck, marry, kill the three brothers?"

"Kill is easy." My first thought is of Connor and the shit-under-his-shoe looks he kept throwing me. If I didn't fuck him, I'm going to have to get offended that it was something less personal that he took issue with, and given the types of cars they drive, it's easy to pick what. I've done relationships with a huge income gap before, and while I don't care about money, it always becomes an issue.

"So which one are you fucking, and which one are you marrying?" Ethan pushes.

"I thought we don't come between brothers."

"This is your loophole. Hypotheticals."

I know he's not going to let this drop, so I might as well play along. It's hard though. Lachie is the one I'm attracted to, but do I really want to spend my life with the other one? It's possible I'm giving this hypothetical more thought than it requires.

"Fine. Fuck Lachie and marry the non-angry brother."

He continues typing away on his phone. "How do we spell Lachie?"

"I don't know."

"Is it some kind of new age, L-O-K-double-I-double-E-Y type of thing? Or short for Lachlan?"

"I ... have no clue."

The look Ethan gives me is withering. "Given how obsessively you've been talking about him since you walked in, a little social media stalking should be the least you can offer me."

"All I know is that animals are weirdly attracted to him, he used to come in all the time, I haven't seen him in years, and then he walks in today looking like a god." I hang my head back with a groan. "Have I mentioned he's really, *really* pretty?"

"Yes. And somehow, I'm even less attracted to the idea of him than I was the last time you mentioned it."

"And you don't think it's weird I knew him when he was a kid?"

"Were you attracted to him as a kid?"

I recoil. "*Fuck* no. When I saw him today, I barely recognized him. He was like an entirely new person, but as soon as I heard the story of the cat searching him out in the wild, I knew it was the Disney Princess. And he has this whole new-age vibe to him now that he never had before. He has his ear pierced and wears rings and this leather necklace, and—"

"Then it's fine. Why would it be weird? Other than calling a grown-ass man a Disney Princess."

"I don't know ..." I scrape my brain for reasons, but there were never any unbalanced power dynamics between us or personal stories shared. Lachie would bring animals in, he'd help out with the grunt work I didn't want to do, I'd tease him about being a Disney Princess, and then he'd leave. We barely had a full conversation in all the years he came by the shelter.

"And the age gap isn't an issue?" Now it's like I'm trying to find a problem.

"What is the age gap?"

"I—"

"I swear, if you say you don't know one more time, I'm going to throw an apple at you."

"An apple?"

"It's the closest thing within reach," he says, pointing at the bowl.

I shift it away. "Leave the fruit out of this. We flirted for about half an hour, during which he strongly suggested we have sex, and I was strongly interested in the idea. There was no exchanging of details other than we both like fucking dudes. And running."

"Like, running out on dates?"

"No, actual running."

Ethan lifts his hands like he's horrified. "Cardio? This man keeps sounding worse and worse."

I run a hand over my jaw, stubble almost reaching the point of full beard. Normally I don't let it get this long, but it's been a few weeks since I went out, so I haven't bothered with it. "Lachie offered to help with the half-marathon day."

"Awesome. We could always use more volunteers."

"I told him we were good."

"Great. Now your sex life is creating more work for me."

"You're supervising a petting zoo. I think you'll be fine."

"I thought you were going to point out that you don't have a sex life."

"Thanks for that reminder." I do have a sex life, just not recently and not with the guy I currently want. It's disappointing, but I'll get over it. Lachie isn't the only guy out there, even if he is inhumanly attractive and exactly my type. The pull I have to him will fade, and I'm half convinced I'm exaggerating him in my head because of my shock over how much he'd changed.

"I think you need to work out if you actually fucked his brother," Ethan says. "If you didn't, then you can fuck Lachie, he can help at the charity run, and all will be right in the world."

"You want me to straight up ask if Connor and I have had sex?"

He guffaws again. Still so weird. "You could, *or* you could ask if he knows why Connor was such a dick."

Right. That's obviously the way to handle it. "Next time he comes into the shelter, I'll ask."

"If he's as much of a Disney Princess as you say, you shouldn't be waiting long."

And thank fuck for that. Hopefully, by this time tomorrow, we'll have everything straightened out … and I can show him what it actually means to beg.

—

Why the hell didn't I get his number?

It's not the first time I've beaten myself up over it, and I doubt it will be the last. As I direct the charity run volunteers putting up the starting line banner, my thoughts keep straying to Lachie and how the Disney Princess allure must be broken. Two weeks? Am I being tortured for something?

I need to shake him from my head because today is going to be a long day. In addition to the half-marathon, we have a 5K, some relays, and booths set up at the end with face painting, a petting zoo, music, drag queen story time, and roaming entertainers. Days like today always remind me what an amazing community I'm a part of. Not only are these people ridiculously talented, but they all volunteer their time to be here and give back.

Maybe I was being selfish in denying Lachie that chance.

Screw it. No more thinking about him today. Just the race that I'll be running in later, and getting everything ready in the meantime.

It's early, but it already looks like we'll be in for a hot July day. There's nothing I love more than being outside and surrounded by nature. My career allows me the flexibility for weekends off to do these kinds of things, and I couldn't imagine anything more soul-crushing than being stuck at a desk all day. Taking work home with me. Never able to switch off.

Sure, I'll never be able to afford to buy my own place, but I have a plan for retirement, and I'm going to enjoy my life until I get there.

The half-marathon isn't an easy one. Most of it takes place along the trailhead in Reynolds Landing, and we have a few hundred people turn up to compete. This is the third time we're hosting it, and it's always a big earner, coming second to the end-of-year holiday event.

I'm proud to be a part of it, but the more that pride grows, the worse I feel. Lachie should have had the chance to feel this as well.

I'll have to make more of an effort to reach out to him for the end-of-summer open day. If I can find him. I thought he'd have already been back in by now, but he hasn't.

Bit by bit, the setup comes together. We're kicking off at nine, so I was up before the sun today, and the closer we get to starting, the more the parking lot fills. We have shuttles to bring people in so that parking isn't an issue—lesson learned from our first year—and with half an hour to go, I hand off coordination to the charity's manager and focus on stretching instead.

Light nerves always sneak in before a race like this. I never expect to win, but the adrenaline of a race is addictive for someone who's usually not competitive.

I'm mid-lunge when, over the general chatter and unloading of shuttles, a roar builds through the trees. It gets louder and draws the attention of every person in the parking lot. A man wearing headphones near me even pulls them away to see what the hell is going on.

We don't have to wait long.

A full-blown motorcade comes along the winding road. Two motorbikes lead the way with a group of shiny black SUVs following them. And when they pull to a stop, I'm not expecting what comes next.

An array of neon headbands, bright pink tutus, and too much multicolored Lycra spills out from the doors. The men are making as much noise as the motorbikes were, and the sudden explosion of color and sound has brought the crowd to a standstill.

Then I clock the G-Wagon right at the back.

CHAPTER FIVE

LACHIE

I have to hand it to the guys; when I told them my plan, they took it and ran with it. The only complaints came from Connor, who is still bitter over Sam flirting with his man, and Foster Grant's husband asking if the costumes were necessary. That guy isn't even running or wearing a costume, but he hates attention. Why he married an NHL player if he has social anxiety, I have no idea, because as a hockey player, I have to say, we're a pretty social bunch. That probably explains why of all the Collective, I've spent the least amount of time with Foster.

All active players of the QC, plus Connor and two other recently retired members—Oskar Voyjik and Radimir Novicov—have shown up to run, as well as Alek's partner, Gabe, who's a fine-ass firefighter. Easton has dragged his boyfriend, Knox, along, and Novi—who refused to wear a neon tank top like the rest of us, so has gone shirtless instead because he's a stubborn Russian—brought his boyfriend, who's an NHL coach. We're all fit and ready to run this bitch.

Some of us more than others. Like me, for instance. Because not only is my point to grab Sam's attention, but it's also to run away from Ezra and Anton.

All that "I want to be Ezra Palaszczuk when I grow up" stuff? I take it back.

Just because they happened to win the Stanley Cup last season, they think it's hilarious that they brought the Cup with them on this trip. They're going to have their "Day with the

Cup" back-to-back, and their brilliant idea was to put it in a wheelbarrow so they can run with it. I originally thought, "Amazing. That should get media attention and bring in even more donations to the charity." But no. Those bastards have ulterior motives.

And as they pull good ol' Lord Stanley out of the trunk of their rental and put in it *our* family wheelbarrow, Ezra runs it right for me.

"Touch it. Come on, Little Kiki, touch it."

I take off, yelling, "Anton, make your husband stop hitting on me!"

"You little—" Ezra cuts himself off and stalls when he notices all the kids and the grown-ass adults staring at the giant manchildren that we are. "Now I'm really going to make you touch the Stanley Cup!" He stops chasing me and turns to the crowd. "And anyone else who would like a photo with it?" He waves people forward, and suddenly, I'm forgotten.

When I finally stop looking back to make sure Ezra's not chasing me down, I almost run into someone. A giant someone. Big arms crossed against his wide chest. Pleasant smile on what is otherwise a terrifyingly large, muscular body. Yet, as intimidating as he is, my gaze still goes to the man beside him.

Sam's wearing teeny, tiny running shorts and a running tank, and … and … and … I think my brain has short-circuited. I'm trying to remember if I've ever seen him out of his khakis, and I can't have. I would have remembered him looking like this.

"Why is that guy chasing after you with a wheelbarrow and yelling about a cup?"

"Because he has no self-respect. Uh, hi." I glance back again, paranoid as hell. Ezra is in his element, shmoozing everyone who approaches him. Damn it, that whole idol envy thing is back.

"What are you doing here?" Sam asks. The big guy next to him elbows him hard. "Ouch," he hisses, glaring at the monster. "This is Ethan."

"Ah. Ethan. The roommate and best friend." Intimidating-as-fuck roommate and best friend.

Ethan nods. "Lachie. The little brother of the guy Sam fucked."

I choke on air. "Wait, what?" I turn to Sam. "You hooked up with Easton?"

"No!" Sam says. "And I don't even know if I slept with the other one. Ethan is being a dick." He slaps his hand over Ethan's mouth. "Do *not* say anything about Lachie's brother's dick, I swear to God."

Maybe this is my answer to whether brothers act like we do because Sam and Ethan certainly seem familiar in the same way.

"Connor?" I screw up my face because that makes no sense. "There's no way that happened. He's only ever been with one dude, and that's his current—oh, unless he lied." Is Connor, Mr. Follow the Rules, a big fucking liar?

"If that's not what happened, then why does he hate me—" Sam's stare gets stuck on something or someone behind me. "Ohhh, this all makes so much sense now." He puts on a wide smile and steps past me. "Hey! It's my favorite rat daddy and ... you again."

I turn to see Connor and Parker, Parker carrying little Conishkin—their pet rat—in his carrier.

"I figured you might want to see how he's doing," Parker says. My brother stands next to his partner, head down, hands behind his back, not saying a word.

Sam approaches the carrier as Parker holds it up for him. "He looks good. Healthy. Happy."

"He is," Parker beams. "He comes everywhere with me."

"*Us*," Connor grumbles.

Parker stares at my stupid brother, doing that couply telepathy trick.

Connor sighs. "Apparently, I need to ... apologize to you or whatever."

Sam looks up from Conishkin to Connor. "Me?"

"Allegedly—"

"No allegedly," I cut in. "Factually."

Connor's sigh is even louder this time. "Factually, I have been a dick to you for no reason, even if I believe there's a reason because you flirted with my boyfriend right in front of me."

"We didn't hook up?" Sam's face lights up.

Is that why he rescinded his invitation for me to help out at this thing? Is that why I've had to take a squirrel with some kind of skin issue all the way across town to another shelter so I wouldn't embarrassingly throw myself at him again?

"Us? Hell no. No. I've only ever been with Parker. Only. Ever."

I'm sure the countless women before him would love to hear that. Though I get it. He'd never been in love before Parker. And if that's how body count works now, I'm a virgin. Go me!

Sam inches closer to me. "Everyone here in a tutu belongs to you?"

"That depends. Are you ... happy or sad about the tutus?"

"Very happy. This event is supposed to be about having fun."

"Oh, I definitely brought the fun."

"What are you guys?" Ethan cuts in. "Some kind of athletes?" His voice is so deep and loud, the small group of people around us all stop.

I'm pretty sure Connor's mouth is on the patch of grass beneath our feet. How dare someone not follow hockey. That's blasphemous, especially here in Colorado. Then again, it's not like we're in Canada. That would be way worse.

I'm trying to think of a way to tell him we're pro hockey players when Connor speaks up.

"Seriously? They don't even know the greatness they are in the presence of?"

"Why? Are you famous?" Sam asks in a snarky tone.

It's not like I need Sam and Connor to get along for the chance to fuck him, but considering I've been obsessed with this man since I first discovered what jerking off was, I need Connor to stop cockblocking me.

"Not me. That." Connor points to where Ezra and Anton ... were a moment ago.

"Wait. Where's Ezra gone?" Panic claws at my chest, and a chill shoots down my spine.

Horror movie music plays through my mind. Or maybe Ezra and Anton are blasting the *Jaws* soundtrack on their phone. I wouldn't put it past them.

"Hi, Little Kiki." Ezra's voice makes me jump and run.

I duck behind Sam and Ethan. "Save me."

"From what?" Sam asks with amusement in his tone.

"I can't touch the Stanley Cup, or I will never win one."

A weird snorting sound comes from Ethan, hard to explain. I think it's a laugh. Sam laughs too.

"Really?"

Ezra steps forward, trying to get the wheelbarrow between Sam and Ethan.

I grab the back of Sam's arms and use him as a human shield. "Really."

"And is the thing in the wheelbarrow the Stanley Cup, or is it the wheelbarrow? Or is it the hot man wielding the wheelbarrow? It would be a shame to never be able to touch him."

I assume the growl that follows comes from Ezra's husband, but nope. It's apparently coming from me.

And Connor. "Is there anyone you don't flirt with?"

"Nope."

And there's the confirmation I needed. Sam was not seriously flirting with me, he's not actually interested in fucking, and now I'm standing here, in a pink tutu, like an idiot.

Before I can get too down on myself though, someone on a megaphone says it's time to line up for the race.

"You better run fast, Little Kiki," Ezra says. "Lord Stanley is coming for you."

I step backward, bringing Sam with me. "Are you even allowed to race with that thing? Where's its babysitter?" The Stanley Cup has an official handler who goes wherever it goes over the summer.

"Oh, George? We gave George a motorized scooter so he can keep up."

Damn it.

"Are you sure it's a good idea to motivate me this way? I might win the whole thing, and you will lose."

"Pfft. There's no way in hell we're going to win if we're carting this all the way around."

Oh yeah. "Good point. Good luck catching me." With that, I turn on my heel and start jogging toward the starting line, where everyone is lining up.

It's not until I'm in position that I notice Sam followed and is right next to me.

"Good luck catching *us*."

I cock my head. "You don't want to touch the Stanley Cup?"

"Not if it means I'll never win one." He knocks me lightly with his elbow. "I could be good at ... wait, what sport competes for the Stanley Cup?"

I slump. "You're lucky you're hot."

CHAPTER SIX

SAM

Lachie and I are side by side the entire race. He's running so close his scratchy tutu keeps bobbing against my hip, and every time the breeze kicks up, I get a nose full of his fresh sweat. Damn, it's hot.

Unlike me, who probably stinks at this point.

My lungs are tight, and I'm putting all of my effort into finishing this race. We're about three-quarters done, and I'm making good time, but I suspect that he's purposely sticking by my side instead of trying to win. Every time I glance over at him, he looks like a freshly oiled model in neon.

Meanwhile, my tank top is drenched through.

Along the trail, I've seen flashes of those tutus up ahead, the occasional one overtaking us with way too much energy and way too many expletives. The guys with the wheelbarrow must be long behind, but that doesn't stop Lachie from glancing back over his shoulder every few minutes.

"Still ... worried about that thing?"

"Me? Worried? No. No way." Of course, he isn't out of breath at all. I've always prided myself on being fit, but I might need to reassess that idea.

"What's so special ... about it anyway?" I'm trying to match his even tone and failing.

Lachie mutters something under his breath. "It's the Stanley Cup."

"Right."

"*The* Stanley Cup."

"And I'm assuming ... Stanley is an important guy ... in your sport."

"You're killing me. And not just because you have those thighs out."

Now that I know I didn't fuck Connor, there's nothing to stop me from flirting with Lachie. Lachie's presence brings that gut-swimming, pulse-thrumming excitement that's almost addictive.

I know sleeping together is a given, but ... I can't even name the "but" to myself. I get this feeling that I need to hold back. That hesitance is still there. It isn't something I've experienced before, and I'm kind of annoyed about it, if I'm honest. Like my subconscious keeps coming up with excuses about why I shouldn't fuck him when it's something we both want.

Ignoring this gut feeling, I focus back on the man beside me.

He thinks *my* thighs are good when his are a work of art. It's obvious he keeps in shape, and I'm assuming whatever sport he plays helps with that.

"So are you going to share what sport it is? Or is it a secret?"

I sense a brief hesitation. "Hockey."

"Ohh ..." I dated a guy in high school who played ice hockey, and if anything he said could be believed, those locker rooms are homophobic as hell. He refused to come out, I refused to hide, and the minute the team found us together at the movies one night, he joined in on the not-so-nice name-calling and pretended he didn't know me. I'm trying very, very hard not to compare Lachie to that guy. It was ten years ago, and I'm mostly over it, but the association has always stayed. "Are you guys a rec league or something?" Suddenly, the wild outfits are making a lot of sense.

"Yeah ... or something."

I love being active, and I have a group of friends I meet up with to play soccer sometimes, but I've never been involved with organized sports. "Maybe I could join."

A choking noise comes from him. "Have you ever played before?"

"I've ice-skated. How hard would it be to knock a puck around?"

"Oh, yeah, no, not at all."

"You can teach me."

There's nothing but steady breathing beside me, and I look over to check if he heard the suggestion.

Lachie's grinning my way. "Sam ... are you fishing for a date? Because I have to say that's the least romantic thing you could suggest, and you don't need to date me to fuck me."

A laugh explodes from me. At least I never have to worry about Lachie holding back. "No, I actually think it could be fun. My impression of hockey players is ... not the best. Might help to have someone ... like *you* who isn't a complete dick and can prove those impressions wrong."

"You want to prove your impressions wrong?"

"Why not?"

"Feels emotionally healthy to me. Most people I know would prefer to hold a grudge."

"Most people *I* know wouldn't show up with a fuchsia-wearing entourage to a charity run either. I think we can agree neither of us are the types of people we normally hang out with."

"Is that a bad thing?" The vulnerability I detect in that question makes it easy to answer.

"No. I think it might be a—"

There's a squawk, right before a bird lands on Lachie's head.

He ducks slightly but keeps running, glaring up at the thing.

I only realize I've come to a complete stop when he's a few paces ahead of me.

I hurry to catch up. "There's a bird on your head."

"Not the first time it's happened this week."

"*This week*? You've had more than one bird land on your head this week?"

"It happens."

"No, it doesn't."

Lachie gives his head a sudden shake, and the bird takes off. "You're telling me you've never had a bird land on you?"

"Not a wild one, no."

"*Really?*"

"Never." My smile is taking over at the absurdity of the doubt on his face. "You really are a Disney Princess."

Lachie's lips pinch together. "You've always given me shit about that."

"You think I'm giving you shit?"

"Aren't you?"

"No. I think it's really cool."

Our eyes meet for a second, and my toe catches on a stray rock, almost sending me sprawling over the path. Right. Focus. No looking at the pretty man.

"Falling for me already. You're only human."

I regain my footing. "I think we've missed a couple of steps. You should at least buy me a drink before you expect me to fall for you."

"And teach you hockey?"

"Exactly."

"And let you fuck me."

The matter-of-fact way he says it is so confident I have to give him props for that. It also makes me more determined not to make it easy for him though. "You don't give up, do you?"

"Do you want me to give up?"

He knows I don't. It's written all over his sly expression. Unfortunately for him, my blood is too preoccupied overheating my cheeks from the run to rush to my dick, so I can think clearly around him this time. "You know what, I'm interested to see what your moves are."

"My moves?"

"Yeah. How you get a man into bed."

He blinks at me like he's buffering. "I need moves for that?"

I bark out a laugh that makes it even harder to breathe. "How do you normally do it?"

"I say, hey, I'm Lachie Kikishkin. Wanna fuck?"

"You give guys your full name?"

"Of course."

"You're even more confident than I thought." Not that I can talk. A lot of the time with hookups, I don't even bother exchanging names, so he's one up on me. "So ... how would we spell Kiki ... kikish ... shin ..."

"I think you need to learn to pronounce it first. Why do you want to know?"

"Ethan wants to cyberstalk you. While we're at it, how do we spell Lachie?"

"L-A-C-H-I-E, though if you're wanting it for cyberstalking, it's technically Lachlan. But also, you were talking about me with Ethan?"

"That wasn't obvious with the whole fucked-your-brother thing?"

"No, that told me you were talking about Connor." We jog a few more steps. "So what did you say about me?"

"You really want to know?"

He knocks me with his shoulder, the closest he's gotten yet. "*That* good, huh?"

"I might have told him how hot you were enough times to make him want to punch me."

"Ooof. Considering the guy looks like he could take out a tree trunk, that's risky. You really *do* love me."

His words have my skin pricking pleasantly.

The flirting isn't lost on me, and the urge to touch him keeps growing. Lachie is just *hot*. Windswept brown hair, wide jaw, and thick neck, the slutty necklace hanging in front of his tank top, and the way he keeps meeting my eyes, unflinchingly full of the knowledge that we're going to see each other naked. He's the kind of guy who knows who he is and is confident in his skin. That's always been a massive turn-on for me. From what he's saying, he hooks up a lot, and with looks like his, I'm sure he gets whatever he wants in life.

And what *I* want in life is to pull him off the path, press him into a tree, and shove my tongue down his throat. That's not what I'd call falling in love, but I can't deny there's something bugging me to get to know him more.

I have two choices. Finish this race, then take him back to my place for what we both want.

Or make him work for something for maybe the first time in his life.

I'm not sure he's interested enough to play along, but he *did* organize all of his friends to show up here. And if there's any sign that he's losing interest, I can always jump back to plan A.

I rarely get a chance to play with guys. To dive into the tension until it's so strong it hurts. This is my chance.

Looks like summer has become a whole lot more interesting.

CHAPTER SEVEN

LACHIE

The fact that Sam is not balls-deep inside me right now should be illegal. Why hasn't he taken me back to his place and fucked me yet? We flirt the entire race, and it's not like I've been the tiniest bit subtle about what I want.

He hasn't been subtle either.

But as soon as the race finishes, he sends me a smile and says, "Thanks for keeping pace with me, even though you were barely breaking a sweat."

I don't even get a chance to boast about my stamina before he walks away.

The mixed signals are driving me so crazy, my skin is itchy, like horny me is trying to claw his way out of my body just to get some relief.

Does this really all come down to him being a flirt with no follow-through?

If that's the case, I'll be disappointed, sure, and it's his right to be that way. But it will also be my right to jerk off to the thought of him until my dick is raw.

I give him the benefit of the doubt because he does have to stay until after the ceremonies, make a speech about the money they'd made, and then pack everything away, so it's not like he's had a chance to drag me into his office or a cave, or hell, I'd settle for a romp in overgrown grass. So I hang back, tell the guys they can go get ready for the Collective shenanigans we have planned for the night, and help with whatever I can to make packing everything down faster.

Only to be met with, "Thanks for coming today. I'm sure I'll see you at the shelter again soon."

I am so damn confused.

I knew what I was doing hanging back. *He* knew what I was doing hanging back. And he's still walking away.

I've never thought of myself as a cocky guy before, but with how shocked I am that I've been turned down, maybe I am? Or maybe it has to do with that slightly tender bruise of disappointment growing in my chest.

I don't have the time to drive home to Mom and Dad's, shower, and change into something I don't mind ruining with alcohol spills, vomit, and cum, so my tutu and pink tank will have to do. I'm already going to be the last one to arrive.

We're all meeting at a sports bar where everyone knows us by name. Not only us Kikishkin brothers—Denver-raised boys where the older two have done our hometown proud—but every single member of the Collective.

Sam and Ethan might not know who we are, but half of Denver does. Okay, probably less than half, but it would be close.

We're not famous, household names nationwide, but in part of this town, we are.

The Collective is staying out by Lake Dillon, which they'll make their way to later this evening, but for now, we're having a drink or two after making them all run thirteen miles. On me, of course, because I forced them into some light cardio during the off-season. Hey, their teams might thank me once the season starts up again.

I don't have many plans for the summer. I'm going into my last contracted entry-level year, so I figured I need to be more low-key than I usually am.

Though for someone who has never tried to hide their sexuality, I'm surprised I'm the only Collective member who hasn't had a scandal yet.

Am I ... the good boy?

Oh, wait. Foster Grant hasn't either. It's so easy to forget about him when everyone else is so loud.

So it goes Foster Grant, then me on the well-behaved to naughty scale.

Slap my ass and give me my halo, damn it.

Technically, Connor and Novi haven't had huge scandals yet, but it's only a matter of time. My brother "retired" early due to an "injury," but that injury was a horny dick that landed inside the team owner. They're waiting a few years before coming out as a couple publicly. At the same time, like me, it's not like they hide it well. A lot of people in our hockey circles know, but it hasn't hit those gossipy social media profiles who like to post all the details of players' private lives. Now that Novi has retired, I'm awaiting his announcement of being engaged to his old coach from his last team, which will get people talking.

Bottom line is I'm the innocent one, so I deserve some sex.

Okay, eww, that sounds too incel for my liking.

It's not like I wouldn't be able to hook up with someone else. I have no issue pulling a willing participant, but I've wanted Sam since I was a scrawny teenager, and he has finally noticed me. I don't want any random fuck. I want Sam.

The second I step through the doors of Lady Gin, I'm practically attacked from both sides by a cloud of expensive cologne and warring egos.

"Hey, Little Kiki," Ezra taunts. His husband has my other arm, and they start dragging me toward a corner booth where the shiny, slightly dinted, Stanley Cup sits in the middle of a table.

"No! No, no, no." I shake my head and try to backtrack, but Ezra and Anton don't let me. "Why are you being so mean? Is this your way of flirting? Do you two swing? I'll let you tag team me if you stop with the Stanley Cup jinx." I look at Ezra. "You, of all people, should appreciate the superstition. Don't make me bring a black cat with me every time we meet."

Ezra drops my arm and his jaw. "You wouldn't."

"Oh, I would."

"Fine. No more Stanley jump scares."

Anton releases me now as well. "Way to make it unfun."

"You hate black cats too?"

"No," he growls. "I hate people joking about fucking my husband."

Noted. I will put that in my back pocket for later. Not as a reminder of how to keep the peace but of how to get what I want.

"Where are our drinks?" Easton calls out from his seat.

I fish out my credit card from my wallet and throw it at him as I take a seat next to Dex Mitchale, who's cuddled up with his husband, Tripp. "Have at it."

"Oh, little bro, you are going to regret this." East stands and heads for the bar.

Eh, I'm expecting tonight's check to be ridiculous. I'm good for it. We all are. My entry-level contract alone was worth four million a year, and I'm the lowest-paid player in this room. So yeah, tonight is going to get messy.

With the Collective, it always is.

—

Ezra somehow convinces the bartenders to put the replay of them winning this past season on the TV above the bar, and now he's drunkenly standing *on* the bar singing. He's drawing a crowd who all have their phones pointed his way, and I have a good feeling I'm going to see this moment all over my social media tomorrow.

Recently retired Oskar Voyjik is spooning the Stanley Cup, his feet up on his husband's lap as he lies across the vinyl booth, slurring words like "We could have been so good together" against the metal. All the while, Lane pats Oskar's legs and replies with some version of "I'm really feeling the love."

George is in the corner, head in his hands, the weight of the world on the shoulders of a man who has seen some shit happen with that Cup.

I'm happily buzzed, not wasted like others, but I learned my lesson with the llama. Getting drunk and then having animals follow you with no memory of who they belong to or how to get them back to their owners? I don't want to go through that headache again.

Contrary to what these guys think, I didn't steal the llama. I'm ninety percent sure of that. Okay, eighty. I definitely didn't kidnap the goats that came with the llama, and if I didn't take them, then obviously, I didn't take the llama. My logic is sound. Ish.

Maybe I'm drunker than I thought.

An arm wraps around my shoulders, and the stinky breath of my brother Easton hits my cheek as he sways into me.

"Psst. We have a brilliant idea."

I think he's trying to be quiet, but he's yelling. Not that anyone close would be able to hear us in the loud bar.

I pull my face away from the alcohol breath. "What's the idea?"

"While the bozos from Boston are distracted, we're going to pry the Cup from Voyjik's arms, then take it to the golf course and send ransom photos."

"Okay, one, brilliant idea! But more importantly, there's no way we can pull it off. If we do somehow manage to distract prison guard Connor, we still have to get by George."

Easton smiles proudly. "Connor and Knox are in, and George is just going to have to follow us."

"Connor is in? Connor. Uptight-as-hell, follow-the-rules Connor?"

"I'm fun, you fucker."

I jump at my other brother's voice coming from behind me. A more responsible person would protest all the ways this plan could turn disastrous. Luckily for this family, that person is usually Connor, so if he's in ... "Let's go."

Seeing as I'm one of the few in this damn group without a Stanley Cup to my name and can't touch it, I head to the bar and throw my arm around Anton's shoulders to cheer on Ezra's surprisingly amazing rendition of "We Are the Champions." I'd worry about only having a couple of seconds to keep them distracted as it's the end of the song, but of course, Ezra drags out the final notes, then asks the barkeep to play the song again. He's probably going to be up there singing the same song for the next three hours while the replay of the Cup-winning game shows on the screen behind him.

As casually as I can, I look over my shoulder to see if they've got the Cup moving yet. They're still trying to pry it from Oskar's hands, but once they get it free, I know I need to up my distraction game because from where Ezra is, standing on the bar, he has the best viewpoint to see what they're doing in the back corner.

But how the hell can I distract the most egotistical couple in the league? Then an idea I know I'm going to regret pops into my head, and before I can rethink it, I pull off my tank top, whip it around in the air, and throw it in Ezra's direction so his eyes are drawn to me. Where I proceed to press in close to Anton. I grab his hand and wrap his arm around me as we sway to the song.

Anton barely pays me attention because he's too busy staring up at his husband like he's in some kind of mating ritual trance. But Ezra notices me. And that's the whole point. Because if he's looking at me shamelessly all over his husband, he's either going to get so turned on, he'll jump down and take Anton to the nearest quiet area to get off, or he'll get so mad, I'll get punched in the face.

I hope for the former but prepare for the latter.

When that moment inevitably happens and he leaps from the bar, I brace for violence. The only thing remotely resembling violence is when Ezra barges me from the side and takes my place in Anton's arms. Somehow, I catch myself before I go sprawling, and the second Ezra grabs Anton's face and smashes their lips together, I take my chance to make my escape and help the guys get the Cup.

At least focused on the Cup, I don't have time to think about the weird hit of longing I get over their claiming kiss.

I run to my brothers and yell, "Go, go, go, they're making out, we have at least a couple minutes to get a head start until they notice it's gone."

"We would be faster if you could help us carry the damn thing," Connor grumbles.

"Not you too. I'm not touching it."

"At least get the door. Wait... what happened to your shirt?"

"Never mind that. Let's get out of here before they notice."

CHAPTER EIGHT

SAM

I can safely say that I've never had an after-midnight callout for zombie squirrels, but there really is a first for everything. Mostly because I'm ninety-nine percent sure they don't exist, and that remaining one percent is only because I'm not so sure I heard the guy properly through all the shrieking.

I climb out of my car in the Ravenna Country Club parking lot, wondering if I'm about to be arrested. This is probably the fanciest place I've ever been to, and sneaking onto the grounds in the dead of night feels like something I could be arrested for. Fuck me.

Still not sure, I pull out my phone and call the number back.

It answers on the first ring.

"I'm, ah, here ..."

"*Ohthankgod!*"

It takes me a second to decipher the slurred words. "Can you bring the animal to the parking lot?"

"We can't! That's the wissue!"

"Wissue?"

"Hurry! They're going to be here soon, and swiwwrels are trying to eat us!"

I stop midway toward the fence line and where the guy assured me there's a space to get through. "Are the animals injured or—"

"*I'm* injured! It bit me. I think I have rabies!"

In the background, I hear someone yell, "It's *about* to be injured—"

"Okay, stop. Back away. Leave the wild animals alone—"

"But the Cup! They have the Cup! You don't understand, it's the Cuuuup!"

A trickle of awareness slips through me. "Does this cup belong to someone called Stanley, by any chance?"

"You're a *fan*?"

I hang up, half a mind to get back in my car and leave, the other half more curious than I want to admit. I have a very good feeling that the drunken men I'm about to encounter might have to do with the one I haven't stopped thinking about all night.

Fuck it. If security spots me, I'll let them know I'm trying to save their golf course from morons in neon. No one would arrest me for that.

I slip through the gap in the fence, moving faster now that I know I'm not walking into a potential murder scene. It only takes a few minutes, but the man was right.

I can't miss them.

As I approach the group, one keeps darting forward, screaming, then backing away again, while the group around him is a mix of rolling on the grass laughing and worriedly watching the scene unfurl.

Except for one lone man. I pass the tired-looking guy who's sitting on the green, cheek propped in one hand while he plucks at blades of grass. I recognize him as the guy who was on the motorized scooter during the race today.

"You okay?"

"All part of the job."

Another shriek pierces the night air, bringing my attention back to the blond man backing away again. "Don't take offense to this, but shouldn't you have maybe *not* let the drunken men break in here?"

"That is *not* part of my job. As long as the Cup is safe, they can do what they like."

I narrow my eyes at him, suddenly understanding that this trophy thing might be more of a big deal than I realized. It only takes me a second to spot it, lying on its side, while a family of squirrels scamper over it. And squatting not too far away, trying to coax them to him, is Lachie.

My stomach flutters at the sight of him, and I force it to calm down before I approach.

"We have to stop meeting like this."

"S-Sam." He shoves to his feet but stumbles so hard I have to catch him. His biceps are warm under my palms, and it doesn't escape my notice that he's shirtless. Again. And that he looks just as sexy at night as he did under the shelter's fluorescents.

"I had a callout for zombie squirrels."

Before he can reply, a heavy arm slings over my shoulders, and I'm hit with the scent of dried sweat and alcohol. "Look who it is. Mr. Animal Man."

"Connor." I ignore my urge to elbow him in the ribs. "Are you the one who called me to come?"

"Call you? Why would I call *you*? I don't want you to come. Not everyone is into you, even with your big smile and muscles. Some guys don't like that kind of thing, and you shouldn't flirt with them or their boyfriends or their brothers or—"

I cut off his drunken ramblings by patting his very large chest. "You're right. Some guys aren't into that kind of thing. But some are." I spare a smile for Lachie. "Ask your brother."

Then I slip out from under his arm and leave his grumbling behind. Lachie follows, but I refuse to look at him because his naked torso is making it very hard to remember that the plan is to tease him. Not fuck him. Yet.

Right.

"Who called about the zombie squirrels?"

Yes, that's a question that just came from me.

A dark-haired man flings his arm in the air. "Me. Bilson. They're trying to eat my Miles."

"Who?"

He points at the blond man with the backward baseball cap who's approaching the Cup again.

I hurriedly get between him and the squirrels, catching his chest and making him back up a few steps. And of course, he has an amazing chest too.

"Is there anyone here sober enough to tell me what's going on?"

Another inhumanly attractive man seems to think that's him. It isn't.

"We kidnapped the Cup and were about to take ransom photos, but then the squirrels kidnapped it back, and now we're in a standoff feud with forest creatures who know that the bigger Kikis are the only ones allowed to touch it, but they're scared of the squirrels, so Miles is trying to scare them off, but he almost touched the Cup once, so now it's getting too risky—"

"Holy fuck, stop."

Connor snorts. "Not going to flirt with Aleks too?"

"Keep going with that attitude and I'll flirt with Lachie harder."

Lachie pops up beside Connor. "You will?" He shoves his brother closer. "Quick, keep being petty. That's easy for you."

"I'm not petty!"

Easton sits up from where he's lying on the grass. "You're very petty."

"Fuck you all."

"But we love you, even though you're an ass sometimes."

He drops his voice. "Parker loves my ass."

"You do have a great ass," I agree.

Connor's face takes on an almost painful expression, like he's torn between having an ally and actually liking me. While he's broken, I turn back to Lachie. His face, not his chest.

"Get the squirrels."

He recoils. "I'm not going near that thing."

"You're a literal Disney Princess, and you got me out of bed to solve a problem you could very easily solve but won't because of some dumb superstition?"

He gasps. "You take that back."

"Superstitions *are* dumb."

"Not *that* part!" His gaze flies between the men around us, who are all staring at Lachie like he's gifted them new cars. "The princess part! Quick, reverse time!"

"My brother is Cinder-fucking-rella," Easton cackles. "Wait until I tell Ezra."

"Do *not* tell Ezra."

"Baby bro, every single one of us is telling Ezra."

Aleks holds up his phone. "I've already texted him. And changed your name in my phone."

"Oooh, good idea," Bilson says, and everyone except Lachie turns to his phone.

Lachie face-palms. "You owe me for that."

The whine in his tone is adorable. "Fine. If I save your Cup, will we be even?"

"Sam! Now you're rubbing in that it's not *my* Cup. Why do you hate me?"

I laugh and ignore him as I take out my thick gloves and pull them on. "Please don't say my name like that. You're giving me ideas."

Connor chokes behind me, and Lachie looks like he's swallowed his tongue.

I turn toward the Cup and the squirrels using it as an obstacle course. As I approach, their alarm calls get louder, and they start showing signs of aggression. They're ballsy little bastards, that's for sure, and when one of them puffs itself up in front of me, I spot its scarred face. At least now I know where the zombie claims came from.

I crouch down, trying to appear nonthreatening, and make a quiet little tutting noise.

The zombie squirrel immediately jumps toward my outstretched hand and latches its little teeth onto the glove.

So maybe these guys were right to keep their distance. Miles screams again, and there's commotion behind me, but I grab the little guy from behind and gently pry him off.

Lachie crouches beside me, close enough to feel his body warmth.

"Careful," I warn him. "The cup thing is right there."

"I wanted to give you backup until you called it a cup thing, and now I'm thinking you deserve to be eaten by rabid squirrels."

I stand as the little thing struggles against my hold, but it's not going anywhere. With the angry one removed, the others dart for Lachie like he's a life raft, and I watch as they scramble up his arms and legs. I've seen the attachment from the injured animals he brings in to me, but this is something else.

They're climbing that man like a tree, and I can't blame them for it.

Maybe I'm just an animal at heart.

We move the squirrels away, and there's a triumphant hoot from the others as Easton hoists the Cup up off the grass.

I don't talk again until we set the squirrels down back by the trees, and I have to give the angry one a nudge with the toe of my boot to get it moving. "You know, technically, I was looking out for you with the Cup. That gets me brownie points, doesn't it?"

Lachie's gaze searches mine, and he seems more sober than I first gave him credit for. "Depends. Do you *want* brownie points?"

"Why wouldn't I?"

"You ran out on me pretty fast today."

I probably shouldn't like the sulky tone he takes on. "And you didn't try to stop me."

Lachie's whole face lights up. "You weren't brushing me off?"

The hope in his voice makes it so hard not to set my stupid plan aside. This feeling, that sizzling attraction before giving in, is addictive though, and I want to indulge in it for a bit longer. I wrap his long necklace around my fist and tug him close enough that I can tilt my lips by his ear. "Asking me if I want to fuck isn't going to get me into bed. I told you, I want to see your moves."

His exhale rushes against my neck. "We don't need a bed. We can do it against this tree. I'm not picky."

"Not my point."

"What's your point? There's a point?" He backs up, eyes squeezed closed as he presses down on his cock. "Can't think with you so close to me."

Him and me both. I'm not hard like he is, but if I keep looking at his chest, it won't be long. I tear my gaze back to his friends on the golf course. Instant boner killer. Maybe I shouldn't be completely honest, but the game is more fun if we're both playing it. "My point is that I have the impression you get what you want, when you want it. So I'm not going to take it that easy on you. You want to fuck, you need to earn it."

"Wait. Why shouldn't *you* be the one to work for it? I'm a catch, damn it."

I take a moment to blatantly check him out. My gaze runs from that stunning face, over his droolworthy chest, and down to where his cum gutters meet the waistband of his still-ridiculous tutu. My voice comes out more gravelly than I mean it to. "If you think I'm not working for it, you'd be very, very wrong."

He releases the sluttiest moan I've ever heard. "Fine. I give in. How do I earn it?"

"That's what you have all summer to figure out."

CHAPTER NINE

LACHIE

I need to earn it? Like having a crush on the guy for the longest time hasn't been enough torture? I finally, *finally*, get his attention, and he's going to make me work for it?

I pause on that for a second. Okay, that's fair, but it's a giant tease, telling me I can basically have everything I've wanted if I'm able to put in the effort. I am so willing to put in the effort, but summer is only so long, and I'd much rather spend the next two months naked with him.

Sam stands in front of me, lips turned upward as he waits for me to say a magic word or some shit, but when my mouth opens and closes with no sound coming out, he huffs like he's not surprised and then tries to walk away.

I grab his upper arm. "Can I at least get your number?"

His smile widens. "Your friend found it easily enough. I'm sure you can handle it." He shrugs out of my hold and begins his trek back to where Ezra and Anton have now arrived to reclaim what is rightfully theirs.

Miles must be filming because as soon as Anton and Ezra charge toward the group, he runs in the opposite direction, holding his phone over his shoulder and pointing it in their direction as he screams, "Your old knees will never catch me."

"Interesting group of friends you have here," Sam says as I fall into step with him.

"Eh, they're more my brothers' friends. They let me tag along so they can live vicariously through me."

"You really do think highly of yourself, don't you?" Sam doesn't sound turned off by that fact, but he's got it all wrong.

"Compared to these guys? No way. It's that I'm the youngest of them all, and they're all coupled up now. I'm the only single one, and if it weren't for my two older brothers, I doubt any of them would want to hang around me."

"Why the hell not? You're an amazing human being."

I ignore the warm glow that fills my chest. "How do you know that? You knew me when I was a kid, and you haven't seen me for, like, three years. You don't know I'm amazing."

"I know you enough. There's a reason animals gravitate toward you, and it's because they can sense that you're safe. You can help them. I have never seen it so strongly with anyone before—"

"You mean apart from Disney Princesses?"

"Anyone real, then. But wildlife and animals see you as one of them."

"Maybe they can sense that I'm as untamable as they are."

"Untamable, huh?" He stops walking and glances at me, tracing my face with his gaze. "We'll see about that."

My feet are rooted to the ground as Sam walks away again, and as my gaze dips to his ass, I begin to think there might be something to this having-to-work-for-it angle.

It's like edging. It's a lot of teasing, a building need, and when I finally get it, the high will be euphoric.

He wants to be chased, and I love a good game of cat and mouse. Of course, I'm usually the mouse, and it doesn't take much chasing for a cat to catch me. Usually a simple "You're hot" will make me give in.

What can I say, I'm an easy guy. But Sam is going to make this anything but easy.

Game on.

—

Okay, game off.

I don't know what I'm doing.

As I lie on the couch of the insanely huge holiday rental the guys are staying at, I mindlessly toss a baseball in the air and hope I catch it before it hits me in the face. It may or may not have already happened once or twice. I'm hoping if I do miss, it might knock some ideas into me.

How do you seduce someone without coming across as creepy or stalkery?

I could show up to his work, but how is that any different to usual? It's not. That's how I met him, developed my crush on him, and then felt rejected every time he didn't pay me any attention.

Now I have his attention, how do I keep it?

I stand and try to find some of the others. They're all in couples, so maybe they can help. The only issue will be finding any of them who aren't having "afternoon naps," which I've learned through the power of using my ears is code for afternoon fucks.

I make a mental note to ask them later that if the whole house is filled with men getting dicked down, does that mean they technically have orgies every time they go on vacation together? Maybe that's how I could get Sam into bed. Offer for him to be my plus-one in this group of obsessively fucked-up friends who are unaware of all the orgies they have.

I head to the basement, where there's a games room filled with board games that have so many missing pieces you can't play them—I know, I checked—and a pool table. It also houses all the lake toys for the summer and the snow necessities for the winter.

Ezra and Anton are playing pool. Or they were. They're currently making out against the pool table.

I clear my throat.

Ezra waves me off and doesn't pull his face away from his husband's.

"Fine. I'll come back. Just don't get cum on the felt."

Ezra mumbles against Anton's lips, "We can afford to clean it."

"I don't care about that! I want to play pool later."

They both laugh, so I head out the side door to the backyard that leads down to the lake. Ayri Quinn and Vance Landon are on the small jetty, swinging their legs as they sit with a fishing rod between them.

I give them a wave and head their way. "Catch anything?"

"Nah," Vance says, "we're not even using bait. We wanted to get some peace and quiet from all the chaos inside that house."

"I'm surprised you're not joining in on the orgy."

Quinn splutters as he chokes on ... air? His spit? Who knows. "They're doing what in there now?"

"Not literally. But with the noises coming from some of the rooms, I feel like they're all doing the same thing."

"You're welcome to hang with us," Quinn says. "We're talking about the future."

"I'd rather listen to everyone around me have sex than think about that."

Vance looks surprised by that. "Why? You have an amazing future ahead of you. You're going to be one of the greats."

I've been told that my whole life. All three of us Kikishkins have. We are the future of hockey. Apparently. Which is awesome and all, but sometimes it's hard to see what else there is. "Considering the only guarantee I have for my future is hockey, that doesn't reassure me at all. Because hockey is never a guarantee, not even for those who are great. Anything could happen. And being around all these couples ... it makes me realize I've never been serious about anyone ever."

"You're twenty-one. You don't need to be serious about anyone," Vance says.

That's true too, but it's exactly what I was saying to Sam last night. I'm a lot younger than all of these guys, and some of them have started retiring already. Maybe I am too young to be thinking about a serious relationship, but if I don't even know how to ask someone on a date, how to actually win over someone's heart instead of only their dick, I'm never going to find the type of love the rest of the Collective has.

"How did you two fall in love?" I ask. "Who asked who out, and—"

"Uhh, Quinn's dick let me know how he felt about me whenever he was on my physio table."

Quinn shoves Vance. "Can you not tell everyone that story?"

"Okay, that won't work for me," I say before Vance ends up in the lake. "There's this guy—"

"The guy from the race yesterday?" Vance asks.

"Yes. Him. We've basically told each other we want to bone, but he says I have to work for it. Apparently, my usual tactic of straight up saying 'We going to do this?' wasn't good enough of a try for him. How do you ask someone on a date?"

"Vance took me geocaching."

I screw up my face. "Is that where you go around looking for hidden treasure and shit?"

"Yup." Quinn smiles.

"Not my style. I don't need to nerd out around Sam when he already thinks I'm a ..." Nope, not going to say it.

"Disney Princess?" Vance smothers a laugh.

Damn it. "Exactly. I need him to see me as awesome."

"Geocaching is awesome." Quinn legitimately looks confused. Not sure I can take "awesome" advice from someone with that much hair riding his top lip.

I put my hands up. "It is. It is. Just ... not for this. What the fuck is romance, and how do I do it?"

"As you said, you have a house full of couples. Why don't you ask the others?" Vance suggests.

"As soon as they stop boning, I will."

It's only half an hour before the first couple emerge. It's Lane and Oskar. I jump up from the dock and head their way. "How did you two fall in love?"

Oskar smiles, making his scar along his cheek crinkle. "He had to babysit me to make sure I kept my dick in my pants. It turns out, he couldn't keep his in his pants."

Ugh. "That won't work either."

"Huh?" Oskar asks, but I'm already headed inside, where I find Miles and Bilson.

"How did you two fall in love?"

"Uh, we started fucking as bros and did the whole 'it's not gay if you don't look your bro in the eye as you dick him down.'"

I'm beginning to think the Collective is not going to give me the answers I need.

CHAPTER TEN

SAM

My phone lights up with a DM, and I hurry through my remaining set of sit-ups to check it. I'm panting, overheated, and when I see the name in my inbox, I assume sweat has gotten into my eyes and I'm seeing things.

I grab my towel and wipe my face down, then try again.
Nope.
The name hasn't changed.
Lachie Kiki.
His message isn't what I'm expecting either.

> Do you know how many Sams there are in Denver?

I'm grinning and not entirely sure my racing pulse is from my workout or him contacting me.

> Can't say I've ever done a headcount.

Considering my profile is literally *Sam T*, I'm surprised he managed to find me. I don't even know if he knows my last name is Travers.

> Let's just say I started my search days ago. There were at least three times I worried that you weren't on social media at all and that I was completely wasting my time.

But he still kept looking? Considering my impression of Lachie is that he likes to have a fun and fast time, I'm impressed. I guess he's not as opposed to my game as I worried he might be.

Which is good for me, because I love a good flirt over text.

> Why didn't you get my number off your friend?

His response is so fast I assume he was waiting for that question.

> I did. It went through to the animal rescue line and someone else answered. Smartass.

Considering my on-call ended at six, I can imagine Lachie spluttering his way through that one.

> Guess I should have mentioned that wasn't my direct line.

> We both know that wasn't an accident. But I hunted you down, are you impressed?

> Impressed and turned on.

Yes, that was mean of me, but I don't want him to doubt my interest, even though we're not immediately jumping into bed together.

> Ten points for you.

> We're working on a point system now?

> Why not? A kiss has to be worth twenty points.

> I should probably tell you now that math is my most hated subject.

> Then let me break it down for you: you're halfway there.

> Halfway to a kiss, you mean. Don't get me wrong, I'm dying for that, but it's nowhere near halfway to what I really want.

> Has anyone ever told you that you're so good at playing it cool?

> Fuck that. I might be into your game but I'm not going to act like I don't want to see you naked. That is the whole point of this.

> Another point for honesty. I like a man who's clear about what he wants.

> What else do you like?

Him asking me an actual question about myself catches me off guard. It's hard to know if he's asking sexually or in general.

> I like a man who doesn't take things too seriously. Who's ready for fun.

> Have you dated many guys like that?

> A few. But what I like in a guy I fuck versus one I date is very different.

> In what way?

> Guys I fuck need to be into it, sometimes adventurous, and attractive to me. That's basically it. Guys I date need to be someone I can have fun with but can also trust. Trust is something I struggle with.

I don't mean to type that last part, but somewhere deep down, I guess I'm warning him that this is strictly fun. He's here for the summer, we're both into each other, and from what little I know, he likes to sleep around. I've tried dating guys long distance, or who were closeted, or who wanted an open relationship. Those things don't work for me, and I know it.

His answering question is expected.

> Why?

It's too early to get into a deep conversation, so I leave it at:

> Just my personality.

And because this whole conversation has been centered on me, I turn his question back around.

> What kind of guys do you date?

> I don't. My career makes it hard.

I guess he's not a teacher, then, because I can't imagine that being a career that gets in the way of a relationship. Because I can't help myself, I probe a bit deeper.

> Is that something you want?

I'm tense as the dots bounce and disappear and bounce again.

> One day.

I breathe out in relief. He's not looking for a relationship, which is perfect for our arrangement. Sex and then back to our regular lives.

Part of me wants to send through my address so he can come over and we get this thing started; summer only lasts for so long. But stretching things out a couple of days can't hurt. Right?

I look down at where my cock is tenting my pants. *Right?*

Before I can decide, his reply comes through.

> You busy today?

> Why?

> I have points to earn and moves to make.

That gets a laugh from me.

> Have you figured out your moves already?

> I went to the guys for advice.

> How did that go?

> Depends. Would burning down my house impress you?

> What the fuck?

> Or I could accidentally force you to marry me?

> Is there a third option?

> You don't want to know.

> Actually I'm sort of invested now.

> In that case I can taunt you about being bad at sex until you prove to me you're not.

> Genuinely: who are you hanging out with?

> Come on a date with me today and you'll find out.

Well, that's an offer I can't say no to.

—

I look around at the explosion of mayhem in front of me. "Quick question: do these guys have a drinking problem? The two out of three times I've seen them, they've been drunk."

Lachie hands me a beer. "We're good boys for eight months out of the year. Summer is the time to have our fun."

My gaze sweeps the scene in front of me as I try to count how many people are here. There's the group from the golf course. Easton is kissing some strawberry blond guy up against the side of the lake house, while Connor argues with a man with a giant scar down his face. Ezra is being chased down to the jetty by a black-haired man with a Super Soaker, while his husband is stretched out on a sun lounger beside a man with a sexy mustache and another who's completely covered in freckles, and that's not even all of them.

I look from one cluster of men to the next, taking in the familiarity, the casual handholding or kissing, and turn back to Lachie.

"Is everyone here queer?"

"That is why we're called the Queer Collective."

"Is it?" A man passing stops in front of me. "I thought it was because we're queer and Ezra is collecting us."

Lachie snorts. "Considering you're married to the smartest man I've ever met, Foster, you of all people should know the answer to that."

"I dunno. Zach calls us a cult. Are we a cult?"

Lachie takes a swig of his beer. "Pretty much."

"Shit." Foster shoves a hand through his hair and glances around. "I need to call Beck. He has experience getting out of those."

I have no clue who Beck is, but it sounds like someone needs to be worried about him.

I take in the extravagance before me. If it is a cult, I wouldn't mind joining. A multimillion-dollar lakeside house, an international music icon, the line of luxury SUVs down the side, and bottles and bottles of expensive alcohol ...

Oh. Oh no.

"Lachie ... you're not in a rec league, are you?"

"Rec league," Foster snickers and stumbles away.

"*Technically*, I told you we were *or something*." Lachie gestures to the hooting and hollering mess around us. "This is or something."

"And 'or something' in this context, means …"

He takes another sip and says into his beer, "NHL."

"NHL, as in the *pro* league? The best of the best?"

"We brought the Stanley Cup to a fundraiser. The signs were there."

"It was a trophy. In a wheelbarrow. Surrounded by men in ridiculous outfits. The signs were very much not there."

"You haven't spent much time around professional athletes, have you?"

"I think I need another beer."

Instead of showing me to the alcohol, Lachie takes my hip and turns me toward him. "I'm basically famous. Tell me that doesn't make you want to sleep with me."

At least it's making sense why he's never had to work for a hookup before. Even the hottest men strike out sometimes, but being this sexy *and* a professional hockey player, the odds are definitely in his favor. "If anything, it means you need to work harder."

"Harder?"

My grin tugs outward. "Now I know how easy you have it, yes. But for the record, I wanted to sleep with you before I found all this out, and that hasn't changed."

"You want me for my body and not my status?"

"Your status means nothing to me." I glance down at his T-shirt-covered chest. "But I might need another glimpse at that body to be sure."

The smuggest smile I've ever seen him wear crosses his face, and he reaches for the shirt. "It *is* a lake party. It's almost rude to be clothed." He lifts the material slowly, revealing his abs, his nipples, and his chest, then tugs it over his head and tucks it into his shorts. "Your turn."

Who am I to argue with the dress code? I'd worn my nicest button-up, thinking this was a *date* date, but I'm grateful to be getting rid of it. I'm not a dressy guy, and I won't tell Lachie, but a casual party is way more my speed than sitting down in a restaurant and eyeballing each other.

"Holy fuck," comes out in a strangled breath. "You are such a tease."

"You asked for it." I flex my pecs, and Lachie covers his eyes and spins away from me.

"Torture. This is fucking torture."

And because I want to torture him some more, I step closer, one hand casually resting on his hip and soaking up his warm skin, and murmur by his ear, "You've only seen the half of it."

He shivers, but we're interrupted before he can respond.

"Whoa," comes a loud voice from behind me. "Mr. Animal Man hasn't been skipping chest day, has he?"

I turn toward Ezra—the one who was taunting Lachie with the Cup—and the bluest eyes I've ever seen. "I take care of myself."

"Yeah, you do." Then he turns to shout over his shoulder. "See, Anton? There is no letting yourself go. Got it? No excuses!"

The *GQ* model with the slick black hair and big sunglasses flips him off. Judging by what I'm seeing, I can't imagine that man ever looking like anything other than the Greek god lying there.

"He loves me," Ezra sighs.

Lachie snickers into his drink. "The fact you have to tell people that during every conversation is a worry."

"You don't believe me?" Ezra asks.

"Nope."

"Watch this, then." He pulls sunscreen from the back of his shorts and holds it out to me. "Be a dear and rub this into my back, won't you?"

"Fuck off, Ezra," Lachie snaps. "Sam is mine."

His? Ohh, this is fun. "Just to confirm, if I do that, it'll make your husband jealous?"

"And turned on."

"Will he kill me?"

"Nope. I'm the one who gets punished." The excited way he says that—and the pouty expression on Lachie's face—has me all in.

I snap open the lid. "Turn around."

Then I proceed to massage cream into his back while Ezra makes so many turned-on noises we get the attention of everyone close by. I can feel his husband's stare on us, and despite what he said, I'm very worried I'm about to be punched.

But then I glance at Lachie and the needy puppy dog eyes he's giving me, and my excitement kicks up again. "Like what you see?"

"*I* want a back massage."

Ezra moans louder.

"Will you be as dramatic about it as he is?"

"No." He pauses for a *Sam, oh, Sam!* then adds, "My moans will be real."

Imagining that is almost enough to get me hard, but I focus on keeping my dick down while my hands are on Ezra. I don't want anyone to get the wrong ideas about what's causing it.

Even with all the sexy, shirtless men here, there's only one of them I have any interest in.

"And that's exactly why I won't be doing it."

Lachie groans at the exact moment Anton appears in front of us like he's popped out of thin air.

"Baby, Sam's got my back so creamy and wet."

I never want to hear Ezra say "creamy and wet" again.

I immediately let him go, kinda scared for my life, but all Anton says is, "Inside. *Now*," and Ezra does exactly what he's told.

I glance over at Lachie as they leave. "I'm not sure what happened there."

"Anton gets turned on seeing Ezra flirt with people, and Ezra gets turned on when Anton goes all caveman."

"Ohhh."

Lachie crosses his arms tightly. "I maybe might understand where Anton is coming from."

I lift my eyebrows for him to go on.

"You're both really hot."

A laugh bursts from me. "Did that turn you on?"

"At this point, I think everything you do will turn me on." He steps close enough that our chests brush, and this time, the surge of attraction is out of my control. "Except unlike Anton, that just made me really jealous."

"Jealous?" I know he wants to sleep with me, but that's taking things a bit far.

And then, in the midst of half the Collective screaming out of tune to a Jay Jackson song, another of them car surfing, three wrestling each other off the jetty, and the spares filling up water balloons that can only mean trouble, Lachie leans in by my ear and utters the last thing I'm expecting.

"I've wanted you to touch me like that since the first day I saw you."

CHAPTER ELEVEN

LACHIE

Sam stumbles away a couple of steps and echoes, "The first day? You were ... like, ten."

"Twelve, actually."

"Yeah, that isn't any better." He screws up his face.

Okay, so I made it weird instead of the endearing tale I thought it could be. "Yeah, now that I'm thinking about it, telling you I had a crush when I was a child and you were an adult is probably not as cute as it is in my head."

"Not cute at all. In fact ..." He glances around at the chaos that follows the Collective—the god of mischief's fault, not our own—and frowns. "Putting everything into perspective—"

"Noooo. Don't do that. Perspective is bad. Ignoring red flags is good."

He laughs. "My point is, throwing me back to those days where you'd come into the shelter with whatever animal you had rescued that day, your big bright eyes and an eagerness to work with the animals, it kinda reminds me of how much younger you are. Your group of friends don't really help with the immature image."

"Pfft. These guys are as old as you are."

"That doesn't help either!" But he still sounds amused, so I hope he's joking.

"Trust me, I knew back then you would never look at me in a romantic way. Hell, that might be why I'm still playing your game. Because I never thought you would look at me as anything more than a sucker volunteer who did all your grunt work because he had hearts in his eyes. I was a dumb kid back then. Unaware of how the world works. I moved away and grew up, Sam. You're allowed to see me as someone new. I'm not a kid anymore."

"You've definitely grown up. Physically. The last two days of shenanigans you and your friends have pulled make me question how serious you can be."

"I thought you said you want your hookups to be fun and not serious."

"I do. But ..."

The guys' chaotic shouts and hollers echo around us, a loud splash from one of them being shoved into the lake, but that's nothing to the ringing in my ears.

I feel like he's on the verge of walking out of here and cutting things off before we even get started, but I have no idea why or what I've done wrong. I swallow hard, not wanting to ask him to elaborate but needing him to. "But what?"

"There's a difference between having fun and treating everything as meaningless. Maybe it's my trust issues getting to me, but even if we agree to hook up, have a summer fling, whatever we're deciding to do here ... I don't want it to make me feel disposable afterward. How do I know if you're only chasing me because you had this big crush, and once you get what you want, that you won't ... forget I exist in front of all your friends?"

I let out a loud breath of relief. "So you're asking for basic levels of respect, and you think I can't do that? Because I don't mind proving to you that I can. Respect is a two-way street, something I've very much learned in the years I've been away. Trusting hookups to keep my secret, making sure the hockey gossip doesn't get loud enough to tip off the media. That kind of thing."

"Wait. You're not out?"

God, that's probably going to turn him off even more.

"I'm not *not* out?"

"What does that even mean?"

"It means the life of a professional athlete is kind of complicated, which is one of the reasons I didn't want to tell you what I did for a living, but if you're wanting to understand me better, I'm willing to show you."

Sam takes one more glance around the lake party, still hesitant, and I know if this is going to happen, it's a conversation I can't have around the Collective. They'll ruin all my credibility with something ridiculous like carrots in the shapes of penises. Not the first time Ezra's done that.

"Let's get out of here," I say. "Away from the chaos. There's a trail that runs along the lake if you want to go for a walk?"

Sam thinks about it for a second before nodding softly. I hold out my hand for him as we head for the lake, and he takes it, his soft fingers interlacing with my callused ones.

"Your hands are surprisingly rough," he says.

"It's from all those years of ... stick handling."

The breeze by the water is refreshing from the stifling heat.

"How long have you been playing hockey?"

"Forever. I could skate before I could walk. Probably. That's what my parents tell everyone, anyway. My older brothers were already playing around that time."

"Aww, and you wanted to be like them?"

"I don't think it was ever a conscious decision. It's always been my future to play hockey."

We walk hand in hand, strolling our way along a well-worn but unpaved trail, and he actually takes in the words I'm saying. It's as if he's processing it all before he speaks again.

"Do you love it?"

"Luckily, yes. I'd like to say I wouldn't be playing if I didn't love it, but not going to lie ... my family, mainly my parents, they've put pressure on all three of us to do well. They're supportive, for sure, but everything we've done in terms of our hockey careers has been calculated and meticulous. And that's why I'm not out officially."

"Is being out a bad thing in the NHL?"

That's such a loaded question. Because while it's not as big a deal as it once was, hockey has notoriously been known to be filled with bigots. "It's not a bad thing, but it still draws attention. That's attention our parents didn't want on any of us. Easton is the only one officially out. Connor is dating Parker, who actually owns Colorado's team, and there's been speculation about them, especially after Connor retired early with an injury that no one believes is real. Spoiler alert: it's not. But they haven't actually taken that public leap yet. Though, like me, it's not like they hide it. We just haven't addressed it in the media. The media can't be trusted at all. They'll spin anything."

Sam frowns again, and it makes me want to reach over to smooth his brow line and say something to make his lips turn upward.

"That's pretty heavy."

I shrug one shoulder. "It's the only thing I've known growing up. So yeah, I guess the reason I'm so chaotic and wild is because when hockey season comes along, I have to slip back into PR mode. Summers are for partying. Having fun." I stop in my tracks and tug on his hand so he turns in to face me. "Having flings ... respectfully."

Sam steps closer. I'm only the tiniest bit taller than him, so we're eye-to-eye as he presses his shirtless body against mine. "Respectful flings."

"Full of fun. Can't forget the fun part." My voice has dropped low, almost a whisper.

Sam's Adam's apple bobs as he swallows, and when his pink tongue darts out to wet his lips, I almost give in to the instinct to surge forward and capture his mouth with mine. But I hold back.

I'm discovering Sam is a hot-and-cold kind of guy. He says he's making me work for it, but part of me thinks he's only doing that so there'll be a chance I'll give up and he won't get hurt. Just because emotions aren't involved when it comes to hooking up, that doesn't mean you're invincible to pain that might come with it.

Still, my hand itches to cup his face. My lips tremble at the thought of having his mouth on mine.

"What are you thinking about right this second?" Sam asks.

I give a half smile. "I'm not sure you want to know."

"I think you'd be wrong about that."

This is my moment. Am I going to take it or turn away and continue to walk with him? This tension building in my chest already has disappointment clouding the idea of walking away without having kissed him. If I chicken out now, I might never get the guts to ask for it.

So, in a squeaky voice I have to clear my throat to get rid of, I rasp, "I can't stop thinking about kissing you."

CHAPTER TWELVE

SAM

Funny. We're having the exact same thought.

His lips are right there, full and defined and begging me to kiss him.

Literally.

I've never been so torn.

He's not officially out, and he exists in this toxic culture where it's a risk for him. I've heard it all before. And while I know it's valid, it's also perfectly reasonable for me not to want to get involved in all that.

On one hand, my game is doing what I thought it might and bringing out all the red flags.

On the other hand ...

"Fuck it."

I grab his face and crash our mouths together. My teeth hit his, and our tongues meet as this desperate need explodes from the both of us. A rush of want passes from my scalp to my toes, and even though my self-control is face-palming, I ignore the little fucker. I lasted ... a whole week. Granted, I haven't seen him or spoken to him in that time, but I still deserve some sort of credit, and I'm assuming this kiss is my reward.

I wrap my hand over the back of his neck to force the kiss deeper, and my skin prickles as Lachie grabs my hips. His rough hands feel incredible, the gentle scrape getting my cock excited for what they might feel like on it, and when he closes the last of the distance between us, it's bliss.

His hard chest meets mine, long necklace trapped between us, and our kiss moves from a desperate need to pure hunger.

His experience is obvious in how confidently his mouth moves against mine, and it goes a long way toward extinguishing the doubts I was having. He's a man who knows what he wants, and so am I.

I almost moan when he shifts and our hard cocks press together. He's wearing thin swim shorts, and I'm seriously regretting the cargo shorts I'd pulled out in anticipation of some stuffy date. The rough zipper of my fly is stopping us from getting any real friction, and we might be in the trees, hidden by a bend from the rest of his friends, but they barely register.

Lachie's smirking mouth breaks from mine to leave heated kisses along my jaw. He reaches my throat, and the sensitive nerves there go wild, anticipating the rush his lips are bringing.

His labored breaths hit my ear as he tugs my earlobe with his teeth.

"Your turn. What are you thinking about …" His fingers link into the front right of my shorts, nails brushing pubes. "Right now?"

"How much I want you to move your hand to the left."

It's like I can hear him grinning. "Like this?" The movement is tiny.

"More."

"This?"

Fucking tease. "*More.*"

His lips press to my ear, making him sound louder and more intimate. "What about now?"

Then his fingers skim over my tip.

The desperate sound I release is embarrassingly uncontrolled. "Fuck. Yeah. That's good."

Bastard has me exactly where he wants me. I'm goddamn putty. And I can't say that I'm complaining about it.

His rough fingers stroking over my tip are making it difficult to breathe right. Why did I want to put this off again?

Oh yeah. Because I'm a dumbass.

I'm sure there *were* reasons why I shouldn't do this, but fucked if I remember any of them. I thrust against his hand, needing more.

"You know ... I bet I could guess what you're thinking now." He sucks on my neck.

"What?"

"You're thinking about how pretty my lips would look wrapped around your cock." Lachie pulls back so he meets my eye. "And you'd be right."

Heat rages through me, and all pretenses of denying this are long gone. "Prove it."

The way his pupils dilate so quickly will be something I remember for a really long time.

Lachie plants his hand on the middle of my chest as he presses me back against a tree, and then he pins me there as he undoes my shorts one-handed. His eyes don't leave mine, and his confidence is a huge turn-on I wasn't expecting.

With my fly open, he shoves down my shorts and underwear at once, and my cock falls forward into view. He stares at it for a full couple of seconds.

"Should have guessed."

"Guessed what?"

"That Mr. Animal Man would have a snake in his trousers. Or however that saying goes."

If I weren't so horny, I'd probably laugh. "Stop killing the mood."

He wraps a large hand around my shaft and looks up at me through his eyelashes. "Am I killing the mood *now*?"

Fuck. "No, no. The mood is good." My head falls back against the tree trunk. "Very, very good."

I was right. Those rough hands feel incredible against my skin.

"Hey, Sam?"

I look back at him in time to see him sink to his knees. "Yeah?"

"Feel free to tell me if you like it."

Before I can ask what he means, Lachie stretches his mouth and swallows me down.

Curse words explode inside my head at the warmth that wraps around my cock. There's nothing like a blowjob, and there's nothing like one that you've been trying not to dream about for weeks.

Lachie's mouth is as skilled and sinful as I'd assumed it would be, and as his lips move over my shaft, taking a fraction more of me each time, I know I won't survive this for long.

Just the sight of him on his knees is killing me.

Those broad, strong shoulders, messily styled hair, his piercings, his steady gray eye contact ... and that big hand jerking off his cock, which is hanging out the front of his pants.

I can't get a good look at it from this angle, but the tease of him touching himself is making my balls throb.

"That feels so good," I tell him, and I swear his eyes light up.

As if I could say anything else when his tongue is doing wicked things to the underside of my shaft, but knowing that he wants it to be good is a turn-on. Being with him is a turn-on. Watching the way my dick disappears into his mouth and reappears shiny with his spit is a goddamn turn-on.

I'm trying not to screw my eyes closed and sink into the pleasure since the view in front of me is so enticing.

I give in to the urge to reach for him and run my fingers through his surprisingly soft hair. He hums around me at the touch, and the vibrations run through me, adding to the ache building behind my balls.

I don't know if I'm so close already because it's been longer than normal since I last got off with someone or if this is all my attraction to Lachie, but I'm rapidly losing control of this thing. I want to push it out. Want to make it last to the point he's sucking my cock all day, but my self-control isn't that good.

Not when his mouth feels like this.

Lachie moves faster, hollowing out his cheeks and adding his free hand to drive me out of my mind. My hold on him twists tighter, and even though I'm practically naked, I swear I'm overheating with the way sweat is prickling all along my skin.

"Fuck, Lachie, your mouth is incredible."

He hums around my cock in response, and I can't stop myself from thrusting forward to meet him.

"You're going to make me blow. Whatever it is you're doing with your tongue, don't you dare stop."

He doesn't; instead, he does it faster. Harder. Coaxing me to the edge while he sucks me like it's his life's mission.

I'm panting, fighting hard to keep this going, but he's not making it easy on me.

Especially when his ungodly moan makes me want to hear him make that sound over and over and over.

"I'm so close," I warn him.

Not like he wouldn't know that. My dick is oversensitive to the point I'm unsure how much more I can handle, and my balls are aching and tight. Every time I think I've gotten control of my orgasm, Lachie sucks, licks, strokes in a way that shatters the illusion.

I'm so close.

Reaching that high that will turn me into Jell-O.

"Shit." My grip on his hair pulls tight.

I'm ready. So ready.

The pressure behind my balls is too much.

I'm thrusting uncontrollably, and when Lachie lets go of my cock and reaches for my balls, it's all over. I slam into his mouth as my orgasm crashes into me. My groan echoes in my throat, and I wait as rope after rope of cum floods his mouth. His mouth moves as he swallows me, and instead of looking down like I so desperately want to, I turn my gaze upward as I wait for the high to settle.

I'm panting, staring up at the sky like it has all the answers, because I know that it's safer than looking down. And when I slip from Lachie's mouth and finally give in to the urge, I was right.

His eyelashes are clumpy and wet, lips swollen, soft dick hanging out of his pants with lines of cum on the dried leaves he's kneeling beside.

"Damn, Lachie."

Something softens in his gaze. "Yeah ... damn."

We're both trying to catch our breath.

"You came?" I check, even though it's obvious he did.

"Before you. I've never gotten off so hard from sucking a cock before."

I tuck myself away and do up my shorts, him reluctantly pushing back to his feet.

"Are we going back to the party now?" I ask.

His gaze immediately drops to my neck. "As much as I want to show off that hickey I gave you, I'd rather have you all to myself a little longer."

I was hoping for that answer but was unsure if I would get it. I suppose I was anticipating him leaving as soon as he got what he wanted.

I'm learning I shouldn't underestimate Lachlan Kikish ... Kikshki ...

Lachie Kiki.

CHAPTER THIRTEEN

LACHIE

We continue to walk along the trail. Birds are singing, the sun is shining, and his warm palm in mine is so comfortable it's like we've done this a million times. The taste of him lingering in my mouth only adds to the surrealness of the moment. I'm certain my cheeks are flushed a shade of pink with how warm they feel, and even though I try to keep it inside, a small laugh escapes me.

"What's funny?"

"Hmm, you probably don't want to know."

"Now I doubly want to know."

Considering the last time I brought up my childhood crush, he wanted to run the other way, I'm reluctant.

So I'm cautious with my answer. "Life is ... weird sometimes."

"How so?"

I squint, thinking about how to word the jumbled mess running through my head. "Hockey has always been a given for me. You know how kids have these big dreams of being a famous athlete or an actor or even being a policeman or pilot or whatever?"

Sam holds up his free hand. "Veterinarian."

"Exactly. I never had that because it's *always* been hockey for me, and ... this is going to sound conceited, but I never doubted making it. And you were right about me basically getting everything I've ever wanted. But there was one thing

I was certain I would never have ... and that's any kind of ... *thing* with you."

"And now that you've blown me, you're going to be all triumphant and gloaty?" Sam's tone makes him sound resigned to that happening, and I hate the thought of him being disappointed in this.

"Not if you don't want me to be. I was laughing because I wondered if all those other little kids with big dreams thought getting what they wanted felt as surreal as this does. Right here." I pull our interlaced fingers up to my mouth and kiss the back of his hand. "If you'd rather we kept what we did a secret, I can do that. I'll do anything if it means I could have another shot at it happening again."

Sam stops walking, and I think I've scared him off for the thirtieth time today, but then he tugs on my hand and pulls me against him.

Our skin is sticky from sweat, but he doesn't seem to care, and neither do I.

He leans in, the anticipation of his lips on mine making every hair follicle on my body tingle, but before he kisses me again, he mumbles something—something barely intelligible—but I think he says, "You might just be my weakness."

I want to ask what he means, but then his mouth is back on mine, and as I thrust my tongue between his lips, he moans. He can probably taste himself as much as I can.

My cock is nowhere near ready to go again yet, but it's trying.

Being someone's weakness isn't always a bad thing, is it?

I don't want this kiss to end, but after mere seconds—or maybe minutes; time is an illusion today—something crawls over my foot and tickles my leg.

I've learned from years of experience not to kick and thrash because it's most likely a small animal coming to check out the weird human. Said weird human being me.

Sam pulls away first. "What the fuck is that?" He glances down, and a look of relief fills his face.

I eye him. "For someone who works with animals, you'd think one approaching you wouldn't freak you out." I finally look at the creature that has come to say hello. It's a cute little rabbit.

"Okay, you need to explain the animal thing. Can you go anywhere without attracting some kind of wildlife or farm animal?"

I remain still so the bunny can have a good sniff. "Of course I can. You saw it a few weeks ago. Domestic animals also approach me."

"That's not what I mean, and you know it. It's almost ... supernatural the way they flock to you."

"I know. And I can't explain it. It might have to do with how I was bitten by a radioactive coyote when I was a kid."

"A what?"

"Instead of giving me coyote powers, like Spider-Man, it gave me the ability to talk with the animals. For instance, this little guy at our feet is saying that you are really cute and that if you agree to go out with me for dinner tonight, I'd be the luckiest man in the world."

Sam's lips turn upward. "Oh, really? That's what the rabbit is saying, is it?"

"Yep. All the rabbit. The rabbit thinks you're great."

"Then can you tell the rabbit I think he's also great?"

I can't feel the animal at my feet anymore, so I'm assuming it's hopped back to its burrow now. Sam and I aren't talking about the actual rabbit anyway. He knows that, and I know that, but I'm still going to play with him anyway.

I roll my eyes. "Sam, you're so unrealistic. The animals can talk to me. I can't reply. Duh."

"Oh, sorry. How ignorant of me."

"A man who can admit his faults is extremely attractive to me, so you're forgiven."

"What are your flaws?" Sam steps closer to me. "Because I'm starting to think you don't have any."

I puff out my chest. "I don't. But I don't need to be attracted to myself."

"I can't even with you." He says this, but he hasn't stopped smiling.

"Can't even what? Believe how irresistible I am? Charming? Sexy—"

"Incorrigible."

"Okay, yeah, I'm that too. I'm a lot of things."

"I'm learning that."

We start walking again. "You've learned a lot about me, so now I want to know about you. Why didn't you end up becoming a vet?"

"No money for college—"

"I'll pay for it. You should get your dream."

Sam shoots me a disbelieving look. "Okay, now I might be having my surreal moment. The kid who used to clean out cages for me just offered to pay for college."

I shrug. "I can afford it."

"That's beside the point. I wouldn't accept it anyway."

"Why not?"

"Hooboy. For a whole lot of reasons having to do with the complications of loaning money to people you know, let alone someone you've hooked up with."

"It wouldn't be a loan. It would be a gift."

"And now it's bordering on prostitution."

I have no answer for that, but Sam laughs. I don't fully understand why giving him the money would be an issue, but at least my dumb offer hasn't offended him. I don't think. Unless the laugh is one of those awkward ones people do when they don't know what to say.

"Sorry if I've crossed any boundaries," I say.

"You have, but I also know it's coming from a good place. You're a sweetheart. The biggest reason I wouldn't accept your money is I don't think I'm smart enough to become a vet. I gave up that dream a long time ago because my grades weren't there, and I didn't want to waste my time and money trying to become one. I won't waste yours either."

I nod.

"Besides. I'm happy where I am. In ten short years, I've become manager of the shelter, not that it was some huge goal of mine, then I've taken all these different wildlife handling courses and do that on the side ... I might not have become a vet, but I still get to work with the animals I love. And I don't have to be the one to euthanize them when it comes down to it. That is a win-win in my book."

My heart sinks. "I've never thought of that before. That would be the worst part of being a vet."

"Agreed. Being in the room is hard enough. I couldn't live with being the one to ... you know."

"You're in the room with the animals when they get put down?"

"No creature, no animal or human, should have to go through that alone. We might be a no-kill shelter, but we often get sick or injured animals that we don't have the resources to rehabilitate. In those situations, we don't have much of a choice."

I let go of his hand and wrap my arm around his shoulders instead. "You're amazing for doing that."

"And yet, the animals don't appreciate me the way they do you. I know the radioactive coyote is bullshit, so tell me the truth."

"I was raised by a pack of wolves until the Kikis adopted me."

"More bullshit," he singsongs.

I relent. "I've looked online. A lot. All it tells me is that animals respond to my calm nature or my pheromones. The calm thing would probably explain why I've never been approached by an animal at a hockey game before."

"I'd be worried if there were any animals allowed in the ice rink, so it might not have anything to do with your demeanor at all."

"Oh, vermin get in there all the time. The only rat interested in me is my rat nephew."

"Maybe you really are a Disney Princess."

As much as I pretend to hate it, I'm warming to the nickname. "Until they're making my bed and cooking me breakfast, I refuse to believe that."

Sam pats me on the back. "Sure thing … Princess."

CHAPTER FOURTEEN

SAM

On a list of five things I thought would never happen, going on a date with Lachie would have been at the very top.

We're back in Easton's G-Wagon, heading for the middle of town, and I keep sneaking glances over at him. He's completely relaxed, one hand on the steering wheel and the other elbow propped on the center console.

I don't know what this is, but we held hands, and he said he wanted us to hook up again, and now we're going on a date.

Not a Collective party date.

An actual date.

The kind that I usually hate but am actually ... excited for? No, not excited. But there's something hopeful blooming in my chest.

"You keep looking at me," he points out gleefully.

I push down my smile and turn to look out the window. "Just curious if everyone else noticed the dried cum around your mouth."

"The *what*?" He barely keeps the car in our lane as he turns to the mirror on reflex and swipes at his mouth. "Where is it?"

I laugh, looking back at him because I'll take any excuse, and he narrows his eyes my way.

"You fucker."

"I'm looking at you because you're hot. Obviously."

That placates him. "Obviously."

"And you smell like that lavender bodywash they had at the lake house." Thank fuck we got to shower the sweat off us before we left. I almost suggested we shower together, but I could feel Connor eyeballing me, and as much fun as it is to annoy him, I didn't want to risk him having a heart attack ruining our date.

"Better than the locker room soap, trust me."

"What does locker room soap smell like?"

He thinks for a moment. "Chemicals. Which is a thousand times better than the actual locker room."

I try to wrap my head around that. "Still can't believe you're a professional athlete."

"For me, it's a job just like anyone's. I have to perform, I have to plan and prepare. There's a lot of travel and making sure I eat enough, and for eight months out of the year, I plan my whole life around it."

"That actually sounds horrible."

He grins at me. "It's fine. It's all I know."

"Being that busy, how do you find time to hook up?"

"After a win, if we have the next day off, a lot of us go out to celebrate. Hang around sports bars and you're never short on options."

"Ever had a threesome?"

"Nope, but I've had a lot of offers."

"Why didn't you go there?"

He rubs his jaw like he's never thought about the question before. "I guess I don't see the appeal. I love sex, but one person is enough focus for me."

"That's fair."

"And the teammate I live with has threesomes all the time."

"Lucky him."

"Lucky? So you've had them before?"

That actually makes me laugh. "You're giving me way too much credit. It's not something I'd say no to, but not all of us lead the lives of famous athletes."

"Sucks to be everyone else." Lachie pulls up out front of a restaurant I've never seen in my life, and immediately, a valet approaches the car.

"Are we in the right place?"

"Sure are."

I look down at my cargo shorts and button-up, feeling ridiculously underdressed and too dirty for this place, even though Lachie is still in those tiny board shorts and a T-shirt.

He's already out of the car and talking to the valet when I pop the door and follow him. I'd agreed to this date, and I'm interested in more hookups, but the way Lachie moves so confidently in this type of setting only reminds me of the enormous distance between us.

I've been in this position before.

I'm the hot, rough-around-the-edges guy that men want to slum it with until the fantasy wears off. Which is fine, considering I'm not about to turn down sex, but I'm going into whatever this thing is with both eyes open.

I stuff my hands into the pockets of my cargo shorts as Lachie passes off the keys to the G-Wagon and sets his palm on my lower back to steer me inside.

"Just a heads-up," I say. "I'm happy to pay for my half today, but if we make it to a second date, I won't be able to keep affording these types of places."

"Don't be ridiculous; I'll pay."

I know he can, and I don't have an issue with it exactly, but money is one of those things that has tricky, unspoken attachments. For me, I need it to get through life, but it's transactional. Not something that holds weight. Unfortunately, my experiences have proven that some people have expectations tied to every dollar. "I know you can and want to, but I'm not about that. This is a first date, so if you want to pay as a once-off, awesome. But I've dated rich guys before, and the few times I've called things off, the accusations thrown at me weren't nice."

"Already planning to reject me, huh? Guess I better work harder."

"Calm down." I give his firm shoulder a pat. "We can count on one hand how many actual conversations we've had, and you've sucked my dick one time. It's hardly a long-term commitment."

"But—" He cuts off when a waiter in a vest approaches to lead us to our table. He looks like he's fighting himself to hold whatever it is in as we take our seats and our water glasses are filled. Finally, the man leaves, and he continues with, "I want to suck your dick again. Can't do that if you reject me."

I snort at him saying something so brazen surrounded by all of these fancy people. I like that he's not trying to act like he fits in; he just does. It goes a long way toward helping my self-conscious thoughts. "Interesting." My opinions on whatever this is are all over the place, so I take a moment to drink my water. He's made it clear what he wants: more sex. So what do I want?

"How long until you return to Missouri?"

He thinks for a second. "About two months."

That's an ideal timeline. We could fuck like rabbits while he's here, but it's not long enough for this to get messy or anyone to catch feelings. "When you say you want to do this again, what exactly are you thinking?"

There's no pause this time. "As much as you'll give me."

His enthusiasm is such a turn-on. "Okay."

"And what does *that* mean?"

"We have two months. Might as well enjoy them."

"Together?"

"I can't have a turn sucking your dick if we're apart, can I?"

A choking sound comes from behind me, and the waiter reappears a second later. My whole face burns. It figures he'd come back right at that moment, and not while Lachie was the one talking about sex. Nothing I can do about it now. Lachie orders drinks like nothing happened, and I bite down on my tongue until the man leaves again.

"Fuck me," I whine.

"That was embarrassing for you."

"You knew he was there, didn't you?"

"If I tell the truth, will it jeopardize our summer of fucking?"

I don't think there's anything that could do that. "No. Summer of"—I check over my shoulder first—"fucking is on."

He lifts his beer, and I tap mine against his. "You know, I was really dreading this visit home, but I'm suddenly very happy to be here."

I tilt my head as I take a long drink. "Why? You seem close with your family."

"I am. I love them, and I know I have it good. Connor's also gotten so much better about letting go of things since he met Parker, so that's awesome too. But ... maybe it's because I'm the little brother, but I've always felt on the outer. It doesn't help that Connor and Easton played together and lived next door to each other as well. I've been content to do my own thing, but now they're settled down and Mom and Dad are living their country club life, I'm a bit ... lost."

It's hard not to be shocked by that. "From the outside, it looks like you have your life made."

"Don't get me wrong, I'm super lucky. I love my life. But I question if I fit in at home anymore."

"That must be tough."

He taps his fork lightly against the table. "Yes and no. I think my brothers finding their paths has made it very obvious to me that it's time to grow up and find mine."

"You're only twenty-one."

"I know, but I feel ready."

"That's a good sign, then. Maybe this summer can be your last chance at fun before you go away and ... grow up." If that's what he wants, then good for him. I don't believe in a set of checkboxes you have to do in order to achieve that though. I'm quietly chipping away at my goals, and I know I'm on the path I need to be. It's not flashy or showy, and I love having a roommate I can come home to. This is my version of growing up, and it's awesome.

But it's on Lachie to figure out his.

"I think before we start the fun," I say, steering the conversation back to safer territory, "we should get everything out on the table now."

"Oh yeah, like what? If you're talking about measuring dicks, I don't think we need to get those out. You're bigger than me, and I'd like to not be blacklisted from here."

The way he goes so easily from a deep conversation to dick jokes is warming me to him as well. "No, I mean that because we're in this for the fun, we should get all bad qualities out of the way. I'll tell you mine, you tell me yours, and then nothing will catch us by surprise or get in the way of us enjoying these two months."

He turns introspective as he studies my face. "Okay ... you go first."

"I've had some shitty past relationships that mean I bring baggage to all of my new ones."

"Shocking," he deadpans. "That's total news to me, considering you've only brought it up once."

I give him a dry stare as I take another sip of my beer. "I'm full of surprises."

His gaze dips to where my groin is covered by the table. "Yeah you are."

"Your turn."

"Fine ..." He scrunches his face up as he tries to think of something. "I hate being touched in my sleep."

Considering how many times he initiates contact, that one catches me by surprise. "Noted. Why?"

"I get all hot and sweaty and distracted. If your dick is there, I'm going to get horny, so let me sleep, and we can fuck later."

"Wow. I'm a snuggler."

"Of course you are." He runs a hand down his face. "This is going to be a problem."

"No sleepovers in our future."

"Guess not. What else?"

I set my chin on my hand. "Nope, it's your turn."

"I just went."

"Being anti-snuggling isn't a deal breaker."

"Fine." He gives in quicker than I thought he would. "Umm ..."

"Should I be worried that it's taking you this long to think of your bad qualities?"

"No, I have them, but it's not something I've thought about before."

He's so adorably earnest it's hard to hold anything against him. "Tell me, what's it like to not overthink every little thing?"

"Hard to overthink when you spend your days physically exerting yourself, and all you can do when you get home is eat and then crash."

"You have no extracurriculars or hobbies," I say. "Got it."

"You don't like sports," he throws back. "That might be your worst one yet."

"I think we've both lost sight of what the point of this game is."

He shrugs. "I don't think I ever knew."

We grin across the table at each other, and it occurs to me that we're both sitting here, saying the things we *don't* like about the other ... and it's easy.

I'm pretty sure this isn't how a date is supposed to go, but I'm weirdly into it.

On a whim, I reach across the table and stroke the back of his hand, and even though we're in public, he doesn't pull away. Instead, he laces his fingers through mine and relaxes into his chair.

"Okay, let's move on to childhood traumas. I'll go first this time."

This *definitely* isn't how a date is supposed to go. But we don't stop talking the entire time we're here.

CHAPTER FIFTEEN

LACHIE

As I pull up to the gigantic house we're staying at as a group, I'm tempted to jump in Sam's Honda and head back to the city with him.

"I'd invite you to come up to my room and stay the night, but I get the sense the Collective guys are maybe too intense for that to be enjoyable. For either of us. Between dodging my brother's death glares and dealing with immature comments about us hooking up from the others, I doubt we'd get much sleep. And not for fun reasons."

Sam smiles. "Yeah, I don't think I could sleep without one eye open the whole time, waiting for Connor to stab me."

"I'd protect you. He wouldn't stab me. I'm his baby brother."

"As much as I'd want to see what it's like to use you as a human shield, I should get back anyway. I have an early shift tomorrow."

I cock my head. "You're the manager. You make the schedules, and you chose the early shift?"

"The early shifts are usually the calmest. Plus, if I ever have a wildlife rescue at the house, I can't leave Ethan alone with it for long before he complains. Your life revolves around hockey. Mine revolves around the shelter and animal rescue."

If this were ever going to be anything more than a fling, that would be an issue because I barely get enough time for personal stuff during the season as it is. I'd want a partner who could be there for me when I am home. That's probably selfish of me because hockey is my number one, while I'd want to be someone else's priority, but that's kind of the deal with hockey players. Many relationships in the hockey world fail because of scheduling issues and lack of time spent together. Though Easton and Knox seem to make it work. During the season, they only get brief stretches together, but they make up for it by being glued to each other in the off-season. That might not work for typical couples, but it's the secret to their happy relationship. I think, anyway.

"What's going on in that head of yours? You look lost in thought."

He has a point without even knowing he does. Why am I thinking about a relationship with him and why it wouldn't work when that's not something we've discussed? We've both agreed to a summer fling, so it's a waste of energy to worry about how our lives wouldn't combine well.

"I'm thinking I should bail on the guys and go back to the city with you."

"You don't need to do that."

"I know I don't need to, but I want to. Summer is only so long."

"Exactly. So why don't you go inside, spend time with your *Collective*, and then come see me when they all go home to wherever they live. I'm not going to be able to drop everything at work for the next eight weeks, so we'll see each other when we can."

I might not have a lot of experience with dating—hookups, yes, not actually going on dates and seeing them more than once—but I do know what a blowoff sounds like, and I can't help feeling like this is that.

"If that's what you want," I say, trying to have my usual flippant tone.

Sam reaches across the center console and caresses the back of my neck. "I didn't say it's what I want. I'm saying I'm not going to blow off my obligations, and neither should you."

While that eases my gut feeling, I still want to go home with him, but I relent. "Okay."

"Good. Now, give me a kiss good night so at least when I get home after the hike of a drive back, I have something to think about as I fall asleep."

And there go all my doubts about his interest. I lean in toward him but don't touch my lips to his yet. "How do you expect me to sleep at all if I know you're thinking about me?"

He lowers his voice to a sexy rasp. "Probably the same way I'll get to sleep. With my hand wrapped around my dick and a mess to clean up in the morning."

I lower my forehead to his. "You are so mean."

"Aww, poor horny hockey player will have to wait a week to get off with me again. How will you survive?"

"I don't think I will, to be honest."

"You're so dramatic."

He doesn't let me snark back at him. He cuts me off with his lips on mine and a soft moan into my mouth. Then he does the worst thing possible and pulls away too soon.

I swear I whimper, but all he does is pat my cheek, call me dramatic again, and climb out of Easton's car and into his own.

I have to wait until his taillights have left the driveway before I can even get out without showing off how hard I am. Good thing I wait, too, because they're all in the living room off the entryway when I walk in. All ten thousand eyes are locked on me.

"You better not have gotten cum on my seats," Easton says.

"Would that be better or worse than birthing fluid?"

"Eww, better," Knox says.

Easton elbows his partner. "Way worse. That's my little brother."

"But afterbirth and goop and"—Ezra screws up his face—"other things I don't want to think about. That's a hundred times worse than cum."

Anton cups the back of Ezra's head. "Says the guy whose cum is probably in so many different places he'll have to worry that if a crime is ever committed, he could be implicated through DNA."

"Nah, that's more Oskar's thing," Ezra bites back.

"Fuck off, I'm a good boy now!" Oskar yells.

They're all so focused on bickering and trying to decide which would be worse, cum or amniotic fluid, that they probably don't even hear me when I say, "I'm going to bed," and disappear upstairs to the teeny tiny attic bedroom that barely fits the undersized single bed in there.

Had Sam come up, we could've made it work, but maybe it's a good thing that he didn't. He's left me wanting more of him, and I can't wait to see him again. It can't come fast enough.

—

Three days. I last three days before I snap. "Do any of you ever stop fucking?"

The open-plan living and dining room falls silent. Eyes from every and each direction land on me.

"Uh, I mean … good morning?"

A beat passes, and Easton drops his spoon into his cereal bowl, breaking them all from their shocked silence.

"Is the fucking in the room with us?" East asks.

"No, but it's upstairs …" I strain my ears to pinpoint which room it's coming from. "Second door on the right." I glance around the room to see who's missing. "So it's Dex and Tripp right now."

Ezra steps toward me from where he's making his breakfast in the kitchen. "You can hear them from here? Are you, like, a superhero with super hearing?"

Only when I'm horny and lonely. "I must be, because I swear on Mario Lemieux's grave I can hear every damn orgasm in this house, and it pisses me off that none of them are mine."

Anton frowns. "Mario Lemieux isn't dead."

I throw up my hands. "Bobby Orr's, then."

Connor snorts. "Also not dead."

"Whatever." And yes, I sound every bit the petulant teenager as that word can get. "I need coffee." I storm into the kitchen to someone muttering, "Sounds like you need more than a coffee."

No shit.

"So, what's the plan for today? More bonding crap? Can we play flag football with contact?" At least then I could channel all my frustration into violence. Friendly violence, of course.

"So you can hump us when you tackle us?" Dalton asks. "Not my idea of fun."

Ezra turns to him. "Not what you said when—"

"Shut your face before I shut it for you."

Ezra laughs. "Seriously, this never gets old."

While those two bicker as usual, I make myself a shot of espresso while mixing a protein shake to add it to. If I can't get rid of all this horny energy by having sex with Sam, I may as well do some off-season conditioning. I'm going to turn up to training camp completely stacked.

Slowly, the group disperses, more people enter, and it's a real choreographed rotation to get us all fed breakfast. I sit on a stool at the kitchen island and drink my shake, trying to wake up properly and get rid of the bad mood. I don't wanna drag these guys down with me.

Eventually, Easton makes a reappearance. Don't know when he left, but he's back and no longer wearing pajamas but swimming shorts and a tank.

He puts car keys in front of me and pats my shoulder. And this is why he's my favorite brother. He's telling me with actions and not words that I deserve orgasms too, and I should take his car to go get it.

But then I lift the keys off the counter and get confused. "Wait. Which car are these for?"

"Ezra's rental. I figure you're going to bail out of here soon enough to chase your Prince Charming. I'm just making sure you don't take my baby when you do it."

Okay, kind of a dick move on his part, but it's all the permission I need.

A few minutes later, after chucking my protein shaker in the dishwasher and throwing on any clothes I can find in my suitcase, I'm on the road back to the city.

Even if he's not interested in hooking up again, the mere thought of seeing Sam has put me in a good mood. Any orgasm he might possibly offer me will be a cherry on top.

CHAPTER SIXTEEN

SAM

No, Lachie, you have a fun summer with your friends, Lachie. Spend time with them, Lachie. We have *time*, Lachie.

Fuck past Sam and the horse he rode in on.

It's torturous to know I could have spent the last few days having sex instead of working and eating steak on the couch with Ethan as he detailed his preparations for his next lifting comp. Whenever he's in the lead-up, all his meals are protein, protein, protein to the point that it makes me want to go vegetarian.

You'd think working at a shelter would make that happen, but no. It's my roommate.

At this point, there's only one type of meat I'm craving.

And the way I just called Lachie's dick *meat* is enough daydreaming for today.

I rub my fingers into my eyes and try to ignore this gut-deep feeling that maybe now that he's had his orgasm and done the dinner thing, he's not as keen as he originally let on.

A summer fling sounds perfect in theory, but I wouldn't even know how one works. Is it an exclusive type of arrangement, or do we carry on with our lives and fit each other in when we can?

Considering I hadn't hooked up for a good month or so before he sucked my dick, it's not a huge issue because I could feel myself getting weary of that scene anyway. If Lachie is serious about this being a regular thing once his friends leave, that will be more than enough to keep me satisfied.

Especially knowing the things he can do with his tongue. And how he moaned when I told him how good it felt …

Shit.

I glance down at where my dick is straining in my khaki shorts. That motherfucker. I'm going to be patient and stick to my guns that Lachie should spend time with his friends, given how hard he works, but if the fling comes to nothing, I'm going to be disappointed as hell. I want him. Our dinner couldn't have gone better, and I really shot myself in the foot by ending it with that scorcher of a kiss.

I pick up my phone, wanting to message him something—anything—so he knows I'm still interested in this continuing, but as usual, I come up blank. I don't want him to think it's my way of texting a very unsubtle booty call or that I want him to ditch his friends for me … even though I kind of do.

It takes way more self-restraint than I even know I have when I set my phone down again.

There's a knock at the door, and I glance up as Danika pops her head in. "Going to be a busy morning. We've had a litter dumped on us."

"Kittens?"

"Puppies. Maybe a Lab mix, from what I can tell."

Fuck me. "How old?"

"I'd guess four weeks. They don't look good."

Hooking up is the last thing on my mind as a spike of anger pierces me. The people who can be mean or neglectful to animals are the lowest form of life. I happily work with rangers and the police to try and bring about a charge because the last thing I want is them ever getting their hands on an animal again.

"Have you called Owen?"

"He's on his way."

I follow Danika through to the back, where there's a box waiting filled with puppies clambering over a filthy blanket. I bite back my rage and distract myself. I know exactly what Owen's preliminary checks will be, so I go over them for signs of fleas, emaciation, and any issues with their eyes or teeth. Danika sources the blend of goat's milk and puppy paste to introduce solid food and puppy formula replacers for milk, but we'll wait until the vet sees them before giving them a feed in case one of them needs medical intervention.

These guys are skinny but otherwise look okay, and whenever this happens, I can't stop from questioning *how*.

Danika heads back through to the front, and while I wait with the puppies in their isolated section, I complete the daily check on our cages.

It only takes an hour for Owen to show up.

"How many do we have?" he asks as he enters the room.

"Five." I've been watching the little black furballs crawl over each other and try to seek out their mom. It's heartbreaking.

"Damn. They're cute."

"Very." I nod to the smallest. "I'm worried about that one's eyes."

Owen scoops the pup up and carries him to a table. "Let's take a look."

"We're assuming they're a Lab mix."

"The white belly and paws and longish fur makes me think collie. The face is all Lab though. Aren't you, little guy? You are a cutie tootie." Owen scratches the pup behind the ears and gets to work examining it.

"Age?" I ask.

"I'd say ... close to four weeks."

I was hoping we were wrong about that, but it could be worse. At this age, they're going to need round-the-clock care, which means they're coming home with me for four weeks. Ethan will be thrilled. The good news is that as long as they don't have any issues and thrive, it will take next to no time to home them.

"Her temp is down," Owen says. "When were they brought in?"

"Just before we called. The person who left them said she found the box on her morning jog."

"Good chance they've been left out all night, then."

Poor little things.

"Eyes are dull, he needs a good meal and a flea bath, but the focus is on getting him warm again. Everything else is looking good."

I'm so relieved. Being a dog dad for a few weeks is a small trade-off for making sure these guys get the best reset to life.

"Ah, Sam?" Danika's head pops into the room again. "We have a visitor."

A visitor? Oh, fuck, I bet it's Ethan dropping by with a protein shake. "You okay for a second?" I ask Owen.

"This is the least demanding thing I have to do today."

I'm careful not to step on any paws as the puppies play around my feet, and I escape their pen to follow Danika through to the front.

The person waiting there pulls me up short, and I'm so shocked I forget how to speak for a second.

"Hey." Lachie's grin is way too self-satisfied. "I'm here to volunteer."

"Volun ..." It's taking my brain too long to wrap around the offer, considering he's done it a billion times before. "Ah, right. Okay."

He watches me as I round the desk and grab the sign-in sheet and a badge for him.

"Aren't you supposed to be with your friends?"

"They were pissing me off."

"Why?"

"Because they weren't being considerate of my balls."

Danika's eyes widen. "I'm going to check on the pups."

She disappears, but Lachie lights up. "You have puppies?"

"Just dropped off." My smile is tugging its way free. "How opposed would you be to taking your shirt off again?"

"If I didn't know any better, I'd say you were the one sending all the animals my way to get me to strip off."

If only I had that kind of power. "Unlike your friends, I'm very concerned about your ... balls."

He chokes on a laugh. "Not that I don't love where this conversation is headed—and we'll get back to your concern for my balls soon—but if I'm going to volunteer, I probably shouldn't do it with a hard-on."

He's right, but after days of not seeing him, the sudden appearance has me on edge. The puppies are mostly fine, so it's easier to let go of my anger for now and focus on how much I want the man in front of me.

Unfortunately, there's something we have to fix first.

"You're right. And I'm glad you're here because I was serious about taking your shirt off. We have some puppies we need to warm up, and I don't trust them to stay still long enough for a heat pack to do the trick."

"Wait. I get to cuddle them? I get to spend my day cuddling puppies?"

He's already tugging his T-shirt over his head, and I have to remind myself that I'm at my goddamn workplace, damn it. "If you play your cards right, that won't be the only thing we do together."

The wicked gleam that hits his eyes is too much. "In that case, I promise to be on my best behavior."

Apparently, his *best behavior* includes grabbing me on the ass as I lead the way into the back. I refuse to let myself get hard, but if he keeps it up, I'm going to be fighting a losing battle.

Thankfully—or unfortunately—the puppies are enough to distract him from groping me again.

"Oh, shit, they're even cuter than I thought they'd be."

I turn to Owen. "This is our walking heat pack."

"Fantastic." Owen points at where the smallest pup is sitting off to the side. "Start with her."

Lachie eagerly scoops up the puppy and settles off to the side, cuddling it into his impressive chest.

The other three on the floor scamper over him.

Owen drops his voice. "I'm going to take this one with me. He's got a tick, and being so little, he might need some extra love. He's already looking too lethargic for my comfort."

My worry must cross my face because Owen cuffs me on the shoulder.

"My guess is that he'll be back with his siblings tomorrow. We'll set up vaccination dates and spaying and neutering then."

"Thank you."

"For puppies?" Owen scoops up the one he's taking and holds it to his face. "Anything for these cookie wookies. I wanna bite those widdle paws." The dog bats at his face. "See you tomorrow."

At least that means I'm starting tonight with only four pups.

Owen leaves, and I turn to where Lachie is sitting on the floor, petting the sleeping pup's head. The other three are curled up at his side, already exhausted from their play.

"I was going to offer help, but it looks like you've got it covered."

"If you want to take your shirt off too, that would help *me*."

"I've got animals to feed." I run my gaze over where he's sprawled out like that, liking the sight of it way too much.

We need to hook up again.

"Once those pups are warm though, come and find me. I'm sure I'll have something else to keep you occupied."

CHAPTER SEVENTEEN

LACHIE

My bad mood from this morning is all but forgotten about. Turns out I didn't need sex. I needed an oxytocin boost, and nothing does that better than stealing it all from the puppies. Though, technically, I'm giving it back to them too. We're sharing all the oxytocin, and it's working because I'm in love.

I wish I could take these guys home with me, but during the season, I don't have time for any pets. I couldn't care for them the way they need, and after being dumped in a box, they deserve all the love they can get from families who won't ever leave them. Even for a little bit.

When the door opens, my heart leaps into my throat, because I'm excited for whatever Sam meant by keeping me occupied, but it's not him. It's Danika, and she has a tray of ... what I think is food—looks like slop—and four bottles.

"They need a feed. We should do the milk first because we don't know if they've tried solid food before, so we don't want them to gorge on that and make themselves sick."

The puppies are currently asleep on me, the smallest in my arms, the other three on my thighs, resting in the dip between my legs.

"How do we do this?" I ask.

She puts the slop tray up high on a floating shelf on the wall and then takes a seat to the left of me, facing my way.

The movement makes the puppies flinch, but they must be so tuckered out, they don't open their eyes.

"Here." She hands me a bottle and then picks up the puppy near my knees and holds it to her chest. "It's like feeding a baby."

"I've never done that either."

She smiles. "Just make sure the bottle is always facing downward so air bubbles don't form. We don't want them filling their tummies with so much air they can't eat anymore."

"Got it." I don't really, but I follow her lead.

The puppy in my arms barely stirs as it starts sucking on the soft bottle teat. I get mesmerized as I watch it guzzle down the milk while keeping its little eyes closed.

In all the animal encounters I've had, this one has to be the most fulfilling. Maybe because when I usually bring animals in, or in all the years I volunteered, it's not like I had much to do with the animals once they were here. I'd bring them in, they'd treat them, I'd get a pet and a cuddle in between cleaning cages, but this ...

My chest is full, and it's so heartwarming it practically aches, and when the puppy makes a small grunting sound, I almost melt.

"Who could be so cruel?" I ask.

"Some people don't deserve animals."

"Agreed."

"Okay, if he's done with his bottle, now you have to burp him."

Is ... is she serious? I must pull a face because she holds her puppy upright on her chest so its head is on her shoulder to demonstrate. Then she pats its tiny little back gently. "It's easy. Just like a baby."

It feels weird, and I'm half convinced she's messing with me, but when my pup lets out a hiccup-type burp, I fall even more in love.

"Is it this cute with human babies?"

"Hell no. They scream their little heads off." Danika looks way too young to be a mom, but she speaks like she knows from experience. "I have a million little brothers and sisters. I started volunteering here a few years ago so I could escape the noise of the house. Sam officially hired me last year after I finished high school."

"That's awesome. I used to volunteer here before moving. You must've been my replacement after I left."

"I think Sam took pity on me. Took me in like all of the strays that belong here. We need to switch pups, but let's put these two together so they can stay warm."

We do that and then each feed one of the remaining pups. It's so easy to get lost in what I'm doing that when Sam comes back into the room, I've almost forgotten he's the reason I'm actually here.

"You look like you're having fun."

"I am. Do you know how amazing it is to bottle-feed puppies?"

Both Danika and Sam huff a small laugh.

"Yeah. I might have some experience with that." Sam smirks.

"Oh. Right. Anyway, I'm thinking of quitting my job and making this my full-time work. How much does a puppy feeder get paid?"

"Nowhere near the kind of income you're used to. When you two are finished feeding, Danika, I need you on front reception, and Lachie, I'll be in my office."

I'm reminded of what he said, about him occupying me with something, and as much fun as I'm having with these puppies, this second one seems intent on taking his sweet-ass time.

Hurry up and drink, little one! Get all the sustenance you need, so then I can get what I need.

Though I'm probably reading into Sam's tone. Surely he doesn't mean here.

It takes all my strength not to rush the poor little thing so I can get to Sam, but it eventually happens, and with their bellies full and cuddles done, the four pups crawl around and settle on a warm blanket pressed against one another.

It's the sweetest and most heartbreaking thing I've ever seen. I wash my hands and clean up, and even though I should put my shirt back on to walk through the shelter toward Sam's office, am I going to? Nope.

If he didn't mean we could hook up here, I will at least let him think about it. And if he did, then I'm saving time.

I knock on his office door and let myself in, expecting him to be behind his desk, but he's not. He must have been waiting right behind the door. I've barely gotten it closed behind me when he pushes me up against it.

I'm sure the thud probably echoes down the hall. "I thought you were going to be a lot more professional than this. Here I was, thinking I'd have to coax you with my washboard abs—"

"Fuck being professional," Sam growls, and the throaty sound catches me off guard.

It's still so surreal that he could take that tone with me or be so turned on by me he has to slam me against something because he needs me right now.

"You nursing a puppy shirtless and caring so much for those tiny creatures is probably the sexiest thing I've ever seen."

"Wait until you see me play hockey."

He shakes his head. "Nope. Nothing will ever compare to what I just witnessed."

"Yeah? What are you going to do about it?"

"Something I've been dying to do for days. Return the favor." Sam immediately gets to his knees, and my hand flies out to grip his hair.

My breathing is already heavy, and all he's done is sink to the floor. I don't even have my dick out yet. At least we won't have to worry about being caught if I'm only going to last three seconds.

"I know this isn't the point," I say, trying to keep my voice even but failing, "but you could have had this if you didn't tell me to stay up at Lake Dillon."

He goes for the button on my jean shorts. "Trust me. I've been yelling at myself over that for days. So sorry for trying to be mature and selfless."

"Both of those things are overrated."

Sam lowers my shorts and underwear down my thighs, just enough to free my dick and balls. "Until you, I thought they were good qualities to have." His long fingers wrap around my shaft. "I was so wrong."

I'm unable to speak anymore.

He was so wrong. Because being selfish feels amazing. I throw my head back against the door as Sam strokes my cock. Slowly at first, teasing. I anticipate his mouth, wait for it, begin to beg for it through a whine, when he releases a large sigh. The puff of air on my skin has goose bumps breaking out all over, only heightening the sensation of want lusting through me.

I have to close my eyes and silently count to ten, or I'll be too dangerously close to coming all over Sam's face.

Oh fuck, I shouldn't think about what that would look like.

"You have the most amazing-looking cock," he whispers as he strokes a bit firmer. Quicker.

Where my usual brand of snark or confidence would have me quipping something like, "Wait until you see my hole," I'm stunned speechless, so turned on and full of need that I can't find any words. Only stuttery mouth sounds.

I glance down at him, filling my eyes with as much pleading as I can, seeing as my words won't work, and he blinks up at me through gorgeously long lashes I'm only noticing in this very moment.

"You're not known for your patience, are you?" He laughs.

Most hockey players aren't. If we let our chance to score go by, we miss it.

"Please," I manage to croak out.

His hand slows, and his grip loosens, but he trails his fingers down my tight skin until he's able to cup my balls. He gives them a squeeze as he finally puts his mouth on me, and my breath is so shuddery as pleasure spreads throughout my body.

He starts slow, only taking so much of me with each bob of his head, and it makes me want more and less at the same time.

I'm trying to keep myself from surging my hips forward, but I'm about to snap.

Sam knows it too. He looks at me the whole time, those deep brown eyes never leaving mine, not for a second.

The intensity of his stare, the wet heat wrapped around my dick ... I'm already so close to—

Sam pulls off my cock. "I love watching what this is doing to you, but I'm torn between finishing you off now and kissing those fucking biteable lips."

It's only then that I realize I've sunk my teeth into my bottom lip. His own lips are shiny with spit, and it makes me want to feel them on mine.

I tug on his hair. "Stand up. Kiss me."

He does as I say, his tongue plunging inside my mouth while my hands fly to his pants to get them undone.

As soon as I do, I bring our hard dicks together, wrapping my hand around us both and stroking fast and tight.

With the heat of his cock in my hand and the warmth of his tongue in my mouth, I don't care if it makes this the shortest frot fest in history, it's going to be impossible to hold out for long.

And when he gasps and pulls from my mouth, "Oh fuck" repeating over and over, I only get that much closer. The thing that sends me over the edge is how he throws his head back, exposing the almost healed hickey I gave him three days ago. That's my mark. The thing that screams to others that he's taken. Even if it's only temporary, it says he's mine.

It's that thought that makes every muscle inside me stiffen. My cock pulses, making a mess as I continue to stroke us both. Sam thrusts into my fist, faster and faster until he joins me, riding that wave of pleasure that shoots out of our cocks.

The second we both stop convulsing and coming all over the place, Sam presses his forehead to mine.

"We probably should've thought that through more. Now we're both covered in cum, and I can't go home to change."

I step out from being trapped between him and the door and reach for the tissues on his desk. "Eh, I think most of it landed on me. You should be all good." I swipe a few tissues and then hand the box to him.

As I clean up the evidence on my stomach, I can't help thinking what a brilliant idea it was not to put my shirt back on.

CHAPTER EIGHTEEN

SAM

Wearing a cum-splattered shirt at work is a first for me. Luckily, the puppies give me a perfect excuse to cover it up. I've collected a few different baby carriers over the years that I use for carrying animals around that need the extra love. I could technically crate all four to bring home with me tonight, or I could make the excuse that the small one still needs body warmth.

Which it does. Probably.

Lachie throws himself into the chair opposite my desk and rests his hands behind his head as he looks around. It stretches out his long torso, and I let my gaze run over it, enjoying the view.

"It's going to be incredibly distracting doing payroll while you're shirtless."

"Should have thought of that before getting me naked."

In my defense, I had no idea I was going to jump him at work, but he was with those puppies for-fucking-ever, and with every passing second, I got more and more eager. Being teased by his presence isn't great for productivity.

"So ..." I start, putting space between us as I take my desk chair.

"Uh-oh. That doesn't sound good."

I grin across at him. "Why? What are you imagining comes next?"

"So, get the fuck out of my office? So ... that wasn't as good as I remembered. So, I'm actually married with three kids, and your sister is the baby momma."

"You don't have a sister."

"I never said my thoughts made sense." He anxiously spins his stud earring, like he doesn't realize he's doing it.

"Do you want to know what I was actually going to say?"

"Depends. *Do* you have kids?"

"Not three."

His whole face drops, and it's hard not to laugh.

"I'm screwing with you. I don't care how hot someone is, I'd never cheat."

"Good to know."

I watch him closely for a moment. "Don't take this the wrong way, but athletes have a reputation as cheaters. Is that something you'd ever do?"

He's quick to shake his head, which doesn't necessarily make me believe him, but his words do. "Don't get me wrong, I always have options. It's one of the main reasons I've stayed single for so long. I liked being able to go out and hook up. Especially during that first year in the NHL, it felt like I'd been handed all my dreams. Lots of money, playing the sport I love, freedom from my family, and guys throwing themselves at me. I took full advantage of all the doors that were opening. But ..." He looks less like he's trying to convince me now and more like he's working through his thoughts. "While those things are great, they've lost some of the excitement they used to have, and if I ever settled down, the person would be worth the trade-off. I'd have no interest in looking somewhere else, because I already know what's out there, and I wouldn't say it's bad or anything, more that ... perspectives change. And I think mine has."

Good answer. Not that it matters for me, but if he were a terrible human, it might have dulled my attraction to him. So far, he's loyal, loves animals, and is easy to talk to. On top of being hot.

He's the hookup jackpot.

And he's here with me.

"Question for you."

"Why do I feel like I'm on trial?" he throws back.

"Because I'm nosy?"

Lachie cocks his head. "That's a bad quality you failed to mention the other night. What else are you hiding?"

"Just my foot fetish."

His eyes narrow like he's trying to see inside my brain. "You're fucking with me again, aren't you?"

"You know me so well already." Paying attention is another green flag. "What I want to know is ... you have a lot going for you. So why are you here with me?"

His initial interest made me worry it was some kind of hero worship thing and that he was only hanging around because he wanted to prove he could fulfill the crush he used to have. And maybe it started that way, but if we keep doing this, I at least want to know that I'm bringing more to the table than some kind of wish fulfillment.

"You mean, aside from being stupidly hot."

I crack a smile. "I dunno if that's a valid reason on its own."

"Ah, so you're wanting your ego stroked. I can do that."

"Considering how good you are at stroking other things, I don't doubt it."

We share a look, and he leans forward and plants his elbows on my desk. "Obviously, good-looking was what caught my attention, but then you had to go and be a great person too. Anyone who loves animals is immediately high on my list, then you're funny, into fitness, and have pretty much rolled with every curveball I've thrown your way. I like that."

It might not be deep, but knowing we have common ground that doesn't come from him knowing me when he was younger settles the last of the doubt I was clinging to. "You're the kind of guy I can fuck and then head out for breakfast with the next morning as friends."

He lights up at that. "Exactly the way I feel about you."

I lean back in my chair and cross my arms. "Are summer flings supposed to be friends outside all the sex? I really don't know how this works."

"Fucked if I know. You're currently my longest relationship."

There he goes, reminding me that while there's not a huge age gap between us, our lives have been very different. "I guess we get to make the rules, then."

"Excellent."

"Which brings me back to what I was originally going to say when I sat down and you derailed the whole conversation."

"That was you."

I refuse to be distracted again. "*So* ... will this volunteering be a regular thing? Because I know we just had sex, but I really shouldn't make a habit of doing that at work."

"I guess you'll have to learn some self-restraint."

My groan fills my office because I was worried he'd say something like that. I'm not even mad about it. I like him here. He likes being here. And when it comes to volunteers, there's so much work around here that we can never say no to an extra set of hands.

"Besides," he adds. "We both know the animals wouldn't let me stay away even if I wanted to."

"True," I say. "Then the days you're here, I'm going to have to make sure you have a full schedule. Prepare to work your ass off."

"You don't get to be a professional athlete by taking it easy. Bring it. Especially if it means more puppy cuddles."

Time to disillusion him. "Don't let them trick you. They're hard work."

"Those little angels? Never."

"I'm going to have to get up during the night to feed them, and I have no idea if they'll even settle at my place, so there's a good chance I'll be pulling an all-nighter. On little sleep, they have a way of being less cute. Trust me."

He taps his fingers on the desk. "You're taking them home with you?"

"They need to be fed and tended to around the clock, so we can't leave them here alone overnight. They'll live with me for a few weeks, and then we'll bring them in to find their forever home."

"I want a dog one day."

That makes me laugh. "From what I know about you, you're going to end up with a whole house full of pets whether you want it or not."

"That would be cool though. A house for all the strays that find me."

"As long as it's done properly," I warn. I've seen too many horror stories of people joking about the cat selection system or bringing in undomesticated animals and trying to make a pet out of them. Yes, animals are cute. No, not all of them make great pets.

Lachie sits back suddenly and throws his arms up. "Fine, I'll help."

Did I black out for a second? "Help with what?"

"The feeding. The all-nighter."

My eyebrows jump up my face. "You're going to help me with the puppies."

"After you begged me, it's not like I can say no."

"Begged you." I try to rub the smile from my lips. "Are you inviting yourself to spend the night with me?"

"With the puppies. Keep up."

Even though I know there is no way in hell we'll find time to fuck between the animals and Ethan being nosy over a new person, there's a flicker of excitement in my gut. Lachie in my place? Hanging out together all night.

"Your friends won't care if you're ditching them?" Then I add, "For the puppies?"

"Are you kidding? They'll probably show up on your doorstep tomorrow morning with an entire pet store's worth of puppy toys."

"In that case, you probably shouldn't tell them. My place is no lake house, and a pet store would not fit in my living room."

"Ignore them? Can do." Then he pulls out his phone and shows me the screen full of text and call notifications.

"Fuck me, shouldn't you at least let them know you're alive?"

"Considering being here was Easton's idea, if he chooses not to tell them, it's on him."

I run my eyes over the screen again, expecting it to be Connor freaking out, but it's not. "So why is Ezra the one calling you?"

"That was also Easton's idea. I have his car."

"Let me guess. Ezra didn't know?"

Lachie taps on something on his phone. "Let's see."

Then Ezra's voice message fills my office.

"Look, little Kiki, I know I said I was fine with cum on the interiors, but I was talking in general. That's a rental. Do you know how much they charge for jizz removal? Because I do, and it's not cheap."

Lachie ends the message. "Sounds like he's fine with it."

Fine is a stretch, but there was no shouting, so I'd call that a win. The fact that they're out here renting expensive cars and getting cum in them is ... so strange. I've had to rent exactly one car in my life, and it was a Ford that I was paranoid about the entire time.

I'll never understand the world that Lachie lives in.

And I'll never have to.

"As long as you don't care about making Ezra paranoid, you're welcome to help with the puppies tonight."

"Are you kidding? Making Ezra paranoid is everyone's favorite pastime."

"And now I'm feeling sorry for the guy."

Lachie makes a choking noise. "Have you already forgotten him and his husband chasing me with the Stanley Cup? For two days, I had the *Jaws* theme song on a loop in my head. This is payback. And in fact, maybe we *should* fuck in his car. He'd deserve it."

"Look, I'm down for whatever, but I'd prefer that you weren't thinking about him while we get off."

"Why?" His whole face becomes a mask of innocence. "Would it make you jealous?"

Yes, actually, it probably would. But I'm not going to tell him that. "No, because then I'd have to think about him too."

Lachie scowls, and it's adorable.

I stand up and head for my door, reaching out to make a mess of his hair on the way. "You are *too* easy."

He catches my hand before I can get far. "When we fuck, I want to be the only one you're thinking of."

His deepened tone makes it easy to drop the act. "Deal."

"Deal."

He tugs me down for a kiss, and fuck me, he tastes good. Heat races through me, and I have to pull away sooner than I'd like. "As much as I love when you make me hard—not at work."

"Guess I have all night to do it, then."

That genuinely makes me laugh. "You have *no idea* what you're in for."

CHAPTER NINETEEN

LACHIE

There's an annoying wasp buzzing right near my head, and every time I try to squash it, it mocks me.

"Psst. It's time again," it says. I swat at it like I've been doing for the last few minutes, and I manage to hit it, but it curses. "Fuck, Lachie. That hurt."

And now I feel bad for the wasp. "I'm sorry, little wasp. Here, let me hug you."

Even though it's super tiny and looks like Sam, it gives the best hugs. I'm warm all over, and—

Ouch! The motherfucker stung me. I don't think an animal has ever bitten me before. "Lachie."

I jump scare awake—that sensation of falling hitting for a split second before coming to.

That's when I realize the annoying wasp *is* Sam, and it's time to feed the pups again.

"Struggling to keep awake?" He's enjoying this way too much.

I sit up in his bed, still disoriented but getting there. "Not at all. It was barely a catnap."

Sam laughs. "And here I was, thinking hockey players had stamina. I was anticipating a night full of orgasms in between feeding the dogs. So disappointed."

"I can do that," I say through a yawn. "Totally. After this feed. Let's do it." I swear my eyelids are so heavy, I can't even be sure my eyes are open anymore.

"Let's see if you get through this feed first."

"Just for that, there's no stopping me now." I slide down to the floor, and Sam hands me one of the pups from the crate and a bottle. The pup takes it immediately, making that tiny grunting noise that is the best sound in the whole world. "How long have you been up for?" I ask.

"I got in a twenty-minute nap but set an alarm so they wouldn't miss a feed."

"Smart. Especially if you sleep like the dead like I usually do. Not right now though. Obviously."

"Yeah, I don't know why you were calling me a wasp or why you were trying to hurt me, but I can only assume it had to do with you being extremely passed out, or maybe you were hallucinating."

"I think you incepted my dream, and dream me made you a wasp."

"So dream you thinks I'm annoying? Really? Wow."

"Dream me is sleep-deprived and irrational. He never listens to awake me. Ever. I tell him to conjure me a hot man to dream about, and he gives me ... a wasp. I don't trust his judgment."

My pup guzzles down the formula, and I can't believe how much these little bodies can take. It takes in a deep breath and then sighs as it stretches its tiny legs out.

"I think this is my favorite thing." I'm slowly waking up, slowly becoming more alert, and when I look over at Sam, I realize I'm extremely mistaken. "Nope, I take it back. That is my favorite thing. When did you lose your shirt?"

"While you were asleep. You know, the thing you said you weren't going to do?"

"It's not my fault you didn't distract me with sex."

"Kind of hard to do when you fall asleep with a puppy on you."

Okay, definitely awake now. "I, what?"

"During the last feed. You took the puppy up on the bed, and when I said I didn't want the puppies on the bed because they will piss everywhere, you said, and I quote, 'Don't worry, I'll put him back before I fall asleep. It's more comfy up here.' Spoiler alert: you did not put the puppy back. Though I will say, I got a good photo out of it."

With one hand, Sam grabs his phone from the foot of the bed and unlocks it, turning the screen to show me the evidence of this bullshit story he's made up.

"Looks like a deepfake to me."

"Uh-huh. That's what I've been doing while you've been sleeping. Faking photos of you asleep with a puppy because ... wait, why would I be doing that?"

"Because I'm tired and not making sense? Duh. Catch up."

"You're fun when you're sleepy."

"I'm fun all the time."

"Can't argue with that," he murmurs.

We burp the pups when they're done and then repeat with the next pup.

"It's three in the morning, so they should be good until at least six," Sam says. "After we're done with these two, we should try to at least get some sleep."

"According to you, I've already had sleep. I still don't believe it, but whatever."

"You're right. You weren't so deliriously tired that you imagined I was a wasp and slapped me. Do I have a red mark?" He turns his shoulder, and there is, in fact, a red hand mark on his side.

I gasp but try to cover it. "No. There's, uh, nothing there at all."

"That's so believable too. At least now I know you aren't so perfect, and I've learned from discovering your faults. I am never waking you up ever again."

"Want to know the secret to waking me up? Blowjob. Works every time, and there won't be any hitting."

"Noted."

"Okay, now I really want to go back to sleep so you can wake me up again."

"But I thought you didn't actually go to sleep?"

Uh … "What's that, little guy? You need to be burped now?" I fuss over the pup and ignore Sam's snickering in the background.

It doesn't take either of us long to pass out after we get the puppies resituated.

—

As much as I'm looking forward to being woken as promised, it doesn't happen. I'm not woken by sweet little puppy cries either. No, I'm woken by Ezra-fucking-Palaszczuk standing at the foot of the bed with Sam's roommate, Ethan, behind him.

I focus in on them. Ethan is also holding two of the pups, one under each arm. "Wha … Huh?"

"Oh, good! You're alive," Ezra cries in his over-the-top fashion.

"Dramatic much? You're sounding like Connor more and more every day. Are you getting old?"

Ezra's mouth drops. "What did you say?"

"What's with all the yelling?" Sam asks and sits up. He's still shirtless, and even if Ezra is my idol and I look up to him, I also kinda hate him for interrupting.

"The yelling is about boundaries and Ezra breaking them," I say.

"You want to talk about boundaries?" Ezra yells some more. "How about calling me *old*?"

"Shh. Don't wake the puppies. I've been up with them since six," Ethan says.

He's been up with them? I glance around the room. "What time is it?"

"Nine." Ethan adjusts one of the pups who's squirming. "I heard the pups crying, and you two were dead asleep, so I took over for a bit, but now I've gotta hit the gym, so …"

I hold out my arms for the babies to come to me, but Ezra steps in front of me.

"You can't. We have a game to get to."

"What game?"

"We got ice time, and we all know you already miss it." He's right, of course, but I'm also having fun playing happy dog dad and temporary partner to Sam. It might only be for the summer, but that's why I'd rather not leave. I have hockey the rest of the year.

"You should go," Sam says. "I need to get to the shelter anyway."

"You didn't want to come check out the game? Can you take a morning off, and then I'll come help you this afternoon?"

"What about the pups?"

"Bring them in their crate," I say. "Come on. You said the sexiest thing was me with puppies, and I want to prove you wrong. It's actually while I'm playing hockey."

Ezra nods. "Can confirm."

Sam purses his lips in thought. "I suppose Danika can take care of the shelter and the other volunteers for a few hours."

"Awesome. Now, let's get our babies ready for their big excursion to the great indoors. We'll need to pack extra blankets to keep them warm, and—"

Ezra's brow scrunches. "How long have we been out at that lake for? You're suddenly coparenting puppies and calling them your babies?"

"Sam and I are practically married for the next six weeks."

"As long as you didn't actually get married by accident." Ezra turns on his heel and heads out the bedroom door.

"Married by accident?" Sam asks.

I think of Tripp and Dex. "You have no idea the type of stories the Collective has, but trust me, you'll want to hear them."

"I don't doubt that. Okay, show me how hitting a disc with a stick somehow makes you sexy."

CHAPTER TWENTY

SAM

Armed with a crate full of sleepy pups, I glare at where Lachie and his friends are out on the ice.

Because he's right.

I think I'm a fan of ice hockey now.

Not only is the way he moves out there so incredibly skillful, but he radiates the kind of confidence that attracted me to him in the first place.

"Damn it," I grumble at the puppies. "He's made his point. And I'm very worried that point is that he's hottest in *every* capacity."

I get a tiny *yip* in return.

The thing is, Lachie is covered in so much padding I can barely see him, so it's not like some porn-level display of manliness. The padding makes him look bigger than I know he is, but the way he bounces back from hits, his speed, and how he covers the ice like second nature is awakening that caveman inside me. It's like the typical jock display of skill, but I get to enjoy it because I know that Lachie is a genuinely good person.

For something that's supposed to be a "friendly," these guys are getting really into it. The bickering and smack talk haven't stopped, and while most of it is between Ezra and a black-haired man, the others get in on it too.

I cross my arms as I watch them move up and down the ice, reminding me that this is not the same thing as my last experience with a hockey player. For one thing, every time he takes a break, Lachie skates over to me to make sure I'm suitably impressed. When he scores, he points his stick my way and shouts—so everyone can hear him—"Impressed yet, Sammy?" and I have to pretend I missed it while checking on the puppies.

There's been no awkwardness. No cold shoulder.

This isn't the real world though, and while he can be himself in front of his other queer friends, that doesn't mean it would extend to a real game. With fans and media and all of his teammates.

And that doesn't matter anyway.

Because this is for the summer.

Lachie speeds my way, pulling to a fast stop and spraying ice over the short wall between us. His hair is damp when he pulls off his helmet, but that smile of his is untamable. "You're impressed. You don't even have to tell me, but try to keep it in your pants until we can get back to your place."

Considering I have to go to work after this, and Lachie is going back to the lake house, us hooking up again is a while away. "I dunno ... I thought I was here to watch ice hockey, not figure skating."

With a word, he takes off in a loop, and then as he comes back my way, he jumps up in a perfect spin and lands on one foot.

Okay, *that* is impressive. "What the fuck?"

He grins as he *thuds* into the wall again. "I've done some figure skating training too. It's not uncommon for hockey players because it helps build technique."

Grudgingly, I have to admit that it sounds like a whole lot more goes into the game than I thought. Hockey to me has always been big men fighting and slapping a puck around. Fine for anyone who wants to watch a messy, uncoordinated game that hardly seems to have any rules, but watching Lachie is making me rethink things.

"As much as I hate these words coming out of my mouth ... that's impressive."

"Thank you."

"I mean it. I know that training is hard because motivating myself to go to the gym or for a run is enough, but I've never given athletes a whole lot of credit. To me, you guys live in a world of protein shakes, chicken breast and broccoli, and scoring goals."

Lachie laughs. "You're not half wrong. Except you forgot the pasta. I eat lots and *lots* of pasta."

"I'm trying to say that I recognize you've worked hard for this. Take the win."

"I always do." Then he leans over and presses a kiss to my lips. "Watch me score this time."

I'm still processing that kiss as he puts his helmet on and skates away.

I wouldn't have thought that casual kisses fell under the summer fling definition, but I can't place why. Is it too boyfriendy? I had his dick in my mouth yesterday, so it feels weird to say we can do that but can't kiss just because we want to.

It's not like everyone here doesn't already know we've hooked up. We've already said we're defining this thing together, so I guess casually kissing will be part of it.

Can't be mad about that.

The group gathers at the center of the ice, and a tall guy with strawberry blond hair who isn't in hockey gear drops the puck. He's been reffing most of the game, though can it be called reffing when he watches them put each other on their ass and no one gets called on it?

Lachie's on the same team as his brothers, and Connor scrambles for the puck, gets it free from Anton, and passes to where Easton is waiting for it. He takes off up the ice, Lachie shadowing the other side, and manages to get a pass off before he's slammed into the glass by Ezra.

One of the other guys picks it up, but it's stolen by Anton and then stolen back by someone else. Even with this casual game, it's hard for me to keep up, and I keep losing track of where the puck is because possession changes so much.

It's clear these guys are good at what they do, and they're more competitive than even Ethan, who's always putting pressure on himself to be the best. To think I was going to suggest they teach me a few things, but considering I'd be like Bambi on ice, that idea is hitting the bucket. I have no doubt that even if I spent most of the time on my ass, they still wouldn't take it easy on me.

Lachie steals the puck back so fast that he's taking off down the ice before I even notice. He's got a good gap, but a man with a nasty scar comes at him, and Lachie chips the puck around him. They jostle each other before Lachie pulls away, regains possession, and then charges toward the redheaded goalkeeper.

They're one-on-one, and Lachie's moving so fast I brace for the collision, but he shoots, and the goalie darts left.

Or at least, I *thought* he took the shot.

But the second the goalie moves, he snakes his stick into the gap left open and taps the puck into the net.

The *woo* he shouts as he points my way again is filled with the kind of happiness that only comes from doing what you were born to do. So instead of being a fucker and pretending I missed it again, I put my fingers in my mouth and let out a piercing whistle.

His whole face lights up, even as his brothers slam against him—happily, I guess?—and I can't stop the answering smile.

Then something moves in my periphery and makes me jump.

"You with these guys too?" an enormous, dark-haired, dimpled man asks. He's stupidly tall and has muscles on muscles. Like a real-life Superman.

"Ah … yeah?" I'm half worried he's security and is about to kick me out.

"Tell me there's no cats in there," he says, pointing at the carrier.

"Puppies."

"Thank fuck. I'm allergic to cats." He sits next to me and points onto the ice at one of Lachie's friends. "Regrettably, that one's mine." Despite his words, there's too much pride in his voice to pull off the "regrettably" part.

At least I know he's not about to throw me out.

"Sam." I hold out my hand.

"Gabe." His smile stretches wider. "So you're the Sam people have been talking about."

"Should I be worried people have been talking about me?"

"With this group, always. The rest of the BAHs are cool though. You'll fit right in."

I'm almost scared to ask. "BAHs?"

His gaze flicks to me and away again. "Oh, ahh, just a group of us. Nothing special."

The way Gabe's tone pitches higher has me curious, and I'm about to push when one of the pups gives an impatient bark, and the others follow.

"Shit, I didn't wake them up, did I?"

I open the front of the carrier. "Nope. They've been asleep for an hour now, which I didn't think they were capable of. Want to hold one?"

"Hell yes."

I hand over one of the puppies and pull out the smallest one before setting the carrier on the floor. The other two are feeling adventurous because they sneak out and give the area a sniff. Normally, I wouldn't let them explore without them being vaccinated, but any diseases they could catch aren't going to be living on the cold concrete floor.

"Four dogs. Wow. You've got your hands full."

Yes, I do. "Only for a few weeks. I work at a shelter, and I'm looking after these guys until we home them."

"That's cool." He lifts the puppy, and it immediately licks his face. "I think he likes me."

"I think he does too." Pushing my luck, I say, "He'll be vaccinated, neutered, and mostly house-trained in a few weeks ..."

Gabe laughs, clearly picking up on my very heavy-handed hint. "With Aleks away so much and me working long shifts, plus fostering children with different needs, getting an animal is hard." I can tell he's thinking about it though, and then he surprises me. "But the fire station has been talking about getting a dog for a while. What breed is this guy?"

"A collie-Lab mix. We think. They respond well to training and being kept busy." I leave off that being in a fire station surrounded by people and constant work would be perfect for her, but it's a close call. I can already see Gabe thinking about it.

"Let me make some calls and get back to you."

Unlike most people who say that, I can tell he's serious. "I can give you two weeks. I guarantee these guys won't last long."

"You know, one thing we've done for our local animal shelter in Seattle is take photos with the animals for a social media campaign. Most of them were adopted within hours of it going live. All I'm saying is that you have a lot of very famous hockey players right there, and ninety percent of them need less reason than charity to take their shirts off ..."

I slide a sly look his way. "Are you saying I should exploit Lachie's friends for the greater good?"

"Aleks!" Gabe shouts, and the group turns our way. "Get over here."

His very confused boyfriend comes our way. "What's wrong?"

"Take off your shirt."

"Gladly, but ... why?"

Gabe sighs. "For me."

Aleks takes his helmet off, strips off the jersey, and looks at Gabe expectantly.

"All of it."

"*Really?*"

"Just do it," Gabe says, like Aleks is being the difficult one. He glances over at me. "I swear it's not usually this hard to get him naked."

Aleks rolls his eyes but strips off the padding and undershirt until all he's left in are his hockey pants.

"Perfect." Gabe shoves the puppy into his arms.

And like that, Aleks goes from hot to sexy. He snuggles the little puppy in his tattooed arms, and everything from his sweat-drenched hair to his broad chest that the pup rests its head against is perfect.

Gabe snaps a photo and shows it to me. "See?"

The puppy is gazing up at Aleks with big, starstruck eyes, and it makes even *me* want to adopt him. The puppy. Not the player.

Ezra joins us. "Not that I don't love the view, but why is Aleks stripping?"

"Photoshoot," Gabe replies. "These little cuties need homes, and what better way to make it happen than pictures that go viral?"

At first, I think Ezra is about to call Gabe out on sexualizing them based on the scandalized look that takes over his face. I should already know better. "And Aleks was the first one you asked? Please. If you want viral, you should have come to the source."

"He said viral, not virus," the black-haired player says, joining us.

"Even you can't deny I'm irresistible, Little Dalton," Ezra throws back.

Little Dalton has an evil look cross his face, and I immediately know not to get on his bad side. "Bet Aleks gets more likes than you."

Ezra's eyes go wide. "Aleks? Be serious now."

Little Dalton shrugs. "Me, then. Or Lachie. Connor. Oskar. I'm willing to bet that literally any of us will get more likes."

"It feels wrong to bet on that," Ezra says. "It's such an easy win that—"

There's a bunch of *ohhhs* and echoing disagreements, and before I know what's happening, hockey jerseys and gear are going everywhere, and I'm surrounded by attractive, shirtless men.

Lachie leans over the barrier to press his lips to my ear. "You're drooling."

And while I might be enjoying the view, it's purely aesthetic.

I turn to him and give his jersey a tug. "Not yet. But I'm sure it won't take you long to change that."

And the second his shirt is off, I'm not wrong.

My money is on Lachie blowing the others' pictures out of the water.

CHAPTER TWENTY-ONE

LACHIE

I'm itching to get out of here. Not that the hockey wasn't fun. Or the photoshoot with the puppies and the friendly competition between us players.

No, I'm dying to get out of here because ever since I hit the ice, I've sensed Sam's stare on me. Watching my moves. Being in awe. At least, that's what I'm going to assume the heat in his eyes has been. I can't wait to get him alone so he can tell me how I was right. Me with a puppy? Adorable and irresistible. Me on the ice? If there was room to fuck in his car, I'm sure we'd need a pit stop before getting him to work. Unfortunately, the crate with the pups will take up most of the space. Which means all this peacocking and showboating can't result in sex until after his shift at the shelter. Here I was, thinking I was teasing him this whole time, when all I've been doing is prolonging things for both of us.

I should've told Ezra to fuck off this morning, let Ethan take the puppies, and then had a morning of orgasms.

But I can't deny the high I get walking off the ice and into the locker rooms here in Colorado's practice facility.

This is where Connor and Easton have suited up countless times, been on the ice together, been teammates. Today has really been the only time I've gotten to experience that with them. There was a charity game a couple of years ago, but that was in Vegas. That whole city has a different-ass vibe. This facility, being Easton and Connor's home base ... I wish

Colorado had been able to draft me instead of St. Louis. We knew it wasn't going to happen because I was the favored number one draft pick, and Colorado is a playoff contender every year, so they never get that pick, but it would've been cool to play with my brothers. Now, that will never happen because Connor retired for love.

I only have one more season on my entry-level contract, but I'm still at the mercy of St. Louis for a few more years until I become an unrestricted free agent. The only way I can leave St. Louis and sign with another team is if they let me, and I don't see that happening anytime soon. I'm the team's best chance at a Cup run.

I sigh as I strip down in the locker room.

Ezra appears beside me out of nowhere like a ninja. "What was that weight-of-the-world sigh? You have a man out there waiting for you, cute puppies to cuddle, and you smoked us all out there on the ice. You should be gloating."

"I'll happily gloat about kicking your old ass all over the ice."

"Then what's up? Talk to Uncle Ez about your troubles."

"Uncle Ez?"

"I was going to say Daddy Ez, but despite what you think, I'm not Damon King levels of old yet."

I relent. "Being out there today made me realize we're never going to have the Kiki brothers on the same team at any point. Connor's retired, I'm trapped in St. Louis."

"Aww, you're lonely up there all on your own?"

Technically, I'm not alone. I have my roommate, Hawke, who I moved in with the year I was drafted. It's normal for newly drafted players to have a billet family or a roommate the first couple of years in the league. A few of the guys offered to host me, but I chose Hawke because he knows what it's like to be out but not actually, publicly out. It's why he's never been interested in joining the Collective, because hanging around these guys is like putting a flashing neon sign above your head outing yourself. Hawke and I have each other's backs and have had some fun nights out together, but maybe I was hoping for more from him when I moved in. More of ... this. I might feel like I'm on the outside of these guys—the little brother who hangs around like a fly—but this still feels like a family. I don't have that in St. Louis.

"I guess." It hasn't been a problem before now, but being on the ice with my brothers, having Sam watch ... I always figured I'd be signed to Colorado eventually, and today has made me realize it's still a really long way off.

Ezra looks around the locker room. Most of the guys are in the showers already, but he still lowers his voice anyway. "I get it. Before Anton, I thought I was happy. Then I had a taste of what real happiness is, and I realized all of my friendships, my hookups ... they were all shallow. You need a support system in place, especially when you're feeling like this, so if you ever need me, I'm only a text away."

I nod. "Plus, you make me check in with you every time we play against each other."

Something passes across Ezra's face before he says something I never, ever thought would come out of his mouth. "I won't be in the league forever though."

My eyes widen. "What? Did you just admit that you're getting ol—"

He points his finger in my face. "Don't even say it, Little Kiki. I mean eventually."

"You're probably going to outskate us all."

"That was the plan, and if you repeat this to anyone, I will cut you, but even I know I'll have to re ..." He puffs his cheeks out. "Reti—" He cuts off and clears his throat. "One day, my body won't work the way it's supposed to, and that's so depressing I'm going to stop talking about it. My point is that the Collective works because we're a community, and a community can't thrive if you give up on it. So stop moping, get showered, and go have fun with your man out there."

My *temporary man*.

For some reason, that thought brings me down even more. But I'm determined not to let it affect my mood. I won't.

—

"You okay? You've seemed kind of ... distant since we left your hockey friends. I thought you were going to go back to the lake house with them. Did something happen?"

I'm totally succeeding at not letting my thoughts affect my mood. At all.

After volunteering at the shelter while Sam worked, we're arriving back at his place with the puppies, including another one from the litter which the vet had taken yesterday because he wasn't doing great.

"Just tired. Being a puppy dad is hard work."

We carry the crate inside and place the pups in the small living room between the banged-up wooden entertainment unit and a plant I assume was alive at some point.

"You don't have to stay again. I'm used to these kinds of foster jobs. I thought you'd be eager to get back to the lake house with your brothers."

"Eh. I have forever to hang out with those losers." Something I've been trying to remind myself of all afternoon.

I wouldn't rather be there than with Sam, but my revelation today is still making my mood sullen.

"What happened in the locker room? One minute, you were all smiles and cocky attitude, and now, you're quiet and ... not like yourself."

I wrap my arm around Sam's waist and pull him against me. "I'm good. I promise. I'm a little bummed because I only realized today that summer is too short. Being back on the ice today, I'm already thinking about heading back to St. Louis. Which is depressing because I don't want this to be over."

Sam sucks in a sharp breath, and I fear I've scared him off.

"Summer. I don't want summer to be over."

Sam's hands run up my chest and rest on my shoulders. "We still have so much time. The summer's still young."

It is, but at the same time, I know it's going to go way too fast.

I grip his hips and pull him tighter against me. "We should make the most of it."

Sam looks down at the crate. "We fed them before we left the shelter. How long do you think we have until they bug us for more?"

"The more important question is probably how quick do you think we can get each other off?"

Sam grabs my hand and pulls away, dragging me with him to his bedroom. "I swear before the summer is up, we're going to have sex where we're not in public or have to rush because I'm working or there are needy puppies demanding attention."

"Agreed. It will happen. Not today, but it will happen."

CHAPTER TWENTY-TWO

SAM

Rushed blowjobs, silent frot sessions ... As much as I am loving the orgasms, and as cute as the puppies are, after a week and a half of it, I'm getting antsy. Is it rude of me to shove Ethan out the door with the pups with the threat not to come back until tomorrow morning? Maybe.

We've been considerate of Ethan by not screaming the apartment down every time Lachie comes over, so it's his turn to give back.

Thankfully, he's made plans to stay with a gym-bro friend who loves animals, so it's all worked out perfectly.

I'm pacing the apartment, already hard, and have just finished tidying up all the puppy stuff when I debate whether to start dinner now or wait until later. The knock at the door answers my dilemma for me.

It's been two days since I last saw Lachie, and while I know I'm the one who warned him we wouldn't be able to see each other every day, it doesn't mean I don't want to. Especially because the reminder we're almost halfway through our time together keeps popping into my head more frequently than ever.

Lachie was right. Time moves too fast, and even though it seemed like we still had so much time together, realizing we're already down to six weeks left until he has to leave, I'm dreading when that time comes.

Everything has moved so fast, it's easy to forget what this is. It's happened a handful of times, from when I misinterpreted him saying he didn't want this to be over to when he was baby-talking at the puppies and called us their daddies. I know better, but my body is getting ahead of my brain, and I don't hate the happy flutters.

I'm close to tearing the door off its hinges when I reach it, I'm that eager to get to him.

"Did someone order a pizza?" he asks in a fake professional voice.

I don't have it in me to play along. I grab his arm and tug him inside, slamming the door closed behind us. We're kissing before I've even backed him into the door, and it's unclear who moved first, but I do know he's been wanting this as badly as I have.

My tongue sweeps into his mouth, his hands gripping my ass, and this heightened lust is addictive with how deeply it grips me. I'm tempted to strip him off and suggest we spend the entire night naked, but first, I should probably let him get inside the apartment.

My hands cup his face, and I press one last kiss to his mouth. And then another. And another. "I've been debating," I say between kisses, "whether to have dinner, then fuck you. Or fuck you and then have dinner."

Lachie grunts, and without an answer, his mouth is back on mine. Our kiss is heated, and as we consume each other, he wraps the front of my shirt in his fists and backs me toward my bedroom.

Fucking first, it is.

With that decision made, I grip the bottom of his T-shirt and drag it up his body as we walk. Our kiss breaks long enough for me to shove it over his head, and mine quickly follows, and then our mouths crash together again like magnets.

I'll never get tired of the way his body feels against mine. Hard chest, warm skin, the roughness of his body hair. Those callused palms bring goose bumps up along my skin with every touch, and I don't know why it took me so long to kick Ethan out for the night.

My back collides with a wall, and as I shove him away, he collides with a doorframe. I go for the button on his shorts, yanking them open, pushing them down, while he attacks mine in return. We have no clue where we're going or what we're doing, and our legs tangling together have us plowing into random parts of the house.

Our shorts disappear.

Our underwear goes next.

It's just him and me and this sizzling friction between us.

Somehow, we make it into the hallway. Then my bedroom.

We stumble toward my bed, neither of us wanting to let go, and when my calves hit the frame, I fall backward, taking him with me.

His weight on me is sexy as hell. His muscles, his cologne, the way his mouth breaks from mine and teases the nerves all along my neck. I grind up into him, bringing our rock-hard shafts together, and it's relief and frustration all at once.

"Fuck, Sam," he rasps, the first words he's spoken since he got inside.

I flip us, pressing him into the sheets as I make my way down his chest to suck his nipple into my mouth. It tightens as I lick it, his breathing hitching as his hand plunges into my hair. "*Shit.*"

He leaves a sticky line of precum against my hip as he thrusts against it.

I chuckle, teeth giving his nipple a tug, and then I let it go and continue downward. Maybe later, we can try again and spend the night teasing each other, but right now, what I need is to get my cock inside him. When Lachie mentioned the other day how he's been waiting for me to fuck him already, I haven't been able to concentrate on anything else since.

I kiss and lick my way down his torso, running my tongue along his abs and dipping it into the V by his hip. Every inch of him turns me on, and the more I get of him, the more I want.

"Suck it," he begs.

I move closer, like I'm going to, but I lick the precum from his tip instead and then hitch his thighs up over my shoulders.

"Tease," he whines, but the word cuts off when I drag my tongue over his hole.

"What was that?"

"I said I love everything you're doing, and you should definitely continue."

My laugh puffs against his skin, and I spread his ass cheeks before diving in. He tastes like soap, and he obviously showered as carefully as I did before he got here. At this rate, fuck dinner, because I'd rather spend the night wrapped up in him instead.

I massage his hole with my tongue, slowly working him open until I can push inside. He's not some blushing virgin, thank fuck, so I don't need to handle him gently, but I'm careful not to go too fast. There's impatient, and then there's being an asshole. As much as I want to get off, it's only hot if it feels just as good for the person I'm with.

"Keep going," he breathes, reaching for his cock. I watch his firm, patient strokes, wishing I had a hand free to do it for him. When it comes to Lachie, I get the feeling he's always going to leave me wanting more.

As he loosens up, I work my tongue deeper, and my cock aches at being ignored. I'm edging myself as much as I'm edging him, and hearing the slutty little moans and stuttered breaths has me leaking onto my sheets.

I fuck him with my tongue, moving freer and deeper, before I retreat and fill him with two fingers instead. His hole wraps tight around them, and I watch as he sucks me into his body and then resists as I pull them back again.

"You're going to be so tight around my cock." I'm mesmerized by the sight of him taking me, and I can't stop squeezing his ass with my free hand. I know hockey players have a reputation for glute muscles, but this is next-level. Maybe I have Lachie lust goggles on, but I don't think there's a single thing about him that doesn't turn me on.

His shoulder blades, those little dimples at the bottom of his back, his strong calves, and fuck me, even his *knees* are masculine and sexy. I'm glad we've still got a month to fool around, but I have a feeling Ethan is going to need to get used to sex sounds coming through the walls.

Now that I get to experience taking it slow and doing everything I want to with him, it's going to be hard to stop.

I add a third finger, loving the way his hole is stretching. Being experienced at bottoming makes this so much easier when my dick is a bit bigger than average. I don't need to worry about hurting him, and I trust Lachie to tell me if I do.

Because while the sex is a force on its own, developing a friendship between hookups makes this so much better. We get a chance to talk about what we like, and it adds another level to the experience when I know the man I'm with. When I can trust him to communicate and know what he can take.

I brush the spot deep inside him that drives Lachie wild. His head bows back as his chest inflates, and then he lets it all out in a rush. "I have to be ready. If I'm not, I don't care."

Luckily for him, he is ready. Still, I fuck him with my fingers a couple more times because it turns me on with how it looks. Then I pull them free, loving the way he stays open, and climb off the bed to grab supplies.

My dick is angry and red and has reached the point where it's throbbing with the need for attention. I pull out a condom and the lube, then turn to him.

"Do we need this?" I ask with the little square between my fore and middle fingers.

"I'm on PrEP," he says.

"Me too."

There's a stretch of silence before he decides. "I don't need it. Just fuck me."

That's what I was hoping for. I drop the condom back into the drawer and squeeze lube out into my palm. I'm slow as I coat myself in it, trying to get my cock to settle so that I don't come the second I'm inside him. I'm not sure I manage it, but hey, at least we have all night.

I settle at the top of the bed, back against the headboard, and slap my thigh. "Get up here."

He crawls up the bed, running kisses all the way up the inside of my legs, and only stops once he reaches my balls.

"And you called me a tease," I complain.

His wicked grin is exactly what I was expecting, and I reach for his long necklace, wrapping it around my fist.

"I said get up here." I use the necklace to drag him to me and only stop once he's straddled my thighs and our lips are hovering close together. "Can I kiss you?"

He doesn't answer, just seals our mouths together.

I lean into the kiss, fumbling the lube as I squeeze more out and return to his ass. He's a little tighter as I press three fingers back inside him, but it only takes a few seconds to loosen up again.

Lachie changes the angle, pressing forward so that our cocks are trapped between our bodies, and the sudden contact almost makes me lose it.

"Fuck, stop," I gasp, panting as I fight to stay in control. "Give me a second."

The heated look he's staring back at me with makes me think he already knew that. "I swear to Stanley, if you come before you're inside me, we're going to have our first fight."

I grip the base of my cock hard and count to five. He's still rocking back onto my fingers, which really isn't helping, but screw it. If I come the second I'm inside him, at least I've followed through.

"Lachie," I say, pulling my fingers free and bringing my hand down on his ass with a *crack*. "Sit on my fucking cock."

CHAPTER TWENTY-THREE

LACHIE

The second I sink down on his fan-fucking-tastic cock, an explosion of pleasure, fantasy, and emotions hits me right in the chest.

If I could go back and tell little twelve-year-old me that the hot, older teenager I was obsessed with would one day want me ... okay, past me would probably be cocky about it and ruin it, but to think, I never thought this would happen ...

His cock fills me up to the point I almost can't take it. It feels ... amazing—no, that's not enough of a word for what this feels like.

I can say all I want that this summer is a fling, that it's purely about having fun, and I'll happily return to St. Louis come September, but I already know leaving Denver this time will be even harder than when I was first drafted.

Not only because of my revelation that I want to play hockey for my hometown—sooner rather than later—but because of this here, being with Sam in a way I have only ever imagined.

"Fuck," I hiss when I get fully seated.

I've never been so full. Hell, I've never been this close to someone I've had sex with. Physically or emotionally. There's no doubt Sam and I have become friends. I probably trust him more than I trust some of my teammates, and considering I've been with a lot of those same guys for three years now, Sam has quickly become a staple in my life.

Going back to hockey is one thing—it's my career, my love, my passion. I will do anything to keep that, even move away from my home, my family who I love. For some reason, the thought of having to leave Sam in a few weeks feels like it's going to be so much harder. Daunting.

And yes, all these random melancholy thoughts are running through my head while he's balls-deep inside me.

"You need a minute?" he asks, his voice croaky like he's trying with all his strength to hold on to a tiny thread of control that's unraveling fast.

Physically, I'm ready to go, but I wasn't ready for the emotional gut punch taking this step with him would do to me.

I want to get even closer, have every inch of him against me. But I take the moment he's giving me and play it off like I'm still adjusting to the size of his cock instead of the way he's pushing inside my heart.

"Yeah. Just a sec."

Sam strokes my face with one hand while he keeps a strong palm on my hip to keep me in place. "You've got this."

You've got me, I want to say.

I've never felt this before—this kind of bond—with a hookup. It's entirely possible that in this moment of connection, of intimacy, that I'm being fueled by lust and sex hormones and superficial stuff that makes me think it's deeper than what it is. But as I slowly rotate my hips and more smaller explosions of happiness shoot through me, I can't help thinking it's something more.

I lower my forehead to his and rock forward on his cock.

"Fuck, you feel so good," he whispers.

Good, amazing, incredible, none of these words are enough for how he feels inside me.

I was so eager for this to happen, so eager for Sam to fuck me, that I was certain it was going to be fast and messy, but after weeks of rushing through orgasms to take the horny edge off, I'm going to do this how I do everything else in life: the way I fucking want to.

We have all night—something we haven't had before.

I stare down into Sam's brown eyes as I begin to move, rocking back and forth on his hard cock. It's nowhere near enough to satisfy either of us, but it's an intense connection I want to keep for a little while longer.

"You're killing me." Sam breaks first, lowering his head to my shoulder and biting down hard enough to leave a mark but not to break skin.

I throw my head back as sparks prickle along my skin, but I refuse to give in yet. I'm going to keep my slow and torturous pace because I need to worship this man's body all night.

In saying that, it's an effort not to let go and ride him like a cowboy.

Later. Later. Soon, I chant in my head.

Our heavy breaths echo off his bedroom walls. We've become too accustomed to having to be quiet because when Sam's moan breaks the almost silent room, my first reaction is to cover his mouth with my hand.

He murmurs something against my palm.

"What was that?" I ask as I let his mouth free.

"No one's home. We don't have to be quiet."

"Oh, fuck yes," I practically yell.

Sam laughs.

I lean in and take his mouth with my own, kissing him while letting go of a tiny bit of restraint. My hips are no longer doing all the work as my knees get involved too. I rise up on Sam's dick and push back down again.

It's a mistake the second I do it, though, because the desperation in the noises he begins to make is enough to make me snap. Turns out, adding a soundtrack of needy whimpers and throaty sighs is too much for me to handle.

My cock aches as Sam hits my prostate every time I sink down on him, precum leaking everywhere.

There's no stopping me now because any sense of control is completely gone. His hips meet mine over and over again. Sam grips my ass hard and thrusts upward into me.

"Fucking hell," he curses.

"I know. Holy shit, this is amazing. Fucking awesome dick. No notes."

Sam huffs, like he's trying to laugh again but physically can't anymore. "I was more talking about your glutes and how rock hard they are, but yes. Your hole is amazing too."

"Damn right, it is." I could come like this. I could come any minute like this, but I don't want to.

All night. We have all night.

I force myself to slow down before I reach that moment of no return.

Sam is breathing heavily, a sly smile on his face. "Is this your way of telling me you're into edging or—"

"No. I want to come. I want to come so badly, but not yet. I want you to fuck me every which way, and I only want to come when we're both exhausted enough to pass out."

"That sounds like a challenge I can get behind. Right after I get behind you. Get up." He slaps my ass, not hard, but the *thwack* sound goes right to my cock. "Get on your hands and knees."

I climb off him and do as he says, but instead of flipping over and getting right to it, Sam stands and rounds the bed. I watch him as he goes, my neck craning to see him over my shoulder. Then, without warning, his big, capable hands dig into the front of my thighs, and he pulls me backward, dragging me down the mattress until my feet are hanging off the end, my arms stretched out in front of me, and my ass up in the air for the taking.

My hole contracts, missing being full, and a soft curse comes from behind me.

I hang my head. "Fuck me, Sammy. Please. I need it."

He doesn't give me what I want though. Instead of his fat cock, he goes back to fucking me with his fingers. It feels good, but it's not enough. I push back onto his hand, trying to get deeper, harder.

"I like you like this," Sam says. "So desperate for it. I want to give you everything you need, but to do that, I need a second to come back from the edge. You're so sexy like this. Too sexy. I could watch you fuck my hand all night."

I whine as I lower my head and rest it on the bed beneath me. I want to stop riding his hand so he'll be tempted to hurry back, but I can't help but keep on going. I'm more than desperate. It's no longer a want, a craving … it's a goddamn fucking need.

I want to crawl out of my skin. "I *need* your cock."

"Okay, but if I come the minute I'm inside you …"

"I won't care. I'm sure it won't take me long to follow. I just … I …"

He puts me out of my misery, removing his fingers and slamming that amazing cock inside me. We immediately find a hard rhythm. Every thrust is another one of those explosions of pleasure. Even though he's going hard, he's not rushing it. He slams inside me and slowly pulls out, doing that over and over and over again.

Sam leans over me, his breath trailing up my back, and then his hands wrap around my chest. "Lean up on your knees for me."

I push myself up so my back is flush against his front. His cock slips out of me, but he's quick to kneel on the edge of the bed and then guide his cock back to my hole. Being pressed against him like this, his arms around my torso, it feels like he's surrounding me entirely, filling all of me, inside and out.

Instead of the hard and slow pace from before, he's now taking me short and fast. Shallow.

Sweat drips off my wet hair, and my chest is slick with it. Every muscle in my body contracts and releases as I get closer and closer to that high. Sam's sure to move at a pace that won't get either of us across the line, but he's doing an amazing job of making me want to get there more and more.

I've restrained myself from touching my cock, but I'm not going to be able to hold out much longer. I know when I resort to that, it's going to be all over.

"Are you close?" he rumbles in my ear.

"It won't take me much to get there."

"What do you need?"

"I need you to touch me. Fuck, wrap your hand around my dick while you keep fucking me. Just like this." I stare down at my cock as his long fingers cover my tight, velvety skin.

My hands are behind me, holding on to the side of his thighs as they propel him forward, pushing his cock into me deeper. He strokes me in time with his thrusts, and it feels so good my mind fuzzes over.

I reach the point of no return, but before I can give a warning, my cock pulses, and ropes of cum fill Sam's hand and cover the duvet below us.

My ass tightens around his cock while I continue to erupt all over the place. His free hand pushes me down by the middle of my back, and while I begin to recover, he starts taking what he needs.

He fucks me hard, deep, fast, and if he had done this at any other time, I would've come immediately. My cock leaks with the last of my release, and my prostate becomes oversensitive, but at the sound of his skin slapping against mine, his increased breath, his erratic pace that has lost all rhythm, I know he's close.

When Sam finally stiffens inside me, filling me with his cum, it's a relief and also such a turn-on that I swear my dick tries to get hard again.

My brain, muscles, and limbs are all mush at this point, and when Sam pulls out of me, I fall forward in the puddle of my own release and push my knees out from under me. Because I'm on the edge of the bed, my knees hit the floor, and this is actually really comfortable.

Or Sam did what I told him to and fucked me until I'm so exhausted that I could pass out right here and now.

Actually, I think I do, even if it's only for a minute. Because the next thing I know, I'm startled by a warm, wet cloth running up the inside of my thighs and then over my hole.

He's cleaning me up?

The sex might be over, but those happy bursts of emotion are apparently here to stay.

CHAPTER TWENTY-FOUR

SAM

By the time we nap off the amazing sex, it's getting late, and my options to cook are noodles or ... noodles. Not mad about that, considering how much I've been missing carbs lately.

I get dinner on, basic as fuck but about the best I'm capable of, and Lachie comes up behind me. He presses his naked body against my back, soft cock resting by my ass, and wraps his arms around me. One hand settles on my chest, and the other rests low on my abs as he watches over my shoulder.

"Aren't you worried about the hazards of cooking naked?"

"I think this is a pretty safe option."

"True. And pasta is the way to a hockey player's heart. Though I'm going to have to make sure I slip in an extra workout tomorrow."

This is feeling way more domestic than I'd planned for, and I don't hate it. "Why the extra workout?"

"I always eat pretty good in general, but during the season, we play and train so much that the main focus is on eating enough to maintain my size, since I burn through a lot of calories. Off-season, I always forget to adjust my portion sizes, so I try to throw in extra workouts after a big meal so that I'm not sluggish once training camp starts."

"You know, I could just give you a regular person amount."

Lachie gasps. "Of pasta? Do you hate me?"

I laugh, and he turns his smile into my neck, breaking out those stupid flutters that I have to remind to calm down. And then, the worst thought ever for a summer fling pops in my mind. *Why can't he stay?*

Not only is it stupid because I know the reasons he can't. Hockey is his life, right down to what and how much he eats. It will always be his number one, and considering how hard it is to make it as a hockey player and the work he would have put in to get to this level, I understand it. The other reason the question is stupid is because I'm crossing lines we drew together. I knew what this was going into it, and even if Lachie felt the same way I do, it doesn't matter.

He has to return to St. Louis, and long-distance relationships are the kiss of death for a couple. I don't know anyone who's made it work.

"What are you thinking about?" he asks.

There's no way I can give him the real answer. "How many times we can come before Ethan gets home tomorrow."

"I'm ready to pull an all-nighter if you are."

"Considering we both crashed after the first round, I don't see that happening."

Lachie finally steps away from me to head to the fridge. He pulls it open, the glow from inside lighting up his naked body, and I drink the sight in greedily.

If nothing else, I got to have this. And who knows, maybe we can still catch up whenever he's back in town to visit family or next summer or whatever.

He grabs the jug of water, no clue I'm shamelessly eye-fucking him, and pours us both a glass.

"We should probably hydrate," he says with a wink.

I drain the noodles and then set them back on the stove, dumping the jar of pasta sauce on top. "I was thinking ..." I say in an offhand way and not as though I've been curious since I saw him fucking around with his friends. "Can we watch a game replay anywhere? I'll have no clue what's going on, but maybe you can teach me."

His eyebrows rise slowly. "You want to watch me play?"

"Why not? We need something to do between fucking, and you're right that you look hot as hell when you're on the ice."

"Okay, but don't blame me if you can't keep your hands off me."

"Hockey or not, I don't think that's possible."

He goes to put on the TV while I plate up dinner.

"What streaming services do you have?" he calls back.

"Umm ... none?"

His concerned gaze meets mine. "None?"

"I don't watch TV."

"You don't ... *why*?"

"I keep myself busy. If Ethan's watching something, I'll join him, but I don't actively find things myself."

"You are a giant weirdo." He opens an app on the TV and logs in. "Now you have my account, so feel free to stalk all of my games this season."

There's no way that's going to happen, but I won't kill his dreams like that. As soon as he leaves, I'll be doing everything possible to *not* remember him, and I have the feeling that while it'll be great to watch it with him here, it'll be any other boring sports game without him.

We settle on the couch, and he hits Play on a game against Dallas.

"We absolutely wrecked them this game. It was so much fun, and I almost got into an awesome fight. It was in highlight reels for a good week afterwards."

"Did you get into trouble for that?"

He blinks those gorgeous gray eyes down at me. "Trouble?"

"For fighting?"

"Nah, only a roughing penalty and a high five from my coach."

A high five? From the person training them? "This sport is so weird."

But as strange as it is, I'm oddly into it as we watch him play and Lachie explains all the bits and pieces for the game. He goes over positions, lines, what each person is primarily responsible for.

Yet he doesn't bat an eye as the commentators say, "And here's Lachie Kikishkin, coming right down Dallas's throat!"

I side-eye him, but he's too busy rattling off stats like a second language. He walks me through all the refs' calls and what a face-off is, and goes into the history between the two teams, and points out the guys from Dallas who he likes and the ones he hates for being known homophobic assholes.

"Are there guys like that on every team?"

"Yeah, more or less," he says like it's common knowledge. "The Queer Collective is amazing at keeping representation front and center, but something most people don't know about Ezra is that he's actively trying to dismantle the homophobia and work with the league to bring in new regulations. It's hard work. The league isn't known for always doing what's right when there's money involved, but he's pushing hard, according to Parker." Lachie shrugs. "Connor doesn't have much interest in talking shop now he's retired, so Parker and I have gotten close because of that. Well, that and how much Conishkin adores me."

"That's the worst rat name I've ever heard."

"When I want to piss my brother off, I call him rat baby Connor, and he answers to that too."

"Like I told them: rats are very smart animals."

Lachie sets his finished bowl on the coffee table and leans into me. "You couldn't have picked a better pet for Parker. He has that thing with him everywhere."

"Good. Conishkin"—I can't believe the name came out of my mouth—"deserves all the love."

"He does."

At that moment, the Lachie on-screen drops his gloves against one of the Dallas players he hates. The punches land hard and fast until the other guy drops to the ice, covering his head, and the refs pull Lachie off him.

"Damn ..."

Lachie's smirking, but it looks forced. "He said some not-nice things about my brothers."

"I'm sorry."

"We still have a long way to go in the league."

"Is that why you haven't come out?"

He thinks over my question, arm sneaking around my shoulders and tugging me closer to him. "My team knows. Most of the people in the league do too, and it leads to some shitty comments about the gay being contagious or whatever. But mostly, I don't want that distraction to hit my team. I don't want to *be* a distraction. And when it comes right down to it, my parents have always talked about making sure we come out in the *right way* that I think that got into my head. I'm pretty confident there isn't a right way to be who you are, but I've also never met someone important enough to fight them on it."

"That makes a lot of sense."

"One day, I want to follow in Connor and Ezra's footsteps."

"What do you mean?"

"Connor spends his time visiting schools and talking about bullying in locker rooms and how to be better than that. At the lake house, I overheard Anton and Ezra talking about camps they're spending their summer visiting to help spread the You Can Play message. I think so much of them for doing that, and hopefully, I can find my own thing one day."

"I think you will. You're motivated and not the type of person who'll stop until he gets what he wants." I'm exhibit A, and that's so weird to think about.

He grins and nips at my jaw. "You have way too high of an opinion of me."

"You also have a lot of years ahead before you need to worry about anything like that."

"True." He runs his nose along my jaw. "And there *are* more pressing things for us to worry about."

The way his voice deepens with suggestion has my cock perking up. "Like ... rinsing the dishes?"

"Nope." He runs his free hand over my thigh.

My breath hitches. "Maybe, uh, dessert?"

"Closer ..." His hand wraps around my half-hard cock and strokes it until I'm stiff in his hold. "Bet you can get me off during first intermission."

I pull out of his hold and shift until I'm kneeling on the floor in front of him. "Challenge accepted."

Lachie spreads his legs, and I lean forward, taking his whole length in one. We were considerate enough to lay a sheet down over the couch, but I'm already a big fan of the whole staying naked thing, and hopefully, we can have a lot more nights like this one before he leaves.

I don't take my time like when he first got here, just bob up and down, sucking hard, tongue doing everything it can to drive him wild. Lachie grips my hair as he fucks my face, and it doesn't take long for him to jam his cock down my throat and come.

Once he's finished, I stand up, and Lachie leans forward to do the same to me. His lips, the suction, the way he looks up at me like he's checking he's doing a good job really is my weakness.

I set my hand on the back of his hair but let him do the work. "That's so good," I tell him. "Your mouth is goddamn magic."

Something deep inside his gaze lights up with satisfaction, and those stupid flutters hit my chest again. I tell myself to look away. To cut eye contact and enjoy the blowjob.

But I don't.

I can't.

I thrust into his mouth, getting closer to my orgasm, reassuring him how amazing it is the whole time.

"No one sucks my cock like you," I tell him, and I mean it. A blowjob is a blowjob, but for what's supposed to be a summer fling, this is hitting harder than it should. "You're incredible. So fucking incredible ..."

I come, his mouth working around my dick as he swallows my release, and we watch each other the entire time.

My cock slips out of his mouth, leaving puffy lips and a shadow of a smile. "Just in time," he says. "And during next intermission, you can tell me all about the ways you find me incredible."

I throw myself back down on the couch, limbs feeling weak as I catch my breath.

That will not be a conversation we'll be having.

Because I'm almost scared of what could come out of my mouth.

CHAPTER TWENTY-FIVE

LACHIE

Naked nights at Sam's should be a regular thing. If it weren't for the puppies and Ethan, I'd probably ask to stay every night.

Me? Desperate for him? A little bit.

But he's so easy to talk to and fun to be around. He doesn't want me just because of what I do for a living, and we both have the same interests—minus hockey. Even with that though, he's been interested in learning. He asks genuine questions and didn't look at his phone once when I made him watch the game against Dallas. That kind of attention isn't something I've really had before. Then again, I haven't had this kind of ... fling before.

It feels more like the beginning of a relationship—not that I know what that actually feels like—but I'm worried about what's going to happen when it's time for me to head back to St. Louis.

We've agreed this ends, but I'm finding it hard to walk out the door today, and I'm only going thirty minutes to my parents' house. I wouldn't be going at all if it weren't for them blowing up my phone this morning.

If they were any other parents, I'd think they were worried about my whereabouts, considering I'm supposed to be sleeping there every night and have stayed out more than I've been home, but no. This is agent business.

Having them as our agents has been ... a ride. Sometimes I think they get carried away in excitement and forget to be parents first and agents second, but with the way they've called and messaged for me to get home to take a meeting, I get the sense I should be excited, too, this time.

And the crazy thing?

I stare down at Sam, at his freshly shaven jaw, the dark eyelashes fanning his cheeks while he sleeps, and ... my chest aches. I'm not excited about what my parents or the St. Louis management team have to say. Because it's going to be extension talks.

I don't want the reality of signing my next seven years to the same team. I'm in the last year of my entry-level contract with stats exceeding those expected of a first-draft pick. If St. Louis want to keep me, they basically have first dibs, and they also have the budget in the salary cap to meet any outside offer.

Everyone from the start has said it's obvious I want to play with my brothers, but with Connor retired already, those rumors haven't been as loud, so I wonder if people think it's not the same without the three of us. But it has always been the plan for us to eventually play for Colorado, and that's not a secret. The thing is though, until I become an unrestricted free agent, I don't get a lot of say.

So no, I don't want to go have this meeting, but there's no getting out of it, so I throw on my clothes, kiss Sam on the head, and tell him I'll come by the shelter later. He's so out of it I can't be sure if he understood me or not or if he even heard me.

As soon as I climb into my waiting ride share, I open our texts, planning to send Sam a cute good morning one, but I stop myself before I can. We've been hooking up way too short a time for me to be this gone already. We agreed to a fling, giving my heart an inch to let someone in, and my heart's let in a mile.

When I arrive home and head inside, Mom and Dad don't even ask where I've been.

"Morning," I say in my usual upbeat tone, even if, for once, I'm faking it.

Mom grips my shoulders from behind and directs me to the formal dining area, where a breakfast spread has been laid out with all the food I shouldn't be eating. Maybe I'll run to the shelter to burn off some calories.

I slide into my seat and take a croissant from the pile and my butter knife. It's not until it's buttered and halfway to my mouth that I notice both Mom and Dad staring at me expectantly.

"What's wrong?" I ask and shovel in the pastry goodness.

"What's wrong with us?" Mom asks. "What's wrong with you? We were expecting the first words out your mouth to be 'How much?' or 'Where do I sign?'"

I place the half-eaten croissant back on my plate and swallow hard, unsure if it's the food making my mouth dry or this conversation. "Okay. Then how much are they offering?"

Mom's face lights up. "Seventy million. Seven years."

I blink at her. Then glance at Dad. Blink some more.

Average of ten million a year is a fucking good deal for someone coming out of their entry-level contract. But ... seven years. Seven.

"Why aren't you screaming and yelling with happiness?" Mom asks.

"He's in shock," Dad says. "Let it sink in a bit first."

I shake my head. "It's not shock. It's ... a long time. A long time in a city that doesn't feel like home, on a team with some great guys but who aren't my brothers."

Mom's gaze sharpens. "I thought you loved St. Louis. You're thriving there."

"I know, but ..." There's not really much I can say, is there? Because she's right. On the outside, I'm thriving where I am. I have friends like Hawke. I'm kicking ass and giving St. Louis hopes of holding the Cup again one day.

"But what?"

"I don't know."

Dad chuckles to himself. "You know, but you don't know. Got it."

"If I sign a four-year contract, I'll become an unrestricted free agent. I could go anywhere then. I could come home."

"If Colorado could afford you then," Mom says. "Four years ... they're not going to offer you anywhere near the ten million a year for that."

"I miss you too, Mom," I say dryly.

"You know we miss you, and we'd love to have you home, but we knew going in that it wouldn't be likely or possible before you become a UFA."

I know all of this, and until this summer, I had accepted it.

"Is this because you're homesick and want to be on the same team as Easton, or is it because of the reason you're not sleeping here most nights?"

Am I actually considering turning down a seventy-million-dollar deal because of a boy? That's what she's asking, and my immediate reaction is to be defensive, because no, it's not all because of Sam. Yet, if I really think about it, it's been a very short amount of time to realize I want to be home sooner rather than later. Even four years is too long.

"Do we need to lock away an extension yet?"

"No. Not if you aren't ready to negotiate. But if this is because of a boy—"

"It's not," I lie. Kind of. It's not entirely because of a boy.

"Keep in mind, the more you push back and reject their offers, the more you let them know you want to be shopped around, and the more likely you are to damage your relationship with St. Louis management. And considering they still own you for another minimum five years, it would be wise not to do that," Mom says, switching to full agent mode.

"My current contract doesn't even expire for another season. It's all too ... overwhelming to think about. What happens if I sign this mega deal and then go out and have a shit season? Everyone in St. Louis will blame me for it or say I'm not worth the money they're throwing at me."

All the more reason to sign now. I can blame the pressure of the job all I want, but both Mom and Dad know I'm good under pressure.

Mom runs an assessing look over me. "Maybe we should look at getting Trevor back out this summer."

It's an effort not to sulk. "I don't need a sports psychologist."

"This isn't another Connor moment, is it?" Mom looks panicked for a second. "The only reason we push you is because you said you want to be the best. We're trying to help you do that. If you want to walk away—"

"I don't. I need …" What do I need? More time with Sam. That's what I need. "Time for myself. Outside of hockey."

"You sound burned out," Dad says.

"I wouldn't go that far. You both know I live and breathe hockey, but maybe I need something for myself this summer. Volunteering at the animal shelter. Having fun."

"And you can do that," Mom says. "As long as when training camp time comes, you jump back in with both feet."

I swallow around the lump in my throat. "I will."

Now I have to hope I'm not lying.

My parents' house backs onto the country club golf course, and there's a water trap that marks our property line. That's where I find myself after my talk with Mom and Dad, sitting against a tree and staring into water like it holds all of life's answers.

I can't explain it. I should be over the moon. I should be shouting from the rooftops and gloating to my brothers because their first contracts after their entry-level years were nowhere near this one.

Sam and I are temporary—we've both agreed. It's going to end. I'm going to be in St. Louis for the next year, minimum, so it wouldn't be smart to start something real with him.

But one year versus seven? It gives me foolish hope that if I sign with Colorado next season, maybe Sam and I have a chance of finding each other again. If I spend the next seven years halfway across the country, it closes off any future with him. My gut hollows out at the reminder of that future.

Footsteps sound behind me, but before I can get excited and think Sam figured out where I live, I see Connor and Easton approaching. "Let me guess. Mom and Dad are worried about me."

My brothers box me in as they sit on either side of me.

"You turned down seventy million dollars, so yeah, they're worried," Easton says.

"And so am I," Connor adds.

"I didn't turn it down," I argue. "I asked why I need to sign an extension now when I still have another season to play."

"Uh, because the game is unpredictable, and you don't want to go through a slump and be offered less next season?" Connor says in a tone that drips with "Duh."

"But if that happens, maybe—" I force my mouth shut. It's pointless to even say the words out loud, partially because they'll never happen, but also because I know I won't be able to hide how much I want it.

"Maybe what?" Easton asks.

"My value will go down, and Parker could afford to sign me to Colorado," I say like I haven't thought about this a thousand times already. "Colorado was always the plan."

Connor rubs his chin, but there's regret in his eyes. "It was. A long time ago. And we all knew it would take a while before we would be able to play on the same team. Plus, I'm retired now, so—"

"Just because you're not playing anymore, that doesn't mean we shouldn't give the world more Kiki bro action."

My brothers share a look that can only be described as concerned.

"Tell us this has nothing to do with Sam," Connor says. "I already hate the guy enough as it is. Don't make me hate him more."

And him asking that question suddenly makes me worried that this has everything to do with Sam, because I can't say it. Yes, Colorado was the plan, but Sam's the future I apparently never stopped hoping for. "Why do you hate him? Because he flirted with your boyfriend once? He's a nice guy."

"He's not if he's making you question your entire future and urging you to turn down seventy million dollars. It's *seventy million dollars.*" Connor's screechy voice sounds like nails on a chalkboard.

"It's seven years in a city I don't like," I bite.

"Wait, you don't like playing for St. Louis?" Easton asks.

"I do. I like it *fine*. But … don't I deserve better than *fine*? I want to come home."

Connor's jaw hardens. Easton looks sympathetic, but I swear I hear the judgment behind his soft eyes. He's telling me I'm acting childish. Because I miss my family.

Or maybe it's that they don't believe me, and they think I've been dickmatized by Sam.

I'm glad I haven't bothered to fill either of them in on how deep my feelings go.

At this point, I can't be sure I believe my excuses either. All I know is I should be ecstatic over this contract, but I'm not.

CHAPTER TWENTY-SIX

SAM

I'm surprised that Lachie is gone before I wake up, but it's probably a good thing. Each sleepover, each orgasm, it's only going to make the reality of him leaving so much harder. Instead of being woken with a blowjob, I'm woken by the yap of puppies jumping and playing on top of me.

"The fuck." My voice is scratchy with sleep, and I peek out at the bright daylight to find Ethan grinning back at me.

"Morning, sunshine. Get lots of sleep last night?"

"So much." I squint at my clock and almost fly out of bed. "It's past nine?"

"Yeah, weren't you supposed to be at work ten minutes ago?"

Yes, I was, and I almost scramble out of bed before I remember that I'm naked. "You're going to have to get out unless you want to see my dick."

He tsks. "Girl, I've seen that war hammer more times than I can count. Besides, I'm scared to touch anything in our apartment. Tell me whether I need to get the blacklight out."

"You're safe." I strip off the blanket and go in search of a clean uniform. "We put down a sheet."

The tension leaves his massive shoulders. "I knew I picked a good roommate. Always so respectful."

"Have the puppies eaten?"

"Sure have. Unlike you, they're ready for their day."

With that reminder of how late I am, I push my luck some more. "Any chance you can throw together something for breakfast while I shower?"

He gives me an eyebrows-raised, pursed-lips judging look that I know isn't serious. "You better get your shit together."

"I know, I know—"

"You haven't even complimented me on my new Nikes. I'm feeling neglected."

That almost makes me laugh. I force myself to stop and give him my full attention. "Jordans. High-tops. I love the pink."

He strikes a pose, heavy frame barely fitting in the doorway. "Eggs coming your way, baby."

Ethan disappears, and I shout after him, "I love you and your protein!"

"I know that second part is a lie!"

I shower quickly, and thankfully, Lachie seems to have drained my balls because I skip jerking off and scrub the smell of sex off me instead. It was nice while it lasted. I move quickly, half because I'm late, and half because the sooner I get there, the sooner I'll get to see Lachie. He's volunteering again today, and my eagerness is a red flag in itself, but ... something changed last night.

Well, not changed. That's not the right word for it. Nothing outwardly has changed at all, and we're still stuck in the same arrangement as ever, but there were a few moments where I could have sworn it felt like we were on the same page. The way Lachie would move so he was touching me. How natural it felt to kiss without it leading to sex. The way we washed up after dinner, and even without talking, it felt nice. Like, fuck. It's only been a few hours since I got to touch him, and I *miss* him. Like this deep ache has taken up residence in my sternum and refuses to leave.

Our summer fling is starting to feel a lot like boyfriends, but I don't think it's possible to do the boyfriend thing on a timer. We'd get together and then what? Set a time and date to break up again?

I have to keep ignoring the way my chest feels whenever we're together and hope that when things end, we're able to do it amicably.

I throw back my eggs, crate the puppies, and as I'm heading out the door, Ethan shoves a lunch bag in my hands and kisses me on the forehead.

"Go get 'em, tiger."

I don't know who I'm supposed to get or why I'm an animal, but I don't have to understand Ethan for him to be my best friend. And now lunch is organized. I'm so lucky to have him.

I make it to the shelter in record time, and the plan is to walk in and pretend like I'm not stupidly late, but the second I feel Cherry's judgmental stare on me from behind the counter, I cave. She's one of our part-timers and seems completely pleasant right up until she talks.

"You're late."

I clear my throat as I pull an excuse out of my ass that isn't *fucking my boyf—fling made me sleepy*. Fuck me, I can't even keep my story straight in my head. "Rough start with the pups."

"Right."

"Thanks for opening for me."

"Didn't have a choice."

Where's Danika when I need her? "I know, but thank you anyway."

"You're never late." She's still watching me, heavily lined eyes narrowed like she's pulling the thoughts from my brain.

"There's a first for everything."

"Owen's waiting."

Of course she couldn't open with that. "I'll go right through."

And get away from her freaky-ass stare. She might have the social skills of the color gray, but when it comes to doing the work, she's someone who's meticulous. Nothing's skipped, everything's perfect, and her schedule is exact. We're still working on smiling when people come to the desk, but it's been a fair trade-off.

"I'm so sorry I'm late," I say as I head through to the back, where Owen is.

He glances up from the table we use for inspections. He's holding Skampers, the fluffy white bunny we had brought in after someone found it tangled in a barbed wire fence. It's clearly domesticated but not registered, and so far, no one has tried to claim him.

"It's fine," Owen says, sounding unbothered. "I've kept myself busy checking that these stitches dissolved properly and gave the two new cats a quick check over. All looking good."

That's always a relief. I'd worried with how covered in blood Skampers was that it might not be a good outcome.

"Amazing. Here are the patients you've been waiting for." I set the crate down, because it will be easier for us to take the puppies one by one from there before adding them to the playpen rather than trying to keep track of them all.

"Vaccination day," Owen says, taking Skampers back to his cage. "That came around fast."

"Maybe for you," I grumble. There's no heart behind it though. I love looking after the animals I get to take home with me; it's just bad luck that these few weeks fell in line with the start of Lachie's and my ... thing. The pups are seven weeks old already and will be available to be homed next week. Time is moving way too fast, but at least when the pups are gone, I'll have Lachie for two whole weeks to myself.

I help Owen with the checkup and vaccinations, expecting Lachie to walk in at any moment and fuss over "our babies." By the time Owen is done, I have to admit it's good that Lachie's having a slow start to the day, because this is work, and as endearing as I find Lachie, he has a way of making me think unprofessional thoughts.

Owen doesn't need to be around while that's happening. He leaves, and I get stuck into changing food and water and updating the schedule on which cages are ready to be cleaned out and which ones will be empty after today's pickups.

The morning drags on, and every time Cherry comes through to the back, I perk up for a whole second before I realize she's not Lachie.

Knowing how tired I was this morning, I wouldn't be surprised if he passed out the second he got home. If I didn't have to be here, I'd probably still be sleeping too.

At lunchtime, I cover Cherry's break, and then when she comes back, I can't help but ask—as casually as possible, "Did we have any volunteers come in this morning?"

"It's Tuesday." She looks at me blankly. "We don't need volunteers on Tuesday."

"No, I know …" We never have any on the schedule. "But walk-ins, I mean."

"No."

Okay, that confirms my theory. Lachie is still sleeping off the fun we had, and I'm borderline jealous I wasn't able to do the same. I head back through to my office, and when I pull open my lunch—expecting more protein—I almost melt when I find a salad sandwich instead.

I take a picture and text it through to Ethan.

> Have I mentioned before how much I love you?

> Of course you do. I'm glorious.

He sure is.

As I eat, I'm tempted to message Lachie next, but every time I open our texts, something makes me close them again. I don't want to wake him up, but as it creeps closer to one, my certainty that he's having a lazy day shifts to something else. Something that doesn't make me feel good.

Lachie said he'd be here, and he's always followed through with what he says, but ... I woke up feeling like something had changed; is it possible he felt the same? And instead of feeling good about it, it's made him take a giant step back?

He was gone before I woke up, and I haven't had a single text all day.

I shove the rest of my sandwich into my mouth, not even getting to enjoy it as I choke it down and try to convince myself I'm overthinking. Which is just great that I've already reached that point in our relationship.

Normally, it takes at least a few months before I start getting these shady feelings. I guess being on a condensed timeline is speeding things along. It's only been a few weeks since we started hooking up, but in the proper dating world, that's maybe three days. Lachie and I have spent nearly every day at the shelter and most nights together.

Fuck me, it was supposed to be two months of fucking, and I couldn't even do that right. That gutted, hollowed-out panic is setting in over something that's objectively so stupid.

Lachie has a life. He doesn't *have* to spend what's supposed to be a relaxing summer working for free. Yes, I was excited as hell to see him today, but it doesn't mean he has to feel the same way. That's not how fuck buddies work.

I'm so frustrated with myself that I'm tempted to go out and clean all the cages myself. At least it would keep my hands busy.

Instead, I hook my phone up to my computer and focus on the biggest to-do list item I had for today.

Getting these puppies adopted.

The photos we took at the ice rink fill my screen, and I click through, finding the best ones. After they all took bets on whose would do the best, I decide to turn it into an official competition for the campaign.

I set up a poll on our website, along with all the photos labeled with the men's names. I hate to say it, but Ezra's turned out really good, and Asher's grumpy face as the puppy licked it will make people laugh, at least.

The images are eye-catching, and normally I'm not into this particular kind of marketing, but how often do you have professional athletes volunteering—actually begging—to help you home our animals? If this goes as viral as Gabe claims it will, it'll get a lot of eyes on the shelter, and I'm never going to say no to the types of donations it could generate.

I leave Lachie's pictures for last, and it's only when I can't avoid them anymore that I open the first one.

Fuck me.

A softness blooms behind my rib cage that's unlike the usual *holy shit he's hot* reaction that he normally pulls from me. He *is* hot, but so is literally every other man I have on my screen.

I let my eyes fall closed as I rub them, cursing myself in the process. "I'm an idiot."

Because I've definitely caught feelings for Lachie.

What I should do is end our arrangement immediately.

What I'm going to do is milk every last second with him that he'll give me.

Judging by his lack of contact today though, I get the feeling it won't be all that much longer. Which is going to hurt, but at least I'm prepared for it.

I pick the picture of Lachie with all five dogs snuggled into him—and yes, it easily gives him an advantage over the others, sue me—and then work on my post.

If I'm going with this marketing angle, I'm going all in.

> Get ready for Puppies and Puckboys!
>
> The hotties of the NHL are showcasing the newest fur babies at Downtown Denver Animal Shelter. Get ready to fall in love—with the puppies—and vote for the Puckboys! Who makes you fall for these cuties the best? Voting is open for the rest of the week, and the puppies will be available for their new homes in two weeks.

> Disclaimer: Unfortunately, the hockey players are
> not included in the adoptions.

Then, because I'm planning to milk this for all it's worth, I tag the guys who have their tags still on and hit Post.

Then I cross my fingers that people like hockey players more than I do.

While I try not to pay attention to the time ticking down on our arrangement.

CHAPTER TWENTY-SEVEN

LACHIE

It's not until late afternoon that I realize I've wasted the entire day focusing on seventy million thoughts. Well, seventy million and one.

If Sam noticed my absence from the shelter, he didn't show it. My phone is void of notifications, and that should be a good thing. It should make it easier to decide about committing to St. Louis.

Instead, it makes me question if I'm reading too much into Sam and us. I contemplate getting a ride share out to the shelter in time for him to leave work, but I can't be sure he'll want me to go back to his place after I ditched him today, so instead, I borrow Dad's Ram truck to go see him.

Even though I leave with plenty of time to get there before Sam should finish work, traffic is a bitch, and I worry I'll miss him. I pull into the parking lot right as he's locking up for the day, so my parking job is crooked, and the truck is still running when I jump out.

He glances over, khakis straining over his broad shoulders, boots at the end of his long legs, and sweet brown eyes lined with tiredness.

I jog up to him and the puppies, who are trying to get to me through their crate, jumping up and hitting their little heads on the top of it.

I kneel to their level. "Hi, babies, were we good children for Daddy today?" I stick my fingers through the wire sides, and one of the boys latches on with his razor-sharp puppy teeth. "Ouch, baby. You're a dog, not a land shark."

Sam finishes dead-bolting the front door, and I stand to give him a proper greeting, but something feels off. He smiles, though it seems forced. "Please don't tell me you slept all day and that's why you didn't show."

"I'm so sorry. My parents called me home this morning because of some work stuff, so I've been in a daze of contracts and negotiations. I didn't realize how much time had passed while I had to use my brain and think."

Sam's shoulders lose some tension. "It's fine. It's not like you had an actual shift or we were dependent on you. A text might have been a nice heads-up though."

Fuck, I'm an absolute shithead. "I really am sorry. I'm here to make it up to you."

"You don't have to make anything up to me, but if you're offering to buy me dinner, I won't say no. Maybe you can tell me about your stressful day of ..." He pretends to hold up an imaginary clipboard. "Checks notes: thinking." Finally, the smile that breaks through is genuine, reaching his eyes.

"I'm kind of sick of talking about it. The short of it is my team in St. Louis have offered me a really good extension on my contract, but ... it's a long commitment, and, well ... I ... I don't want to be there for the next seven years. Not if there's a chance I could come home."

"Come home. For good?" There's something glimmery in his eyes that looks like excitement. Maybe telling him he's a factor in my future is too much, so I go with something that is not a lie but not exactly the whole truth.

"My entire family is here. My brothers played here. I want to be part of that. But it's complicated because of how contracts work in the NHL."

Sam nods. "Okay, well, how about we get these babies home, and then we can order in and not have to think for the rest of the night?"

I blow out a breath of relief. "That sounds perfect."

—

I'm catching my breath while completely blissed-out with Sam's naked form on top of me, and our cum is drying between us. We're back to fucking silently, and while I'm not complaining, I want more of letting go. No holding back. I need more of the desperate sounds he makes when he doesn't have to stifle them.

It's difficult to do that when there's a roommate or when we have a crate of puppies in the room.

"I'm worried we've traumatized them," I say.

Sam lifts up, cocking his head in confusion until he realizes I'm talking about the puppies. He rests his head back on my chest. "They've seen a lot in their short lives."

"Yeah, but from next week, they can be adopted. Which means they're no longer babies that are too young to know what's going on." I gasp. "What if they get adopted and all they do is hump anything and everything because of what they've seen? We've perverted a whole litter of puppies!"

Sam laughs, his warm breath hitting my skin. "I'll be sure to add sexual deviants to their online profiles."

"They're up?"

"Yup. By the time I left today, we already had over one hundred applicants. I worry the impromptu photoshoot with your friends was too successful. Finding the right homes is going to be difficult."

"Wait, you used our photos?"

Sam rolls off me but stays curled into my side. "You didn't get the notification? I tagged you and some of the other guys' profiles in the post."

"I don't have my notifications turned on, but I also have that approval thing on for tags, and my team's PR department chooses what to allow and what not to."

"Oh. I didn't think of that. That's ... pretty intense. You don't even have full access to your social media accounts?"

"Not the official ones." I shrug. "Not that I post any personal crap on there anyway."

"Right. That would violate nudity rules, I'm guessing."

I poke him. "I have no nudes, thank you."

Sam leans up on his elbow. "You lie."

"Nope. No lies. I might be pretty lax and chill in person for someone who's technically closeted, but photo evidence? My brother and parents would kill me."

Sam draws a circle on my chest, his fingers soft on my overheated skin.

"What are you thinking about?" I ask.

"Just how different your real life is to … all this. I … maybe we should clean up and have a talk. I know I promised you wouldn't have to think anymore tonight, but we're getting down to the business end of this … fling, and I'm kind of realizing that when you leave, you're going back to this whole famous life I don't know much about."

"I'm hardly famous. Outside of sports fans, no one knows who I am."

"You have PR people who run your socials. That's a level of fame higher than the average animal shelter manager."

I roll on my side so I'm face-to-face with him. "What are you saying?" For a split second, I thought he might be trying to say that he wants me to stay too. But now I'm thinking he might be trying to say that we should end it now. The bright side of that suggestion is it means he's getting as attached to me as I am to him. The downside? Everything else. Not seeing him. Not seeing who the pups are adopted out to. Spending the next three weeks trying to force myself not to come to the shelter or show up on his doorstep.

I've quickly become addicted to him, and it's a habit I'm not ready to break.

Soon, I'll have no choice in the matter, but until then, I want to forget how deep my feelings for Sam go and continue to enjoy every second I can with him.

Sam seems to deflate. "Nothing. It doesn't matter. I forgot for a moment that we have an expiration date."

"It does matter." I'm dying to know what he was going to say. My nerves are an unsettled weight in my gut as words I probably shouldn't say fight their way out. "Because I don't want us to have an expiration date." I hold my breath, worried this will scare him off or give him an excuse to take a step back.

Sam's expression is torn. "We might be on the same page there, but it's not like we can do anything about it. You have to go back to St. Louis. My life is here."

"I know," I relent. And I hate it. "I wasn't lying when I said I want to move home for my family, but ... until you, I was always okay with that being a future idea. I know it hasn't been long. This might be too much for you—"

"It's not too much. When would you be likely to come home?"

"Not for at least another season."

"How long is that?"

I grunt. "I can't believe I'm having this conversation with someone who doesn't even know when hockey season is." I have to tease because if I told him how long the season is, there's a good chance he'd say doing long distance for nine months of the year isn't something he's willing to do. Let alone another four to seven years, depending on the contract negotiations. This frustration of having no control over any of it claws at my chest.

"That long, huh?"

"September is training camp. Season starts in October, and depending on how my team does, it could be over as soon as April. No one ever plans for that though. In our minds, the end of the season is always June."

"And then you could come home?"

"If my team will let me."

"Didn't you say you were talking contracts today?"

"Yeah, but the rules around free agency suck in the first seven years of a career. I don't have the choice to reject my current team. I can say no to contracts, I can even have offer sheets from other teams once my contract officially ends, but I'm not free of St. Louis completely until I become unrestricted or they voluntarily release me, which they won't do. If I get an offer from another team, and they match it? I'm contractually obligated to stay where I am."

"That doesn't seem fair."

"It's not. But two years down, five to go. At a minimum. The team is trying to get me to sign to seven years. Adding that to the year I'm about to go into, that'll be eight before I can come home."

"Eight years?" Sam asks. "That's ..."

He doesn't find the words, but I hear him loud and clear.

Impossible. Eight years is impossible.

CHAPTER TWENTY-EIGHT

SAM

So hockey is basically a prison sentence. Good to know. A well-paid and admired prison sentence, and maybe I missed out on the jock gene, but is all that money and fame worth it if you have zero control over your life?

I don't care what Lachie says, if people know and idolize you, you're famous. It might not be Hollywood or influencer levels, but it's still more than I'd ever want to see in my lifetime.

The shelter's social media went wild after posting those pictures—at least, I thought it did—then Ezra Palaszczuk shared my post. The notifications coming through now are genuinely terrifying, and Lachie thinks he's not famous?

"Holy hair on a horse, this is insane." I stare at my computer screen in shock. We haven't even unlocked the shelter for today, and Danika and Cherry are staring over my shoulder as the *ding ding ding* of comments comes through.

Lachie's opposite, watching us like I've grown two heads, feet kicked up on the desk as he makes his way through the second breakfast burrito Ethan sent us off to work with.

"Should I open early?" Danika asks. "There are already a few people waiting outside."

"Fuck me."

Lachie laughs at the panic in my voice and pulls my attention away from the screen. For a second, we just stare at each other—and then I break into uncertain laughter too.

"Okay, I misjudged this whole situation, so this is on me."

"Agreed," Cherry says. "How you didn't think the Stanley Cup winners, a Dalton brother, and the Kiki brothers shirtless and with puppies would break the internet, I have no idea."

I turn in my chair to stare at her. "Please tell me you're not a hockey fan."

"I can tell you almost every Colorado stat for the last ten years, maybe longer. Test me."

"I don't even know what stats are." Finding out just how much spotlight Lachie has on him, combined with Cherry having an actual interest outside of this place, is almost too much.

"Ooh, I'll take that," Lachie says, his feet landing flat on the floor as he sits up straighter. "Who was the last Colorado player to win the Calder?"

Cherry rolls her eyes. "Easton Kiki, duh."

"Which one of my brothers has more awards?"

"Easton has the Calder, and Connor has a Norris, but the year Connor left, Easton won the Conn Smyth. I figured it was kind of a 'fuck you' to those who said Easton wouldn't be as good without his big brother setting up all those goals for him."

Lachie smiles. "What year did—"

My office phone rings. "So sorry to interrupt this boring-as-fuck conversation about hockey awards, but ..." I answer the phone while Danika pushes Cherry out of the room.

"We'll open up."

The call is someone asking what time we open, so they're quick to get rid of. I forward future calls to the front desk for the day because I'm already getting the sense I won't have time to be in here at all.

Lachie takes another large bite of his burrito. "This is so good. You know, I think Ethan and I could be best friends."

"He has a best friend," I mutter, wondering if I should call in some of our casual staff or regular volunteers for some extra hands. I look over our roster of available people and am mid-decision when Danika comes back in.

"Ah, Sam? There's a local news outlet on the phone."

"There's what?"

"They want to talk to you about the shelter."

I pin her with a look. "And the hockey players?"

"Well ... them too."

I am so unprepared for this. "Can you have them call back? Later. Much later."

She leaves again, and I turn back to my computer. "I need to take this shit down."

Lachie moves so fast he lives up to his pro athlete reputation. He plonks his ass on my lap and rolls my desk chair away from the desk. "I'm not letting you do that."

"But—"

He stands briefly to reposition himself so he's straddling me and sets his hands on my shoulders. "First, you need to breathe. Second, I'm beating Ezra in votes, and that needs to continue."

"You're keeping track?"

"It is being heavily discussed in the chat. The rest of them will be sharing it today, so ..."

"I definitely need to take it down. There are only five puppies in that litter to adopt."

He cuts off my stressing with a kiss. It's enough of a distraction until the *ding ding ding* starts again.

"See?"

"I've got to say that this stressy side of you is hot."

"Lachie ..."

"Fine." He drops the playfulness and meets my eyes. "This is a good thing, remember? There are only five puppies, yes, but there are so many other animals here that need homes. We're getting eyes on the shelter, which was the end goal, and if this ends up going viral—"

"This isn't viral?"

At least he's trying not to laugh at me. "This is fine, and it will trickle away by the end of the week."

"The media is calling us."

"It's the local news, calm down."

This conversation is really putting the differences in our worlds on display. "And for a community shelter, the local news is a big deal."

Lachie turns my face so I'm focused on him, which is maybe my favorite thing to be focused on. Instead of making me happy though, that ache behind my ribs reminds me that while we both might want more, eight years apart isn't realistic. It would be like torture to have him but not have him.

"This is what we're going to do," he says gently. "You'll get some more help in here for the next few days. Once that's covered, we're going to go out the back and take pictures of me with all the animals that still need adopting—"

"How does that solve my problem of this huge, viral moment?"

"Again, not viral. Focus. I'll even keep my shirt on. We're going to post the pictures and have people apply for those animals too. Then we'll go through and discard the people who aren't suitable and go from there. When the journalist calls back, you'll tell them you have professional hockey friends who made the suggestion, and then bring every question back around to the shelter. How people can donate, how you accept volunteers, and ..."

I'm already overwhelmed, and now there's an "and"?

He wrinkles his nose, and it's the cutest thing ever. "You are really hot."

"Thank you, but what does that have to do with all this?"

"You have the face card, babe. Use it."

"The what?"

I'm guessing this is one of those chronically online things Ethan is always talking about that I pretend to understand.

Lachie gives the collar of my uniform a tug. "There's something about this buttoned-up, dorky look that hides all those sexy muscles that really does it for me. Your uniform is so unintentionally slutty, and you could really make that work for you."

"I'm still not following."

"I think you'll get a lot of attention online as well. Teach people what to do if they find injured wildlife. Or abandoned animals. Set up resources. Show people how to care for their pets. All that stuff you know that you wish more people knew. This is a really good opportunity."

It's something that I've never considered before, and while I can acknowledge that it's a good idea, it's all too much to think about.

"How do you know this will blow over within the week?" I ask.

"Because it's the hockey world. We all have very short memories, trust me. When I was drafted, it was like this, then it died down as soon as all the off-season weddings and babies started circulating. Then it picked up again my first season, and now that I have two under my belt, I don't even think the fans remember who was drafted first overall two whole people ago." Lachie's phone pings, and he glances down at it. "Oh, look. The NHL page shared it."

"Fuck me."

That earns me another kiss. "Turn off the computer. We have more cute animal pictures to take."

He climbs off my lap, and I do what he said to. It's easier to lean into his confidence than sit here staring at my screen all day, and at least if I'm not online, it should help with not being so overwhelmed by everything.

I don't care if this whole thing isn't viral; hundreds of comment notifications are enough for me.

We run into Cherry on the way toward the animals.

"The terrier's gone."

"It escaped?"

She gives me a look like I need to screw my brain back in. "Adopted. Just now."

"That's great news!" The poor thing has been here for a few months already. Older dogs struggle to be homed, and she had a lot of energy and some nervous habits that made it even more difficult. "Did you check out the owner?"

"Yep. Older guy who recently lost his wife. He works from home, wants a companion, and has experience with dogs with anxiety."

It's a relief because whenever an animal is here for longer than average, it weighs on me. I want every creature to be happy, and sometimes I'll take them home with me for extra cuddles and one-on-one time. I couldn't do that with her, though, because it takes her way too long to adapt to new environments.

"He saw the post, by the way," Cherry adds. "Said it popping up was like a sign for him to go adopt since he's been thinking about it for weeks now."

Cherry leaves, and I don't need the smug look Lachie sends me to agree that maybe this was a good idea after all. I can survive an avalanche of notifications if it means helping some of these animals who really need it.

"Tell Gabe thank you," I finally say, falling into step with Lachie on the way to the back rooms. "I'm hating every second of this whole thing ... except for that. And the animals are why I do this."

He slings his arm around me and presses a kiss to my temple. "So does that mean you *do* want my shirt off in these pictures?"

I laugh and shove him off me, pulling out my phone as we reach the first cages. "No. The public has seen enough of my man's body. Let's focus on the animals this time."

He links his fingers into the first cage that holds a tan and white hamster, but he doesn't open it. He's still looking at me. "Your man?"

Shit. I probably shouldn't have phrased it that way. Not because I don't believe it on some level, but because it's not fair on either of us to take the conversation to that place again. We're trying to ignore how we both confessed feelings for each other and act like everything is normal, but it's hard to turn off how much I want him. "You know what I mean."

He reaches inside for the hamster. It immediately chirps and snuggles aggressively into his hands like it's never been more excited. "Did you hear that, little guy?" Lachie asks. "Sammy wants me for my body."

And that's one of the best things about Lachie. Even in heavy moments, he can make me smile. "At least that makes sense," I point out. "You think khakis are slutty. I'm worried about your judgment."

"With the way they hug your ass and shoulders? Babe. Come on."

Babe. That fucker. I can tell by the glint in his eyes that he's getting me back for the "my man" comment. Two can play at that game.

"Shut that pretty mouth and get to modeling."

"What will you do if I don't?"

"I have a lot of practice at keeping you quiet. Don't test me."

He lifts the hamster up to his face and speaks to it again. "I know he's not talking about his dick, so how seriously do you think I need to take him?"

The hamster head-bumps him, and I get the perfect shot. "Motherfucker."

"What?"

I show him my screen. "Clothes or no clothes, this photo isn't going to help matters."

"Why?"

"Because you're fucking stunning."

And as Danika brings a family through who immediately recognize him, I'm reminded that he might be hockey royalty, but I'm still a nobody.

They didn't make hundreds of years' worth of movies about princesses finding their prince only for him to end up with the animal guy.

CHAPTER TWENTY-NINE

LACHIE

"You're not allowed to pick favorites." Sam's voice makes me jump, and I scare poor little Angelica, who I may or may not be cuddling on the floor of Sam's bedroom because she woke me up in the middle of the night with her crying.

Now the pups are getting closer and closer to being adopted out, they no longer need round-the-clock feedings, and Sam says we need to teach them some independence, but, but, but … Angelica is the sweet, angelic one who was the smallest. She's a miracle, and I love her.

"Put. The puppy. Down," Sam says as if negotiating a kidnapping situation.

"She was wonely." I pout and lift her front paws. "Yeah, Sammy Wammy. I was wonely."

"I will not fall for your emotional manipulation."

I mock gasp. "Did you hear that, Angelica? He said you were emotionally manipulating him."

"You named her?"

"She doesn't suit her shelter name. Just because she's the only all-black pup of the litter, she got the name Shadow? Pfft. It doesn't even suit her."

Sam sits up in bed. "It does when it comes to you. She is practically your shadow, following you everywhere, even when her siblings are playing."

"Eh, that's not new for me. She suits Angelica so much better. She's so …"

"Angelic? Wait until she's in between six months and two years old and turns into a velociraptor. You'll be changing your tune then."

It's in that moment, the second the words leave his mouth, that we both realize we won't be around to see it. A stale silence settles between us as we readjust to reality. In no time at all, we won't be with each other, and Angelic—Shadow will be with her new family.

"I wish I could be around to see that," I say. "If it was possible to take her to St. Louis with me, I would."

"They do have crates you can take on airplanes."

My heart sinks that it can't be that easy. "It's not the flight. It's that I wouldn't have anyone to look after her when I'm not there. And I'm not home a lot. Even if I got a dog sitter, she deserves to have someone with her always." The pup stares up at me, tongue lolling out the side of her mouth. She looks so adorably derpy, like her two brain cells are competing to form a single thought. I wish I could keep her. Not only her, though. I glance up at Sam.

He sighs. "Bring her up here, and come back to bed."

My eyes widen. "But what about all the pee and not allowing the pups on the bed?"

"I'm not saying to bring all of them up here. Just her. And you will be washing my sheets tomorrow if she pees anywhere."

"Deal." I jump up so fast, Angelica yips and thinks it's playtime. Oops. I hold her close to me. "Shh, shh, shh, baby. It's not time for zoomies. It's time for cuddles with your daddies."

"Temporary daddies," Sam says through a yawn.

Whether he's throwing that in my face to remind me our time is coming to an end or himself, either way, it's probably needed. Anytime I think about what will happen in a few short weeks, depression punches me in the gut. I've always been a go-with-the-flow kind of guy, but I dunno, something about getting my childhood crush turns me into a whiney baby.

Connor and Easton would always complain that, because I'm the third child, I'm the spoiled one. I get everything I ever want. And while I can't dispute that, it's not like I haven't had to work hard for what I have. I worked hard to become the number one draft pick. I worked hard to keep my shenanigans on the DL because my parents and Connor asked me to. I've compromised a lot in my life, despite still getting everything I've ever wanted, but Sam ... Angelica ... these are impossibilities, the only things I've ever wanted so desperately but can't have.

Sure, I could suggest long distance, and sure, I could adopt a puppy and pay someone to take care of it while I'm away, or I could ask Sam to give up the job he loves and move to St. Louis with me, but how are any of these options fair? I would get what I want, but at what cost? Puppies need consistent love. Sam's entire life is here in Denver.

Sam's already back asleep before Angelica even settles, but when she finally curls up against my chest as I lie on my side, I place my hand on her side, which basically covers all of her, and do what I have to. I hold on to the warm and fuzzy feeling inside me and shove down the reminder that soon all this happiness will be over.

—

Time is a deceptive bitch, and I hate her.

Each time someone comes to the shelter to check out the litter of puppies, I've been sure to keep Angelica with me. Sam pretends he doesn't notice me disappear with her and even buys my excuses when I say she needed to go to the toilet or needed a bath or was lacking in vitamin D, so I took her outside.

Each of the puppies are slowly finding their forever homes, and I know once the other four are adopted, I will have to let Angelica go, but I don't want to.

Could it be possible that Angelica is a metaphor for the entire summer, the fling with Sam, and I'm not ready to leave it all behind yet? Not at all. That sounds like psychology talk. This is just me being a brat and wanting to keep a puppy.

"Lachie, have you seen the last p—" Sam stops as he enters his office, where I'm hiding with Angelica in his puppy carrier thing on my chest. I've been pacing back and forth with her, thinking of ways I could smuggle her out of here. Maybe I could convince Connor to adopt her. Or my parents. I don't want to say goodbye.

And I'm still only talking about the dog. This has nothing to do with Sam.

"The last what? Pop-Tart in the staff kitchen? I didn't eat it. Wasn't me."

Sam's shoulders sag, and a small smile crosses his lips. "Are we going to keep pretending like you're not carrying a puppy around like a baby?"

"What puppy? I only see a baby. A real human baby." I start bouncing while I walk, as if she really is a baby and I'm putting her to sleep.

Her little tail is wagging, and she's practically trying to climb out so she can get to Sam.

"Okay then." Sam turns on his heel and leaves me be, but I know it won't be long before he'll have to pry her from my hands.

When he inevitably comes back in, papers in hand, I want to cry. I'm expecting him to say it's time, but what does come out of his mouth shocks the hell out of me.

"There has been a new application. Normally, I wouldn't approve it because these weeks are important to the imprinting phase, and there's a long line of applicants who could take her now, but ... this person ... They want to adopt her but can't take her for another two weeks. Other than that, they're perfect for her."

It takes a moment to process what he's saying. "I could keep her for two more weeks until I leave?"

"That's what I'm saying. But if we do this, are you going to be able to say goodbye when the time comes? You're already struggling to do it."

"Honestly ... it doesn't matter either way because I know saying goodbye is going to destroy me." My heart squeezes, and this time, I can acknowledge I'm not only talking about the dog.

"Then I'll push this application through. Even if it means sharing our last two weeks together with a dog."

The fact that he's even willing to do that for me only cements how I feel about him. It's entirely possible I'm too far gone for Sam to pull back now. Or ever.

It's entirely daunting to realize that heartache isn't only a possibility when I leave. It's inevitable.

CHAPTER THIRTY

SAM

As soon as we're home, I remove Angelica from the carrier Lachie is wearing and hand her over to Ethan. She cries for him, but for once, the little whimpers don't work on me, and I give Lachie a stern look when he goes to retrieve her again.

"I need you to take Angelica for a walk," I tell Ethan.

"Angelica?" He lifts her to his face. "What a perfect name for the little princess."

"Because she's angelic," Lachie explains.

Ethan scowls at him. "Don't make me revoke your gay card. It's obviously because she's a pampered princess like all the iconic women before her. Cher gave birth to Angelica Pickles, who grew up into Regina George. Don't argue with me, girl. It's science."

Lachie's about to argue back, so I cut off this conversation before it can go any further.

"Either way, iconic Angelica needs a walk. Now. Please."

Ethan catches on. "You know, I've just been hit with the need for a matcha. Angie is coming with me."

"It's Angelica."

"She needs a lesbian name for when she's doing lesbian things, like physical exercise and leaving the house after five p.m. without it involving alcohol."

I have no idea where Ethan gets this stuff. "Tell me you've never met a lesbian before."

"Do you want to argue about lesbians, or do you want to get laid?"

"The second. No question. Now, get out."

Ethan attaches Angelica's harness, even though she'll end up in his arms after a few steps, and blows us a kiss. "Bang hard, boys."

I move to the sink to wash my hands as he leaves, and Lachie joins me.

We're silent for a long moment and then, "So … laid?"

I flip the tap off and round on him. Before Lachie can get a word out, I cup his jaw and press my lips to his. Fuck, it's been a long, emotionally charged day, and the one thing I need is to fall into our time together and think about nothing else.

I know Lachie feels the same way as I do, but once he leaves, he'll be jumping straight back into his hockey world and leaving this bubble of us behind.

While I'm left here with all these Lachie-sized holes in my life. It'll be impossible to exist in my office without looking up and expecting to see him smiling across at me. Every time someone brings an animal in, I know there will be that split second where my heart hopes it's him. Coming home and eating dinner when it's just me and Ethan again. Sleeping in my bed, walking to the park, running a marathon …

And every day spent with Angelica, holding on to that tiny link to him.

He moans into my mouth, tongue sweeping mine, and I know I'm going to miss this too.

I'm trying so hard to focus on the moment, but when every moment keeps racing ahead of us, I don't know how much more I can take. We still have some time, but I can already feel the end looming over us, shadowing every experience, and the more I fight against it, the harder it hits.

I back Lachie up until he's against the wall and I'm pressed even tighter to his chest.

My gut is trying to tell me so strongly that this is how we're meant to be, him and me, putting the outside world on pause.

If Lachie had any choice at all, I'd hope he would pick me, but that's not a question I'll let myself ask.

So, yeah. This feels right because it is right.

But it's not our fucking time.

I break my mouth from his and kiss my way down his throat. I want to worship his body, want him to walk away from me knowing if I had any choice at all, it would be him. I'm not mean enough to say those words aloud, because I won't make this harder on him than it already is, but the trueness of it is infecting me.

Lachie is mine.

He's *mine*.

Until he's not.

The pain that shatters through my chest almost has me begging him to stay. I have to stop torturing myself. It's not fair to either of us.

So I shove the thoughts back and focus on him.

His skin, his scent, the way his hands are gripping me like if he lets go, I'll disappear. Being with him is addictive, and the more he runs his hands over my back, the more he squeezes my ass and grinds his hard cock against mine, the easier it is to shut all those voices up and have this.

No regrets.

No worrying about a few weeks' time.

He's still here, and I still get this.

"We're wearing too many clothes," he complains, voice hitched and head bowed back under my lips. "I need more."

I'm only too happy to give it to him. I strip off his T-shirt and then unbutton the front of my shirt. I'm so horny it's hard to think, and all I can do is shamelessly watch as he holds my gaze and slides his shorts and briefs down his thick thighs.

"Where do you want me?"

Everywhere, somewhere. On the ceiling, for all I care, as long as I'm there with him.

I squeeze my dick through my shorts, trying to get my brain online long enough to answer his simple question.

"Kitchen. Island. Bend over."

"I like the way you think."

While he does that, I duck into my bedroom to grab the lube and finish stripping off in there. My dick is standing straight upright, begging me to hurry up, and I pump some lube into my hand and jerk myself off as I walk back out to him.

And find the sexiest scene waiting for me.

Lachie's bracing himself against the island with his forearm, while he's bent over and fingering himself. That sexy hockey butt is arched up waiting for me, and it takes every ounce of self-restraint I have not to jerk off until I come.

"You're killing me."

"Good." He rocks back onto his fingers. "I couldn't wait."

Me either, baby. I catch that thought before it slips out and instead settle for setting the lube on the counter next to him and gripping his jaw instead. I meet him in a deep, filthy kiss, knowing I'll never get enough of this.

"Please," he pants against my lips. "Need you inside me."

"It's so sexy when you use your manners."

I coat my fingers in lube and then move around behind him. Lachie's already done a fast job stretching himself, so I fill him with three fingers straight away. His back arches onto me, and his breath is heavy with lust. "More."

I give it to him. I fuck him with my fingers, getting them as deep as possible while he loosens up. I've never been a jealous man before, but I'm hit with this blinding flash of it, imagining all the men who get to see Lachie like this in the future.

All those men who aren't me.

It almost ruins the moment, but then Lachie pleads, "*Sammy*," and it's enough to bring me back to him.

Fuck all the other guys.

No one will ever have with him what I do.

I pull my fingers free and line my cock up with his hole. "You ready?"

"Do it."

As much as I want to slam home, I take my time.

Sink into the feeling of his body molding around me. Of breaching that ring of tension before his body gives up the fight and tries to suck me deeper.

I sweep my hands up Lachie's broad back, watching my dick disappear inside of him. As far as I'm concerned, this is heaven.

When I'm pressed tight against him, I lean forward, leaving kisses along his neck and shoulder, letting him adjust to my size, while I give in to the way I want to kiss and touch and pleasure him everywhere.

I commit his scent and the way he breathes to memory, giving in to the urge to move. I grind deeper inside of him, loving the way he grips me, planning to spend as much of the time we have left together doing exactly this.

"You're not going to make me come like his," he grumbles. But I can tell he's turned on by the way his voice is all gravelly.

"Want me to move?"

"I want you to fuck me until I can't breathe."

Damn, I want that too. I'm pretty sure Ethan is going to give us plenty of time, but considering we're in the middle of the kitchen, I don't want to risk him walking in and seeing us. Lachie's body is for me and me only.

For now.

I straighten and set my hands on his hips as I pull out and slam home again. Sex with him is addictive, and the more we do it, the more I need. Maybe it's because we're on a timer and I know our opportunities to do this are limited, but I crave him constantly.

At work.

At home.

Even in those few moments I've spent watching him sleep.

Only the way I crave him has changed, and that's the part that scares me. If this was all sex, it'd be easy to move on. But the way Lachie's got something deep in my chest in a vise warns me this is going to be the relationship I have the hardest time walking away from.

"Sam ..." He rocks back onto me. "Harder."

Harder. Right. Focus. This is about the sex and only that.

I pick up my pace, hands steadying him as every thrust sprawls him further over the counter. The sounds of my hips slapping against his ass are echoing in the kitchen, and my gaze is locked onto the way his cheeks jiggle as I fuck him. His back muscles are tight under his skin, forearms flat on the counter to hold himself in place in a way that makes his shoulders look so good I want to sink my teeth into them.

He pushes back, taking my cock easier, arching his back, and my gaze slips to those slutty little impressions over his ass and back down to where he's wrapped around me.

The visuals are such a turn-on that I'm close to losing it, but there's something else I need. Something else that will get me over the edge.

I reach for the back of his necklace and pull it until it's tight around the front and then twist it in my hand. I give it a tug, and Lachie doesn't even try to fight me as I pull him upright, plastering myself against his back.

It's harder to fuck him fast like this, but we find a rhythm and work together as I bury my face into the dip where his shoulder meets his neck.

I'm so obsessed with his scent, with the way his breathing has deepened, and how he moans when I kiss his skin.

My cock is aching, and I try to hold out a little bit more. I want this to last.

So ... much ... longer ...

"Touch me," he begs.

"Not yet."

"But—"

I bite down on his shoulder. "I said not yet."

His half sob almost makes me give in, but the last thing I want is his cum covering the kitchen.

My balls tighten, because apparently I do love that thought, and all I can picture is filling him with my own. I'm so damn close, balls aching in a way that has me ready.

I fuck him harder, panting, overheated against his body but not ready to let him go.

My orgasm swells, then finally releases, and I groan as my cock throbs deep inside him.

My sweaty forehead rests against the back of his sweaty neck, and Lachie wriggles his ass against me. "Now is it my turn?"

"In a second." I pull out and rest my hand on his lower back, pushing him forward over the counter again. "I want to see something first."

"What?"

"My cum running down your legs."

He trembles, tilting his hips toward me, and I watch as my cum slips out of his ruined hole.

Fuck, he's so damn sexy.

Before he can beg me again, I flip him around, drop to my knees, and swallow him into my throat.

Lachie lets out a strangled sound, head tilted back, hands gripping the counter behind him, and I wish I could take a photo of him like this because I'd hold on to it forever.

I reach between his legs and slide two fingers into his hole while I blow him. Lachie's leaking already, and I let him take the lead. He thrusts into my mouth and rocks back onto my fingers, faster and faster as he gets closer to the edge.

I love him like this. Messy. Needy. Giving himself over to the way I'm making him feel.

"I'm gonna come," he warns me.

I suck him in deep, then wait for him to do it. It doesn't take long. His cock twitches out rope after rope of cum, and I swallow it all down, wanting everything he can give me.

I'm still catching my breath when he slips from my mouth, and I lean in to rest my forehead against his hip. All the happy, swampy feelings settle over me, and I turn my head to press a kiss to his thigh.

Lachie runs his fingers through my hair, giving the strands a gentle tug to pull my focus up to him.

I do, and a long moment stretches between us while we just breathe.

I don't want you to go, I tell him silently.

I wish I could stay, his eyes tell me right back.

All the wants ballooning between us have nowhere to go and fizzle out instead.

I knew what this was when I signed up for it.

I just didn't realize I was signing up for heartbreak as well.

CHAPTER THIRTY-ONE

LACHIE

I blinked, and now it's over. It's the last morning of waking up next to Sam. That's how fast this whole summer has gone.

Flings are supposed to be that—flingy and quick. So it makes sense that today is our last day together, but I also fucking hate it, because all I want is for this summer to continue forever.

There's a very strong, panicky part of me that wants to burrow back under the blankets and fuse myself to him forever. Today is going to be one of the worst days of my life.

Because I know what's coming. We have to let each other go.

The itch to get back on the ice is there, but it's being smothered by the pain I'm trying to ignore. It's impossible to imagine retiring at this stage in my life, especially for a man who I've spent one summer with—I don't know how Connor did it for Parker—but my longing for Sam is what's holding me back from signing that perfect contract.

After I rejected it, it's probably not even on the table anymore. Whenever Mom or Dad have brought it up or tried to call, I've kept saying that now's not the time. I have an entire season to sign an extension. I blame myself for having two great rookie seasons. I should've hidden my talents better.

"I hate that I'm so good," I say to myself, not realizing that Sam is awake next to me.

He snorts. "I love that you're so humble."

"Humble is my middle name."

"Lachlan Humble Kikishkin. It has a nice ring to it."

I pull back and turn my head to look at him. His eyes are still sleepy, and he looks so cozy and sweet I never want to get out of bed. "You finally learned how to say my last name correctly in time for me to leave? It's like you want to make this harder on me."

I'm joking, mostly, but my voice gives a little crack, giving away that there's some truth in there too.

Sam reaches for me and pats my cheek. "Sorry. Lachlan Humble Kinikishton."

"Much better."

His thumb strokes my cheek softly before he realizes what he's doing and breaks the contact. We've had too many moments lately that get close to showing how we feel before we avoid it. "So, what are you so good at that you're upset? Your ability to make me come so much last night, there's no way I'll be able to get it up again before you leave?"

I pout. "No. But now I'm upset over that too."

"What was it, then?"

"That I'm more talented at hockey than either of my brothers, and I'm in high demand. If I wasn't so good, maybe my team would let me go."

His eyes soften. "They'll let you go eventually."

I sigh. "Minimum five more years. Anything could happen in that time. You're probably going to fall in love, get married, and have babies by then."

"I doubt children are in my future, considering I need Ethan to look after me half the time." Of course, he avoids the main point. So I push harder.

"Maybe you'll fall in love with Ethan. Roommates falling in looooove, having baaaaabies."

"One, Ethan and I are completely incompatible. Two, even if we weren't, do you really think I'm waiting for you to leave so I can go and meet someone else?"

Maybe I should have kept avoiding it too. "It would be easier if you were like that."

"In that case, I actually have two guys lined up after you."

I screw up my face. "Okay, nope, nope. I take it back. That thought is so much worse."

"Then let's not think about what happens after you leave for your flight tonight."

I've been trying not to think about it all summer, but he makes a point. I can wallow on the plane. Today is a day for making a lasting memory, because as tempting as it is to push for long distance, everyone knows it doesn't work. If it was only going to be for the season, maybe, but next season is so unknown, and I don't have faith this contract mess will sort itself out. I can't let myself get my hopes up.

"We need to get up." I throw the sheet off me and stand.

"There's a plan?" he asks as I slide on my underwear and shorts.

"Yup. I made a booking and everything."

"A booking? For what?"

I want it to be a surprise, so I say, "Something I've always wanted to do but have never had the right amount of rage to do it. Sometimes being a chill kind of guy has its disadvantages."

"Should I be scared?"

"Never with me." And I don't only mean when it comes to fun activities.

—

"You know how you said I never have to be scared with you? I'm officially scared." He looks down at what he's wearing. "What kind of date are you taking me on where I need a hazmat suit and protective eyewear?"

"It's a paper jumpsuit. Not quite hazmat material. It could be a sex den and I'm trying to protect you from all the bodily fluids we're about to be covered in."

"I knew I shouldn't have let you convince me to sign the waiver without reading it."

"It's not a sex den. It's a way for us to get all the anger and sads out about me leaving." And I have so many to get out.

Sam is thinking it over, trying to figure out what it could be, when our attendant comes into the locker room.

"All dressed and ready to go?"

"Apparently," Sam mutters.

"All set," I say, remarkably upbeat compared to how depressed I fucking feel.

Push it down. Ignore it. Feel it all later.

We're led down a hall that's all concrete flooring, weathered doors, and graffiti covering the walls.

She taps a key fob in front of a door and opens it. "Have fun," she says and leaves us to it.

"You go first," Sam says.

I smile. "Gladly." This is going to be so much fun. Or at least cathartic.

As soon as he follows me through the door, he frowns. "Murder room? This looks like a murder room."

I pick up a baseball bat that's lined up with other sticks, broom handles, and anything else we can use. "The only thing we're going to be murdering is our anger." I turn toward a barrel that has some drinking glasses on it and swing, loving the shattering sound as the bat connects.

Sam winces. "The eye protection makes sense now, but ... what if I'm not angry at anything?"

"You're not mad I have to leave?"

"Mad probably isn't the right word," he murmurs. "Sad, maybe?"

"Then this was probably the wrong kind of date to take you on. That's all right. All the more things for me to smash!"

There's a dinted old microwave, so I take a swing at that too. It makes an echoey sound but doesn't break any further, just dents it some more. "That's for summer being over." I hit it again. "And that's for my stupid brothers being so good at hockey that they couldn't tank Colorado for my draft year so I could've been drafted at home." I'm on a roll, so I keep going. "This is for stupid rules about restricted free agents." *Thwack.* "And to St. Louis for offering my dream in the wrong fucking city." *Thwack, thwack.*

"I get it now," Sam says. "My turn." He picks up a crowbar and gives a tentative, piddly, weak hit to the busted microwave.

"You really don't have much rage in you, do you?"

"I'm warming up. That one was for you leaving, because like I said, that doesn't make me mad. But this one ... this one is for ..." It takes him way too long to think of something, but then he points the crowbar at me like the perfect thing comes to him. "People who dump helpless animals on the side of the road." This time, he smashes it so hard the glass on the front of the microwave cracks. "Anyone who doesn't spay or neuter their pets and only adds to the stray population with irresponsible breeding." *Smash.* It cracks some more.

"This is good." I bounce on the balls of my feet. "Keep going!"

"This is because Ethan force-feeds me protein!" The whole front glass on the microwave shatters.

"Perfect! My turn."

We throw all of our complaints out there. I complain about my brothers some more. My parents and how they can treat us more like their clients when we actually need them to treat us like their children. I whine about away games. The loneliness of being the only Kiki not in Colorado. It doesn't take long for me to start panting, but I'm still full of rage. Especially when I think of the contract. The seventy-million-dollar contract.

"This is for all the stupid emotions that made me turn down seventy million fucking dollars." I hit a wooden crate on the floor over and over again until it breaks into pieces.

My muscles ache when I stop, and I try to catch my breath, but it becomes evident really fast that my breath is the only sound filling the room.

My gaze finds Sam's widened eyes.

"Wh-what did you say?" he rasps.

"Uhhhhhh." The word is dragged out so long, I think my mouth is stuck.

"Did you say seventeen million dollars?"

Well, shit. First, because I wasn't going to tell him how much it is, but secondly, because if he thinks seventeen is a lot of money, he's going to flip at seventy.

I can't lie, but telling the truth? I know I have to, but I'm hesitant because I'm about to walk away from him, and neither of us can stop it from happening. Maybe this summer has only been so amazing because we've both known it's going to end. We've been able to tolerate the annoying little things because we know we won't have to put up with them for long.

Before I find the right words to say, he blurts, "I'm the one!"

For some reason, I think he's talking about being my soul mate or some other romantic thing that almost has me dropping to my knee and making a promise I definitely won't be able to keep, but then he clarifies what he means.

"I adopted Angelica."

Fuck. I thought declaring he's the one for me was romantic, but this? It brings tears to my eyes. "You ... *you* did?"

He hangs his head, soft, dark hair making me ache to touch it. "I didn't want to tell you until you came back to see me because I didn't want her to be the only reason why you'd visit, but ... if you're saying you turned down seventeen million dollars because you'd rather be here—I know it's mostly for your family, but I'd like to think I'm a factor in it—then you should know how deep my feelings go for you. And seeing how much you love her, I couldn't let ... *her* go."

I drop my bat, and his crowbar clangs to the ground a second later.

We charge toward each other, bodies pressing in close as my arms wrap snugly around his waist, and I fuse my mouth to his. Our tongues twist together. I put all my feelings into the kiss because I want him to know that I've fallen hard for him.

I know I wasn't supposed to, but I did.

When I pull back to tell him that, he beats me to it.

"I don't want this to end."

I touch my forehead to his. "Neither do I."

"But long distance ... and you turning down that much money ... you can't do that."

"I have a confession. If it was actually seventeen million, I would have no trouble turning that down for you."

He pulls his head back. "What? But you said—"

"You misheard. I actually said seventy. Seven zero. *Seventy*."

Sam stumbles back. "Seve... Seventy?" He stumbles back some more and almost falls over a broken plate.

Maybe I should've let him think it was seventeen.

CHAPTER THIRTY-TWO

SAM

And like that, the rage Lachie has been looking for unlocks, and I take a timber plank to everything within reach.

Seventy million dollars?

Every second our time has been ticking down, I've been waiting for the answer. The moment when we work out how we can do this. His flight is hours away, and I *still* thought there was a way we could work through all of this, but it's finally hit me.

We're over.

The summer wasn't long enough.

Not waking up to Lachie tomorrow, not seeing him hanging out around the shelter, not watching on in mock exasperation as he breaks all the rules for Angelica ... oh, wow. This pain has caught me completely off guard.

It's not until I've smashed a washing machine to the point it's unrecognizable that hands grab me from behind.

Lachie wraps himself around me, and I almost wish he wouldn't, because it reminds me of that time he stood behind me while I cooked dinner, and I'll never get to have that again.

I swallow thickly, fighting my tears, but one slips out and is thankfully caught by the goggles.

No one, absolutely no one, can walk away from seventy million dollars. That sort of money isn't real money. This being Lachie's dream career makes it even more impossible.

I don't have the money to relocate, and even if I did, giving up my entire life for someone that I've spent a couple of months with is the definition of ridiculous. Everything I've worked for is here, just like everything Lachie has ever worked for is in St. Louis.

I bite down on the inside of my cheek until the pain there helps the one in my chest dull. Then I clear my throat and turn back to him when I'm ready to smile. I refuse to make this harder on him than it needs to be. Because I don't doubt he feels the same way I do, and he's the one being forced to walk away.

"You're right," I say. "That was exactly what I needed."

He tries to smile back, but I guess he's not at the stage of faking it either. His reddened eyes almost break through my willpower as it is. "I am a genius," he jokes weakly.

The buzzer sounds to signal our time is done, and I'm glad because I need to get out of here. But even outside the room doesn't make it easier to breathe.

"We have time to grab lunch," he suggests.

I'll cling to any opportunity to extend our time together. "I'm starving."

I'm not. I don't actually know how I'm going to eat. All I know is that I cannot think about the flight if I want to hold my shit together.

Apparently, whatever broke in me has sunk in for Lachie too, because we both try to make conversation over lunch, but it's useless. Every time I go to mention something about Angelica—an appointment, the next stage in her development, training—I remember he won't be there to see it. Whenever he brings up training camp, it brings us back to hockey and the reason we can't be together.

All those future things that have always been so easy to talk about are sinking me further and further into regret.

This was *supposed* to be a fling.

I insist on paying for our half-eaten food, and when we stand and walk out, all I want is to reach for his hand. To pull him against me and make sure he's okay.

We haven't done the public affection thing outside of our friends, and it's way too late for that conversation now.

We get out the front, and he gives me a shrewd look. "Couldn't eat?"

"I'm more surprised that you couldn't. You've never met a food you didn't demolish."

"I'm just going to say it: this sucks."

"It really does." I flick my sunglasses down over my eyes in case I'm in danger of crying, and I refuse to do that in the middle of the street.

Lachie slides his hands into his pockets. "You know ... we'll play Colorado this year. And when I have a handful of days off—which is rare, but it happens—I always make a visit home. Then I should have a week off in early February ..." His words fade away. February. Six months away. His voice cracks when he speaks again. "Maybe we could catch up?"

"Yeah." I keep my tone light. "Angelica would love that." *I'll* love that. "She'll miss you." *I'll* miss you.

He holds my gaze. "I'll miss her too."

I blink and look away. I'm trying so hard to make this easy, but I only have so much self-control. "You really have to get moving," I point out. "Or you're going to miss your flight."

"Yeah ..."

"Can I drop you at the airport?"

The whole plan was that I'd drop him home and his brothers would drive him over, because neither of us wanted to say our goodbyes there. But I'm not ready yet.

Truthfully, I don't think I'll be ready there either.

"Yes."

He directs me to his parents' place, a huge property that's intimidatingly scary, and I pull up in the driveway, my Honda and I feeling distinctly out of place. Maybe it's a good thing this is ending when it is because our financial situations haven't even factored into our fling other than trying to beat each other at paying for dates. If it turned into more, we'd have to face the challenges that money always brings. At least this way, we'll still be on good terms.

He unclips his seat belt and goes to climb out but pauses. "Do you, uh, want to come in? Let my parents give you the third degree? One last glare from Connor?"

I'm a real fucking mess because I'd kill for one last glare from Connor. But doing the whole meet-the-family thing when we're down to our last hour? No way. "I'll wait here."

"Right."

He climbs out, and I watch him walk all the way up to the house, wishing I could have given him any other answer. But it's time to protect my heart since I haven't bothered to do it once this summer.

I'm restless while I wait, questioning whether I should leave and save us both from that moment, but I can't do it. Picturing the look on Lachie's face to walk out and find me gone is enough to make me stay put. I can deal with the pain once he's gone.

It takes half an hour for him to reappear, Connor and Easton both with him, and the suitcase almost has me lose it again.

I end up getting that one last glare from Connor as Easton rounds the car and knocks on my window.

I slide it down, forcing a happiness I don't feel. "Hey, how are you?"

"Good..." His gaze lingers on my sunglasses. "If you want to catch up for a drink at any point, Connor and I will be around."

The lump in my throat grows, and I glance back at Connor. "Why do I get the feeling that's not willingly?"

Easton laughs. "Connor has always been the protective one, but he's a big softie underneath. And you have no idea how weird it is for me to be saying that."

"Thank you," I say, hearing Lachie climb back in. "I appreciate it."

"I got your number from Lachie. I'll text you."

"Thanks." But considering the family resemblance between Lachie and his brothers, I think it'd be less painful to run myself through a shredder than spend time with people who remind me of him.

We leave, and Lachie waves them off before turning to me. "Sorry it took so long. My parents were trying to guilt me into letting my brothers drop me off. It was only when Connor pointed out that you were doing them a favor by taking me that they finally shut up."

"Wait. Connor was on my side?"

Lachie cocks his head. "Surprisingly, mine. I think he's making a real effort to not be so meddling. Easton says he's like a whole new guy, but I think that was the first time I've really seen it."

"That's good, right?"

"Yeah."

Because it's easier to think his down mood is about them, I add, "Sorry you didn't get to play on the same team as them."

"Me too. But I have a career most people can only dream of, so ..."

So he'll do whatever he has to to keep it. I can't even hold that against him, because I get it.

"Please let Angelica sleep on the bed tonight. Just tonight."

Like I'm going to tell him no about anything. "Just this once."

"Thanks. That'll make it a bit easier."

Honestly, I think it will only make it worse for me.

As much as I appreciate Denver traffic holding on to our time together, we're so close now, I'm anxious to get it over with. To get into the airport, and rip off the bandage, and then ... have him walk out of my life forever.

We pull up later than we were planning, and I follow Lachie inside. There's no line for him to drop off his bags since he's flying first class, and everything from climbing out of the car to reaching security is a blur.

Until we're there.

Then it all hits me with sharp clarity.

We linger outside the security hall, and it hits me that our last kiss was in that break room. I don't want that to be it. We were too distracted getting in here that I didn't even stop to think.

Now we're in public. And he might say he's not famous, but in this city, where his brothers are big names with anyone who knows sports, there's too much of a risk that someone might recognize him.

I want to feel his lips one more time so much that it's killing me.

But because he's not out, I leave the decision up to him.

"Can I kiss you?"

His gaze snaps to mine, and I see the same longing I have reflected back at me. A million little things pass between us before his lips tighten.

"No."

All my hope crashes. I should have expected it, shouldn't have asked at all. With that one word, reality finally pierces our bubble, a timely reminder that if it didn't end here, I would have been forced back into the closet. As much as it hurts, maybe this is a good thing. Maybe—

"If you do"—his voice cracks—"there's no way I'll be able to get on that plane."

I stagger back from him, grateful for my sunglasses as I press my lips together in a way that I hope doesn't make it obvious I'm about to cry.

A tear sneaks out from under his sunglasses, and I drink him in, committing him to memory. That messy, light brown hair, his strong jaw, the piercings, his long necklace that hangs perfectly down his hard chest.

I'm dangerously close to testing out his theory and grabbing him anyway.

"You need to go," I choke out.

So he does.

And I'm forced to watch him all the way down security until he disappears from view without a backward glance.

Someone bumps into me from behind as they rush past, jolting me out of the numbness that still has me standing there, and all I can concentrate on is getting back to my car.

The airport is a blur, too many people and things that I shut out.

I've parked in the outdoor parking lot, and once I reach my car, I'm still not ready to drive. Even if I were, I have no idea where I'd drive to. I'm not ready to go home. I'm not ready to see Angelica. I'm not ready for Ethan to fuss over me and try to make everything better.

So I climb up on my hood and sit there, staring at the sky, watching the planes come and go. Until I don't think I have any tears left in me to shed.

CHAPTER THIRTY-THREE

LACHIE

Skating, reconditioning, training camp media, home, repeat.

I'm managing to keep my shit together for the most part, but it takes every single ounce of energy to pretend to be my carefree self on the outside when I'm messy spaghetti on the inside.

Which is why, when I get home from a particularly grueling session on the ice where old guys like my roommate, Hawke, were skating circles around me, I only make it to the couch before I face-plant onto it.

Hawke, following me into the living room, dumps his bag on the floor next to me. "Are you okay?"

Nope. "Yup."

"Because ever since you got back from Colorado, you've been ... different."

I turn my head so I'm not talking into the cushion this time. "How so?"

"Less annoying, for starters." He grins when I side-eye him, but then he shrugs. "You're ... quieter than usual."

"What I'm hearing is I never shut up normally."

"Exactly my point." He's still smiling, but then he takes a seat in the armchair and settles in for an explanation I don't want to give.

I sit up. "Maybe you can help me with something, seeing as you're ancient and all."

He stands again. "There he is. Never mind. You're fine."

"I'm kidding. I'm kidding. Sort of."

Hawke cocks an eyebrow but sits back down and waits for more.

We've always had this easygoing friendship. He's been an amazing mentor when it comes to hockey stuff, but we've never gone too deep into relationship crap. I don't really know much about his personal life because during the season, neither of us gets much of one.

"Have you ever had to tell team management that you're grateful for the opportunity to play for them but really, really don't want to anymore?"

"Ah. So the rumors are true, then? You turned down an extension any other rookie would kill for?"

"Yes, but not because of the money. It's no secret that the Kiki brothers have always wanted to be on the same team, and while we all thought it would happen when I become a UFA, I really want to move that timeline up. Especially now Connor isn't coming back. What happens if Easton up and decides that he's done too?"

I don't think I've ever experienced Hawke's analytical stare before, but it makes me uneasy.

"I call bullshit." He's so matter-of-fact, I almost want to be offended. Can't really be when it's true though.

"And I might have had a thing with this guy this past summer, and it only makes me want to move home even more."

Hawke's lips purse as he nods. "This industry is rough on relationships."

I wait for more elaboration, but it doesn't come. "That's it? That's your whole advice? Actually, I don't even think that can be considered advice. It's just a fact."

"It is, but you're probably not going to like what I have to say on the matter."

"I want to hear it anyway."

"St. Louis has invested a lot of money in you. They've hyped you up as the player who can turn the team around and get us a

Cup. If you leave after everything they've done for you, you will be burning that bridge. There's a reason most of the partners of people in the NHL are stay-at-home parents or have business ventures that can be done from anywhere. Trades at the drop of a hat, being locked into contracts ... when it comes to NHL players, it's the partner who always has to compromise. That isn't advice either. Just more facts."

"Facts suck."

"Yup. Of course, there is one way to be the one who compromises, but at your age, I would advise against it."

"Why my age?"

"Because it's retiring. And doing that for love when you're what, eighteen?"

"I'm twenty-one, jackass."

He lifts one shoulder. "Same thing. My point is, changing your career or abandoning your dream for a love that may or may not work out in your early twenties? Imagine how much resentment you would hold. Have your fun while you're young, sign the contract, and think about huge life changes when you're my age."

"Pfft. I'm never going to be as old as you. I've made a deal with the devil, and I'm going to be young and cute forever."

"You're definitely one of those things."

"It's cute, isn't it?"

"Nope." He stands. "Okay, now that we've gotten deeper than we ever have before—"

"That's what he said."

Hawke throws up his hands. "I give up."

"I love you too," I sing as he walks away.

I hate, hate, hate that he said the same thing I've been telling myself this whole time, but it makes the most sense.

That doesn't mean I have to accept it so easily.

I miss Sam already. It hurts to think about him. I've refrained from texting him or calling him other than a "landed safe" text when I got here, but I don't think I can hold back anymore.

Texting him is only going to make things worse, I know this, yet I can't stop myself anyway.

> If I bought you your own animal shelter in St. Louis, would you move here? Jk.

Yes, because putting jk at the end isn't the universal sign for "Not really joking but will say I am in case what I said makes it awkward."

> Miss me that much already?

> You have no idea.

> Actually, I do.

A picture message comes through, and my chest aches at the sight. It's of Sam and Angelica in bed, and she's cuddled up to him, her nose nudging his cheek.

> One night might have turned into letting her sleep on the bed every night. I blame you.

> Good. That little princess deserves to be spoiled. Being that adorable is tiring.

> Are you still talking about the dog or me? Need I remind you, you're the Disney Princess.

> Adorable isn't the word I'd use to describe you. Hot, maybe. Sexy, definitely. Especially in bed.

A response doesn't come through for a really long time, but when it does, it's not the flirty reply I'm hoping for.

> How's hockey going? Winning all the games?

We're setting boundaries, apparently.

> You thinking there are games on at the moment when it's still training camp makes me sad. Mainly because it means you haven't been stalking ESPN to try to catch any of my non-existent games I haven't played yet.

> I haven't had the time. Between training Angelica and the influx of strays and wildlife I've been called out to, I'm crashing immediately after I get home most nights. I used to blame you for all the wildlife calls or for being so busy. Turns out, I'm still as busy but I don't get cute men bringing me the sick and or injured animals. It's a lot less fun without that part.

Now he's flirting? I thought changing the subject was his way of putting that barrier in place, but now I'm more confused than ever.

> Ethan tried to bang you yet? Cheer you up with his dick? Proposed? (again, jks)

But not really jokes. Ha. Ha. Fuck, I hate myself right now.

> Totally. All those things. I'm a very desirable man.

I know he is. That's the problem.

I think about what Hawke said. How I should have my fun while I'm young.

> Let's make a pact. No matter where we end up in five to eight years, we meet up and give us a real shot.

> Are you asking me to wait for you?

Fuck, that is so not fair of me to do.

> No. I can't hold you back from living your life. And I know we were only a summer fling, but it got way too real in the end there, and now I have to learn how to live without talking to you every day. Without waking up next to your smile, and no more tricking you into adopting animals. It absolutely sucks, and I already hate it.

> Me too. Have you spoken to your team's boss people about a shorter contract?

> Not yet. I did speak to my teammate about it, but he said what we already know. If I burn this bridge with a team who has built me up and invested in me, I might become untouchable.

> Does that really matter? You want in with Colorado, and your brother's boyfriend owns the team. Wouldn't they protect you?

It's not as easy as that.

> Owners don't get a whole lot of say when it comes to players. They have input, sure, but it's really up to the GM and coaches. If they hate you, they have the power to ship you off to any team. And if you have the reputation of being difficult and ungrateful? Maybe no team would want me.

> Hockey politics is frustrating.

That's never been more true than right now.

> Tell me about it.

CHAPTER THIRTY-FOUR

SAM

I've deleted three messages today. Which is an improvement over the seven I deleted yesterday. Though I don't know if it could be called an improvement because I called out sick to work so I could stay home and wallow. If anything, that's a step back.

Lachie confirmed what we both knew, and his contract isn't going anywhere. You don't offer someone seventy million if they're interchangeable to you, and I only wish I had that kind of money to make a counteroffer.

Lachie belongs in Colorado.

I'd try to hide it and say that I mean with his brothers, but I really don't. He belongs with me. There's no maybes left in my mind.

It's why I'm actually considering waiting five to eight years like he suggested. Which, yes, is ridiculous.

But no one else has ever stuck before, and the thought of hooking up before Lachie was getting old. Now, it's painful.

Ethan's tried to remind me that hooking up will make moving on easier, but what I failed to tell him is that I don't actually want to move on. Even though I know that I need to.

I climb out of bed once ten o'clock passes, and Angelica follows. I've thrown all my rules out the window when it comes to her, and she's exactly as spoiled as I always swore no pet of mine would be. Without her though, I doubt I'd even be getting out of bed.

I change, brush my teeth, then head out for a run. It's nice having company for this now, and with how much energy she has, it makes sure I don't skip a day.

The stray thought to text Lachie a hot and sweaty picture once we're done flits through my mind, and I have to forcefully push it out again.

He has a career he needs to focus on.

We cut through the park down the street, and just when we're passing under an enormous tree, Angelica goes to dart off and hits the end of her leash before jerking back.

"What are you ..." My words trail off when I spot what's caught her attention. There's a squirrel at the foot of the tree closest to us, and immediately, I flash back to the golf course and the family climbing all over Lachie.

I can't do anything without thinking about him.

I try to tug Angelica away, but she barks and pulls me closer.

The squirrel doesn't run, which is weird in itself, but on second glance, I realize why. It's injured.

"For fuck's sake." I throw Angelica a dirty look. If she turns out like Lachie and attracts all the sick and injured wildlife, I'll fly to St. Louis myself and leave her on his doorstep. Until then, I have to deal with this little guy. It's lucky I'm the one who found it and not someone else with the best of intentions and no clue what they're doing.

Lachie's suggestion of making videos to help educate people comes back to me, and for the first time since he left, a memory of him doesn't make me want to curl over and die.

I hastily set up my phone and hit Record, and then I tie Angelica to the nearest bench and get to work handling the animal carefully without any of the proper equipment. Once I'm back at the shelter, I can film some more and show people what they really should be using if they need to contain an animal until help gets there.

I drop Angie off at home before heading into work.

My day is taken up by helping Owen with the squirrel, making excuses to Danika about why I called in sick, filming some more, deleting it, and filming some more again, so that by the time I head back home, it's late.

Angelica sits next to me on the couch while I inhale my dinner, and it's almost peaceful.

Almost.

Except for how much I want to tell Lachie about my day and can't.

My video does well, so I spend most of the next day filming some more, and it's almost distracting enough to get my mind off Lachie. Until the quiet moments in between when I remember he's gone all over again.

I'm not sure if it's a good or bad thing that it's the weekend because it means no having to get up for work—and begging Ethan to do an early morning with Angelica tomorrow—but it also means no distractions.

I'm definitely going to text him.

One week down, and since he mentioned ESPN, I went to create an account to watch hockey and found his still logged in to my TV. Considering I'm only using it to watch him, I have no guilt whatsoever leaving it there.

Where there are still no games.

How long does training camp go for?

I know Google is *right there*, but I'm trying to hold back from looking up anything to do with hockey.

It's past seven, and I'm contemplating putting something on for dinner while I wait for Ethan to get home, when someone pounds so hard on the front door that it sounds like they're trying to beat it in.

"What the hell?"

I grab my phone, unsure if I need to call the police, but when I check outside, it's not a home invasion. I don't think.

I tug open my door to find Easton and Connor Kikishkin on my doorstep.

"Ah ... hi?"

"Let us in," Connor says, then, without waiting for an invitation, pushes past.

"He meant to say please," Easton assures me as he follows his brother.

I close the front door, pinch myself to check that I haven't passed out, and then head back inside.

"Not that I don't love this surprise"—I don't—"but what are you doing here?"

"We're going out," Easton answers, picking up some random sculpture thing that Ethan made, inspecting it, and setting it down again. "And we're dragging you with us."

"Umm, why?" I barely know these guys, and they look way too similar to Lachie for me to handle having them in my home.

"What kind of brothers would we be if we didn't do the overbearing grill-the-boyfriend thing?" They share an evil grin.

Ouch. "You're excused from duty. I'm not Lachie's boyfriend."

Connor's eyes narrow, and he doesn't hide the way he paces to my bedroom door and looks inside.

"What are you doing?"

"Making sure you don't have some other guy in here."

I sigh. "You really don't like me, do you?"

"I don't ... not *not* like you."

"That sounded painful."

Easton gives Connor a look that has him dropping the asshole big brother act.

"I love my little brother. You and I didn't get off on the right foot, and all he talks about or not talks about is you every time we call him, and so I figured ... I would give you a chance."

"Again, bit late for that."

"It's not our fault," Easton scoffs. "Lachie wouldn't let us near you. Every time I dropped him here and tried to come in, he threatened to trip me during our first game. Not cool."

"I'll be sure to let him know you stopped by." The next time I *don't* text him.

Connor crosses into the kitchen and starts opening cupboards at random. "Where do you keep the alcohol? I think we need pre-drinks before—"

"We don't have any."

He screws up his nose and turns back to me. "What?"

"Ethan and I aren't big drinkers."

"Who the fuck is Ethan?"

Easton cackles. "His roommate, dipshit."

There's a distinct whine in Connor's voice. "Why doesn't he ever tell me these things?"

"No clue. That reaction was totally appropriate and chill."

Connor flips his brother off and closes the cupboards. "Fine. Let's go."

"I can't." I point at where Angelica is sitting on her bed, waiting for permission to greet the newcomers. "She needs to be fed soon."

"So feed her now."

"But—"

Ethan uses that exact moment to enter. "Girl, wait until I tell you what happened at the—" He cuts off as he rounds the corner and finds our place full. "Huh. You know, when I told you that the easiest way to get over Lachie was to get under someone else, I didn't mean find two look-alikes to double-team you. This feels like the opposite of progress."

While the brothers gag, I slap my hand over Ethan's mouth before he can say anything else. "You are so close to losing your best friend card. This is Connor and Easton. Lachie's brothers."

"Oh ... I am so relieved."

"Can you look after the dog?" Easton asks.

"I am the queen's third daddy."

"Who's the second?"

"Okay, okay," I cut off Ethan's reply. "Let me get changed, and you can drag me away."

There's no point in arguing with them, and hopefully, the sooner we go out, the sooner they'll figure out how boring I am, and the sooner they will leave. This whole thing is completely pointless, considering Lachie and I are over, but if I can get the barest scraps from them about what he's been doing, I'm still in a painful enough place to want it.

We end up in a bar downtown, and Connor orders us a round of shots before I can grab a beer. I'm going to fight him on it, but ... what's the point? I don't have to make a good impression, and honestly, getting good and drunk, then passing out, might be exactly what I need.

"To Lachie's seventy-million-dollar contract," Connor says, eyeing me like he's waiting for a reaction.

"You're an asshole," I throw back.

Which, for some reason, draws a genuine laugh from him. The brothers tap their shots against mine, and we all throw them back.

"So he told you about that." Connor signals for another round.

"He did. Right before he left. It was at that point I knew that we were *done* done."

"You have no idea how rare it is for a rookie to be offered that kind of contract. St. Louis has basically told him and everyone else that Lachie is their future. They're invested in him. For the long term."

He can stop rubbing it in now. "Hockey is weird."

"It's a beautiful sport."

"I've only ever watched one game."

Easton makes a sound like a record screech. "*What*? Your life makes me sad."

I grab my second shot as soon as it's set down. "If it helps, I plan to watch every single one of Lachie's games. He gave me a crash course on the rules, and I still don't understand any of them, not that it matters. I won't be watching for the hockey."

"Fifty bucks says you'll be a fan by the end of the season."

"I'm not taking that bet." I am dropping some of my attitude with them though. Connor seems to have let his jerk side go, and if he can move on, so can I.

"More shots?" I ask, because we might as well do this thing properly.

"I got it." Connor signals again.

"You don't have to pay," I point out. "I can get my own."

Easton stops me. "He can pay. His boyfriend is a billionaire. That's with a *B*. He will pay every single round until the end of time."

"But you're a millionaire," I point out. "That's also not a small amount of money."

"True, a round of drinks isn't something we notice. So if we say we're paying, let us pay. Don't get all weird about it."

I'm about to point out that I'm *not* the one who gets weird about it, but ... my instinct is to push that I can afford some fucking drinks. It's not so much a pride thing, but there's something simmering under the surface that makes me want to prove that while I don't have the money they do, I'm still worthy enough to be sitting with them.

"You won't think I'm leeching off you?" I ask. "And throw it back in my face when you're mad about something?"

Easton does a double take, while Connor almost looks offended. "Are you serious? Why would I think that?"

Holy shit, I *might* be the problem. "No reason."

"Has someone done that before?"

I search my memories for an example of when it's happened and ... *have* they? Or has it been my insecurities the entire time? "I think I need another drink."

"Ask and you shall receive." Connor hands my drink over. "And no more money talk. Or Lachie talk. I want to hear the reason behind these hot animal videos." He pretends to glare at me. "Yes, Parker was watching the one where you conveniently took off your shirt to help the squirrel."

I throw my head back with a laugh, brain already feeling happily fuzzy. "What did he think?"

"Said it was educational," Connor says with a side-eye.

"Then what are you grumbling about?"

"*And* hot."

Easton snorts into his shot. "You are way too easy to rile up."

Connor's lips hook upward in a smile, and he reminds me a *lot* more of his brother like that. "I reminded him of why he's with me. Don't worry about that."

Before Connor can get into his sex life, I turn to Easton. "Shouldn't you be at hockey camp too?"

"First, it's not some summer camp where we're all locked up. Second, only rookies and baby players report so early."

"Lies," Connor cuts in. "I always reported early."

"Yeah, but that's because you always played the part of the golden boy. Experienced players *can* start early, but I'm not a dumbass. This is my last weekend of freedom before my life is taken over again."

"It really *is* your whole life, huh?"

"Yep. Makes it worse that my boyfriend is a ref and his schedule is as bananas as mine is."

I tilt my head at that. "So how do you guys make it work?"

"We know that being together is better than being apart, so nothing was too big for us to make it happen. Yeah, we're long distance for most of the year and find every opportunity to be together, but he's the one for me. Nothing else matters."

"He's nowhere near as in love with Knox as I am with Parker. I *retired* to be with him."

"Actually, I'd argue I'm *more* in love," Easton throws back. "Neither of us asked the other to give up their dream jobs. We *support* each other and know that we're allowed to have a life outside of the relationship."

"Parker didn't ask me!" Connor splutters. "I did it for him. I chose to. Like a grand gesture."

I tune out the brothers' bickering, smiling for the first time in days as everything gets blurry at the edges. From what I can gather, they were both in relationships that shouldn't have worked, and they made it happen anyway.

Because they found their person.

Lachie is my person. I *know* he is.

Maybe in the real world, one summer isn't long enough to know, but I do. Because he's a Disney Princess, and I want to be his Prince Charming.

But unlike Easton, long distance isn't an option, because Lachie doesn't come home anywhere near as much as Knox does. They see each other every week or two at least, whereas for me and Lachie, it's months.

And Connor gave up hockey, but it wasn't his dream career like it is for Lachie.

So that isn't an option either.

But the alcohol is making it so hard to remember what I was all worried about.

Nothing else matters.

The answer feels so close, and as I'm ordering another beer, it feels easy to pull out my phone and click open our messages.

> Your brother is so wise. Nothing else matters.
> Just that I love my princess so much.

CHAPTER THIRTY-FIVE

LACHIE

> Your body is so wired nuthatch else matter just like i love myself princesses sorry Michael.

My alarm goes off at stupid o'clock to get to the practice facility, but the cryptic message Sam sent last night stares up at me. I have no idea what to make of it.

Michael? Who's Michael? Is he sorry to Michael or sorry about Michael? Does that mean he's already moved on with someone else? Someone I'll have to track down and murder with a puck to the head?

I read over the text for the millionth time, but when my second alarm goes off to make sure I'm up and walking out the door, I have to put my phone away and try to forget it while I do what I'm paid to do.

I'm distracted all the way to the rink though, trying to decipher what that text was. I'm annoyed that I told Hawke I'd drive us in today because all I want to do is keep looking at that screen. Maybe reply.

No. I shouldn't do that. Especially if he's only going to turn around and tell me Michael is some guy he met. Sam deserves happiness, and I'm not going to hold him back, but damn. It's only been a couple of weeks.

"You're grumpy again," Hawke says.

"Not again. Still. Just like you're still old. You're not old again."

"Fuck you, then. I won't be a good teammate and try to help you out, but when your mood starts affecting your game, don't come crying to me about it."

I really don't like this side of me. I'm usually so easygoing and calm, not a tense ball of anger and frustration. "I got a text," I say.

"From him?"

I nod.

"What did it say?"

"I have no fucking idea."

"What do you mean?"

I gesture at my phone in the center console. "Have a look for yourself."

He pulls the phone out and holds it up to my face to unlock it, but before he presses anything, he hesitates. "I'm not going to see anything I shouldn't see when I open your messages, am I?"

"Pfft. You think I'm dumb enough to have nudes on there when you know my agents are my parents?"

"I've never thought of that before. Poor you."

"Wait, does that mean you have nudes on your phone?" I almost swerve into another lane from the idea of that, but he doesn't reply.

He goes into my messages, and out of the corner of my eye, I see him frown. "Was he drunk?"

"God, I hope so. Have no idea what he was trying to say though."

"Maybe he was trying to say you have a weird body."

"How is that any better than wired? And why is he talking about my body at all?"

"We should send this to the team. Maybe they can decipher it."

"No." I lean over to grab my phone out of his hand, and the car swerves again.

"Fuck, calm down. I know you say I'm old, but I'm not old enough to fucking die yet. Watch the road."

"I don't need my humiliation going through the entire team, thanks."

"Why is it humiliating that you met someone and like them?"

When he puts it that way, I don't have a real answer. "Because I got dumped?"

"Did you though? You're still in contact with the guy, and I'm sure he doesn't actually mean your body is wired. Unless that's a new thing you kids are saying. Like, oooh, that's so wired. Meaning hot."

"You really are old."

"Nuthatch else matter could easily be nothing else matters. So, 'Your body is so hot, nothing else matters.' He loves himself, which is a good thing because you need self-love before you can give anyone else love ... but then 'princesses sorry Michael'... I have no idea what that could be."

"While I like your interpretation better than mine, I read it as 'Your body isn't good enough, he loves himself, so he chooses to be with Michael.'"

"Who's Michael?"

"That's what I want to know!"

"So ask him." Hawke taps away on my phone.

"What are you doing?"

"The mature thing. I'm texting him 'WTF.'"

"So very mature," I say dryly.

"There you go. Now you won't have to wonder once he replies."

If he replies.

—

He doesn't reply.

Not by the time I have to hit the ice. It makes practice difficult, and Hawke's words really sink in. If I can't somehow get over Sam, this shitty attitude is going to start affecting my game. I'm already slower on the ice. Sluggish.

Everyone's eyes are constantly on me, though that might be paranoia. Every time I've walked past someone from management or Coach has wanted to talk to me, the hairs on my neck have stood up. No one has said anything because contracts and deals always go through agents, but I can't help feeling like they're death staring at me and will continue to do so until I sign my extension.

I swear there have been rumblings within the team too, complaints about me not taking a team-friendly deal and wanting to push the team toward the salary cap. I swear I'm two seconds away from yelling in the locker room, "It's not about the money!" But on the off chance they're not talking about me and it's all in my head, I don't want to come across as unhinged.

When Coach dismisses us for the day, I hang back on the ice and let the others file out first. Am I eager to get to my cubby and check my phone? Of course I am. But what if he still hasn't replied? What if that rambly message was the last I'll ever get because he has *Michael* now?

A chorus of "Aww" catches my attention, and there, past the ice exit, is a black Labrador puppy. Not Angelica, which is disappointing, but this is one of those purebred Labs that will eventually be trained to be a service animal. Right now, it's in its very early puppy stages and is probably here to be desensitized to all types of noise.

The pup only makes me miss Angelica and Sam even more, which makes me mad. And sad. I'm smad.

At least some puppy cuddles should cheer me up.

I leave the ice, and I even find a smile buried deep down somewhere, but then the weirdest thing that has ever happened in my life shocks the hell out of me. The puppy recoils as I approach it.

What the fuck?

I take another step closer, and it lets out a little growl and a yip, and then runs behind its handler. I step back and stare at it wide-eyed. It growls again.

"I'm so sorry," its handler says. "He's never done this before."

"I've never had an animal hate me on sight before." I sidestep the woman and the pup and head for the locker room, confused as fuck about what that was. I don't know what's more confusing: Sam's text message or that dog's reaction to me.

Is everything backwards today? Is this some kind of dream? Did I get hit in the head with a puck yesterday, and this is some coma-induced hallucination? It probably doesn't say much for the state of my mental health if I'm hoping it's that last one.

I take my phone out of my bag, and my breath catches in my throat when I see Sam's name in my notifications. I'm tempted to throw it back in my bag and go shower so I can prepare myself for whatever it says, but who am I kidding. I open it so fast and hit the icon so many times I almost delete the message I'm trying to read.

No, *messages*. A slew of them.

> I am soooo sorry. So so sorry. I was drunk, and if I'm honest, I don't remember exactly what I was trying to say but it wasn't ... whatever that is.

> I hope your lack of response is because you're busy with hockey, but in case it's not, can I call you? Can you give me a time you'll be available?

> Actually, you can call me when you want to. I don't want to push.

Because he's so eager to talk to me, that has to be a good thing, right?

"Did he message?" Hawke's voice makes me jump. He's standing in front of me in only a towel.

"Yeah. You were right. He was drunk and wants me to call him."

"So why haven't you done it yet?"

"Give me a minute, geez. I was practically attacked by a beast of a dog, and what happens if he wants me to call so he can tell me he slept with someone else?"

"Why would he want you to call if he did that? And oh no, you get attacked with all those puppy kisses?"

I wouldn't be complaining if that was it. "No, you don't understand. It growled at me. And tried to get away!"

"Finally, a dog or animal with good taste. I should see if he's available for adoption."

I gasp. "You wouldn't dare."

"No. I wouldn't. But you should forget about it and call your guy." Hawke keeps walking, heading for the showers.

He's right.

> Is now a good time for you?

My phone rings a couple of seconds later.

"Hey," I answer.

"I blame your brothers!"

Uh, what? "My ... brothers?"

"They showed up to take me out drinking, and maybe I was drunker than I thought because I didn't think I'd actually sent that message, and—"

"Wait, wait, wait. Hold up. My brothers took you out drinking? Why did you say yes to that?"

"I didn't. I didn't put up a huge fight either, but it was clear they weren't going to take no for an answer."

"*Why?*"

"Because they were being pushy."

"No, why did they take you out?"

"That's probably a question for them, but they said something about you being ... uh ... kinda whiney when they've spoken to you."

Of course they did. "That ... might be true. Might not be."

"If it helps, I've been whiney too. According to Ethan, anyway. Though, today it's mostly about the hangover I wish I didn't have."

"If I was there, I'd help soothe your hangover."

He exhales loudly. "When was your first game in Colorado again?"

"Not until the end of November."

"But that's so far away."

"I know," I murmur.

A depressing silence falls between us, and while I want to change the subject, I can't. Not until I know for sure.

"What was that message supposed to say?"

"I think I was trying to say your brother is wise?"

"That makes even less sense than saying my body is wired."

"They made some things clear to me, is all, and that's ... I want to give us a try."

"And by that, you mean—"

"A relationship. I don't know that it will work in the long run, but we can do long distance until we figure it out. I have no interest in anyone else. It will suck for a bit, but ... I want my Disney Princess."

For the first time since I came back to St. Louis, something deep in my chest loosens. It's like all the strength I've been pouring into the last few weeks breaks, and I want to curl into a ball of relief. "About that. I think I'm broken. A puppy literally growled at me and tried to run away."

"You're lying, but also, you dare cheat on Angelica?"

"Not lying. Maybe being away from you, that calm zen that supposedly attracts animals is all gone because all I'm doing here is missing you."

"Uh-oh. I broke you. You lost your superpower! Guess I'll just have to figure out a weekend I can get up there to see you, then."

"Yes. We need to right the imbalance."

"I'll see what I can do, but I should get back to work." He hesitates for a second. "I miss you."

The distance between us grows heavy on my chest. "Miss you more."

"It's not a competition."

"Don't you know? I'm a hockey player. Everything is a competition."

CHAPTER THIRTY-SIX

SAM

On Monday, I send Lachie a picture of me and Angelica all cuddled up in bed.

On Tuesday, I get a post-workout shot, where his abs are accidentally on purpose in the frame, looking as mouthwatering as ever.

Wednesday, we cave and video call each other. It doesn't take long for the phone sex to start, but it's considerably less hot with Angelica scratching and whining at the door because she can hear Lachie's voice.

Moping around because we couldn't have each other didn't work, so something had to give, but I'm not sure if this arrangement is better or worse.

Dating someone I never get to see is the ultimate tease. The whole time his body was on-screen, all I wanted was to reach through the phone and touch him. Taste him.

Then the sex was over, and the need to hold him was even worse.

I'm going out of my mind, and it doesn't seem to matter how much I jerk off, I only get hornier. And more irritable.

"You need to get laid," Ethan mutters as I stab at the chunks of beef in the dinner he's cooked.

"I'm working on it." And I am. I've been saving all the money I can get together for a plane ticket out to see Lachie. "I did the numbers, and as long as nothing else comes up, I'll be able to go two pay days from now and not touch my savings."

That part is important to me. I'll never own my own place, but I want to make sure I have a fallback fund, and it's nothing special, but seeing it grow bit by bit keeps me motivated.

Ethan sighs, playing with his phone, and a second later, my screen lights up.

I choke on the bite I've just taken. "A thousand dollars? I can't take this."

"Girl, you think I'm giving you a choice? It's a small price to pay to get some damn peace around here. Angelica and I are sick of seeing you all depressed."

"I'm not depressed." I am still staring at my phone though. I don't want to take it, even though I know Ethan has more than enough money, but I do really, *really* want to see Lachie.

"We're not doing this back-and-forth thing. You're taking the money and going and seeing your man for the weekend. And Angelica and I are doing mani-pedis and watching *Golden Girls* reruns, and we both know you'll ruin the vibes by being here."

I so desperately want to accept. Don't ask me why I'm comfortable taking money from Ethan but not from Lachie. It probably has to do with knowing there are no strings when it comes to Ethan. With Lachie ... I'm not at that level of trust yet. I desperately want to get there though, and to do that, I need to see him. "Are you sure?"

He leans over and kisses me on the head. "Please don't make me go so far as to book the flight for you. That seems like too much work."

I lean into him, hugging him but not hugging him, still so grateful for the day he answered the roommate wanted ad.

Who would have thought that going on ten years later, we'd be here?

"Thank you."

"Anything for you."

I jump off the couch and immediately call Lachie. As much as I'd love to show up and surprise him, I have no idea what his schedule looks like or where he lives.

"Please tell me you have the weekend off?"

He chuckles warmly into his phone. "Sort of. I have to make time to skate and work out, but there's nothing specifically scheduled. Why?"

"I'm coming to see you."

"Wait. *What*?"

"If you want me to."

"Of course I want you to! This weekend? As in two days away?"

His excitement fills my chest with warmth. "Hold on." I put him on speaker and sit on my bed, looking up flights. The more I look, the more my heart sinks. "Oooof. Okay. Last-minute flights are expensive." I keep my tone joking.

"I'll pay."

"What's your schedule like next week instead?"

"Hold on." All I can hear is him breathing for a second. "Wednesday is a light day, then we leave late Thursday for our first preseason game. Back early Sunday morning."

"Okay ... when do you finish on Tuesday?"

"Usually about five."

"So if I aim to get there Tuesday night and fly out Thursday?"

He immediately perks up. "That works for me."

The cheaper flight options have a late arrival time, but they're all I can afford with Ethan's money. That leaves the question of accommodation ... "It's two nights. Is there a hotel close to you or ..."

Lachie snorts. "You'll be staying with me."

"Don't you have a roommate? Will he care?"

"Hawke!" Lachie yells, and I'm sure he covers the phone, but it's still loud. "Are you cool if Sam stays with us two nights next week?"

A deep voice answers him. "Sure. But same rules as always."

"No sex noises, got it."

I screw up my face at the reminder of how many times Lachie has probably had sex there. It's no different from him being here, of course, but I don't like the thought of his roommate thinking I'm just another guy.

I want to be more than that.

It doesn't matter right now though. I'm smiling properly for the first time in days, nervous excitement filling me over the thought of being with him in a week. I book the flights while he's on the phone.

"Okay, I'll land after eight your time. If you want to send me the address—"

"I'll be there waiting for you."

Again, I'd hoped for that but didn't want to push. "I'm so excited to see you."

"Yeah ... you have no idea."

—

I stare up at the departures board and the bright *DELAYED* next to my flight number. My gut twists over being late. It's bad enough that I won't get there until after eight, so every minute later that my flight leaves is a minute less I get to spend with Lachie.

Thankfully, I only packed a carry-on, so I can get off the flight and into his arms as soon as possible.

I order a coffee while I wait, try to watch mindless videos on YouTube before getting restless and posting one of my own. Normally the comments on the animal videos are enough to keep me distracted, but as the questions come in between the borderline inappropriate ones, I don't trust myself to answer any of them.

I get up and pace instead.

Then realize I look unhinged.

Sit.

Try not to vibrate out of my chair.

Check the screen again.

Try not to look.
Fail.
Look again.

I swear, every time I look up, the expected delay keeps increasing. At this rate, it'll be after nine by the time I land ... after ten ... after eleven ...

I break and message Lachie.

> Still not sure when we're leaving, but I'll be getting in late. If you need to sleep, I'm okay with grabbing a hotel tonight and catching up in the morning. Just let me know x

"We're now boarding for the flight to St. Louis. All passengers in—"

Thank fuck.

I all but launch out of my seat, eager to board and get us in the air as soon as possible. It feels like forever before my group is called, and I hold in the very strong urge to remind people to have *their damn boarding passes out*. This is okay. It's fine.

I get to see Lachie at the end of this, and that's all that matters.

After what feels like a thousand years, I reach the front, scan my pass, and as I'm about to head down the gangway, an attendant stops me.

"I'm sorry, sir, we have a full flight today, and I'll need to check your bag."

Every last ounce of frustration seeps out of me.

"Of course you do," I say weakly and hand it over with a smile. It's not his fault, and I refuse to get mad at someone doing their job, even though the universe is *really* trying to push me to it.

I take my slip and board with nothing but my phone and earbuds.

Then I take my seat, cue up a TV show Ethan downloaded onto my phone, and hope Lachie replies before we leave.

He doesn't.

And as the onboard announcement declares before takeoff, economy doesn't have Wi-Fi on this flight.

That tracks, with how today is going.

This is going to be the longest flight in history.

CHAPTER THIRTY-SEVEN

LACHIE

When a tired-looking Sam appears in the arrivals hall, I don't care if anyone recognizes me. I can't help but throw myself at him.

As relieved as I am to see him, as much as it warms my chest and has that ache of longing disappear, the scowl on his face makes me want to do everything I can to turn this around.

If we're only going to have a short time together, I'm going to make the most of every single minute.

Starting now. I slam into him and dip my head to kiss him, but he puts a palm on my chest to hold me back.

"Everyone is looking. You're technically not out."

"I don't care."

He still looks worried. "I haven't brushed my teeth since I left for the airport."

"Still don't care. Hurry up and kiss me."

His lips turn up as he leans in, and I anticipate the sense of calm, that balance of the world righting itself, but the second his mouth lands on mine, all I feel is hollow. Not because of him. He's perfect. His lips are soft, he tastes like coffee, and I can't wait to get his clothes off. But having him in my arms doesn't settle the unease inside me because I know in forty-eight hours, he'll be gone again.

I pull back. "We should go. Get you home."

"Home?"

"My home. Or, more specifically, Hawke's home. Maybe I'll have my own place the next time you visit. It's probably time I be a big boy and move out." I hold his hand as he leads me to the baggage claim belt. "I didn't even notice you don't have your bag. How much did you bring when we're going to be naked for most of the short time you're here?"

"Full flight. They made me check it."

Damn. That, plus the three hours delayed, it's no wonder he looks wrecked.

"After my new contract kicks in, I'll fly you out private." I'm joking, but that gets me thinking. "How much does it cost to buy a private plane?"

Sam shoves me. "You're not buying a private plane."

"No, not me, but I could probably convince Parker to."

Sam shakes his head and tries to cover his smile, but I still see it. I want to see it more though. Every day, if it were up to me.

I have no idea how this long-distance thing is going to work. All I can do is try to make the most of every time we're together.

Sam's bag is one of the first out, thankfully, but we still won't be getting back to my place until close to midnight. At least traffic won't be a pain in the ass at this time of night.

I pay for parking on the way out, and it's not long before we're on the road. "Are you hungry? We can get drive-thru somewhere if you need to eat."

"I'm only hungry for one thing, because the last couple of weeks without you means I won't even be able to think around you until you've drawn at least one orgasm from me."

"Damn. If running red lights wasn't risking not getting home at all, I'd pay as many fines as it took right about now."

"I'd be willing to pay half, and I don't even have the money."

"Our video call not enough for you? We might have to do it more often if I'm going to keep you satisfied."

Sam is silent for a beat, and for a moment, I worry I've said something wrong. Is he already doubting this?

I try to glance at him but have to keep my eyes on the road.

"So when your roommate says no sex noises, how serious was he?" he asks.

"Very serious. But also, his place is a mansion, and my room is on an entirely different floor than his. Noise is pretty well insulated, compared to your small apartment, anyway."

"Oh, thank fuck. I was worried about having to be quiet and self-conscious. All I want to focus on is you." Sam's hand lands on my denim-covered thigh.

"At this rate, I might come before we even get back to my place. You have no idea how on edge I've been today. Luckily, hockey pants can cover hard-ons, or my teammates would've thought I was hitting on them."

"Aww." Sam's hand moves up to the back of my neck. "Didn't get a chance to jerk off because you've been working too hard?"

"I've made myself refrain."

"For how long?"

"Oh, only today. I knew I would see you, so I didn't want to waste any cum."

Sam laughs. "Saving it all up for me?"

"All for you," I say as I pull in to the drive and park my car under the giant arch between garage and house.

I'll put the car away later. I can't wait to get Sam inside.

"Are you sure this isn't a hotel?" he asks.

"It's actually not that big. You should see Easton and Knox's house. They bought it off Connor when Connor realized buying a big house when he was lonely wasn't smart." I grab his hand and start dragging him toward the house. "I'll give you a tour later."

"What about my bag—"

"Later," I growl.

I drag him through the house, refraining from touching him other than where our hands are joined because I know the second my hands are on him, we're getting naked, no matter where in the house we are, and Hawke will kill me if I get cum all over his twenty-thousand-dollar couch in the sitting room he never uses.

Hawke has upstairs all to himself, while I have a guest bedroom at the back of the first floor, and only now am I realizing how far in the corner my room is.

What I'm regretting even more is not prepping before I left, because I want Sam, and I want him now. I've cleaned out and am ready to go, but I'm not stretched and ready for his cock. Lesson learned.

I'm so hard, so needy. It hasn't even been that long since we saw each other, but it might as well have been years, because as eager as I am to get his cock inside me, I might be more excited about holding him in my arms and not letting go for the entire time he's here. If I have to practice and work out with him on my back, I'm okay with that.

When we get to my room, I close the door with a loud bang because I'm too impatient to close it gently, and before Sam can even blink, I'm tearing at his clothes to get them off his body. I'm dying to kiss him, but once I do, I know I'm not going to stop, not even for enough time to get naked.

Once we're stripped bare, I can finally let myself kiss him the way I want. With no boundaries, no overthinking who could be watching, and no obligations to a team, my family ... no one but Sam.

Our mouths fuse together, my tongue pushing past his lips, and it's possible I'm too fast or have taken Sam off guard because our teeth clang.

He pushes at my chest. "We have all night. Slow down."

"I don't think that's possible." I cup his face and kiss him again, just as hard but more controlled this time.

Sam groans into my mouth, and our bodies press against each other. Our cocks weep with happiness at being reunited, and I'm so close to the edge already, I'm tempted to let it happen and then go for a round two later.

But no, I want him to come inside me.

We fumble our way to the bed, letting out shared grunts as we fall on our sides. There are limbs everywhere. One of my arms is trapped under him, my thigh is between his legs, and as our hips move instinctively, the friction on my cock is too much to bear. But I don't stop.

"Fuck, I've missed you," I say, breaking my mouth from his and kissing down his jaw. "So much."

"Me too."

"It hasn't even been that long." I rut hard against his hip. "But fuck!"

I freeze and slam my eyes closed, begging to myself, "Don't come, don't come, don't come." Though it must come out loud because Sam laughs and pulls out of my hold.

"Where're your supplies? Getting you ready will at least have you holding off a little longer."

I point to my nightstand and throw my other arm over my eyes to try to gather some sort of sense of control. There's none to be found.

Sam comes back to me and taps my thigh. "Roll over."

I'm so horny, even his voice almost makes me come, but I do as he says and face-plant into my pillows with my ass up. I hear him fiddling with the lube, and then where I'm expecting his fingers to get to work, I'm hit with a whole different sensation.

Sam's warm mouth lands on my hole. His tongue licks at the tight ring of muscle before pushing past. I lose my breath, forget how to breathe. I'm going to die, and I don't even care. Because with his rough stubble on my ass, his tongue doing wicked things, I could die and die happy.

Having said that, living would mean getting a lot more of this. Sporadically. Whenever we can manage a visit.

I shake that thought free and focus on him. On what he's doing. He's turning me inside out, and his cock hasn't even been anywhere near inside me yet.

"Sammy," I whine. "This is … It's too much."

He stops what he's doing and kisses his way up my back. "Don't like it?"

"I love it, but I've been thinking about you fucking me for weeks, and I don't want to come until your amazing dick is inside me."

"I don't think I've ever seen you this desperate before." I hear the click of the lube bottle again.

"I don't think I've ever been this desperate before."

He proves me wrong when a second later, he pushes a finger inside me, deeper than his tongue could reach. I push backward, and before I know it, I'm rocking my hips, fucking myself on his finger because I can't stop myself. I don't even want to at this point.

"You're so sexy." He adds another finger. It goes in so easily, and while there's a big difference between two fingers and his cock, I don't care.

"I'm ready," I whine.

"And now you're impatient. Still sexy, but annoyingly impatient."

I lift myself onto my hands so I can glance over my shoulder at Sam. Our eyes connect, and the lust filling his face is so much more than attraction. It's so much more than looking at me like a fling. I realize it's the way he's always looked at me. We were fucked from the beginning because it was never, ever a simple fling.

What we have is deeper. A real connection.

And when Sam finally pulls his fingers free and lines up his cock, I feel that connection in my bones. In my gut. Most of all, my heart.

Sam's shaky to get started, probably worried I'm not as ready as I should be, but my chest is so full I don't care about the sting of stretching. My body sucks him in to fill me all the way to his base.

I've been craving this. Craving a good fuck. But the fact that it's Sam makes everything ten times more intense. I'm not going to last long, but with the cautious way Sam's moving inside me, I get the impression it's for his benefit more than mine. He's close too.

We can drag out our orgasms tomorrow. Now that the slow part of prep is over, I want him to take me.

"Claim me," I rasp.

It must be what he was waiting for. Either that or telling him to lose control has let him let go. Either way, he pushes all the way inside me and then drags out slowly. Fast thrust, slow pull out. Over and over again, he fucks me hard but slow. And just when I think it can't get any better, he reaches for my hair and pulls my head back by my roots.

Pain mixed with pleasure sets me off, and as he speeds up, I ride that line between climbing to the top and jumping off the ledge.

"Lachie," he breathes. "You're so amazing. You're perfect."

Says the man with the perfect dick currently turning my world upside down.

He leans over me, moving his hand from my hair to rest beside mine on the bed. He thrusts harder, faster, and then when his lips land on my shoulder and he lays a gentle kiss, I shudder. I think I'm coming. He bites into my skin, and that's when I know I'm coming.

I fall. Figuratively.

Physically, I'm puffing and panting, gripping my top sheet in my fists as I come completely untouched. That rarely happens, but it's all I need tonight. Sam is all I need.

He thrusts hard two more times, and that's when he tenses behind me. The moan he lets out is long and deep, and as he trembles through his release, the high slowly fades between us, and all we're left with is a sticky mess and the realization that his short visit will be nowhere near enough time to get our fill of each other.

I'm already missing him again, and he hasn't even left yet.

How is this long-distance thing going to work?

CHAPTER THIRTY-EIGHT

SAM

I'm woken up by kisses running over my cheek, and at first, I'm in that groggy, half-unconscious place where I think Angelica is getting overly affectionate, but then my brain catches up with me.

I peek through my lashes to find Lachie curled up beside me. My heart goes fucking haywire.

"Morning."

He grins, and it's the most beautiful thing I've ever seen. "Morning. You crashed hard."

"I haven't been sleeping great this week." A yawn tears through me. "What time is it?"

"After ten."

"*Ten?*" I sit up and grab my phone, sure he's screwing with me. He isn't. Which is ... depressing. "Why didn't you wake me earlier?"

"You looked so cute sleeping."

I fall back into the pillows that are possibly the most comfortable things I've ever slept on. "I've wasted half the morning I could have spent with you."

His expression doesn't fill me with reassurance. "Actually, it's the whole morning. I have to get a skate in, and we're leaving now. But I'll be back with lunch, and then we'll have the whole day together."

Half of the day. And then I'm leaving tomorrow morning. I try not to let those thoughts get me down; there'll be enough time back in Denver to wallow. Today, I'm going to get up, shower, have breakfast, and brush my teeth, then hopefully he'll be back, and I'll take whatever time with him that I can get.

His lips meet mine, and I hold him there, so insanely happy I can do this again. I really have missed him. "Hurry back."

"Mmm, I'll try," he mutters against my mouth.

He doesn't leave though. The kiss deepens, and I sink into it, loving the way he feels in my arms.

A throat clears by the door. "You got me up early to go, so let's go."

Lachie rolls off me, and I catch sight of his roommate leaning against the door. Fuck me. No wonder Lachie was worried about the hooking-up-with-a-roommate thing when his looks like that. Wavy hair, deep eyes, a jaw covered in stubble.

We eye each other up for a moment, and then he cracks a smile.

"So you're the seventy-million-dollar man."

I cover my face. "People need to stop saying that number."

"Why?"

"Because it's not a real number."

"I dunno, my house feels pretty real to me."

"Stop freaking out my boyfriend," Lachie says, shoving Hawke out the door.

The word *boyfriend* makes my heart warm and happy, but they've already gone. It's only as they're walking away that I hear Hawke say, "Wait until he finds out about the brand deals. That's going to blow his mind."

Brand deals?

I know all about those because Ethan has them, but I've never stopped to think about them applying to Lachie too. Overwhelm threatens to hit me, but I shove it back.

Not here.

Not today.

Even after the shower, as I'm exploring the enormous house, I don't let it take hold. When Lachie jokes about buying a place, this is what he means. A mansion like this.

And yes, this *is* a mansion. I never want to see the monster Easton and his boyfriend live in.

I poke around in the kitchen to see what I can eat and find the fridge packed with labeled containers of names and dates. Seeing *Lachlan* and the words *Lunch* is weird enough in itself without the actual date on there. I guess with two professional athletes living together, it makes sense to have a personal chef. They probably have nutritionists too. And as I look around at the spotless room, I figure they have a cleaner as well.

It's a far cry from Ethan's and my very lived-in place.

I sort of hate it.

Too scared to touch any of their food, I look up what's close and walk to a cafe down the street. It's a nice neighborhood—a very nice neighborhood, considering the car brands passing on the street and parked in the long driveways.

The cafe is in a line of specialty shops that give it a small-town vibe, and the more I see, the more I like.

At least three people say good morning, and when I take an outdoor table and look around—mostly at the parking lot on the other side of the road—it feels ... nice.

On a whim, I look up animal shelters in St. Louis. There are a lot, the closest one a short drive away, and while I sip my coffee, I read through the list. There are a lot of adoption centers, animal rescue, the Humane Society, and a few others.

Before I can finish reading, Lachie calls.

"Hey, where are you?"

"Walked to the cafe down the road."

He laughs into the phone. "You know we have a coffee machine here?"

"There is no way in hell I would have figured out how to work that thing."

He tells me to wait where I am, and it doesn't take long for him to pull up in his Jeep Wrangler. I wasn't paying much attention last night because I was so tired, but there's no way that matte-black paint and those huge wheels are standard.

"Hey," I say as I climb in and kiss him. His brown hair is still damp, and he's wearing a tank top that shows off his arms. I guess when you play on ice all the time, you don't feel the cold.

"Any sightseeing you want to do?"

"Take me to your favorite place."

"The arena?"

I should have guessed. "Your second favorite."

"Oh ..." He throws the car into drive. "The practice facility."

I'm about to request any place without ice, but he winks at me. Shithead. I'd call him out on it, but it's been too long since I've gotten to see him like this. Relaxed and happy. Even before he left Colorado, I could tell the upcoming flight was wearing on him.

It takes twenty minutes for Lachie to pull up in another parking lot.

"Where are we?"

"Forest Park." He closes his door and then rounds the Wrangler to open mine.

"Romantic of you," I say, climbing down, but Lachie only shrugs.

"Have to make sure you want to come back again."

He doesn't have to do romantic things for that. Him being in this city is all it takes, and I don't have the heart to tell him that flying out here at the drop of a hat isn't going to be something I can do regularly.

Before I can ask, Lachie takes my hand and tugs me after him.

"You sure this is okay?" I ask, pressing a kiss to the back of his hand. "This isn't another trick to lure me back here?"

His smile softens as we make our way along a path. "I said it was fine last night, and I meant it. Sure, my parents wanted to make some strategic coming-out moment, but Easton did his own thing, and I always planned to as well." His gorgeous gray eyes meet mine. "I'm not out because I've been having fun. I've been starting my career and wanting that to be the focus, and it has been. But I always knew that when I met someone, I wouldn't hide it, no matter how much people want me to. And a guy like you isn't someone who should be kept hidden."

I don't think he could have given me a more perfect answer. It helps shut up the guilt in the back of my mind that says he's only doing this to impress me. I don't want to date someone who isn't out, but that has to be Lachie's decision, not mine, and knowing that he always planned this, even before I was in his life, is a huge relief.

Our shoulders bump, and I realize I've moved closer. It feels right.

"I've always wanted to do this, you know?" he asks.

"What?"

"Walk along here, holding hands with my boyfriend. I was happy not being committed, don't get me wrong, but I knew that one day it would happen."

"That's the second time you've called me your boyfriend."

"If you tell me you're not, you'll break my heart." But there's a teasing note to his voice, and he squeezes my hand gently as he says it.

"Never. It's good to know we're on the same page." As much as it hurts, as much as I don't know how we move forward after this, he's what I want. "Question though. If the plan was always to move back to Colorado, why did you picture that you'd be walking with your boyfriend here?"

His head snaps to me, and it takes him a moment to process the question. "I ... I actually don't know."

My gut sinks at that answer. If Lachie really planned to move back to Colorado, wouldn't all his future plans take place there and not here?

"Hey." He tugs me out of my thoughts. "I know I'm stuck here for a while. That's all."

I stop us and set one hand on his jaw as I kiss him softly. "There's no pressure from me."

Lachie sighs, and it's like everything I've been trying not to think of pierces our happy bubble. "I have to take the contract."

"I know." As much as it hurts me to say, he doesn't have a choice if he wants to keep his career. "We'll work it out."

"Will we?"

I kiss him again, mostly because I'm not ready to consider the question, and also because he's here and I'm here and I want this.

"What comes next?" I ask.

"What do you mean?"

"You're walking along here, holding your boyfriend's hand ... what's next in your fantasy?"

He lets me pull us back from the edge. "I don't usually get much further than that because usually the group chat starts going off or an animal finds me or I'll reach that point of my run where my mind goes blank."

"Guess that means that we get to choose." I point up ahead. "What's that?"

"The museum. There's a zoo here too, and you can go paddleboating and—"

"Museum first. We have all day. Let's make the most of it."

Lachie and I are at the park until it gets dark, and then he takes me to a grungy little hole-in-the-wall restaurant for dinner, where we eat tacos and listen to the live music before going back to his place.

I have a happy buzz from the beer and being with him, and we exchange blowjobs before I pull him into my arms and he curls in around me.

"I'm so happy you're here," he says sleepily into my chest.

He falls asleep before I can answer him. I'm so happy, right here, but I think I made a mistake coming to St. Louis. I'd had a stray thought when I was drinking with his brothers that maybe I'd fallen for him, but now I know.

I'm so goddamn in love with him it hurts.

And saying goodbye tomorrow is going to be so much more painful than the last time.

CHAPTER THIRTY-NINE

LACHIE

I hate, hate, hate contract negotiations. Sure, this is the first one I've really had to deal with, but I'd been there for my brothers when they went through this. My entry-level contract was an easy one to sign, but this one ... I still haven't signed it, even though I told Sam I was going to.

Tonight is our first preseason game—an away game against Nashville—and even though I won't be able to hear the commentators covering it, I have no doubt they'll be talking about the deal I've turned down. How I'm holding out for more money because I'm an egotistical diva.

The money isn't an issue for me, so if we could negotiate less money for fewer years, I'm okay with that, but Mom and Dad seem to think that asking the team to only hold me until I can go elsewhere is disrespectful because it gives off the image that I'm not committed to the team.

I am. I've come to love St. Louis. But I need Sam like I need to breathe.

Does it matter if I sign a four-year or seven-year contract? Four years may as well be seven when it comes to Sam. Both are a really long-ass time to not be living in the same city.

It's easy to say "We'll make it work" without actually having a set plan, but at what point do I stop ignoring the obstacles and really think about how we're going to do this? Deep down, I already know the answer is that he's going to have to move here. Maybe not soon, but what kind of relationship is it if I only see my partner whenever he can take days off work to fly out to me? The team only plays Colorado three times this whole season, one in November and then twice in January, but only the one in November is in Colorado.

Sam also has his thing about money, so even if I were to offer to fly him out here on his days off, I know he's going to say no. We had a great time while he was here, but he also made it clear the next time I'll see him is when I'm back in Denver at the end of November.

I'm already back to my new cranky self, according to Hawke, and we've already established the world doesn't need that. It fucks with the ecosystem. A stray cat hissed at me the other day. I'm not saying that Sam is the reason animals have always been drawn to me, because it's been happening since I was a child, but maybe it really does have to do with my emotions. I've never had to deal with anything difficult in my life. I've always been a go-with-the-flow kind of guy, and even when Easton and Connor were freaking out about how we all come out or whatever, I never had those kinds of stressors. I can acknowledge the privilege in that, but it also means that I don't know how to handle this situation. Missing someone so much it hurts. Not getting what I want.

I was never the tantrum-throwing child, but I really want to throw myself on the ground and kick and scream. Not that it will do any good.

If I can put Sam to the back of my mind and focus only on hockey, I might be able to make it to November without being attacked by a pack of rabid raccoons. If I can't be with Sam, at least I still have hockey.

When it's time, I head to the lobby to get the team bus to the arena.

Being the first preseason game, I'm on the starting line, but I'm not expecting to get much ice time because the coaches will be playing a lot of our prospects to see who deserves a permanent spot on the team and who needs to go back to juniors or the AHL for more conditioning.

Still, I miss being out there, so I'm going to make the most of every minute I get. When I'm on the ice, I'm fast, agile, and ... a brat. It's seriously fun messing with the other team. Chirping them, totally legal trick shots that always find the net, drawing penalties, getting under their skin, I'm amazing at it all.

I'm hoping I'll be able to be a total chaos gremlin out there tonight. And when I skate up opposite Cody Bilson for the opening face-off, I don't waste any time.

"I'm gonna score on your boyfriend so hard tonight."

Bilson laughs. "You couldn't score your way out of a paper bag, little boy."

"We'll see about that."

The puck drops, and I dig it out while shoulder checking Bilson. This game is already fun.

Only, the forty-five-second shift on the ice isn't long enough for me. The short shifts are so we can go hard, then rest hard, but I have too much energy to rest. I know this game is to test our prospects, but how better to check their chemistry with the team if they're not putting me on their lines?

The game is fast, both teams getting shots on goal, but no one has gotten on the board yet.

Each time I get out there and my blades touch the ice, I feel alive, like I'm recharging and becoming my happy self. Yet, no matter how many times I shoot at the net, Miles Olsen is there to stop me. Or the crossbar is.

I love playing hockey, that's true, but I love scoring and winning more, so when the seconds tick down on the first period and I get a breakaway, I know this is the moment. I'm going to get the first goal of the night. But right as I'm about to send a beautiful shot through Miles's five hole, someone trips me from behind.

I lose my balance, hit the ice, and go sliding all the way into Miles. He lands on top of me, the net goes flying, and even though I missed getting a goal, I'm strangely excited about the shitstorm that's about to happen.

Even though it was one of their guys who tripped me, the fact that I took down their goalie makes me enemy number one.

As suspected, when Miles helps me get back on my skates, his teammate Stoll has already dropped his gloves.

It's cute he thinks any of my team would let me get in a fight—I'm St. Louis's star player and can't risk injury with frivolous fights—but I jump scare him with a fake punch anyway, just to rile him up more.

Hawke swoops in and takes Stoll out, but then Bilson jumps on Hawke. I see Nashville's biggest D-man coming right for me, so I skate behind Miles and try to use him as a human shield.

Before too long, both teams are in an all-out brawl. When Hawke hits the ice, though, and Stoll punches him repeatedly while he's down because the officials are too busy trying to break up other fights, I can't keep standing by. I launch myself toward the scrum but barely make it a few feet before I'm tugged backward as Miles grabs my jersey with his glove and pulls me away like a mother kitten grabbing her young by the scruff.

"Nope. Your brothers will kill me if I let you jump in there."

I glance at him over my shoulder. "Why you ruining my fun?"

"Why are you determined to get punched in the face tonight?"

"Because it's fun. Duh."

"Right. And it has nothing to do with that guy you were fawning all over at the summer house."

"Don't bring him into this. I'm a chaos gremlin. And look at all the chaos. Isn't it beautiful?"

"Yeah. You know what else is beautiful? Not being in denial. You should try it sometime."

"If all my teammates weren't getting misconducts, I'd punch you and keep this glorious chaos going."

"I get a feeling the only chaos going on with you is your mental health." Miles and his *bromotions*. "Are you okay?"

Not a question I can deal with right now. "Nope. But I'm hilarious. That's something."

CHAPTER FORTY

SAM

The phone rings, and I hope I've left it late enough for him to be showered and out of there by now. That game was ... well, from the one we watched together, I wasn't prepared for an all-out brawl to take place.

Lachie looked fine after that, but I still want to call him to make sure.

"Hey," his warm voice comes down the line, and immediately, I feel better.

"First question," I say, launching straight into it. "When the commentators said you were being double-teamed, were they talking about when those two guys slammed you against those board things, or do they have insight into your personal life, and that's the way I'm going to find out you're sleeping around?"

I can hear the grin in his voice. "Sports commentary is so homoerotic, and everyone knows they do it on purpose."

"Okay, good. Second thing: Are you hurt?"

"It's hockey—I'm always hurt. But if you mean the fight, I'm fine. Miles wouldn't let me play."

Miles might be my new best friend. "As your boyfriend, it's my duty to tell you not to fight ..."

"But?"

"But as a man with a pulse, that was hot as fuck."

Lachie's laugh is exactly what I need to hear. "Very caveman of you."

"I'm sure I'm supposed to be more evolved than that ... but I'm just not." I cover my face with my hand, wondering what Lachie's turned me into.

"Good. Never evolve. I love this side of you."

Angie's ears perk up at Lachie's voice, and she whines at my side.

"Put her on," he says, and the notification comes through to switch to video call.

I accept and hold the phone down to her. She immediately jumps up, tail wagging, bounding all over the cushion, and as Lachie talks to her, she *rowr, rowr, rowrs* back.

"Huh," he says when I pull the phone back. "She's gotten bigger than I realized."

I'm determined for this conversation not to go there tonight. "Puppies grow fast."

"Yeah ..."

It's then I notice his background. "Are you out?"

"It's a Queer Collective thing. Whenever we play each other, we have to catch up afterward."

"That's ... really nice." I'm glad Lachie has that kind of support when he's mentioned that hockey isn't the most queer-friendly place. Even if it means interrupting my plans for phone sex tonight. That can wait. "I'll let you go so you can get back to them."

For a second, he looks torn, and it's nice to know he wants to hang on to this conversation as much as I do.

"It's okay." I smile so he knows I mean it. "Call me tomorrow?"

"We fly out early, so it'll be once I'm back home."

"That's fine with me."

I kiss the screen at the same time he does, and then we hang up. Angelica slumps at my side, head between her paws, and I lean over to cuddle her, pressing my face into her fur. "Me too, Angel. Me too."

A long-distance relationship is surprisingly easy.

All I have to do is take Angie for two runs a day, go to the gym with Ethan, work, meal prep, film more content, tend to injured wildlife, watch every single goddamn hockey game Lachie plays, and then by the time we chat, I'm usually too tired to stay awake after our call, so I crash before the pain can kick in.

My videos are doing well. Better than I expected them to, and they're even mostly finding the right audience, which is exactly what I was hoping for. I underestimated how much time they'd take up, but I'm thankful for it now.

It's something to fill my time, and I need it.

I really think November will go faster than October, but it's more of the same.

Waiting all day for the phone call, text message conversations that start and stop depending on what we have going on. I go out with Connor, Easton, and Parker a few more times, and Ethan comes with us when he gets over his "athletes are all narcissists" monologue, "and I should know, because I am one."

I lie on my bed, breathing through my daily orgasm, cum pooling on my abs as Lachie jerks off on-screen, while he fucks himself with a dildo. It doesn't take him long to get there, and his husky *Sammy* makes me wish I'd let him come first.

He's panting, hair sweaty, and I can't wait until he's back and I can push that hair from his forehead and kiss it.

"Only three more days," he reminds himself.

"I'm so glad you're here for the entire weekend, because I plan to do very filthy things to that body for the entire time I have it."

"Hold that thought because other than my game, we do have one other plan we have to fit in."

"Other than orgasms?" I whine.

"Unfortunately, other than orgasms." He cleans himself up, while I wait for him to let me in on whatever it is. "My parents have organized a family dinner. Them, my brothers and their partners, and me."

Well, there go a few more hours I won't get to see him. Coming home to Colorado, it's always going to be like that though. I'm not the only one who misses him. "Of course. That makes sense that—"

"Can I ask them to book for one more?"

I try to meet his eyes through the screen, but he's also doing the same, which means we're never actually making eye contact. "Are you sure about that?"

"Yes. I wanted to show you off last time, but I know why I couldn't. We're together now, so ..."

So it makes sense for me to meet his parents. Technically, we've been dating for months at this point, and after that long a relationship, I'd agree it's time. But something's holding me back, and I know it's the same for him, or he would have just asked me to come instead of getting my permission to *book for one more*. "What night?"

"Friday. Right after I land."

"Yeah. I'll be there."

"You don't sound sure."

I try to give him a look that's everything I'm feeling, but again, it doesn't work through the phone. "I want to meet them. I want to have these moments with you. I ... fuck, I want to be with you so much, I'm doing the long-distance thing. But are you *actually* happy?"

"Yes." He hurries to sit up, getting closer to the screen. "You're not?"

"Lachie, you make me happier than every single person I've ever met." But I can't lie to him. "You also make me the saddest as well."

His gaze drops away. "I know. I'm sorry. We just have to ... to ..."

Make it through seven years? Actually, eight because he still has this season to finish. Eight years of this. I told myself I'd do everything to make it happen, and I still believe that. "Tell them I'm coming."

He smiles, but it's not a full one. Not the kind that lights him up inside. I have to get us back on track.

"Only three more days," I repeat, going back to the hopeful place the conversation started. "It sucks I can't bring Angie to the game."

"Bring her to the warm-up skate. I'll tell Parker you're coming, and he or Connor could meet you outside so you don't have any issues with security, and—"

"Okay, okay." I actually manage a real laugh, because it's so easy to be caught up in the excitement of his visit, and I know Angelica is going to go absolutely berserk when she sees him. I have to film that. "Send me a message with the times you'll be at hockey ... *stuff*, and when the dinner is, and I'll plan our time between then."

"Perfect."

"Ethan's already made plans to clear out for the weekend, so you can stay here with me." I run my hand back through my hair as I settle deeper into my pillows. "Tomorrow afternoon, we're cooking up a whole lot of protein and broccoli so I can feed you while we're here."

"And pasta?"

"Bought extra packets when I was out yesterday."

He sighs happily, and these are the moments that make all the other shit worth it. "I have the most romantic boyfriend ever."

"I'm going to use every second you're here to spoil you."

"I need to come home more often."

"We can both agree to that." And before the longing kicks in, I keep the conversation moving. "Did you sign the contract yet?"

"Nope."

"What are you waiting for?"

"I ..." He huffs. "Nothing. I'm waiting for nothing. I keep hoping the solution is going to fall into our laps and ..."

"Sign it," I say firmly. Delaying it doesn't make sense, because solution or not, he's not leaving St. Louis. We both know it, and leaving that door open for hope isn't helping. "Whatever we work out, we'll do while you're there."

"I'll talk to my parents about it once I'm home." He yawns loudly. "I think I've gone back to them with all the stupid little negotiations I can think of. I'm shocked Coach hasn't benched me yet to get me to pull my head out of my ass."

Especially considering what I've been seeing online. It's not something I've been looking for, but I guess it's true what they say about our phones listening to us. Since watching hockey—even under Lachie's account—my social media is filled with animals and hockey content. It's not the worst thing, but whenever something about the St. Louis team is posted, there are inevitable comments about Lachie looking elsewhere. Fans of other teams taunting that the golden boy won't be there much longer. That he's after a Cup team … It depresses me that I understand so much of it now, but I can't deny hockey is an interesting—and toxic—environment.

I can only imagine the comments when Lachie officially comes out.

He yawns again, louder this time.

"Go to sleep," I tell him. "I need to shower, then I'm going to do the same."

"Two more days tomorrow." We share a smile, and this time, it finally feels like we're connecting. "I'm going to kiss the fuck out of you in that airport. The second I reach you."

"I'd be disappointed if you didn't."

CHAPTER FORTY-ONE

LACHIE

I'm so eager to fulfill my promise of kissing Sam the second I see him that I don't even look around as I approach him in the arrivals hall. I flew ahead of the rest of the team on a commercial flight so I get more time with family and Sam. The sight of his face has me so lightheaded as I reach him that I forget to breathe. It's not until Sam places his hands on my chest and gently pushes me back that I notice said family is here.

"Mom. Dad." Plus my brothers.

"Your whole family came," Sam says, trying to be upbeat, but I can tell by his widened eyes and manic smile that he's freaking out.

I put my hands on his shoulders and lean in and kiss his cheek. When my mouth is near his ear, I whisper, "Breathe." He's so telling me how this eventuated later. Then I pull away and do what I do best: put all the attention on myself. "What's with the welcoming party? I know you all miss me and I'm the only thing that holds this entire family together, but I thought we were meeting at the restaurant." You know, after I've had a chance to blow my boyfriend on the drive there.

"We wanted to be here when you got in," Mom says. "We don't like having you across the country."

Then why aren't you working on a contract that could bring me home? I want to say. I don't. I'm smarter than that. It's got nothing to do with Mom and Dad not doing their job and everything to do with how NHL contracts work.

"It's not exactly fun for me either," I say and wrap my arm around Sam. "Are we going straight to dinner from here? I'm starving."

"You guys go on ahead," Easton says. "There's still half an hour before Knox's plane lands, so we'll meet you there."

"He coming home from a game?" I ask.

East nods. "I told everyone Sam and I could handle picking both of you up, but as usual, no one listens to the middle child."

I laugh, but it's not really funny. When it comes to my family, we really do fit the quintessential three-child home. Connor, the eldest, responsible protector with the weight of responsibility on his shoulders that he sometimes takes way too far. Easton, the one who has ideas, dreams, and desires that are ignored until he loses it and punches someone—in his case, it was Connor. And then there's me. Everything comes easily to me, and with my parents having been through drama with the older two, the leash they put me on is longer.

Though turning up to the airport is new for them, and I get the impression their hold on my leash is tightening with each day the contract negotiations go on.

The five of us get into Connor's car, with Dad getting in the back seat with Sam and me. While I'd like to put my boyfriend in the middle seat because he's smaller than me—not much but still smaller—I take one for the team and wedge myself between them.

"It would've been a lot more comfortable if we'd met at the restaurant," I say.

Sam squeezes my hand and gives me a *drop it* look. Okay, I really need the story of how we're all crammed into this car.

"Nonsense," Mom says from the passenger seat. "We wanted to be here for our baby, so we are."

"Uh ... huh."

After the longest and most awkward drive in history, we get to the restaurant we always go to as a family. It's an old-timey steak house with private rooms where the owners are season ticket holders and always make a big deal when we eat here.

Connor's partner, Parker, is already in our private room when we're led to our table, and I beeline over to him, possibly even faster than Connor does, so I can get the chance to talk his ear off about playing for Colorado as soon as possible.

With there being eight of us, they've set up a square table, so while I sit next to Parker on the corner with Connor on his other side, Mom and Dad sit opposite me and Sam. That's not ideal because I know Sam feels intimidated, but at least he'll be able to sit next to Knox or Easton. That's probably the best-case scenario.

I'm starting to think I shouldn't have invited Sam, but the bottom line is, I am all in with him. It feels right, and I've never been so head over heels for someone before.

They're going to have to get used to the fact that I have a boyfriend, and I don't care who knows it. They don't even know Sam.

I tell myself to calm my thoughts and not to get ahead of them when I don't know for sure that's what this ambush was about, but my gut rarely lies to me, and it's screaming that something's brewing.

Our server takes Parker's and Sam's drink orders, already knowing what to bring the rest of us, including drinks for Knox and Easton for when they arrive. While we wait for them, I fill Sam's and my water glasses with the water on the table.

Parker must sense the same weird energy I do, because he says, "How was the drive over here?"

"Good," I squeak. "Great, even. Tell me, how's that cap budgeting going?"

His gaze flicks to my parents and then back to me. "I know how much you want it, and trust me, I want to bring the Kiki brother publicity back to Colorado, but because we replaced Connor with Woodrow, we're at the cap ceiling. We can't beat the offer St. Louis gave you, and even if we could, they have the space to match."

He's already told me all this, but I guess I'm still holding out for a miracle.

"You could always trade the highest-paid forwards. You only need Easton and me anyway. We can be on the first, second, and third lines. Be out there for forty minutes a game."

"Can you even do that?" Sam asks.

I snort. "No. We would die. But it was worth the suggestion." I put my hand on top of his on the table.

"Well ..." Mom cuts in. "I was going to wait until everyone was here to tell you the good news, but now's as good a time as any. St. Louis came back to us with another deal."

"Four years?" I ask.

"Close. Five. The downside is it's for forty million."

Five years. Including this season, that's ... I may as well sign the seven and use the extra thirty million to buy Sam his own animal rescue in St. Louis. Not that I'd get that money up front—it's split unevenly over each year of the contract, but it's not the worst idea I've ever had.

The easiest solution here is to have Sam move to St. Louis, but how can I force that on him? How can I pressure him to do that? It has to come from him.

"You haven't said anything," Mom says as our server returns with our drinks.

The air crackles with awkward tension while he works his way around the table.

"This is the best offer you're going to get. In terms of years, anyway."

"And," Parker cuts in, "we'll have some players finishing out their long-term deals by then. We'd have the budget to sign you or even get you on trade your final year of your contract."

"But we won't be going into that in too much detail here," Mom says. "You know, we don't want rumors of tampering."

I shrug. "Come on, it's not like it's a secret I want to play with Easton. It's all everyone has talked about since I was drafted. If I become an unrestricted free agent and don't sign with Colorado, people will be shocked. Whoever claims tampering was always going to anyway."

"Still," Mom says. "We don't want to actually be guilty of it. So we're going to focus on the contract in front of us."

With the timing lining up with Colorado regaining cap space, the five-year deal is promising. Yes, it's a lot less money, but I don't need to be the highest-paid player in the league—not that ten million a year is anywhere near the highest paid. My point is, I'm lucky enough that the money doesn't need to factor into my decision.

"The five does sound like a better deal," I say.

"Are you crazy?" Sam pulls his hand out from under mine. "Take the seven."

I turn to him. "Huh?"

"Thirty million dollars for an extra two years, and you're going to turn it down? For what? To come home earlier? I know you say that you're hesitating because you really want to play for Denver, but you've also said from the beginning that it was always a future plan. The only difference between then and now is me. Is our relationship. And if I cost you thirty million dollars, I will never forgive myself."

I shake my head. "I'm not losing that money. That money wasn't mine to begin with. I'd rather sign a shorter deal for less money than tie myself to a place you …" I can't finish that sentence because I haven't even asked him to move to St. Louis yet.

"A place I what?"

"You might not like spending time in. And I want you to be there with me as much as you possibly can. I want you to love it so that one day, you'll consider moving there. With me."

"Moving?" Mom says. "That's all a little … soon for you two, isn't it?"

And there it is. The whole reason I think they ambushed Sam tonight. My gut never lies.

"It's not like I'm faking an injury and quitting completely to be with him." I turn my attention to Connor.

"Don't bring me into this," he complains.

"That was a different situation," Mom says. "You're only twenty-one."

"What does age have anything to do with it?"

"You haven't had a chance to live. To explore."

Connor smothers a cough. "Oh, you sweet, delusional woman."

Okay, now I'm glaring at Connor.

Mom waves him off. "I know he's had his fun as much as I like living in denial about it, but this is your first actual relationship. It's been, what, one summer and two months of long distance? This isn't a relationship you rearrange your life for."

Somewhere in our conversation that's getting heated by the second, Knox and Easton appear.

They take their seats, and Easton leans forward. "So ... what're we talking about?"

Bullshit. Absolutely bullshit. That's what we're talking about.

CHAPTER FORTY-TWO

SAM

A stale silence answers Easton.

This isn't the relationship you rearrange your life for.

Then why the fuck does it feel like it is?

When we're apart, it's so easy to tell myself it won't work. That I want him, but it's never going to last, and I think I do that because it stops me from facing the truth. I can't let this relationship go.

Sitting here, holding his hand, close enough that I can kiss and touch him all I want, that I can just be in his presence, *this* is what I want.

And knowing that Lachie is still thinking long term, still making plans for that perfect one-day moment where we've succeeded.

I can't let him down.

Under the heavy weight of his parents' stares, I lift the hand I'm holding to my lips and kiss the back of it.

It pulls Lachie's attention to me. Those clear gray eyes meet mine, and his lips twitch upward in the corners.

"I love St. Louis," I tell him. "I already have a list of all the things we can do when I visit again."

"You do?"

"You're severely underestimating the lengths I've gone to to keep myself busy while you've been away."

This time, he leans in and kisses me, right on the lips, in front of his whole family. I'm still nervous and borderline afraid of his parents, but I'm not going to shy away this time. They don't think this is real? Fuck them. The only people who matter in this relationship are me and him.

Yes, Lachie is young. And thinking back to when I was twenty-one, this kind of commitment and maturity would have scared me off. Hell, at twenty-seven, it's still daunting to think about rearranging my whole life for one man. But Lachie is the most confident and sure-of-himself person I've ever met. He knows what he wants, and I do too. We both want a chance to make this work.

I pull back before Lachie can push the kiss deeper, which I can tell he's about to do. As much as I've craved reconnecting with him, that's going to have to wait.

My hands find his jaw, slightly rough under my palms, and I pull back enough that I can see him properly.

"Take the deal you want to take. The one that makes sense for you. There's no point listening to me or your parents or your team if it's going to end up with you miserable. We've all told you our thoughts, and we'll support whatever you decide."

He stares at me for a moment, like he's trying to figure something out. "Why do you want me to take the seven years?"

"Five years ... seven years ... they're both a stupidly long amount of time, so it doesn't make a difference to me. But you want to be one of the best. You love hockey. A seven-year contract means you're locked in, and you have your dreams guaranteed. Not to mention the thirty *million* dollars—that is no small amount of money to walk away from."

"He's right," Connor interrupts, and I can't believe he's the one to back me up. "Ask me how I know."

"Bit of a different situation when your boyfriend is a billionaire." Easton tears into a piece of bread.

"It doesn't mean I don't want to make money of my own."

"Speaking of," their mom cuts in. "What do you do, Sam?"

I think everyone at the table can hear her real question. *What do you earn, and are you only with my son for the money?* "I manage an animal shelter."

"Like a vet?"

Ouch. "No ... like a manager."

"He also posts animal education videos," Parker pipes up. Connor immediately side-eyes him while Parker struggles to keep a straight face. "You should watch the videos, Kate. I think you'd enjoy them."

"Hopefully not the same way you do," Easton points out under his breath.

Then his boyfriend speaks up. "Yeah, I've seen those too. Considering ninety percent of them are shirtless, tell the truth. You're doing it as a thirst trap, aren't you?"

It's a struggle not to laugh. "I'm doing it for the *animals*. Unfortunately, I've found that the more skin I have showing, the more the video is pushed out to people who need to see it." And who don't need to see it. Thankfully, there have only been a few comments I've needed to delete that were wildly inappropriate.

"Thirst traps?" Kate repeats, sounding close to passing out. "This isn't an OnlyFans situation, is it?"

"No. Completely PG."

Lachie stretches his arm along the back of my chair with a grin. "And now *everyone* knows why I was willing to turn down seventy million dollars. You don't say no to a body like that."

"*Lachlan*," his dad says sternly.

"It's a joke."

"Not a funny one."

I slip my hand in front of my mouth and mutter, "*I* thought it was funny."

The longer dinner goes on, the harder it is to focus on anything but Lachie next to me. I think I like his family? His brothers and their boyfriends, at least, are warming to me, and while his parents don't manage anything rude again, it doesn't stop the comments about him being young and focusing on his career.

To their credit, they're protective of him, and they're trying to steer him toward the logical choice. If I were objective in this situation, I wouldn't know why he was still thinking about it. But it's hard to be logical when the distance between us hurts so damn much.

It seems to take forever for Lachie and his brothers to finish eating, and I'm so fucking glad I'm not the one picking up the bill for tonight, because goddamn hockey players can eat.

It's not surprising they're paid the big bucks—they need it to afford their groceries.

I'm ready to jump out of my seat the second the bill is paid, and Lachie obviously has the same idea.

"Thanks for dinner," he says, standing and giving me the *get up now* eyes. "We're going to head out."

"You don't want a ride?" Kate asks.

Easton snorts. "Mom, you do not want to witness whatever they're about to do on a back seat."

Kill me now.

She gives Easton a disappointed look before turning a smile on me. "It was nice to meet you."

I can see why she's so good at her job. She can pull off a blatant lie and almost make me believe it. I lie right back and shake his dad's hand, then Lachie has a grip on my arm and is pulling me toward the exit.

"Get me home," he whines.

Damn, it feels good to hear him say that.

It's a torturously long wait for the car that's a few minutes away, and the whole time we're huddled up against the side of the restaurant, I can't help kissing my way along his throat. He can't stop gripping my ass or sliding his hands under my shirt.

"Fuck, I want to kiss you," he complains.

The problem with that is that when the kissing starts, my brain stops. Until I'm back home, I can't afford for that to happen.

Mostly because we won't make it back home.

I'm determined to be good in the back of our ride, but that goes out the window the second Lachie's hand slides over my thigh and finds my straining cock. I'm so goddamn hard, and him squeezing me through my pants feels incredible.

Before he can let go again, I grab his hand and hold it in place, trying to stay as still as possible while I grind up into his grip. I can feel him watching me, and I refuse to meet his eye because the second I do, I'll break down into laughter.

The building tension needs a release somehow, and even I know how ridiculous it is that I'm dry humping his hand in the back seat of a stranger's car.

He leans in, lips pressing against my ear. "You're making me so horny doing that."

My cock throbs, and I know I need to throw his hand off me, but I only press down harder.

With his game tomorrow, we really need sleep tonight, which means we're only going to get one shot at an orgasm, and I'm not going to be doing it in my pants.

No matter how much he turns me on.

It takes forever to get home, and I barely manage a thank-you to the driver before I'm pulling Lachie away from the car. I can't get inside fast enough.

All this lingering need that's been building since the last time I saw him is ready to explode out of me, and the second we're inside, front door kicked closed behind us, I'm on him, but he pulls back. "Wait, where's Angelica?"

"In her crate in the laundry, where she's going to stay until I'm done with you."

"Mm, I love someone who thinks ahead."

How he can be so familiar after all this time is a mystery to me, but as our mouths meet, hands tearing at whatever clothes we can reach, this part of my chest settles. It's like stepping inside after a freezing cold day. Like climbing into bed when you're exhausted to your bones. Lachie feels ... he feels like home.

I sigh into the kiss as all the tension of our time apart leaves me.

"Missed you," he murmurs into the kiss as we separate long enough to get our shirts off. I refuse to answer him. We're not talking about distance or longing or any of the realities getting to us.

Right now, we get to be together.

It happens too little to do anything else but enjoy it.

I pull him back against me, loving the feel of our torsos pressed together as we breathe into each other's mouths.

"How do you want me?" he asks.

It's a dangerous question because I almost say *forever*, but I catch myself in time.

"Bed," I tell him. "I've been thinking about you under me ever since you left."

He leads the way, walking backward, kisses running down my neck. I'm barely able to keep it together when he does that, and he knows it. It's one of my many, many weaknesses when it comes to him.

Lachie strips out of his remaining clothes while he climbs onto my bed, and I round the mattress to grab the lube, eyes glued to his body. All those hard lines, his long legs, the naked confidence. I've missed his slutty necklace, and those sexy studs in his ears, and the way his gray eyes go stormy when he's turned on.

"What are you thinking?" he asks, tucking his hands behind his head.

"That it's probably lucky I only have access to this body in limited doses, or you'd never make it out of bed to play hockey again."

He crooks a finger at me.

I toss the lube beside him, and while I finish stripping off, he holds my eye contact as he reaches between his legs and then ... pulls a long, silicone plug out of his ass.

My jaw actually drops. "Where did that come from?"

"If you need to ask, you're probably not ready to be having sex yet."

He's such a smartass. I climb up the bed until I'm hovering over the top of him, and he tosses the plug aside. "Were you wearing that all through dinner?"

"You're not the only one who thought ahead. I learned from when you visited that I do not have the patience for prep after not seeing you for so long."

"When the hell did you put it in there?"

He kisses along my jaw again. "Do you want a play-by-play, or are you going to fuck me already? All I'm going to say is it's lucky I chose the silicone one and not the one that would have had airport security on alert."

My eyes roll back as a shiver runs down my spine. Definitely the second option. But fuck, knowing he was ready for me all night has my cock so hard, I'm worried I'll blow as soon as I'm inside him. Not that it won't be good for me, but I'd love to give him a fuck worth waiting for.

"Since you're all about taking matters into your own hands, don't stop now. Lube up my cock for you."

His eagerness to grab the lube does nothing to hide how much he wants this. Between that, his hard cock resting on his abs, and the need deep in his eyes, he's showing me how much he wants me.

No games or trying to play it off.

Just us.

I catch his mouth in another kiss, lingering against his lips before I open my mouth and deepen it. Lachie's callused fingers rub lube over my needy dick, and I have to keep very purposely still to stop from thrusting into his grip.

"That plug was a bit smaller than me," I point out between kisses. "Do you need to prep more?"

"No. I want you to stretch me as you push inside. Make me feel it."

My eyes fall closed, forehead meeting his as I reach down and position myself at his entrance. His hole is still well lubricated, and it only takes gentle pressure for me to slip inside.

He's so tight as he embraces my cock, body slowly giving in as I press forward, careful enough not to hurt him, but insistent enough for him to know how much I need this.

It's not even completely about the sex when it comes to Lachie. I think I knew from that very first blowjob how differently we fit together. It was explosively hot, but it took the need I felt for him and twisted it into something unrecognizable. That's never happened before. I've never had a hookup, or even a partner, who I craved so instantly right after I got what I wanted.

Maybe it's because we were doomed from the start. Maybe that's why everything is so fast and consuming.

All I know is that if this is doomed, I'm glad I got to experience it.

"Sammy ..." he breathes as I stretch him open around me. It feels incredible to me, but he's losing some of his hardness, so I reach for his dick to make sure this is just as good for him.

"You okay?"

"Sorry ... got in my head for a second."

"It doesn't hurt?"

"Not ..." His eyes suddenly meet mine. "Not *that*."

He doesn't need to say more. If there's anything I've learned from our time apart, it's that physical pain isn't the hardest thing to get through. "Out of your head," I say, partially for him and partially to remind myself as well. "I'm here, Princess."

Lachie wraps his arms around my neck and pulls my lips to his again.

We don't talk again after that.

I sink into the high of kissing him, keeping my thrusts slow and deep as I jerk him with the same steady rhythm. He's completely surrounding me, and it almost feels like too much after so long with nothing that I'm scared I'm overindulging. Scared that nothing will ever make me feel the way Lachie does when he's with me.

The feel of his warm skin.

His stuttered sighs hitting my mouth.

His sharp cologne mixed with his scent. It's a smell I want to drown myself in.

By the end of the weekend, I want my bed smothered in it.

Lachie's hands map patterns into my back, while I memorize the shape of his cock in my hand. He's leaking, and it's so hot, I'm struggling to stop from pounding my way to the end. If this is all we have time for tonight, I'm making the best of it.

To give myself a second to recover, I pull out of him and squeeze his hip. "On your side."

He rolls over without complaint as I lie behind him and push back inside.

It's taking all my effort to keep things going. Every time I'm worried I'll come, I pull out and make him change positions. I fuck him doggy next, then up against my door, then he rides me on my desk chair, and when that gets too much, I pull out and replace my cock with my fingers while I get back in control.

Every time he begs me, those sinful "*Please, Sammy. Fuck, please*" filling my quiet bedroom, I respond with a "Not yet" and slow myself down even more.

I taste his muscles, bite his nipples, and tug on that *fucking* necklace until Lachie is putty under me. We're both panting, I'm sweating from how much control it's taking to hold back, and my brain has completely checked out as I sink into the lust haze taking over.

"I need it," he says, rocking back on my fingers harder than before. "Need to feel you come inside me."

My teeth sink into his shoulder because those words almost make me spill. "Back on the bed."

He hurries to do just that, and I have to tug on my balls as I approach him. His hole is all shiny and stretched, and as I kneel between his knees and push back inside, I can't help the groan that leaves me.

"Stop holding back," he warns, blunt nails digging into my ass cheeks.

"Way ahead of you."

I fuck him like we've both been waiting for. Not only tonight, but for too long. Between Lachie's moans, the bed bouncing off the wall, my grunts, and our bodies slapping together, we're long past being quiet. My thrusts are fast and messy and desperate, and I'm slipping further into the pull where it's too late to pull back.

Lachie reaches between us to jerk off, one hand still planted on my ass, while mine bunch fists into the sheets as I thrust as fast as I can. A line of sweat runs down my back, the mattress is askew, and when I glance down at Lachie's face, it's too much.

He's blissed-out, puffy lips parted, and as I watch, his head tilts back into my pillow, and he gasps as he comes.

The way his ass clamps around my cock is all it takes to get me there. I shudder as I empty inside him, all these months of longing and need finally being fulfilled. It's like half of me is missing while he's gone, and having him back, in my arms, makes everything feel better.

I pull him closer and bury my face in his neck. "I've missed you so much."

"I know." His breath is so heavy, I feel the weight of it under me. "I think I'm going to take the seven."

It's what he should do. It's what I told him to do.

But it doesn't stop the panic spearing through me anyway.

When I pull back though, I'm smiling. I said I'd support him with anything, and this is anything.

"Okay." I brush his sweaty hair back from his forehead, and looking at him opens up all these feelings I've never had before. Not with anyone. It's not only his face either, but like I'm seeing all of him. The whole person that I've fallen for. He's so beautiful it hurts, and it's impossible to think that in a few days he'll be gone again.

I still have no answers for how we're going to last, but we have to.

We *have* to.

CHAPTER FORTY-THREE

LACHIE

For the whole game against Denver, I feel like I'm playing for the wrong side. I'm on the ice with my brother, but it's unnatural to be facing off with him.

I've been here before. This isn't my first game against Easton; my rookie year, I played against both of my brothers. But this is different. I wanted to beat them then to prove I'm the better player, the faster brother, the one with all the talent. Now, I just want to be on their team. Brothers and teammates.

Of course, that doesn't stop me from showing off and kicking Denver's ass. Not only because it's in my competitive nature but because I know Sam is currently in the owner's box with Connor and Parker, watching me. It's his first live NHL game, and I've been telling him for months that watching hockey in person has a completely different feel than watching it on TV.

He didn't believe me. I hope he's up there eating his words. Especially when I make a pass to Latrell and force Flores out of position, only for Latrell to pass right back to me when I'm next to the net, and it's the easiest shot I've had to make all season. Granted, the season is still young, but it was one of those plays that is seamless. I open my arms wide for teammate hugs as I glide backward into the boards, and in the next second, I'm swallowed by all four of them.

Still, I dream of a day when I can do that in this barn and have the horns blaze and the crowd go wild. It's so anticlimactic scoring at an away game.

Easton follows my goal up with one of his own, saluting me as he skates by me on the bench.

I flip him off—under my glove, of course—and Hawke taps my helmet from behind me.

"You know he can't see that, right?"

"Yeah, but it makes me feel better."

"You'll have to get back out there and score again to show him who's the best Kiki."

"Oh, I plan to."

And even though it's hard won and takes me to the third period to do it, I do get that second goal, along with an assist in the second period.

When we take the win 3-1, I can't help skating by Easton before he can run down the tunnel. "Now, I'm not great at math, but by my count, that's three points to me and ... how many points does one measly goal get again?"

"You're a little shit," he mumbles before turning to head to his locker room, but at the last second, he looks over his shoulder at me. "Safe flight."

As easy as that, my good mood from the win crashes because we're immediately flying back to St. Louis for another game tomorrow night. Why couldn't the NHL schedule a longer stopover here in Colorado for me? Don't they know they should make decisions about all thirty-two teams around my love life?

We're heading right to the airport from the arena, so I rush through dressing down and showering so I can get out of the locker room before the rest of my team, where I told Sam to come meet me. Parker said he'd bring him down and put us in one of the press rooms that aren't being used.

We won't have a lot of time, and the few short days I've been here haven't been nearly enough to get my Sam fix. Or Angelica fix. I'm worried she's starting to not remember me already. I missed so many of her imprinting weeks, and while she's not even my dog—she's Sam's—I don't want her to forget me. Fuck, I want to see them both every single day, and the thought of having to say goodbye to Sam again hurts. We've only been doing this long-distance thing for a short time, and I already hate it.

It makes me question whether we can truly make this work, but I'm going to try, if for nothing else than to prove my parents wrong. I'm not too young for this relationship. Is Sam my forever person? I really hope so because I love him so damn much, I can't imagine us not working out. Or I don't want to imagine. The reality of it is already too close to a possibility.

Parker meets me in the hallway and opens the door to the empty press room. No, not empty. My man is standing there, and beside him is Angelica … Fuck, I'm getting teary at the sight of both of them because I don't want to go.

"You brought Angelica?"

"She was very well-behaved watching her first hockey game. It was so cute. Parker got her these noise-canceling headphones." He takes out his phone, and I close the gap between us to look at the photo on his screen.

"Can you please send that to me?"

"Already did. I'm guessing you didn't have the chance to check your phone yet."

"Nope. It would have held me up from getting to you." I bend down to give Angelica some face scritches. Out of nowhere, the sudden urge to blurt, "What if I quit?" takes over. And once it's out there, I can't take it back. It's not fair of me to say things like that because while the idea of it is nice, actually giving up hockey? I could never, and I don't want him to think it's possible.

But he knows me better than I thought because he smiles. "You won't."

I stand. "You're right. What if I quit for this one game and stay here instead?"

"Your team won't allow it."

"Stop using logic on me." I take him in my arms, but Angelica rubs against my leg and yips. I laugh as I pick her up to join in on the hug. Holding them makes my chest ache.

"I miss you already. Do you get time off around Christmas?"

That's so long away. "I get three days, but I have a game the day after, so traveling for it isn't ideal."

"Maybe I can come to you. Though I usually do my Christmases with Ethan because he doesn't have family. We're each other's family."

"Ethan could come too?"

"Who will look after Angelica?"

"Parker and Connor?" I croak, but I already know what he's going to say.

"When Angie met Conishkin, she tried to eat him."

Yup. That. Knox and Easton are out because their schedules are insane too. "Danika? The shelter?" The desperation in my voice is loud now.

"Hey," he soothes. "We'll figure something out. Maybe I'll spend the next month training her to the point I'd feel comfortable bringing her on the plane with me."

"Yes. Do that. Please do that. But also, a month?" My voice strains. "That's so fucking long."

"We'll figure it out."

We keep saying that, but neither one of us is actually saying how. We're not even letting ourselves ask it because if we think too deeply about this, we know long distance isn't going to work. I want to ask Sam to move for me, but how can I do that when it's a lot of pressure to put on him. Asking will lead to an ultimatum, and that will lead to resentment. If I wait for him to bring it up, I could be waiting for years.

I don't want to admit that my parents are right, but they do have a point. Damn them.

I put my forehead against his, and Angelica struggles in my arms.

My heart thunders in my chest. This moment will be over way too soon because I need to get out to the team bus. We're running out of time. I'm torn between asking him to move to St. Louis with me and continuing in our denial about us being able to magically make it work with no real plan other than "See you when I see you." My voice breaks.

I can't do it. I can't walk away tonight without at least throwing the idea out there. "I know you have a life here. A life you love. You have Ethan and the shelter, and maybe this is way too soon to ask you this, and I don't want you to feel any pressure, but have you ... or would you consider moving to St. Louis at all?"

He pulls away from me, staring into my eyes. His expression is soft, but it's not from sadness. It's apologetic. That's what he's saying without actually speaking. He's sorry, but he can't move. "Maybe down the road, but you live with Hawke—"

"I already told him I'm moving out as soon as I find a place I love."

"But I wouldn't be able to afford a place of my own, and it's probably way too soon to live together. We might want to kill each other by the end of a week. Maybe we should start there. I'll organize some time with the shelter to have a week off, and we'll see how it goes."

I want to argue that we basically lived together over the summer, but I need to remind myself that pushing this issue will make all those things I'm scared of—pressure, resentment, breaking up—happen.

My throat gets thick. "When do you think you could get time?"

There's a knock at the door, and Parker sticks his head in but has his eyes closed. "I hope you're decent."

"Do you really think I'd have sex in here?" I ask.

Parker opens his eyes. "I've heard stories. Something about a storage closet? Anyway, your team is looking for you."

Fuck. Okay, so we haven't solved anything, and now I have to leave. I shouldn't have said anything. I should have spent this time kissing him and showing him how much I love him.

Now it's too late.

CHAPTER FORTY-FOUR

SAM

Regret is a word I'm becoming very familiar with.

I get home, and as soon as Angie is off her leash, she makes her way, head down, to her bed. Ethan comes out of the kitchen, tank top showing off his hairy shoulders and arms, and looks from me to Angie and back again.

He disappears back into the kitchen as I slump on the couch, long exhale rushing out of me like a balloon giving up hope.

When Ethan gets back, he sets down a glass of water and a bowl of soup before sprawling on the floor and offering Angie a treat.

"You know I don't like when you bring my queen home unhappy," he says.

I try for a smile, scrape it out of the depths of my soul, and by the time it reaches my face, I don't know if I look happy or deranged. "He's gone."

"I know. Why do you think I'm home already? Now, eat your soup. It'll help."

I pick it up and eye what looks like vegetables. "No protein."

"Momma knows what you need."

The soup really does help. At least with pushing back the need to cry. Again. "I'm exhausted," I confess, letting the words out. "It shouldn't be this hard."

"Says who?"

That's a great question. "I actually have no idea. He asked if I'd move."

Ethan claps excitedly. "Shut up. What did you say?"

"Nothing. Then he was gone and ..."

"And?"

A happy sigh rushes from me. "I wanted to say yes. So badly."

"Then say yes."

"But—"

"Girl, you know I love a good *but*, but let's sideline that for a minute. You're miserable. And luckily for you, Ethan is a care bear, and I'm happy to look after people I love, but I'm even happier when the people I love are happy too. Lachie makes you happy. I've never seen you like you are with him."

"I don't feel very happy right now."

"And that's a *you* problem. Not a Lachie problem. Why are you standing in your own way?"

I set my bowl back down on the table. "Because there's ... work. And Angie. And you—"

"Leave me out of it!"

"If I move to *St. fucking Louis*, I'd be abandoning you. You don't like living alone."

His eyes soften. "That was ten years ago. I stay here because I like living with *you*. Also, it's home."

"Ethan ..."

"I can manage the rent on my own. You were there for me after my last tumultuous breakup, now I'm here for you. Go to St. Louis. You keep looking at it like an all-or-nothing option. Maybe you show up and hate it and things don't work out. In that case, your room will be here waiting for you when you get back. But—and I'm pretty good at reading these things—I think tonight could be our last night as roommates."

I'm with him right up until the end. "Tonight? But ... work. Angelica can't fly, and—"

"You have a car. Last I looked, St. Louis is a twelve-hour drive."

Drive? Twelve hours in a car sounds about as enjoyable as a protein-fueled weights session, but if Lachie is waiting at the other end? Nerves build way down deep in my gut, and I stare at Ethan as the pieces click into place. "I could drive to St. Louis."

"You could."

"I could be there by tomorrow night. Once his game finishes."

"You could."

"Angie and I could surprise him and—"

Ethan bounds to his feet and crosses the small room to plant a kiss on the top of my head. "Genius idea. I'll help you pack."

One thing brings reality crashing down. "I'm due at work in the morning."

"Get Julia and Aleisha on the phone. You haven't taken time off in years, and those two adore you. After the media buzz you've given the shelter lately, they owe this to you."

It was literally my job, so I don't think they do, but I've always been committed to the shelter. I'm reliable, I work hard, and until recently, I never took so much as a sick day.

I love working there.

But there are animals in St. Louis.

And Lachie.

I rub both hands over my face, a world of scary possibility creeping over me and filling my limbs with helium.

I could go to St. Louis.

There are still so many reasons not to, but Ethan's right. I'm miserable. Lachie was willing to give up *thirty million dollars* for me. He put all his cards on the table.

It's time for me to do the same.

I call Julia, one of the owners of the shelter, and I tell them about everything. That I'm in love, and I understand if the time off isn't possible, but even if I decide St. Louis is where I want to be, I'll come back and help them fill my position. If it's not, I'll be back in a month like nothing has changed, and at least I'll have my answers.

It's the not knowing that's killing me.

Lachie and I could do the long distance for seven years, then he comes home to Colorado and we realize it wasn't meant to be.

It's better to figure it out now.

Even though there's something certain and sure filling me, the strongest gut feeling I've ever had, that says that it won't be the case.

In the end, they grant me ten paid days off, five days of sick time, and five days unpaid.

A whole month.

In St. Louis.

Four weeks to figure out my forever.

After uncontrollable *I'm so proud of you* sobbing from Ethan, and an embarrassing number of Angelica kisses, we get on the road before the sun has broken the horizon.

I have a suitcase of clothes in the trunk, a phone full of text messages from Lachie, who's as miserable as I am, and a very happy collie mix on the front seat, where she'll be allowed to sit until she starts to misbehave.

She *should* be in her crate—Lachie has ruined me as a dog dad—but reaching over when we finally hit traffic and running my hand over her fur keeps all the rattling nervous excitement bearable.

She's still a puppy though, which means we have to stop more than I'd like, and every time I pull over, I've missed a bunch of texts from Lachie, telling me about his day.

I call him from a roadside diner, and the only way I keep my plans from spilling out of my mouth is Hawke shouting in the background that they have to head to the arena.

"Good luck," I tell him, having an out-of-body moment that I'm actually doing this. I don't think of myself as a boring guy, but I'm not spontaneous. This is pushing so many of my limits, and it would be too easy to turn around and head home, but then Lachie *breathes* down the line, and the only thing that has me holding it together is knowing I'll see him soon.

"It's going to be okay," I tell him. "Everything will be okay."

His laugh is soft. "It hurts, but ... I've never missed anyone the way I miss you. I think that helps. It's how I know this is real."

I love you.

It almost spills out of my mouth, but I'll be damned if I say that over the phone.

I'll see you soon.

I want to tell him so badly. Want to give him something to be excited for.

But I wait too long.

"Shit. Hawke's giving me *the face*. Gotta go, but I'll call you tonight."

Then the line goes dead, and Angie pulls my attention to where she's spinning in circles at the end of her lead.

Five more hours to go.

"What do you think, girl? Should we go get Daddy?"

She barks in response, like she has any clue what I've said, and I order fries to eat one-handed as I drive. We stop once more for Angie to pee and me to hastily create my own subscription to watch his game tonight.

Then we're on the final leg of the trip.

My shoulders and back are stiff. My leg keeps cramping up. I'm struggling to follow what's going on with the game that I'm listening to on my phone in the center console, but with every hour that ticks away, my excitement is overriding the rest.

I know from summer that a month will fly by, but this time, by the end of it, I'm determined that we'll have a solution.

The way I feel about Lachie is forever. Now I get to prove that to him. No more uncertainty, no more holding back my feelings. St. Louis won't be forever, but Lachie will be. That's the only part that matters.

We hit the billionth stop-start traffic of the day when I'm about an hour out. Time inches by, and the game wraps up with St. Louis winning in overtime. The glow of brake lights is burning into my vision, and even Angie is getting impatient.

"We're nearly there, girl. Not much longer."

The hardest part is that I don't know Hawke's exact address. I navigate to the general area I remember him living in, and it's not until I find the cafe I had breakfast at that I know where I am.

I make one last stop, let Angelica out for *another* bathroom break, and then call Lachie.

"Did you watch?" is the first thing he asks.

Watched. Listened. Close enough. "I did. Congratulations."

"Thanks. We have the day off tomorrow, so I think the team is going out for drinks."

My heart dives because I didn't consider that in my plans. I'm all geared up to see him any minute, and now I have to wait hours more?

"I want to go home and crash though," he says, and I hear the grin in his voice. "Someone wore me out this weekend."

"Hockey will do that."

"I was thinking more of all the orgasms you gave me." It's strangely quiet in the background.

"Where are you?"

"Just got home. Hawke wanted to change first, but now that I've collapsed on my bed, I don't want to move."

Knowing Hawke, he'll convince Lachie to get his ass up, and I need to catch them before they leave. I'm only minutes away, and it's a struggle to get Angie back into the car without either of us making a noise.

My phone notification lights up to show Lachie is trying to switch the call to video.

I decline.

"Oh." He sounds thrown. "Are you busy?"

"Having dinner with Ethan. Give me five and I'll see your face."

His *actual* face.

"That's a late dinner?"

Shit. "New diet ... thing."

"Right ..."

Great. Now he sounds suspicious.

I get the door closed behind Angie.

"Was that a car door?"

Double fuck. "Yeah, we, uh ... went out for dinner. We're home now."

"Are you okay? You sound weird."

"I'm fine. I promise. Can I, uh, call you back in five?"

There's a long pause. "I think Hawke's going to make me go."

"Five minutes. Give me that. Please?"

Another pause. "Okay."

"Don't go anywhere."

I must sound eager because it gets an uncertain laugh. "Five minutes."

I hang up, throw the car in drive, and make my way to Hawke's place. My heart pounds. My hands are shaking with excitement.

I smell, my body aches, and I could use a very long sleep, but when Hawke's huge house comes into view, nothing matters except that I've made it.

I'm here.

I pull up, car still running, and grab my phone with a minute to spare.

I open our messages, staring at the screen, remembering all the conversations we've ever had before now.

With a deep breath to try and get my nerves in check—it doesn't work—I hit his name and wait for the call to ring.

"Hey ..."

Hearing his voice and knowing he's so close is the weirdest mix of relief and longing. "Remember how you said you'd buy me an animal shelter if I moved to St. Louis?"

"Yes?" His voice is confused, but with a hint of amusement.

"I never needed the shelter."

"Yeah ... It was a joke. That's what the J-K stands for."

"What I mean is, I just need *you*, Lachie." That cuts off whatever he was about to say, and I have to wait for a response.

He swallows hard. "You've had me since I met you."

My heart squeezes tight at the honesty that comes through with every syllable, and I've never felt more amazing in my life. "Did you know there are five animal shelters within a ten-minute drive of Hawke's place?"

"I actually had no idea."

"Hopefully, one of them is hiring."

"H-hiring?" I give him a second to wrap his head around my words. "S-Sam ... what ... what do you mean?"

"Come outside."

Another long pause, and this time when he answers me, his voice is a harsh rasp. "You're supposed to say joke."

The almost scared hope in his voice tells me I'm exactly where I'm meant to be. "I'm not joking."

CHAPTER FORTY-FIVE

LACHIE

I'm in a coma. I took a huge hit during the game, fell to the ice, and am in the hospital with a brain injury. That's more believable than what is actually happening.

I was mid-changing when I flopped on my bed, so I'm shirtless and not wearing shoes, but at least I have pants on as I run to the front door of the house and throw it open.

Sam is leaning against his car. The one with Colorado plates. The one from home. He drove all the way here? With Angelica. She sticks her head out the passenger window, her tongue lolling out the side of her mouth.

I'm still blinking in surprise when Angelica's yip finally gets me moving.

I run across Hawke's lawn, the grass soft beneath my bare feet. "What are you ... how are you ... *What*?"

Sam pushes off his car, and we clash. He laughs into my mouth as I slam my lips down on his. I push him back against the car once again and move my knee between his legs.

Him driving across the country to be here doesn't make sense, and I have a million questions, but I don't want to stop kissing him. It's only when Angelica half climbs out the window and starts licking and nibbling my ear that I'm able to pull myself away from Sam.

Angelica attacks me with kisses. Her paws are on my chest, she's nearly the whole way out of the car now, and I'm still stuck in this surreal headspace where I'm not even sure this is actually happening.

"You've got your hands full tonight," Sam says.

"Huh?" I turn my head back to Sam.

"Having to divide your attention between this little angel and me."

"That's a problem I'm more than okay with having." I pull Angelica all the way out of the car and hold her while I lean in toward Sam and press my lips against his again, softer and less desperate this time. "You're here. You ... Wait, how long for? Please don't tell me you drove all this way for only a day or two."

Sam shakes his head. "I did a thing. On a trial run."

"Trial run?"

"I'm here for at least the next month. To see if we have what it takes to go the distance. To see if my heart knows what it wants or if this summer only seemed magical because it was supposed to end. Who knows, maybe in a week you'll beg me to go back to Denver."

"Never going to happen."

"How can you be so sure?" he whispers.

"Because I've never been so sure of anything else in my whole life. Not hockey, not animals, nothing. I should've told you last night, but I ran out of time, and I didn't want this to be rushed. But you deserve to know. And you're here. You drove all this way. It's only cemented everything I already knew—I'm in love with you. I'm so deeply in love with you, it hurts having to leave you. I miss you before we're even apart. I don't want to be apart anymore."

"Same," is all he says.

I chuckle. "That's it? That's all you have to say?"

"You have to know by now how much I lo—"

"There you are!" Hawke yells from the open doorway. "Oh. And you're not alone. I guess that answers my question on whether you're coming out with me tonight. Have fun, kids. Nice to see you again, Sam." He rounds the house to get to the garage so he can leave.

"House all to ourselves. I have nowhere to be tomorrow until the afternoon ..." I waggle my eyebrows.

"I'll grab my bags later." Sam takes my hand and starts to drag me toward the house.

I laugh but pull back. "Do you at least have some dog food or toys to distract Angelica with?"

"Oh. Right. Good idea." Sam opens the back door to his car and pulls out a box of Angelica's things. "This won't keep her occupied for long though."

"Eh. I read it was good to make sure puppies have alone playtime. Prevents separation anxiety."

We head toward the house, and even though Angelica has her leash and collar on and could walk on her own, I still carry her anyway. Because I've missed the fluffball so much.

I've missed both of them, and I saw them last night. It's difficult to comprehend how I fell so hard, so fast, but I don't need to understand it. All I need is Sam. And Angelica. But mainly Sam.

It's so hard to resist stripping him down and getting off with him as soon as we close the front door behind us, but we need to get Angelica settled first.

I fill a bowl of water while Sam puts some food out for her, as well as treats, her favorite chew toy, which is almost at the point of needing to be replaced, and then puts treats in one of those toys where they need to use their brain to reach the treats.

"That should keep her busy for a while," Sam says.

"Good." I grab his hand, and we leave Angelica out in my personal sitting area. This house is huge, and I have my own space, but if Sam's going to be here for the next month, I want to sign a lease of my own. I've been talking about getting my own place anyway, and until I find the right one to buy and invest in long term, I'll be renting, so we may as well rip off that Band-Aid as soon as possible. As soon as tomorrow morning, if we're not too exhausted from all the orgasms we're about to share.

I lead Sam to my bedroom and close the door behind us. That's when any patience I had leaves my body. I turn and pull him against me, our bodies slamming together.

"I've been on the road for fifteen hours. I probably need a shower first."

"Perfect. I had one after my game, but that's not going to stop me from having another. Especially if you'll prep me while we're in there."

Sam groans. "Definitely made the right choice coming here."

"No argument from me." I go to move toward the attached bathroom, but Sam grabs my hand and pulls me back to him.

"Before we get too distracted, I need to say something. I didn't get a chance outside."

I frown because I have no idea what is about to fall out of his mouth.

"When I said 'Same,' I meant to all of it. I love you too. I wouldn't be here if I wasn't all in with you. Will I miss Denver? Absolutely. But I know we'll be back there one day, and that I'll only regret not trying with you. You're the most amazing man I've ever met, and even though you're young and your parents have no faith in us ... I do. Or I'm optimistic you won't be sending me home in a week."

I cup the back of Sam's head, gripping his hair and pulling him closer to me. "There is no way of that happening. I'm more than optimistic. I'm sure. And when it does work out and you decide to move here permanently, I'm going to make the next seven years the best of your life. Well, so far. After that, when we're back in Colorado, that's where our future will happen."

Sam swallows so hard, I see his Adam's apple bounce. "And what does our future hold?"

"Happiness. Whatever you want."

"All I want is you." This time, he's the one to lead me. He drags me into the bathroom, turns on my shower, and shows me exactly how much he wants me.

He takes care of me. He strips me bare, pins my arms to the tiled wall under the spray, and proceeds to wash me, massaging the soap into my sore and tired muscles. Despite my arguments that I should be the one taking care of him, he shushes me and says, "This is why I'm here. I'm here for you. Because I love you."

"I love you too." And I love having his hands on me, but I'd prefer to have his whole body against me.

His hand moves down my front, gripping my hard cock and jerking slowly. We're in no rush, but I'm desperate to get closer.

As if reading my mind, he leans forward, his mouth landing near my ear. "Why don't you go dry off and wait for me in bed while I wash fourteen hours of road trip off me?"

"Want me to prep my hole for you? It's doable, but I wasn't expecting you, so—"

He cuts me off with a kiss. "We don't have to do that tonight. I just want to hold you. Love you. There are a thousand ways I could make you feel good."

And I'm excited to experience each and every one of them.

I'm in a fuzzy daze as I towel off and wait for Sam, but he washes fast and catches up before I even reach the bed. His arms wrap around me from behind, and his soft lips land on my shoulder. I turn in his arms and bring our mouths together for a kiss that could last a lifetime and still be too short. Our naked bodies slot together like two puzzle pieces clicking into place.

Sam lays me down, climbing on top of me. He's in no rush, and neither am I. Despite being painfully hard, I ignore our cocks for now and allow myself to feel him. All of him. His hard muscles against my own.

He kisses me constantly. His lips travel all over my mouth, jaw, and neck.

We might have showered, but it's already going to waste between the sticky precum pooling between us and the sweat of sharing body heat, but I'll gladly be sticky and sweaty for him. With him being here, driving all this way to declare his love … I will give this man anything he wants. All his desires.

Even though he's started slow, Sam doesn't take long to begin frotting against me. He rotates his hips and thrusts against me.

This isn't about sex. It's about connection. Not wanting to break away from one another. It's a different kind of high, a different kind of chase toward that release. So much so that when that time comes and we both spill over, our mixed cum landing between us, I barely notice that it happened.

The emotions of love and respect, a promise of a future, it feels so much more than an orgasm. It's ... euphoria.

Lying in bed, my arms around Sam as he collapses on top of me, I'm sated and happy. I have to pinch myself because I still don't believe it. It comes in waves—the disbelief, the wondering if I'm imagining all of this. If it's a dream, I never want to wake up. Ever.

My eyes are heavy, and I'm so tired, but then Sam shifts.

"Angelica is suspiciously quiet. Hawke doesn't have anything expensive lying around she could destroy, does he?"

My eyes fly open. "Fuck."

I'm out of bed so fast, I almost forget to find underwear to throw on. If she's gotten into Hawke's part of the house with all his expensive throw pillows and whatthefuckever, I might not be able to afford my own place because it will all go to him.

But as soon as I open the bedroom door, my angelic baby lifts her head from where she's resting on my couch. I sink to my knees, and she runs over to me, her paws slipping all over the tile. She tackles me, and I let her. I fall backward, and then I'm getting Angelica kisses.

This really is the best night ever, but tomorrow will be even better. House shopping. For our future. For us.

CHAPTER FORTY-SIX

SAM

I didn't know that open practices were a thing, but I grab a thick jacket and climb into my car, planning to head down and watch it. It's hard to be bored in a home with a digital golf setup, a huge heated pool, and a state-of-the-art gym, but almost as soon as I got Lachie's text to come and watch, I was out the door.

St. Louis is different. Different streets, different traffic, a different community vibe to what I'm used to. The more I see, the more I think I really like it.

We've spent the last few days trying to figure out a place to lease, and we were really hoping to get it done before Lachie leaves for an away trip tomorrow.

Him leaving again doesn't hurt anywhere near as much as it usually does. Because I know he'll be back in four days.

I'll keep looking for us, catch both games on Hawke's enormous TV, and hopefully, once he's back, I'll have the contracts ready to sign for our temporary home.

As generous as Hawke is by having no issues with me staying, if we're going to do this properly, we need to do it properly.

Own place. Own routines.

And no more freaking out over Angelica potentially ruining Hawke's things.

It's lucky that Lachie sent me the address of the practice facility because it wouldn't have occurred to me that they don't practice at the arena. Logistically, it checks out, but I've never given any thought to hockey players and their ins and outs before.

I arrive at the community ice center, and one look at the line of luxury cars gives away that a hockey team is inside.

I pat my Honda affectionately as I climb out and lock up, like anyone would want to steal her with an Audi only a few feet away.

"It's okay, girl," I say. "I still love you."

She made a twelve-hour drive with no issues, so I'll forever be grateful for that.

It's colder inside than I'm expecting, and I tug my jacket on as I make my way toward where practice is. The team is on the ice, and there are a few people sitting in the stands to watch.

I'm not sure if Lachie will see me here or not, but I find a free section and slip into the front row, scanning the bodies on the ice for him. Even with his helmet on, it doesn't take long.

His smile is infectious, the way he carries himself is familiar, and just like the day I watched him and the Collective play their "friendly" game, I'm in awe. I'm hit with this weird moment of *this is where I'm meant to be.*

Lachie is born for hockey. Even a noob like me can see that when he's out there, the ice is his. I'm too focused on him that I don't notice someone skate over and leave the ice until they throw themself into the seat beside me.

"He's good, huh?" Hawke asks.

"Yeah ... I know nothing about hockey, and I'm probably biased, but—"

"Nah ..." He takes off his helmet and runs a gloved hand over his sweaty curls. "Any player who makes the NHL is really good. I'd say the majority of the league is made up of them. The guys who are better, faster, more accurate. It's why we're professionals. Then there are your greats." He tilts a gloved thumb toward his chest. "That's what I'm aiming for. When it comes to hockey, people know my name. My stats are excellent. And when it comes to injury, I'm one of the few D-men without an IR list a mile long." He knocks on his head. "The Kiki brothers are greats. Anton Hayes. To a lesser extent, the Dalton brothers, though Asher is more or less legendary at this point. Greats are looked up to. Their skill is unmatched. Except ... by generational talents."

My gaze moves to where Lachie effortlessly does this spin thing around one of his teammates and scores. He doesn't lose his grin. He makes it look easy.

"Lachie is a generational talent. His handwork is ridiculous. He's fast. And his stats are way above where you'd expect them to be at his age. But it's even more than that. When Lachie is on the ice, he makes the entire team better. *That's* why St. Louis was never going to let him go without a fight."

"Makes sense," I murmur, trying to wrap my head around it all. "It also sounds like a lot of pressure."

"*So* much. Fuck being a generational talent, is all I can say. But Lachie handles it like it's nothing. He has this emotional maturity that I've never seen in another rookie. It comes naturally to him."

"I think everything comes naturally to him."

"Hawke!" We both look over to where a graying white man in a team tracksuit is waving our way. "Get your lazy ass back out here."

He smothers a laugh. "See you at home."

I watch as Hawke skates off and catch Lachie's gaze instead. I've never seen him look so damn happy, and it helps settle the doubts that pop up every now and then saying that I'm risking it all for him.

"Hey, you're the animal man!"

I glance over at a group of three girls in the next section, all of whom are staring my way. "Ah, yeah. I think so?"

The blonde squeals and moves closer. "Can I grab a picture?"

"Of ...?"

"*Us*. I love your videos. Lachlan Kikishkin shared one, and now they pop up all the time."

It's one thing to know that people are watching your videos; it's another to actually meet someone who does. "Thanks." Brain. Online. Stat. "Yes, photo. Of course."

I take a selfie with her, and then the other two girls do the same. Thankfully, I'm not as exciting as a professional hockey player, though, because after a few minutes of monologuing my videos back to me, they say goodbye and go back to watching the team.

My videos might not be viral—as Lachie loves to remind me—but that's proof that they've escaped the little Denver bubble I'd intended them for, and it's making my head spin.

I have no clue if it's my shameless exploitation of my body that caught their attention or if they're genuinely watching for the animals, but I don't let it bother me. My mindset has always been for the video to reach the people who need to see it, and if that means going through a few thousand who don't first, it's fine by me.

Training is enough to take my mind off myself anyway. They run drills, they do fancy moves that I'd never even think to do with blades attached to my feet, there are pucks everywhere, and more than one coach—again, something that had never occurred to me.

I'm really paying for my lack of interest in any sport now. Thankfully, Lachie is always happy to teach me.

When it finally wraps up, he skates over, using the same exit Hawke did to take the spare seat.

"You will never guess what."

"Your brain has been replaced by an alien infestation that survives by consuming hockey-related content."

He stares at me. "That would explain a lot, actually."

I slap his thigh. "What?"

"Brotevic bought a new place, and he said his house is being staged this afternoon for sale. As long as we keep it clean, he said we can stay there until it sells. It's a bit further away than Hawke's place, but he offered it to me for cheap, and we were talking about something short term while you're here …"

Because Lachie's parents pushed for a portion of his seventy million to be paid as a signing bonus that should come through at any point after he signs his new contract, it means that Lachie will finally be able to buy his own place.

Rookie years can be short, so he was cautious about anything permanent, but with a promise of seven years in this city, he says it's time. Even if I wasn't in the picture, the house would be, and I'm excited that he gets to do this. Generational talent or not, he's worked his ass off to get to this point.

"And Bruh—your teammate, really doesn't mind? Like, he knows it would mean me staying there too?"

"Yep. I haven't shut up about anything else for days. I think Hawke is starting to get offended I'm so desperate to get out."

"I don't want to piss him off."

"Nah, he said he'll apparently have a lot of visitors this season—whatever that means—and it'll be easier with me gone. I'd believe he's sick of me if his lip didn't quiver at the end there."

They might not have the close brotherly relationship Lachie always wanted, but it's clear they care about each other. And with the way his teammate made this offer so easily, I get the feeling they all do. "It's great that you have all this support."

"Yeah, I love them. And since we're together, they're your support too. I'll introduce you to the WAGs, and the BAHs will call the second someone finds out we're living together—"

"I have no idea what you're saying—"

"Because hockey isn't just about me. It's about you now too." He takes a deep breath. "It's no secret that a hockey player's schedule is tough, especially on families. People like to make fun of how so many players have traditional little housewives, but the reality is that our careers don't have a lot of room to give. If we're traded, sometimes we have to drop everything and get on the next flight. It makes it hard for partners to build their own careers. And then if you want kids on top of that ... it's almost impossible to balance both. Dating a hockey player isn't easy."

Some of his nerves are sneaking out, and I want to reach over and take his gloved hand, but with him not officially out and this being a public arena, I hold off. "Being away from you isn't easy. Everything else doesn't matter."

"I'm going to remind you of that every time I make you eat protein."

I hang my head back on a groan. "Not you too!"

He laughs, then grabs my chin and presses a lingering kiss to my lips. "Gotta go. See you at home, babe."

I try not to melt into my chair.

See you at home.

This is actually real life.

And I get to live it.

CHAPTER FORTY-SEVEN

LACHIE

Having Sam here is everything I hoped it would be and more, but with every day that passes, there's doubt building that he's going to choose to stay at the end of the month.

Things are going well, great even. Each morning I don't have practice, I wake to Sam making breakfast. On the days I'm up and out the door before he and Angelica even begin to stir, I come home to a cooked meal with lots of protein. And away games? I thought I would hate them. But knowing my man and baby girl are waiting for me means it's all the more exciting when I get home. And when I do, I'm welcomed with the warmest hugs and kisses a guy could ask for. From both of them.

And since they've been here? Balance has returned to my relationship with random animals. That same pup in training who growled at me? Every time he's been back to the rink, he tries to follow me wherever I go. Perhaps it's because he can smell Angelica on me, but I like to think that now I'm not full of heartache and longing, my sunny disposition makes me an animal magnet once again.

But while everything in my life is balanced, I'm low-key worried Sam might hate the idea of him being the stay-at-home boyfriend. He might choose to go back to Denver, where he has a job. He's already looked into a few shelter jobs here with no luck, and I don't want him to become resentful. Telling him being the partner of a hockey player is difficult and him experiencing it are two different things.

He hasn't complained once though, and if I wasn't so chickenshit, I'd check in with him and flat out ask, but I'm scared he's going to say St. Louis isn't for him.

I should check in. It's what good partners do. And he's already shown how much better he is at this than I am. He moved here for me. He put his real life on hold to see if our love has what it takes to make it. He's the one who's done all the work so far.

We're about three weeks into this thing, and Sam has to make a choice within the week about what he's going to do, so when I come home from my second road trip since he's been here, I pluck up the courage to ask where he's at.

Or at least I think I do. Because when I walk through the front door of Brotevic's place and find Sam sitting on the couch, his head buried in Angelica's fur, with his phone on the coffee table trying to vibrate its way off the edge, my confidence dies.

I don't think I'm going to have to ask because whatever's wrong is about to come out anyway. "Sammy?"

He lifts his head. "I didn't even hear you come in."

"Obviously."

Angelica struggles free of Sam's grip, but I ignore her jumping up on me and go sit next to Sam. I wrap my arm around his shoulders and prepare for him to tell me that he's going back home to Denver.

His deep brown eyes meet mine. "Did you get in trouble?"

"In trouble for what?"

"You haven't seen it?"

"Seen what?"

Sam leans forward and picks up his phone. He hands it to me unlocked and already open on a post. It's a photo of him and me at practice a couple of weeks ago, where I kissed him and didn't even give it another thought.

"I'm sorry," Sam whispers.

"Why are you sorry? Are you the one who took it and splashed it everywhere?"

"No, but—"

"Then you have nothing to be sorry for. It's not like I've ever been careful about not being outed. To me, I've been out for a long time; it's just no one noticed. This is a good thing. I promise."

"What if your parents think I did this to boost my videos on socials? They're going to think I outed you on purpose and I'm only using you, and—"

I rub my hand over my face. "I go away for a couple of days and come back to a freaked-out boyfriend and no idea what's going on. What are you talking about?"

He closes out his app and pulls up his phone notifications. He has new comments upon comments on his animal videos, and his subscriber count has jumped a couple of thousand every hour.

"This is amazing."

He doesn't look amazed.

"Isn't it?" I ask.

"Not if you had to be outed to get there."

"Again, I haven't tried to hide it. I've been discreet, but never with you. I don't want to hide you, and this is in no way your fault."

"Can you say the same thing to your parents, please?"

"Why? What did they do?"

"They must have got my number off Easton because they called and said I'm not to respond to anyone online or talk to the media and told me to say no comment every chance I get."

I stand and grab my phone from my bag to find missed calls from my parents. "I'll deal with this." I go to leave but hesitate as I look over my shoulder at Sam. "But first, are you okay? Are you freaking out about going viral for real this time?"

"A little. But I'm more freaking out about you."

I shake my head. "Do not worry about me. You've made me happier in the last three weeks than I've been in my entire

NHL career. I love hockey, but I love you too. I hope ..." I bite my lip. "I hope you still feel the same about me."

Sam jumps up and approaches me. "I love you more and more every day, and I've already called the shelter back in Denver to ask for more time. I might not be ready to quit completely yet because I'm scared something will go wrong. I don't know what, but this scandal, for instance—"

"Not a scandal, but go on."

"This is working ... right?"

I hug him tight. "It is for me, but I was worried you weren't sold. And I guess you're not if you still don't want to quit—"

"If I let go of my job permanently ... there's no turning back. Not that I want to turn back. I don't." He grunts. "I've lost track of what I'm saying."

"That makes two of us. But as long as you're staying another month and you trust me when I say this whole outing thing is not a big deal to me—I'm happy about it, even if my parents aren't—I can do my best to make those last few insecurities disappear for you."

"How did I get so lucky to find you?"

"You didn't. I found you. Or ... more specifically, the animals I rescued did."

Sam cups my face. "My Disney Princess."

I don't hate that name so much anymore. I lean in and press my lips against his. "My Prince Charming."

—

Even though my parents wanted me to do a huge coming-out speech, blah, blah, blah, I told them no. Because I never wanted to make my sexuality a big deal. Easton walked so I could run, so when the inevitable question has come up in press conferences or inappropriately by rink-side reporters, my story has always been consistent.

"I didn't realize it wasn't already known. I've never tried to hide it."

Sam has gained over one hundred thousand subscribers on his content channels, enough to start earning money by putting ads in his videos. He didn't plan on becoming a content creator, and it's not a lot of money right now, but it's enough for him to pay for his car, his phone, and any personal bills. He argued he wants to contribute to the rent, but I won't let him. Not until he gets a full-time job, and even then, I'll fight him every step of the way.

His content covers his bills, and his free time is filled with doing what he loves most: volunteering at any animal shelter or organization that will take him. I don't want him to feel obligated to get a paying job when he's doing amazing things for the community.

I'll support anything he wants to do, and if that's work, then I'm all for it. I just don't want him to feel *obligated* to do it.

Sam comes to every home game, and so far, it's working like a good luck charm because I'm still in that phase of wanting to show off to him. We're up to six wins and one loss for home games, and the only reason we lost that one was because of a fluke goal by Aleks Emerson. Fucking Seattle.

Sam has extended his leave once more, still not confident enough to let it go completely, but when I come home from practice to hear him on the phone with them, I can't help laughing at what they're saying. He has it on speaker, so it's loud and clear.

"Sam, by this point, you don't work here anymore. You don't live in Denver."

I snort.

He ignores me. "Are you saying you're firing me?"

"No, but I'm pointing out that you were doing this on a trial run. Do you really still need to hold on to it?"

I fold my arms and lean against the wall by the entry to the kitchen, where Sam's sitting at the counter. It's a question I've been wanting to ask.

We're happy. Other than him thinking I was going to flip out over the photo of us spreading online, we haven't had any disagreements or worries.

Sam meets my eyes and smiles. "No. There's absolutely no reason I'm still holding on to it. I'm happy here. And you're right. I'm quitting. Officially."

"Congratulations! Don't go on and forget us now you're all famous and with a professional athlete."

Sam scoffs. "I'm far from famous, but I could never forget you all anyway. Lachie and I will be back. Eventually."

"In seven and a half years," I cut in. But who's counting.

"Lord, I might be dead by then," the owner of the shelter says.

"Maybe I can buy the shelter off you before that happens." I'm half joking, half not, but Sam's eyes widen as if to say *what the fuck are you doing?*

"I'd love to hear your offer sometime."

"It'll be my wedding present to my husband," I say.

Sam drops his phone on the counter, and I laugh.

"In the future," I clarify.

"Can't wait," Julia says. "Talk soon, Sam."

"Definitely." Sam ends the call and stares at me, his mouth slack, eyes still panicked.

"What?" I ask innocently.

"I finally quit my job, and you're already mentioning weddings?"

"I'm not going to force you down an aisle if you don't want it." I shrug. "But the more I have you here, the more I can see it in our future ... uh, again, if you want it. If not—"

"I do. It's scary to think of in this moment, but I could see it happening in the future too."

I step behind him, wrap my arms around his front, and lower my head to his shoulder. "I want everything with you."

"I want everything with you too."

EPILOGUE

SAM

I'm not intimidated ... exactly.

We look at house after house, and while I'm stuck on the seven-figure price tags, Lachie goes through them with all the enthusiasm of a dog on the hunt.

"Angelica will ruin these floors," he mutters. "No yard, no good."

Every time I start getting overwhelmed, it's brought down again by the way he's thinking in *us* terms.

"My parents will visit a lot," he says as we head to the next house.

I throw him a sly look. "Even with me here?"

"Of course. They weren't ..." He tightens his jaw before he can get frustrated with them again. "They just worry, and it's misplaced. Now that I've signed the contract and they don't view you as this big, bad guy getting in the way of my career, they'll love you."

"Even though I earn significantly less than you?" I watch him for a reaction.

He grabs my hand and squeezes it. "You've given up your entire life for me. The least I can do is buy us a big, pretty house for you to enjoy until you've found what you want to do."

"That's far from the least." It does sound nice though. All of my stuff is still at Ethan's, where he said I can leave it until I'm back for all he cares, but I know how much he's always wanted a weights room, and freeing up my bedroom will give him that.

Once we find our place, I'll be able to officially change my address on everything, have my measly furniture brought over, and then ... I'll be here. In St. Louis. Officially. With Lachie.

Because of his schedule, most of the moving in will be down to me, so I haven't been trying seriously to find a job until we're settled. I've been filming videos, and apparently, being the very gay, very animal-loving partner of a professional hockey player has its perks beyond his stamina in bed. I'm *actually* going viral, according to Lachie. It's very overwhelming and almost too much sometimes, but I've learned that if I post and log out, I can cut myself off from the mayhem.

I'm even earning money through the apps, and I don't expect it to last, but at least it's carrying me through this unemployed stage of my life.

It was a very strange mix of emotions I dealt with initially, because I wouldn't say I was necessarily *excited* for the move. I love my life in Denver. I'm going to miss Ethan. The shelter. The people there.

But none of it comes close to how much I missed Lachie.

In the space of a couple of months, when I look ahead, my whole future looks different. It's St. Louis I think of. The small cafe I visited that first day that has become my regular coffee stop. The park we walked through, but now with Angelica by our sides.

I might not have been excited to leave my whole world behind, but it felt right.

Moving here wasn't abandoning my life; it was doubling it. New friends, new favorite places, but most of all, Lachie.

And if we're lucky, in seven and a bit years, we'll be back where we started.

"You know what I find funny?" I tell him. "What rich people spend their money on. Can you please tell me why that last place had a bubble-gum-colored kitchen and orange-and-white checkered bathroom?"

"Yeah, that was a choice."

"I've noticed a trend where it's either something so awful I don't believe they want to sell their house, or white. Everything white. There's no in-between."

"You don't like white?"

I hold my hands up. "I will like whatever you like. You're spending a lot of money, so you need to be happy with it."

"And you're going to be living there." Even through his sunglasses, I can feel his assessing gaze. "I want you to love it as much as I do. So spit it out. What's your issue with white?"

"Not ... an *issue*, really. With the apartment back home, it gave me this cozy, warm hug feeling when I walked into it. Obviously, that's easy to do when the place is one one-hundredth the size, but between how *big* and white everything is ..." I don't know what I'm trying to say. "Brotevic's place is huge, same with Hawke's, but both felt like a home. There's something about them that ..."

"Hugs you." His lips twitch, and I pinch him playfully as he pulls up at the last house before he has to head home and get ready for *work*.

"At least if the house doesn't do that, you will," I say as we climb out.

He rounds the car and does exactly that—makes me feel at home. "Just try and stop me."

I look around as he pulls away. There is a *lot* of front yard space, and the house, unlike most of what we've seen today, is all one level.

"How many bedrooms was this one again?"

"Five. One for us, one for my parents, Connor and Parker, and Easton and Knox."

"It'll be a full house."

"And then when they're not here, lots of space for the Collective to visit."

"I change my answer. *That* will be a full house."

We haven't even stepped inside though, and I can already see this yard sprawled with drunken hockey players.

I'm struggling to remember this listing amongst all the houses we've seen, but it looks like it has two wings spread out from each other, with a circular foyer in the center. The agent we're meeting is waiting for us there, flanked by the stained glass on either side of the enormous front door.

"It's nice to meet you," she says in that same pleasant but efficient tone I've been hearing all day. "I know you're low on time, so why don't you explore the house and meet me for any questions. Just a reminder, we've had a price drop on this one as the owners are looking for a fast sale, but the negotiation margins are tight. I think once you've had a look, you'll agree it's worth every cent of the two point five asking price."

My head swims at the amount of money they're talking about, especially after Lachie pointed out that he'd have that covered in three months' worth of pay. The fact that she's suggesting we *explore* a house when I'm used to ones where you can see everything from the front door is also going to take some adjusting.

Lachie's hand closes around mine, like he can sense my almost freak-out, and he tugs me into the house.

And I get that feeling.

Almost as soon as we walk into the main living area, the homey, cozy vibe wraps around me. It's huge like the last places, but a stone fireplace runs from floor to ceiling between the long glass doors that have a view of the trees and pool in the backyard. The ceiling is timber, the kitchen is right beside us—not white—and instead of being completely open, it has a pass-through, which makes them feel like two separate rooms.

"Wow," Lachie says, looking around. "I mean ... we should probably see the rest of the house."

"Probably."

His gray eyes lock onto mine, sunglasses pushed up and making his brown hair wild. "Our budget was two million more than this ..."

"It was."

"I was looking for something like Hawke's."

I try not to let my gut drop. "His does look like a big, fancy hockey player's house."

"But I think I want this one."

Relief rushes through me. I try not to give myself away. "Like you said, we should probably see the rest of the house."

But the rest of the house goes on being amazing. All-natural stone look in the bathrooms, a huge bedroom that looks out to the trees bordering the backyard, a home gym that I have to drag Lachie out of, a sauna, a spa ... it's ticked every single box, yet it doesn't feel *too much* like everything else did.

The more we look around, the quieter we both get.

Until we reach the enclosed backyard, and all I can see is Angelica running around.

"Lachie ..."

"Yeah?"

"I think I love it."

A relieved laugh bursts from him. "Then why do you sound so terrified?"

"Because this is it." I turn to him, searching his face for any doubt. "We buy this, I move, and then ... we finally have nothing keeping us apart."

"You say that like you haven't been living here for months already."

"Technically, but this ... this makes it all official."

The amusement in his eyes fades. "You have no idea how much I want that."

"I know *exactly* how much you want that." I tug him to me and wrap an arm around his waist. "I'm almost scared to say yes. It's like once we do, everything changes. Good change, and I'm so ready for it, but I don't think I know what I'll do with myself when I'm not missing you all the time."

"*Volunteer*," he says for the millionth time. "I've seen you at work, and I've seen you when you're doing the things you love. You're meant to be doing things that make you happy."

When Lachie says it, it's so easy to believe him. Moving makes me happy. Being with him makes me happy. Posting my videos, and being around animals, and even this house, make me happy.

I reach up to cup his face, caught up in this weird, throat-clenching moment of awe. "You're amazing."

He grins, and I don't think I've ever seen him as happy as he is right now. "So can I put in an offer?"

"Yeah." It's barely more than a hoarse croak, but at the end of the day, the house doesn't matter. All that matters is that we get to be together, and I know the rest will fall into place. "I love you."

"It still blows my mind that it took you so long to figure out how awesome I am."

"Lachie, the second you walked in, covered in amniotic fluid and confidence, I was a goner. You're amazing. And I'm going to spend the rest of our lives proving it to you."

"Pfft, I prove it on the ice every day. I don't need anything from you except to love me. Because you're it for me, Sammy. You always have been. This moment, right here, it's what I've been waiting for. My entire life starts with you."

THE END OF AN ERA

LACHIE

It's happening. It's finally happening.

As much as Sam and I loved how St. Louis treated us, with the trade deadline looming, a Stanley Cup win under our belt, the team knowing I'm not going to sign any new extension they send my way, and Colorado's irresistible trade offer, St. Louis has released me to go home with one year left on my contract. They were smart when they drew up the extension seven years ago because even though my average per year was ten million, they worked it to give me a signing bonus up front and then only pay me eight mill for the first six years, leaving the last year to pay out the most of my contract. In the trade deal with Colorado, they keep none of that salary and have freed up fourteen million from their salary cap. Sorry, Parker.

Sam has been an absolute godsend with the move, selling the house we made a home, tying up loose ends in St. Louis, and traveling with Angelica and her little sister—unsurprisingly, another rescue—across the country.

Knowing the move was coming, Sam hasn't taken on any wildlife rescue jobs for the last six months. Our last rescue was an orphaned coyote cub that stayed with us until it was old enough to go out on its own. If it were up to me, we would've kept it, but Sam wouldn't let me. Something about them not being able to be domesticated or whatever. Doesn't he remember who I am? I'm his Disney Princess, damn it. I could've tamed it.

The last six and a half years since Sam got in his car and drove all day to get to me have been nothing but pure happiness. That's not to say that my schedule made it completely smooth sailing, but because we're both pretty chill guys, there haven't been any real rough patches. It's as if we were made for each other. I don't think I believed much in soul mates until my first-ever crush finally noticed me.

And even though we've been building toward a future in St. Louis, it finally feels like that future is beginning. It's now.

Also now? My first game playing for Colorado. Sometimes trades are fast and take players by surprise. This one was expected, so we were already packed up before we got the official call.

Still, yesterday, I was in St. Louis, and today, I'm suiting up in a jersey color I've never worn before, side by side with my brother, and I'm just hoping Sam makes it in time. He was scrambling to find a flight where he could take both dogs with him in the cabin and not in cargo. He got one, but if there are any delays, he won't be in the arena waiting for me to get out there and fulfill the dream my family has had since the three of us started playing hockey.

Sure, it would be extra awesome if Connor were still playing too, but he is doing the ceremonial puck drop, so that's the closest we'll all get to being on the ice together. Connor chose his happiness the same way I chose mine.

Playing hockey, loving my boyfriend, and helping animals. They're my priorities, and I get to have them all.

"Nervous?" Easton asks beside me.

"Nope."

"Liar."

"Why would I be nervous? Because I've wanted this forever and have built this moment up so much in my head that if we lose, I'll be devastated and think I've made a huge mistake and should have stayed in St. Louis? Nah. None of that is happening."

Easton claps me on the shoulder. "We've got this."

"Totally."

"And even if we don't, I happen to be married to one of the refs tonight. Maybe I can bribe him with sex to look the other way."

I shake my head. "All these years, he's never once shown favoritism because he knows his job is on the line if he does. If anything, he's been extra cautious with calls around you." It's only happened about once a year, but for whatever reason, the person who schedules the NHL has to be high on something. It was widely publicized when Easton and Knox got married, yet despite that, Knox still gets rostered to ref Easton's games. He can be impartial, but why put him in that position? Schedulers being high as fuck while working is the only explanation.

"You ready to get out there?" Easton asks.

I check my phone one more time to see if there's an update from Sam, but there isn't. I want him here for this. But as I'm about to put my phone away, it vibrates in my hands, and it's a pic from the owner's box of the empty ice, saying, "Made it."

"Now I am. Let's do this." And hopefully not choke.

When we hit the ice earlier for warm-ups, the arena was still filling up. I saw a couple of signs with my name on them saying "Welcome home" and some loud screams as I waved to the crowd, but that has nothing on this. Where the seats are full, the lights are down, and everyone is so loud the whole arena is deafening.

Nothing beats this atmosphere. This high. Maybe having sex with Sam, but that's for only us to enjoy and not in front of eighteen thousand people. I don't think Sam would go for that. Even Oskar hasn't had a single scandal since he settled down.

Easton and I are both there for the ceremonial puck drop against Buffalo's captain, Ayri Quinn. He recently announced that this is his last year, and he'll be retiring to become a stay-at-home dad to the baby he shares with Buffalo's head trainer, Vance.

Photos are taken of the puck drop, and then a few with all the Kiki bros together.

When the time comes for the game to get going, I skate up to the face-off and look Asher Dalton from Buffalo right in the eye.

"Hope you don't think I'll take it easy on you," he says.

I snort. "If anything, shouldn't I be taking it easy on you? You're getting up there, old man. Are you next in the retirement line? Your baby bro going to get called up from the AHL to take over your spot?"

"Fuck off. I've still got three years on my contract, but keep going. You know how taunting me fuels my rage, and when I'm ragey, I play like a god."

Knox's face appears in my peripheral. "You two kids done shit-talking yet? Let's have a good game. I don't want to have to put you in adult time-out."

"Little Dalton likes it," I say, only pissing Asher off more. His brother retired a billion years ago, but he's still known as Little Dalton, and it'll stick at least until his youngest brother joins the league.

"Game on, *Little Kiki*."

Unlike him, the Little in front of my name doesn't faze me.

Knox drops the puck, and I dig it out first, passing it off to Easton.

All these Collective guys are getting older, some already retired, others refusing to—only need one guess to figure out who that is—but we've never wavered in our support for each other. In the beginning, I might have felt like an outsider, but year by year, we've grown closer and closer. Sam is friends with all the boyfriends and husbands of both active players and those retired.

Having said that, we may all be supportive, but we're also just as competitive with each other as ever.

Which is why I revel in it when I draw a penalty from Dalton, skating by him in the penalty box, taunting, "Naughty, naughty."

And when Colorado walks away with the win? He doesn't hear the end of it.

—

It's rare when the Stanley Cup doesn't come home with one of the Queer Collective teams, but this year is one of them. The Collective is slowly growing, but not fast enough for Ezra's liking. He says once we have a member on every team in the NHL, then the Cup will be coming home with one of us every year. He still has high hopes of that happening one day, but as the years pass, those who were some of the first, the ones who paved the way for the rest of us, are retired or nearing it; we now have fewer active out players than ever.

When Ezra decided to make this season's end-of-year Collective gathering in Boston—in the city, not some cabin in the middle of nowhere Massachusetts where we can be our loud, crazy selves—I got the sense of impending doom. Okay, maybe not doom, but there's something in the air as my brothers, their partners, plus Sam and I arrive at a ping-pong-themed bar in Boston's Seaport district.

"Is it just me, or is there something alarming by this choice of venue?" I ask.

"If you're wondering if it's like a stripping ping-pong show type situation, it's not. I triple-checked," Connor says.

Of course he did.

"It's not that." I can't put my finger on it exactly. "It's … like, if it was a strip show, that would make sense. This is …" I shudder. "Completely normal and not over-the-top. Something is afoot." I hope for fuckery, but my gut tells me it's something else.

Something big.

"You're extra dramatic tonight," Easton says and swings open the door.

Sam squeezes my hand. "I believe you."

"You do?"

He nods as we follow my brothers into the venue. "Considering how many post-season parties, trips, and Collective gatherings I've been to over the years, the crazy shenanigans, the drunken antics, the near misses, fires, and—"

"Do you have a point?"

"I do. This is super tame. It's unnerving."

"See, you get it!"

Sam leans in and kisses my cheek. "Not even remotely. I don't understand a lot when it comes to you hockey players, but I get you. I know how you think." He knows parts of my soul even I wasn't aware of until he showed me.

"Will you protect me if something scary awaits us?"

"Of course I will. You're my Disney Princess. Even if you're the one with knife shoes and could kick anyone's ass."

"I knew I should've packed my skates."

"Tell you what. Seeing as Ethan is looking after the dogs while we're away, and we have an empty hotel room with no sick or injured animals, the moment you begin to feel too uneasy, we'll leave and go to bed."

"Not to sleep, I hope?"

"Pfft. You're not getting any sleep this entire trip."

Man after my own heart.

"Oh no! I'm sooooo uneasy. We should leave." I try to drag him back toward the door, but he doesn't let me.

"You need to make an appearance."

"Do I?"

"Yes. Because if you don't, you know Ezra will somehow figure out how to get a key to our hotel room and then come jump on our bed—even if we're naked in it—until we make our presence known."

I relent because, "True."

Ezra likes to play the role of annoying pest, but we've grown closer over the years. I've joined him and Anton on charity work, at volunteer centers, and whenever one of us needs something, Ezra is the first one there. He started as my hero, and that's never changed.

There's a server with an array of drinks on a tray, welcoming us. He rattles off each one, and I grab the fruity cocktail because why the fuck not. It sounds fun.

My brothers have already dispersed into the groups of people hanging around the lounge area, while the ping-pong tables remain untouched. For now. I'm going to kick someone's ass later. Don't care whose.

The space has been taken over by hockey players, retired and current, Ezra having rented the entire venue to host this. It makes me even more suspicious that something is happening.

As I look around the industrial brick, the metal beams and poles, the retro furniture mixed with modern, colorful art on the walls, I realize it might be the perfect venue to represent us. It's a chaotic mix of different styles that somehow gels to create something amazing.

My eyes catch on Caleb Sorensen and Ollie Strömberg sitting on a couch in the corner of the lounge. Their heads are close together, hunched over a phone, looking at God knows what. They're the oldest of us all and my heroes. The first two out players in the league deserve all the respect from those of us who have followed in their footsteps. A Collective gathering where I'm not in awe of them is never going to happen. I still haven't managed a full conversation without stuttering, but there's Hawke, just chatting to them like old friends.

At the bar, there's a line of retired players. Tripp and Dex, who retired a few seasons ago, are double fisting drinks, probably happy to be away from their kids for a beat. Next to them, there's Novi, Oskar, Aleks, Bilson, and, newly retired this season, Quinn.

Novi and Oskar still reside in California. Novi's married to the head coach of LA, and Oskar's husband, Lane, still works for King Sports—mostly remote, but he often drops into the King Sports office in LA. Novi and Oskar are living their best retired lives—Oskar doing nothing but being a pain in the ass for his husband, and Novi continuing to live out and proud after having kept it a secret for so long.

There was speculation and conspiracy theories when Novi came out and said he was going to marry his coach from when he played in LA—all of which was true. They did start their relationship when they shouldn't have, while there was a power imbalance and careers on the line, but they've stuck to their story and never wavered so they could protect their organizations, but more importantly, each other.

The bigger scandal was when Connor and Parker announced their relationship. Team owner and the player who was dropped after an injury? No one believed their story of spending time in the Owner's suite every home game made them grow close. Their whole past was dredged up. How they went to high school together, how Connor was a jock and Parker was a nerd. They didn't react to any of it, and if either of them were asked anything, they simply said that not everything online is factual. The chatter died down eventually.

Aleks and his partner, Gabe, basically run an orphanage at this point. That might be exaggerating, but they have about six foster kids at any given moment. They're giving those children in need the stable home environment none of them ever had.

There were trade rumors swirling around Miles this past season, but he's still with Nashville for now. He's been a solid starting goaltender, but the team hasn't won a Cup with him in net. As Bilson tells it, instead of fixing their defense, who often leave Miles out to dry, they're making him the scapegoat. He's threatened to un-retire and become a D-man to protect his Miles because he would do it better than anyone left on the team. Wherever or whatever happens with Miles's future, there's no doubt in my mind that Bilson will be right by his side.

And Quinn? He's enjoying being a stay-at-home dad now, while Vance is still with the Buffalo organization. They're all grown-ups now. Technically, I guess I am too, but I'm still in my twenties, so seeing them all close in on forty, it's scary to think I'll be there in a short ten years. I hope I'm still playing then, but at the same time, I promised Sam once upon a time that I'd buy him an animal shelter. While it might have been a joke then, the idea of running a shelter with him one day sounds like heaven to me. I can have all the animals as pets without them actually being pets. That's still a future plan though. I'm nowhere near done with hockey yet. I've got what I wanted, and I foresee an amazing career in Colorado with Easton.

My gaze skims over Foster, his husband, and the group around them that includes Asher's partner Kole, Westly Dalton and his partner, two men I recognize from a hockey camp I visited with Ezra, and someone else who might be Foster's brother. The only people I can't see are Ezra and Anton. Which is weird because this is their party. Then again, every Collective gathering is an Ezra-and-Anton affair. Ezra is the glue that keeps us together and makes sure our support system doesn't crumble.

I'm about to ask if anyone has seen them when they appear, emerging from the hallway that has a sign above it saying "Restrooms." Seeing them hand in hand, most likely coming out from what would be an obvious hookup, almost settles that gut feeling swimming around, but then I see Ezra's red-rimmed eyes and Anton watching his husband like he might start crying too.

Oh, fuck. What the hell is happening?

The world is ending, someone's dying ... oh my God, the daddies of the Collective have broken up. The OG couple. The first to win a Cup together. That's why tonight is so topsy-turvy.

The thought sucker punches me.

They move in slow motion, and when Ezra breaks from Anton to head toward a small stage under a spotlight, my heart is in my throat.

Ezra picks up a mic and forces a smile as he says, "Now that the Kikis have finally decided to grace us with their presence, we can get tonight started. Anton and I have some news."

No! They can't break up. They're so perfect for each other, and—

"As you all know, or should know because you are all obsessed with us, Anton's and my contracts came up for extensions, but we haven't signed yet."

Because they're breaking up and going to two different teams? Why does it feel like Mommy and Daddy are sitting us all down to tell us they love us and it's not our fault they're separating?

"We've been telling everyone the offers haven't been right, but that's a lie."

I hold my breath as he continues.

"The truth is ..." He pauses. "The truth ..."

Anton climbs the stage beside him, wrapping his arm around Ezra's back and taking the mic from him. "The truth is, we decided last year that this was going to be our last season. We finally did it. We're ... We're ..." He gags like he's trying not to vomit. "Reti ..." He finally gives up trying to say it. "I mean, come on, Ezra's fucking old now, and even though we feel like we could go on forever, our game isn't like it was seven years ago when we last won the Cup."

"Wait, that's the news?" I call out.

"Yes," Ezra says.

"All of the news?"

"What do you mean?" Ezra frowns.

"I thought you were breaking up. I was having a full-blown panic while trying to come up with ideas on how to parent trap you two back together. You can't fucking break up."

Ezra and Anton laugh. "Break up? Fuck no. Anton couldn't get rid of me even if he tried."

Anton nudges him. "And trust me, I've tried."

I let out a relieved breath. "Thank fuck."

Ezra holds his heart. "You really care about us. See, this is why you're my favorite Kiki."

"Hey!" Connor and Easton whine at the exact same time.

I can't say that I'm not relieved about them still being together, but retiring? Ezra and Anton were the two out of all of us who I thought would be here until the end. Boston *is* Anton and Ezra. Without them there ... this next year isn't going to be the same. Hell, the NHL as a whole isn't going to be the same.

"What this means though," Ezra says, ignoring my brothers, "is there're only five active Collective members in the NHL, and I need to hang up my Collective C. We need a new captain."

"Did anyone ever actually elect you captain?" West Dalton shouts out.

"Yes," Ezra says. "Me. But the time has come"—on cue, the *RuPaul's Drag Race* lip-sync battle noise comes through the sound system. Trust him to create a whole choreographed deal with sound effects and lights—"for you all to compete for. The. Win."

Have to say his RuPaul impression is on point, but is he ... is he going to make us lip-sync to become the next him?

"What we're going to do is—"

"I'm out," Asher says.

"Little D, please. Just ..." Ezra cocks his head. "Just ... come on. Okay? Just ..."

"My brother Emmett can take my place when he's inevitably called up. Will happen any day."

"No substitutions. Plus, he's not a Collective member yet."

Asher sighs.

"Woohoo, that sigh means you're on board," Ezra continues. "The five of you, come up here." He crooks his finger, and I'm the first one up there. It takes Foster Grant, Miles Olsen, Asher Dalton, and my brother Easton significantly longer to join me, probably because they're hesitant about what's in store. I'm shocked that Asher is going along with this at all, and I can't help but think he's as thrown by the retirement news as the rest of us. Sure, he tried to fight it, but not Asher Dalton levels of resistance.

Me? I'm up for anything. Always have been. Let's do this.

"Okay," Ezra says. "How do I choose?" We're lined up, and he's walking behind us, back and forth. "We're going head-to-head on this. Playoff ladder style. Let's go. Our first head-to-head is ..." He takes on an announcer voice like he's ringside at a boxing match. "Miles Olllllsen and ..." Using his normal voice, he says, "Little D."

"Oh no," Asher deadpans. "How will I ever win with your enthusiasm the way it is?"

"This is a difficult choice," Ezra says seriously. "On the one hand, Miles Olsen has what it takes. He's fun. Always shows up for Collective meetups. Has the personality that will make it easier for him to recruit more Collective members. But most of all, he's nice to me. On the other hand? He's a goalie, and I don't want to be attending pet rock parties anytime soon. Little D takes this round."

"What?" Asher shrieks. "How is that fair?"

"You *won*," Ezra emphasizes.

"Exactly! This is bullshit." Asher folds his arms.

"Stone and Seddy also think this is bullshit. Just so you know." Miles jumps down off the small stage.

"Moving on," Ezra says and steps up to Foster Grant. "Okay, even if your husband wasn't a socially anxious cutie who makes you miss Collective meetups, you're too responsible for my liking."

"Zach doesn't *make* me. I choose to skip them. To be with him."

"Thank you for illustrating my point. You're out. Congrats. You lost a head-to-head against ... no one." Ezra pats his shoulder and directs him off the stage. Foster walks off with a laugh, uncaring.

Then he stands between Easton and me.

"Ah, the two brothers," he says. "I would've loved to have made you fight to the death or something slightly less dramatic, but if I'm choosing out of you, based purely on who I think would do a better job of taking care of the Collective, I'm going to have to go with Little Kiki."

I grin, proud.

Easton smirks. "Not that I care, but why?"

"One, Lachie is up for anything."

"True." I nod.

"He's the youngest, so he can hold the position for the longest."

I put my hands under my chin, the universal sign for "I'm cute."

"But mostly? He and his boyfriend save animals. Which means they know how to wrangle them. Which also means they could handle this group." Ezra gestures to all the drunkards in the room, who proudly shout woohoos. They don't even deny it.

"And now, for the final round! Little D versus Little Kiki."

"Fucking hell," Asher grumbles. "You're going to choose me to punish me, aren't you?"

"Nope! I'm not leaving my legacy in your hands. The winner is Lachie Kikishkin! Bow down to your new leader!"

Now, everyone breaks into boos and rounds of "Fuck you."

"They already love you more than they love me," Ezra says. He holds up my hand, victorious.

I murmur out the side of my mouth, "This isn't much responsibility, is it?"

He makes a "Pfft" noise. "Nope."

Everyone else's attention is already drifting elsewhere, back to their conversations, but Ezra turns to me.

"It's basically checking in on everyone, making sure shit isn't going sideways, other players aren't being dicks to anyone, and then making holiday plans around your own schedule and telling them all they have to be there. They mostly show up. But I'll also be here if you need advice."

That seems easy enough, and the way he sees something in me finally has that last sense of belonging click into place. This group of guys might have started off as my brothers' group of friends, but now? I'm not only one of them, but I'm going to be the future Ezra. The glue.

"I can do that," I say. And I can. As I stare out at the countless faces around the room, I realize it doesn't matter who takes on this role because no matter what, I know without a doubt that every single person in this room has each other's back.

Ezra drops some of the bravado. "Look after my legacy. I'm so proud of what we've built here, and I really hope someday that the Collective will be overflowing with members. These guys are special, and they should be reminded of it always."

I pull Ezra into a hug, loving that he lets this side of him out. It's rare, but after the handful of times he's allowed me to see it, I admire him even more. He's right that the Collective is special. The NHL still isn't where it needs to be in terms of acceptance, and I don't doubt there are plenty of queer players still in the closet, but I'm ready to take the lead. To keep pushing for the respect we deserve.

Then my gaze lands on Sam, and I'm so unbelievably happy, I could burst. He's my future, but so is the Collective, and I am ready to slay in every aspect of my life.

"The Queer Collective isn't all about getting drunk, setting fires, and bringing party llamas to gatherings."

That damn llama. I haven't heard the end of it, and it's been years.

"It's so much more than that," Ezra says.

"I know. It's about hockey. Family." My gaze finds Sam's across the room. "And love."

"This is the end of my era, but yours is only beginning."

And I'm the luckiest man in the world to have everything I've ever wanted.